PULP
FRICTION

PULP FRICTION

Uncovering the Golden Age
of Gay Male Pulps

Edited by Michael Bronski

ST. MARTIN'S GRIFFIN
NEW YORK

www.stmartins.com

Excerpts from *A Different Drum* by Chris Davidson, *Gay Revolution* by Marcus Miller, *Gay Whore* by Jack Love, *Gay Rights* by John Ironstone, and *Song of the Loon* by Richard Amory appear by permission of www.readmagic.com and www.adonisboyz.com

Excerpt from the novel *Kyle* by Bruce Benderson, copyright © Bruce Benderson 1972, 2002; reprinted by permission of the author

Excerpts from *The Gay Haunt* by Victor Jay, *Whisper His Sin* by Vin Packer, *Lost on Twilight Road* by James Colton, and *My Purple Winter* by Carl Corley reprinted by permission of their respective authors

Library of Congress Cataloging-in-Publication Data

Pulp friction / edited by Michael Bronski.—1st Griffin ed.
   p. cm.
  ISBN 0-312-25267-6   ISBN 978-0-312-25267-0
  Includes bibliographical references (p. 369).
  1. Gay men—Fiction. 2. Erotic stories, American. 3. Erotic stories, English.
I. Bronski, Michael. II. Title.

PS648.H57 P65   2003
813.008'03538'086642—dc21

                                     2001058895

To Victor J. Banis, Bruce Benderson,
   Joseph Hansen, Marijane Meaker,
and all of the other authors, living and dead,
who for decades before Stonewall pioneered
what we now call gay and lesbian literature

And to Joseph Canarelli
for thirty-five years of friendship and love

CONTENTS

PART THREE
Truly Pulp: "Gay" Life in the Shadows

PART FOUR
Out of the Twilight World: The Sexual Revolution Goes Lavender

ACKNOWLEDGMENTS

This book would not have happened without the patience and encouragement of my editor, Keith Kahla (whose idea it was), and his assistant, Teresa Theophano. Thanks also to my agent, Jed Mattes, who was always available, understanding, and supportive.

Linda Schlossberg not only read the manuscript and offered expert advice but continually reassured me that, indeed, pulps were not only literature but great reads as well. Patrick Merla also offered his sage counsel and encouragement on the introduction and the entire project. Chris Bram, as always, heartened and inspired me with his persistent love of literature; a well-needed salve whenever I felt that these books, which I had come to love, were less than worthy of rediscovery.

Enormous thanks as well to John Howard, Lawrence Schimel, Katherine Forrest, William K. Dobbs, Larry Townsend, Richard Kasak, Bill Andriette, Brenda Marston, and Hubert Kennedy for their enormous help in tracking down the authors of some of these selections. And to John Mitzel, who over the years has supported my passion for collecting gay male pulps. Stephen Brophy and Brian Gale were incredibly helpful in the preparation of the manuscript. David Bergman was kind enough to share with me some of his own writings on pulp novels, which were invaluable. As invaluable were my friendships with Richard Voos, Carolyn Stack, Paul Van de Carr, and others who tolerated my reading them passages from these books and insisting that they look at book covers whenever they were at my home. And special thanks to production editor Robert Cloud, whose work has made this a better book.

Much of this work could not have been done were it not for the kindness of Linda Schlossberg and Alice Jardine in securing me access to Harvard's Widener Library.

And thanks to all of the men who over the years collected and preserved their pulp novels. Without these books in archives, used bookstores, libraries, and personal collections, we would have lost a history that is invaluable as it is fascinating.

PULP
FRICTION

Introduction

Gay pulps: everyone knows the covers. With their fabulously garish colors, their cartoonish, mock-heroic studs, and tempting titles such as *The Butt Boy, Dirt Road Cousins, Three on a Broomstick,* and *Up Your Pleasure,* they are old-time gay male iconography for a new, younger generation of homosexuals. Falling somewhere between kitsch and kitchen decorations, these images, no longer on book jackets, now grace refrigerator magnets, postcards, and address books. Often they straddle clear-cut categories: they can be both hot and humorous, nostalgic and trendy, historic and emblematic of a contemporary sensibility. They are artifacts from the past that have acquired new, ironic meanings for the end of the last century and the beginning of this one. But these book covers—and the novels they luridly trumpet—are more than camp or a curious slice of gay life past. They are integral aspects of gay male culture and gay history that are as vital as—indeed, inseparable from—our fight for equality under the law and the freedom to live our lives the way we choose. They are records—albeit fictional and reflecting and refracting the tenor and biases of their times—of how gay men lived, thought, desired, loved, and survived. Even with their exaggerations, high-queen dramatics, silly (even naïve) eroticism, and sometimes internalized homophobia, they give us a glimpse of what it meant to be a gay man in the tumultuous years before Stonewall.

This book began as an anthology of paperback pulps that were published before the Stonewall riots in June of 1969. I had intended to draw upon them—in all of their wildly varied manifestations and idiosyncracies—to sketch a picture of what gay male life was like before the enormous changes that the Gay Liberation Movement brought into the everyday social and political life of our culture. But as I read through the books, I discovered that what I had imagined and demarcated as a genre, distinct and discrete unto itself, was actually part of a far broader, older, and more complicated history and culture. The more extensively I read, the more I realized that gay male pulps were simply one of the more visible manifestations of a gay publishing, literary, and public culture that existed before Stonewall.

Gay pulp is not an exact term, and it is used somewhat loosely to refer to a variety of books that had very different origins and markets. By the 1950s the publishing industry in the United States had reached a new level of production. The printing and distribution of cheaply produced and cheaply priced paperback novels, which had begun in the late 1930s, steadily grew until it reached its full force in the early 1950s. Their eye-catching, provocative covers created and defined a new artistic and marketing genre; screaming damsels in distress represented a favorite motif, as did risqué clothing for both women and men. While mystery, crime, romance, and action stories benefited enormously from these graphic designs, authors from Shakespeare to Aldous Huxley to Edna Ferber also found a new readership. From joke and cartoon books *(Out of My Trunk: Milton's Berle's Joke Book)* to informational guides *(Bantam Books' 1,000 Facts Worth Knowing)* to current events (1945's *The Atomic Age Opens)* the burgeoning paperback industry created new books and new markets.

This advance in the publishing world, particularly in the late 1940s and early 1950s, also included huge numbers of original novels focusing on illegal or taboo sex—adultery, prostitution, rape, interracial relationships, lesbianism, male homosexuality—topics that were, in the words of the cover-copy writers, "controversial," "explosive," "shocking," and ready to "reveal the sordid truth in a way you have never read before." Often these books traded on current social obsessions and "headline news"—juvenile delinquency, motorcycle gangs, wife-swapping, teen drug use, college scandals, mob racketeering, suburban malaise, and the erotic dangers of psychoanalysis. They represent, beneath a veneer of enticing exploitation, a compendium of the not-so-hidden preoccupations and fears of the tempestuous and socially unstable postwar years.

A prominent and bestselling subgenre of these exploitation paperback originals were those that dealt with male and female homosexuality. With cover copy that spoke in easily decipherable code about "The World of Twilight Lovers," "The Love Society Forbids," and "The Hidden Shame of . . . Secret Love," these books promised to expose the "Hidden World of the Third Sex." From the very beginning of their publishing history, however, clear distinctions were drawn between paperbacks and pulps that dealt with lesbianism and those that portrayed male homosexuality.

Lesbian-themed books were more numerous and popular than those that dealt with male homosexuality. This was undoubtedly because a huge percentage of their readership was made up of heterosexual men (and probably heterosexual women as well). Lesbians, of course, also read these books; those by Ann Bannon, Valerie Taylor, Paula Christian, Ann Aldrich, and Vin Packer (the last two were pseudonyms of Marijane Meaker) have become classics of modern lesbian literature. The earliest lesbian pulps were written by these authors (all of whom worked for Fawcett Gold Medal), and they present an honest, even positive view of lesbian life. Even when the dictates of the genre demanded an unhappy ending (often in response to the very real possibility of censorship), the details and textures of the narrative resonated with truth. As a genre, lesbian pulps were extraordinarily successful: Vin Packer's 1952 *Spring Fire* sold millions of copies at twenty-five cents, outselling a new edition of Erskine Caldwell's ever-popular *God's Little Acre*. Their popularity was so great that, along with these paperback "original" novels, it was common for publishers to reissue older works—often serious novels by respected writers—in pulp formats. Anna Elisabet Weirauch's *The Scorpion* (1932), Gale Wilhelm's *We Too Are Drifting* (1935), Elisabeth Craigin's *Either Is Love* (1937), Claire Morgan/Patricia Highsmith's *The Price of Salt* (1952), and even

Radclyffe Hall's ur-lesbian novel, *The Well of Loneliness* (1928), were all pulped up in new editions.

While these writers, both old and new, were notable for their nuanced, "insider" views of lesbian life, the great majority of pulps portrayed a homophobic, overly sordid vision of lesbian culture rife with self-hatred, misery, and violence. These books were usually written by men using female pseudonyms. Ironically, these books were always the mainstay of the lesbian pulp market, and their numbers only multiplied as the increasingly relaxed censorship standards of the early 1960s permitted more explicitly erotic content. The Golden Age of lesbian pulps was over, and the market was now essentially produced by and directed at heterosexual males. By the late 1960s most censorship laws had been abolished, and lesbian content moved from "romantic" pulps to the more overtly pornographic books (all written by and for men) that had now become legal.

The trajectory of the gay male pulps is very different. There was no burgeoning market for gay male novels in the 1950s because they apparently had little crossover appeal for a substantial heterosexual readership. The titillating nature of lesbian sexuality seemed to outweigh any potential threat it might present to the social order. Thus, while the lesbian pulp genre thrived on original works that sold well, gay-male-themed paperbacks were generally made up of reprints of previously published novels from established, respected houses. Titles such as Charles Jackson's *The Fall of Valor* (Rinehart, 1946), Gore Vidal's *The City and the Pillar* (Dutton, 1948), Michael De Forrest's *The Gay Year* (Woodford Press, 1949), Fritz Peters's *Finistère* (Farrar, Straus, 1951), Douglas Sanderson's *Dark Passions Subdue* (Dodd, Mead, 1952), and Gerald Tesch's *Never the Same Again* (Putnam, 1956) were quickly issued in inexpensive paperback editions that sported predictable pulp images and cover copy. These reprints were augmented by a few paperback originals such as Vin Packer's 1954 *Whisper His Sin* and the 1964 *Lost on Twilight Road* by James Colton (the pseudonym of Joseph Hansen). While it is difficult to ascertain exact sales figures, it is reasonable to assume that no gay male titles sold the tremendous quantities attained by the most successful of the lesbian pulps. A curious paradox thus emerges. On the one hand, books with male homosexual themes had a better chance than lesbian titles of being published in cloth by mainstream presses; on the other, once they were issued as paperback pulps, they didn't sell as well as their lesbian counterparts. They were considered to be more literary, yet less commercial.

Gay male and lesbian literature of the fifties and sixties thus came to operate in very different cultural and social contexts. The first, as suggested above, was that gay-male-themed books received greater critical recognition than lesbian ones. Writers such as Gore Vidal, Lonnie Coleman, John Horne Burns, and Charles Jackson were accepted as important American writers, even when they received attacks from homophobic critics. This recognition placed them in a literary and cultural tradition denied to most women writers. The mantle of "literary quality" also granted some protection against censorship.

Secondly, most of the novels dealing with gay male life and culture were written by gay men drawing upon their own experience. This was a very different situation from what was found in lesbian-themed pulps, which were overwhelmingly written by outsiders from a voyeuristic, "pornographic" perspective. Most of the gay male pulps from the 1950s and early 1960s—regardless of their questionable literary quality—have an emotional veracity and truthfulness that is missing from the bulk of lesbian pulps. Because there was a modest but moderately lucrative market for this gay-male-themed fiction, there were more publishing opportunities for gay books by gay men than there were for lesbian books by lesbians.

The third major difference between the lesbian and gay male pulps occurs in the mid-to-late 1960s. More than a decade of challenges to U.S. censorship laws—mostly by book publishers and film distributors—were yielding results. It was now possible to publish work with more explicit sexual content as well as to portray homosexual (and other erotic) themes outside the realm of "literary" publishing. In many ways, the history of gay publishing is also the history of the ongoing battle against censorship in this country. A Supreme Court decision in 1958 reversed a 1956 ruling by a federal district court that U.S. postal authorities were correct in prohibiting the mailing of the Mattachine Society's *ONE* magazine. The lower court had ruled that *ONE* was not protected by the First Amendment because the magazine's contents "may be vulgar, offensive, and indecent even though not regarded as such by a particular group . . . because their own social or moral standards are far below those of the general community. . . . Social standards are fixed by and for the great majority and not by and for a hardened or weakened minority." Thus defined, any writing that promoted or even presented homosexuality in neutral terms was ipso facto pornographic. Such standards were, of course, applied selectively, and while prominent publishing companies had less to fear than small, gay-oriented magazines, the possibility of censorship was always present.

It is a commonplace assumption that in the fifties and sixties "homosexuality" was a taboo topic, that it was never spoken about, or only in hushed tones. This is completely untrue: As the excerpts from these books attest, homosexuality was very much in the public consciousness. If anything, it was more integrated into popular culture than it would be in the late 1960s and the early 1970s. This is not to say that the public discourse about homosexuality in the 1950s was more enlightened or tolerant—although many of the writings included in this collection will surprise you with their frankness and their level of acceptance—but it was understood and discussed in very different ways.

When assembling *Pulp Friction,* I was repeatedly pushed to reconsider my preconceptions about the material. I had to rethink how I, and other scholars of gay history and culture, have long viewed the position of homosexuality in the two decades before Stonewall. In a startling reversal in my thinking, I realized that thinking of all gay fiction written after the war up to the Stonewall riots as a separate literary category was a mistake. I would now argue that the very concept of "gay fiction" is most usefully understood as a post-Stonewall invention, one that serves a specific political function. This concept enabled the newly emergent homosexual community to label and identify books that spoke to or about it. (It also became a marketing tool, as the new community was seen by publishers to be a lucrative niche market.)

The opening section of this anthology shows that many postwar novels featured explicitly gay male characters. These novels were published by respected publishing houses whose books regularly received critical attention from mainstream critics. Some of the novels were written by men who were (with varying degrees of openness) gay, and some were not. While they were certainly read by gay people, they were never labeled "gay novels" or marginalized with accusations of special pleading. While some publishers did market their novels to a more distinctly homosexual readership, even these novels were advertised and reviewed in conventional, mainstream newspapers and magazines.

My second major preconception going into this project was that the majority of novels published before Stonewall, with the possible exception of some of the more explicitly pornographic works, had tragic endings. This is one of the most deeply inscribed myths of the last three decades—the gay novel or film in which the long-suffering, usually self-hating hero or heroine is doomed to die at his or her own hands, thus enacting the inevitable, implicitly deserved fate of all homosexuals. Critical studies such as Roger Austen's *Playing the Game: The Homosexual Novel in America* and Vito Russo's *The Celluloid Closet: Homosexuality in the Movies*—as well as endless offhanded references to the phenomenon in popular fiction and nonfiction—promote this myth. But I discovered that many pre-Stonewall novels end (if not completely happily) with optimism, understanding, or a degree of self-knowledge. Even novels that do end "badly" are not necessarily promoting antihomosexual sentiments or themes. Take, for instance, Fritz Peters's exquisite 1951 *Finistère*, a book that has repeatedly been classified as a "tragic gay novel." Here, Matthew, a sixteen-year-old American schoolboy, has an affair with Michel, a young male teacher at his French school. Matthew does drown himself in the book's final pages, but it is clear that his suicide is the direct result of the attitudes of his uncaring and self-involved parents, the sexual harassment of his stepfather, and the temporary unkindness of his lover.

The third preconception about pulp novels that I had to overcome concerned sex. I presumed that in some of the bolder pulps, gay male sexual activity would be mentioned, even described in some vague detail, and that it would be more explicit in the later, "pornographic" novels of the mid-1960s onward. But I was completely startled by how much sex was described in the earlier novels. While none of it is anatomically explicit, the sexual references, the indications of erotic interest, the importance of sexuality to the char-

acters' lives, and the sexualization of the male body are equal to—
and in some cases go further than—what we find in comparable
heterosexual novels of the period. This is particularly astonishing in
the novels from mainstream publishers in the late 1940s and the
1950s. The reader has full access to the erotic imagination of the
main character in Stuart Engstrand's 1947 *The Sling and the Arrow*
as he negotiates his overt sexual fantasies of sailors with his tenden-
cies to transvestism and transgenderism. In Thomas Hal Phillips's
1949 *The Bitterweed Path*, the main character goes to bed with both
his best friend and his best friend's father, and the author stops just
short of describing, but certainly leads us to imagine, what happens
next.

While pulp novels functioned as validation for gay male sexual
desires, they performed other functions as well. Without denying the
enjoyment—sexual or otherwise—that came from reading them,
these books also functioned pedagogically. Hidden within their plots
and their characters' lives were maps, hints, and clues that told gay
men how they might live their lives. All literature has an element of
tutelage—we are being told something, are learning something,
whether it is how people dressed at grand balls for the Russian no-
bility in Tolstoy's *War and Peace* or what it was like to work in an
abattoir in Upton Sinclair's *The Jungle*. Because so many of the novels that dealt with homosexuality were written by gay men who
drew, to some degree, on their own experience, they are filled with
glimpses into how gay men of this period lived. This is not to say
that they are documentary in intent and effect, but rather that they
provided windows into a half-hidden gay world that was not completely accessible to those who were not members. Reading through
these books, we see how gay men dressed, what their homes looked
like, where they lived, and how they spoke. Certainly most of this
knowledge is filtered through the lens of art and storytelling—
bounded also by the pressures of the marketplace and the limits of
good taste—but it is present and useful to those who needed to
know.

What is it exactly that gay men might learn from these books?
Sometimes it is just finding out in which neighborhoods and communities gay men lived. In book after book—from Michael De Forrest's 1949 *The Gay Year* to Lonnie Coleman's 1959 *Sam*—we

are treated to scenes set in apartments in Greenwich Village. The decor and the furnishings of the rooms are described as are the characters' clothing and colloquial speech. We learn what the inside of a gay bar and a gay bathhouse look like, and how people behave in them. In Jay Little's 1952 *Maybe—Tomorrow,* we see gay life in the French Quarter of New Orleans. In "Spur Piece" from James Barr's 1951 *Derricks,* we see what life is like for gay men in small towns in the Midwest.

The importance of these novels as educational, self-help, and how-to manuals cannot be underestimated. No one is brought up to be gay, hardly anyone (even now) comes from a "gay family." Having sexual desires is one thing, finding people with whom to act on them is another, and finding a community is yet another step that is as liberating as it is fraught with peril and often confusion. These books were the maps and the signposts, the etiquette manuals and the foreign-phrase books, for gay men entering the half-hidden world of homosexuality. The fancifully lurid language of pulp covers was not altogether wrong: Homosexual culture was a shadowy and obscure world whose social presence was becoming increasingly prominent, but whose inner workings and interior life were only barely visible to the mainstream world. These novels often present us with a lovely through-the-looking-glass effect, for just as the fictional characters find their way through the emotional and psychological labyrinth of coming out and discover what their gay life and world might be like, so did the homosexual readers of these books turn to them for guidance.

As important as the social function of these books was—not only for helping homosexuals discover new worlds, but in securing and maintaining for those worlds a place in the heterosexual imagination and the material world—it is vital not to lose sight of them as literature as well. First and foremost, they are works of imagination, written primarily by gay men, that commit to the hard reality of paper the passions and longings of same-sex desire. They vary in form and tone, and certainly their literary quality ranges from high to idiosyncratically low, but each of them exhibits a rebellious, radical urge as they bring the possibility, and pleasure, of same-sex eroticism to a world that is both fascinated by and fearful of it.

After reading just over 225 novels (and some nonfiction) in preparing this anthology, I came to the inescapable conclusion that one of the traditional, post-Stonewall measures that we have been using to judge fiction with gay characters or themes is not particularly helpful, but ahistorical and quite useless in judging literature of any quality. This is the perennial question of "positive" and "negative" images in gay and lesbian literature, film, and theater. Echoing the age-old "Is it good for the Jews?" query, "Is it good for the gays?" has been a staple of how gay men and lesbians have evaluated the enormous variety of cultural products that have been produced over the past century. The question itself is the product of a survivalist impulse. Given the overwhelming prevalence of queer hatred in the world (not to mention general confusion and ambivalence over homosexuality), worrying about whether a book or movie was "good for the gays"—whether it would engender more dislike or even suspicion of homosexuality—is, in many ways, a reasonable response. Thus, in evaluating a work, we tend to ask: Are gay men or lesbians represented in such a way as to make them appear heroic, likable, or even neutral? Or are they presented in ways that draw upon injurious and untrue stereotypes that reinforce preexisting prejudices?

One problem of using the "Is it good for the gays?" argument is that it is not equipped to account for nuance, shading, or even irony and literary seriousness. To take the extreme obvious: Is Radclyffe Hall's *The Well of Loneliness*—which is fundamental to contemporary lesbian literature—"good for the gays"? On one hand, it is a dour, unrelenting study of unhappiness (hence its title) and unfulfillment populated by confused and stereotypical characters. With its doom-and-gloom plot, its arguably unlikable protagonist, and its unending emphasis on the sheer unmitigated pain of female homoeroticism, it is hardly an advertisement for joyful lesbian passion.

Yet it was written as an impassioned plea for tolerance and understanding. And while only the most stalwart "good for the gays" advocate would give a thumbs-down on Hall's novel, it is true that it has fixed in the popular imagination—through its myriad editions from high literary to decidedly pulp—an image of lesbianism that confirms the worst preconceptions about lesbians. The same arguments might also be used against James Baldwin's *Giovanni's Room* or *Another Country* as well as against John Rechy's *City of Night*.

Yet each of these books was an enormous breakthrough in bringing the topic of homosexuality to a broader public discourse, as well as presenting—through their empathy and artistry—complex images of homosexuality and same-sex desire to a reading public. To judge them as "not good for the gays" is not simply to misunderstand their place in history, but to misread them as literature as well.

The idea that some books were not "good for the gays" is closely tied to why they are not better known today and why they were lost to gay history. What created the myth that there were few (or no) books about homosexuality before Stonewall? Or the contradictory, but equally strong, myth that all of the pre-Stonewall novels about homosexuality had tragic endings? Part of the reason is that only a few of these books were actually read by many people in the gay generations after Stonewall and the Gay Liberation Movement. While *Finistère, Quatrefoil,* and *The Gaudy Image* were rereleased in the 1980s, most of these titles were out of print and available only in secondhand bookstores and the occasional library. Often writers who had once had acclaimed or productive careers such as Charles Gorman or Fritz Peters had faded to obscurity. Even a writer who continued to publish and thrive, such as Lonnie Coleman—who achieved considerable popularity, and a smaller degree of critical acclaim, with his *Beulah Land* series in the 1970s and 1980s—found his earlier work, with and without homosexual themes, ignored.

This historical literary amnesia is curious. Certainly the advent of the black civil rights movement led to the desire to uncover an obscured and hidden African-American culture, from the political writings of W. E. B. DuBois (which were rereleased in mass market paperbacks) to the poetry of Phyllis Wheatley and the novels and other writings of Harlem Renaissance writers. The same was also true of the second wave of feminism, which engendered and encouraged the massive cultural project of uncovering centuries of women's thought and literature. Writers as diverse as Aphra Behn, Christina Rossetti, Charlotte Perkins Gilman, Jessie Redmon Fauset, and Jean Rhys were rediscovered and republished in popular editions. Within this great recovery of feminist culture was included the revival of lesbian writers from the 1930s such as Gale Wilhelm and from the 1950s such as Claire Morgan (Patricia Highsmith), Ann

Bannon, and Valerie Taylor. So why wasn't there a similar rush of rediscovery for gay male writers?

A great deal of this was, I believe, due to the need to believe in the myth that the Stonewall riots and the emergence of a Gay Liberation Movement was a decisive break with the past and a radical beginning for a new future. This attitude was apparent in the dismissive attitude that many gay liberationists took toward the older homophile groups such as Mattachine, SIR, and Daughters of Bilitis and their publications. Certainly these pulp paperbacks with their cover illustrations of unhappy men wandering uncertain in a lavender fog and the tag lines "Lost in a Twilight World of Loneliness" or "The Shocking Story of Unnatural Love Between Men" were the nightmare embodiment of everything that the post-Stonewall world imagined past gay life to have been. They were the sad, sorry, and sordid manifestations of life before liberation. There was no need to celebrate this past and no emotional or psychic possibility for nostalgia or even camp enjoyment.

One of the great projects of the Gay Liberation Movement was to create a new gay culture that was both to replace the older oppressive gay culture and to salve the wounds and scars that had been inflicted on homosexuals. There was no doubt in the minds of gay liberationists that the progenitor of queer hatred was what Christopher Isherwood labeled "the heterosexual dictatorship," but that did not prevent gay activists from mounting a similar—and at times even more forceful and ferocious—attack on pre-Stonewall gay culture as well. It would be overdetermined (as well as vulgar Freudianizing) to view this impulse as a scenario of oedipal fury and a mistake to call this cultural rejection a form of "political correctness." The rejection of pre-Stonewall gay culture by the gay liberationists had none of the censure and moral condemnation that is usually associated with how "political correctness" is used today; nor was its rhetoric (as is true today) that used by the right to attack progressive or left-leaning causes. Like most of the social movements of the 1960s—the antiwar movement, the music and drug counterculture, hippies and yippies, environmentalism, black power, radical and separatist feminism—gay liberation was a youth movement whose sense of history was defined to a large degree by a rejection of the past. Not surprisingly, the works of some earlier gay writers, such as Allen Ginsberg and other beats who carried their antiestablishment 1950s political agenda to the antiwar and counterculture movements, were accepted as post-Stonewall literature. After witnessing the Stonewall riots, Ginsberg was said to have commented to a friend that "the fags have lost that wounded look." But with a few exceptions the liberationist rejection of the gay culture of the 1950s and 1960s was decisive and was, in many ways, a frightened response to the pain and the suffering that had visibly stalked gay life in the decades before Stonewall. In the excitement of reinvention we had missed the comfort of continuity. The richness of the literature in this anthology is an example of the wide array of visions and possibilities of gay male life and culture that were available in U.S. culture, particularly after World War II. Most of this was created by gay men in a variety of venues, from the mainstream to the alternative. It was created not only in opposition to a culture that frequently condemned homosexual behavior, but also in concert with that same culture, which was simultaneously fascinated by, even obsessed with, it.

Midcentury America was a unique historical moment for homosexuality. The Second World War had generated profound dislocations and disruptions of traditional ideas of sexuality and gender. As Allan Bérubé documents in *Coming Out Under Fire,* traditional ideas about masculinity, maleness, and male sexuality were profoundly altered by men's experiences during the war. The tremors from these cultural and psychological events continued to reverberate deeply through U.S. culture for at least the next twenty years. The revolutions of the 1960s were, in many ways, the logical and karmic aftershocks of the cultural eruptions of the postwar years. America in the 1950s was a society eager and extraordinarily anxious to redefine itself, to hold on to the securities of the past as desperately as it was attempting to understand its possible futures. Two of the major preoccupations within this cultural flux were sexuality and gender, which, in combination with one another, produced a cultural fixation on homosexuality.

This cultural fixation on homosexuality was already in progress by 1948, the year Alfred Kinsey's *Sexual Behavior in the Human Male* was published. The Kinsey report was a massive, dense, compendium—804 pages of tables, charts, and statistics based on interviews with 5,940 men about their sexual histories and activities. Kinsey, a scientist whose expertise was in the study of gall wasps, had enormous faith in the simple collecting of raw data. When Kinsey's figures disclosed an enormous prevalence of sex between men, the country was shocked: "37 per cent of the total male population has at least some overt homosexual experience to the point of orgasm between adolescence and old age"; "50 per cent of the males who remain single until age 35 have had overt homosexual experience to the point of orgasm, since the onset of adolescence"; "13 per cent of the males (approximately) react erotically to other males without having overt homosexual contacts after the onset of adolescence"; "18 per cent of the males have at least as much of the homosexual as the heterosexual in their histories for at least three years between the ages of 16 and 55"; "10 per cent of the males are more or less exclusively homosexual for at least three years between the ages of 16 and 55"; "8 per cent of the males are exclusively homosexual for at least three years between the ages of 16 and 55"; "4 per cent of the white males are exclusively homosexual throughout their lives, after the onset of adolescence." One of the immediate results of Kinsey's report was a cultural shift that brought such enormous cultural and media attention to male homosexuality that it amounted to a fixation.

The contradictions generated by and embedded within this fixation were tremendous. Here was a country obsessed with ridding its government of "subversive" homosexuals, yet it idolized performers like Liberace and Little Richard and refused to acknowledge their—rather evident to many—homosexuality. The country enshrined motherhood and the domesticated female while at the same time buying millions and millions of lesbian pulp novels and making Marilyn Monroe and Jayne Mansfield stars. The country both savored and ignored rumors about Rock Hudson's "hidden life" while accepting him as Hollywood's leading symbol of manly heterosexual romanticism. This same country embraced the new masculinities presented by James Dean and Montgomery Clift while promoting a revival of patriotic, individualist masculinism to backbone the ongoing cold war against Soviet and Chinese communism. It lionized Marlon Brando in black leather while it editorialized against the national outrage of youth motorcycle gangs. It was the country, finally, that promoted an apotheosis of the healthy male body in slyly homoerotic (and antiqueer) Charles Atlas ads in comics that were sold on drugstore magazine shelves only inches away from copies of *Physique Pictorial* and *Grecian Guild Quarterly.*

The dichotomized thinking of the period not only appeared in thinking about sexuality and gender, but was reflected in attitudes toward other social issues. This was the era that suspected all Jews of being untrustworthy foreigners and possibly communists but made Bess Myerson the first (and still the only) Jewish Miss America; that accepted television's Molly Goldberg as the loving Jewish mother but sent Ethel Rosenberg to the electric chair despite the pleas of Pope Pius XII. It was the country that continued to perpetuate the most horrendous, programmatic, state-sponsored racism against African-Americans while listening and dancing to the seductive (and, to mainstream culture, highly eroticized) sounds of Chuck Berry and Fats Domino.

It is tempting to conjure the 1950s and the early 1960s through Dickens's binary—it was the best of times, it was the worst of times. But the era is far more complicated than that. Neither best nor worst, it was simply the times as they were, and they were complicated, contradictory, confusing, and—to our modern and postmodern contemporary sensibilities—often confounding and unnerving when focused on sexuality, sexual identity, and gender presentation. Gay male literature—as well as gay male culture and politics—grew and thrived through this time. It is a mistake to see it, in any of its manifestations, as moving on a separate track parallel to what was happening in the rest of the world. And certainly a mistake to ignore the very real hostility and oppression—censorships raids on private homes, repeated harassment of gay bars, police entrapment—that the readers of gay pulps faced. Since Stonewall it has been a truism that gay male and lesbian culture of this period was a fundamental contradiction to the established social structures that promoted highly inflexible norms of gender and sexuality. But the mainstream culture of the 1950s and '60s—like all cultures—was constructed of a series of contradictions of which gay culture was one more strand. There is a definite historical and social progression of gay male literature during this time. Just because a culture is riddled with contradictions doesn't mean that there are no means to organize, codify, and discuss them—and they, not surprisingly, both follow and influence the patterns we find in the broader culture.

An enormous and cohesive literature by and for gay men existed before Stonewall. From bestselling popular novels to drugstore book-rack pulps to pornography, these books emanated from, reflected, and shaped gay men's lives for perhaps the most crucial thirty years of this century, from the beginning of World War II to the advent and blossoming of the enormous changes of the 1960s, years that saw the emergence of what we now understand to be the modern homosexual and gay life. These books are crucial to an understanding of this history as well as of the way we are here today. Why have so many of these pulp novels not found a place in the gay and lesbian literary tradition? Their short shelf life is partially attributable to their often controversial content, but it is important to remember that popular American culture as a whole is fleeting. With a few exceptions—*The Wizard of Oz, Gone with the Wind, Valley of the Dolls*—books designated as popular literature have a brief hold on the American imagination. A quick look through the bestseller lists or the Pulitzer Prizes of the past decades demonstrates that enormously popular works, and even books critically praised as "great literature," have vanished from our cultural consciousness. Many novels with homosexual themes published by respectable houses have simply vanished like their mainstream contemporaries.

Another reason why so many of these books are absent from contemporary culture and consciousness is that they have physically disappeared. One of the primary features of the paperback revolution was that the books were, in essence, disposable. Inexpensively produced and priced, paperbacks were not marketed as books to be kept. They were, not unlike characters in a pulp novel, easy, handy, available, and cheap. While paperback copies of novels such as Harrison Dowd's *The Night Air*, Vin Packer's *Whisper His Sin*, Jay Little's *Maybe—Tomorrow* were plentiful when they were published in the 1950s and 1960s, they are scarce now, fetching high prices on the collectibles market. The problem of accessibility is compounded because libraries do not have space, funds, or in some cases the vision to sustain large collections of popular literature. While it might still be possible to find copies of Lonnie Coleman's popular 1970s *Beulah Land* series on library shelves, locating a copy of his 1959 *Sam* is nearly impossible. The novels of Vin Packer, which were issued only in mass market paperback editions, and James Barr's *Derricks* simply never made it into libraries. The gay-themed books that did were at high risk of being stolen by gay readers too embarrassed to borrow them legally, or by self-appointed censors who felt that such works had no place on library shelves.

Finally, many of these books—particularly those with more ex-. plicit sexual content—enjoyed large, but relatively clandestine, circulations. As paperback originals they were generally not sold in general-interest bookstores. Once bought, they may not have been judged as material many gay men would want to display on the open bookshelves in their living rooms or even bedrooms. Often enough, they were stored under the bed or in closets. Unfortunately, while many books were donated to libraries, charity rummage sales, or lawn sales, these titles stood a far greater chance of being thrown away or destroyed so that they would not reveal too much about their owners and their lives.

How, then, did I find the selections included in this anthology? Many of them I knew because I had come across them in my reading over the last thirty-five years. Gay people—whether they are children, teenagers, or adults—often have keen instincts for discovering obscured or hidden information about sexuality. As a teen in the 1960s, I was able to ferret out veiled and shrouded books that mentioned or had principal content about gay men or homosexuality. I was also lucky to grow up during a time before Internet sales when used books were cheap and used-book stores were plentiful, so buying and collecting books with queer content was not only an adventure, but a moderately inexpensive one.

Three sources for this project were invaluable. Roger Austen's 1977 study, *Playing the Game: The Homosexual Novel in America,* is a book so groundbreaking that even when I disagreed with some of its assertions or conclusions, it served as an inspiration and a priceless resource. Ian Young's 1982 *The Male Homosexual in Literature: A Bibliography* is an outstanding work of careful research and dedication. Tom Norman's *American Gay Erotic Paperbacks: A Bibliography*—a massive undertaking performed with obvious love—was indispensable. Another key source was Georges-Michel Sarotte's 1978 *Like a Brother, Like a Lover: Male Homosexuality in the American Novel and Theater from Herman Melville to James Baldwin*, which was helpful in identifying novels and providing new ways of thinking about the material. Barbara Grier's *Lesbiana: Book Reviews from "The Ladder," 1966–1972*, while primarily discussing materials relating to lesbianism, provides a superb overview of "variant literature" of the period.

One of the great joys of putting together this book was the need for literary and historical sleuthing. Because of the half-public nature of homosexuality, many of these books were only semivisible and partially identifiable. Often I would find other titles by looking at the advertisements in book jackets or on the backs of paperback covers ("Other books you might enjoy are . . ."). Pertinent books might be identified through code words: *the twilight world* and *men who live in the shadows* were clear and obvious tip-offs. But less "leading" words were also fruitful: *strange, curious,* and *unusual* generally meant I'd stumbled upon an appropriate find. Needless to say, when the novels were set in Greenwich Village or featured a "bohemian life," the payoff was usually quick and decisive.

Reading through bibliographies and surveys of modern American literature was often useful—particularly when phrases like "unhappy marriage" or "unconventional life" appeared in capsule biographies. Another invaluable bibliographic source was the catalogs from Elysian Fields, a now defunct mail-order company run by the late Ed Drucker that specialized in gay and lesbian literature. While these sales catalogs were not complete bibliographic records but simply lists of what was currently available, they are a gold mine not only of titles and authors but of publishers and publication dates. The latter is an enormous boon for research, as many of these titles have gone through several editions, often from now obscure or nontraditional publishing houses. Copies of the Guild Press mail-order catalog—published in the mid-1960s—were also a tremendous help. Because Guild Press marketed to a primarily gay male audience, their inventory provides a clear indication of what gay men were buying and reading at the time. Searching through old magazines from the 1940s to the 1960s turned up reviews of novels that have faded from cultural memory or passing references to authors who have never been overtly identified with "deviant themes" or "abnormal subject matter." Sometimes, as was the case with Francis Cardinal Spellman's homoerotically tinged writing, I just went on a logical hunch and it paid off.

It was also profitable to comb through used-book stores and see what was on the shelves. Many stores now have a "sexualities" section, or even a "gay and lesbian studies" category, and often odd titles from decades past will appear squeezed in between gay novels from the 1990s and works of gay sociology or lesbian self-help. I was tremendously lucky to have access to Harvard University's libraries, which contained not only many specific titles that would have been nearly inaccessible otherwise, but also a plethora of ancillary works that, while not specifically gay-themed, were vital to understanding both the larger body of work of an author or the context in which she or he wrote. Finally, surfing the Internet provided idiosyncratic access to a wide range of information and connections that would have escaped me otherwise. How else might I have discovered that Stuart Engstrand, author of *The Sling and the Arrow*—an important, if decidedly odd psychoanalytic novel about homosexuality and gender variation—was also the author of the novel *Beyond the Forest,* which became a film with Bette Davis (featuring the famous line "What a dump!")? On the Internet, too, I learned that Harrison Dowd (a writer about whom there is virtually nothing written) was a noted musician, actor, and a major player in the Village arts scene in the 1930s.

Lastly, I relied on the knowledge, goodwill, and generosity of so many fellow queer writers and thinkers who told me of new books, reminded me of books I had forgotten, suggested leads, and provided me with invaluable information. John Howard's work on Thomas Hal Phillips and Carl Corley in *Men like That: A Southern Queer History,* as well as his introduction to the new edition of Phillips's *The Bitterweed Path,* was inspirational, and his helping me secure the rights to Corley's writing was a godsend. David Bergman's thoughts and writings on many of these books and their social and political contexts were also incredibly informative and valuable. Chris Bram, as usual, was an endless source of information about all aspects of literary history.

In my readings, note takings, and collecting of all this material, I began to fear an unintended consequence. While the uncovering of this literature can only have positive effects on how we view our queer past, there is also a danger that these books could become part of what is often referred to as the gay canon. This would be a terrible, and I think, unhealthy fate. Indeed, I believe that the idea of a "gay canon" is not only unnecessary but unhelpful. In his essay "The Personal Is the Political," Edmund White notes, "I myself am in favor of desacralizing literature, of dismantling the idea of a few essential books, of retiring the whole concept of a canon. A canon is for people who don't like to read, people who want to know the bare minimum of titles they must consume in order to be considered polished, well rounded. Civilized. Any real reader seeks the names of more and more books, not fewer and fewer."

It has become clear to me while working on this anthology that if the idea of "gay literature" is to have any relevance at all, any resonant meaning for us today and in the future, it must be a concept that is understood to be ever evolving. Some of the works in this volume—particularly in the first two sections—were not written as "gay literature." They were not understood as such by their authors and often involve concepts of sexual identity and behavior that would not be considered "homosexual" or "gay"—although they would often be understood in contemporary parlance as "queer." Through my research and reading I discovered an ever-unfolding world of writing that was connected to this project, and the idea of the "gay canon" became less and less supportable, less and less possible.

Since Stonewall there has been an ongoing project to uncover, recover, and unearth what is commonly called gay history. Thanks to the work of community and academic historians, to local history projects, to writers and editors, we have a far better—and more complex—understanding of the infinite variety of the lives and loves of all those women and men who came before us. Some of this information has been startling, surprising, or confounding, some of it has confirmed what we already knew (or thought we knew), and some of it has challenged and contradicted accepted wisdom. I hope that the selections in this anthology will do a little of all of these. Readers' responses to these selections will not be the same as responses from readers in 1949 or 1956 or 1968. But the challenge of reading this literature is to think about how we live our lives today, and to imagine how people read and lived their lives thirty, forty, and fifty years ago—times that were very different from, yet not all that dissimilar to, today.

PART ONE

Mainstream Fiction: Not Particularly Hiding in the Shadows

While common sense would suggest that there were few literary images of gay male life before Stonewall, the truth is that as early as the forties respectable publishing houses released many novels with primary homosexual characters. These were not exploitative, sensationalistic potboilers, but rather well received, often critically praised works that were considered excellent contemporary American literature. We know some of these titles today because they have endured the passage of time and the idiosyncratic critical process by which some books become classics. The stories and novels of Carson McCullers, Tennessee Williams, Truman Capote, and Gore Vidal are still in print and read. But these authors and their writings are merely the visible tip of a broad, complex body of work. Placed on a more complicated map of midcentury literature (along with the work of Lonnie Coleman, John Horne Burns, William Maxwell, Charles Jackson, Thomas Hal Phillips, Audrey Erskine-Lindop, Willard Motley, Harrison Dowd, Patricia Highsmith, William Goyen, Isabel Bolton, and Paul Goodman), they can be seen as part of a firmly established tradition of American writing about homosexuality. There are easily more than a hundred novels with primary gay characters or gay themes published by mainstream publishing houses between 1940 and 1969, and hundreds more with minor or incidental homosexual content.

In *Coming Out Under Fire*, Allan Bérubé shows how World War II helped to create contemporary gay identities and communities by reworking acceptable definitions of American masculinity. The patriotic culture of World War II—from recruitment posters to *Life* magazine photo spreads to military novels—both valorized and eroticized the youthful male body. This dovetailed neatly with writings about male homosexuals; beautiful, sexy, well-built servicemen are perpetual inhabitants of wartime and postwar gay fiction, surfacing in works as diverse as McCullers's *Reflections in a Golden Eye* (1941), John Horne Burns's *The Gallery* (1947), Vidal's *The City and the Pillar* (1948), Russell Thacher's *The Captain* (1951), and Lonnie Coleman's *Ship's Company* (1955).

The lure of the sexualized serviceman is also central to Charles Jackson's *The Fall of Valor* (1946). In this novel, John Grandin, a college professor whose marriage is floundering, becomes obsessed with Cliff Hauman, a handsome young marine captain recuperating on Nantucket from battle action in the Pacific. In this work of barely repressed homosexual desire, erotic servicemen are everywhere. Early in the narrative, Grandin's wife finds a newspaper photo he has clipped and hidden under his desk blotter:

> It showed a battle-exhausted marine lying in a burlap bunk fast asleep, his right arm (as if by habit) around a heavy Garand rifle. A packed kit of some kind resting on his chest, and his left hand relaxed and limp on his stomach—the only part of him which did not seem, in spite of his dead sleep, tensed and ready for instant action. He wore a wrinkled shirt open at the throat and loose tropical shorts exposing thick bare thighs and knees, slightly hairy and probably dirty. He had a couple of days' growth of beard so that a potential mustache of some size and width was plainly outlined. His eyebrows were raised, his eyes closed in sleep; his nose was short, almost pug; the mouth was wide and attractive, with tightly closed lips; the chin was strong. He was a very rugged, masculine, and mature-looking young man, possibly a good deal younger than he looked.

Another example of the erotic nature of military men is this passage from *The Risen Soldier*, a 1944 meditation by Francis J. Spellman on the valor (presumably *not* fallen) of the American soldier.

Writing as a military vicar, an appointment from Pope Pius XII, Spellman was archbishop of New York, although not yet awarded the rank of cardinal:

> These young American airmen with whom I was living, wanted to believe and did believe that they too were suffering, and dying to bring salvation and peace to their fellow man. I could not sound the depths of my feelings towards them. All possible emotions in the gamut from fear to love seized me. From my life with them I felt that I knew them; I knew that I admired and awesomely loved them as, realizingly, they grasped my hand in farewell. For some of them it was the dawning of their last morning in the world.
>
> Moments were precious, impressions were vivid, emotions, restrained, were strong; for each of these boys was sacred to me.

> One of the pilots that morning was a boy I had known at home, one of the millions of American soldiers, waging this war for earthly and everlasting victory and peace. It was eight years since last I had seen him on the night of his graduation from high school. Good student and athlete he was . . . a normal American boy, strong and straight in body and mind, with a zest for living, playing, and working.

Spellman's prose—a cross between Walt Whitman, St. Teresa of Avila, and gay pulp—foreshadows the postwar idealization of the male body. It would be easy to say that Spellman, so well-known as an active homosexual that his nickname in gay circles was Fannie, was allowing his desire to overtake his writing, but his vivid and sentimental descriptions of men in the armed forces were common for their time. What is perhaps most illuminating about Spellman's homoerotic imagery is how closely it is bound up with images of the wounded, hurt, or destroyed male body. In *The Risen Soldier,* Spellman's boys are all physically endangered; in his 1951 novel, *The Foundling,* the beautiful male body is constantly disfigured and marred:

No one noticed the solitary, wistful soldier peeling an orange with his teeth. Once this lean, long-legged lad could have taken the fruit in his hands and stripped its skin with his fingers. But that was in other years—years before the war screamed into the world, mastered men, bent them into its vengeful, lustful will and left them, as it had Paul, struck down and maimed in the Argonne.

. . . He remembered big Jack—only twenty-one, gay, handsome, laughing—reading aloud his letters from home, his even, strong teeth gleaming white against the natural tan of his skin. Jack shared his fun, his gifts, his rations, as he shared his life— to bring joy to others less joyful than himself. And then Jack lay a heap of raw agony upon his stretcher, his strong legs and chest smashed beyond repair, even then with death within him, trying to smile at Sam there beside him.

In novel after novel from the period we witness the physical vulnerability of the desirable male body: Cliff, the handsome marine of *The Fall of Valor,* is described as recovering from "ten broken ribs, all his teeth rammed down his throat, his whole face cut open to his jaw, [and having] a fractured skull and concussion of the brain." Beautiful Timothy Danelaw dies in a plane crash in James Barr's *Quatrefoil* (1950), good-looking Bob Ford is brutally strangled by his would-be lover in Gore Vidal's *The City and the Pillar* (1948), and the mouth of handsome Guy Hudson in John Horne Burns's *Lucifer with a Book* (1949) is "horribly scarred and turns upward in a permanent sneer."

Certainly many postwar novels contain wounded males; it is the inevitability of war. Two of the most durable of postwar fictions— Norman Mailer's *The Naked and the Dead* (1948) and James Jones's *From Here to Eternity* (1951)—exhibit a similar preoccupation, which is heightened when juxtaposed with a broader discussion of masculinity prompted by the interplay between straight and homosexual characters. The wounded male body was a potent symbol, a marker of the radical changes that had occurred in the national psyche regarding traditional concepts of masculinity. The wounded male was not only physically but emotionally vulnerable as well and open to a far wider range of psychic and even erotic experiences.

That many of these novels were bestsellers and were read by heterosexuals and homosexuals alike indicates a new public willingness to openly discuss male homosexuality. This was integral to a major cultural shift in how masculinity was imagined, understood, and constructed, and it formed the basis for postwar American literature and influenced the writings of the next half century.

The protagonists in Harrison Dowd's *The Night Air* and Lonnie Coleman's *Sam* are fine examples of the new freedom in depicting psychologically and erotically complicated male characters that was now open to writers of postwar American literature.

HARRISON DOWD

The Night Air

Dial Press, 1950

The cover art and the copy on Avon's 1952 mass market paperback edition of *The Night Air* are grim. The art features a single man in the foreground emerging from a night fog, with a heterosexual couple behind him in a passionate embrace. The cover copy above the art reads, "A Homosexual Looks at Himself," and the flyleaf states:

> As a youth, Andy Moore had gone through the frightening experience of being drawn to members of his own sex—had fought against it, and thought he had won out.
>
> Feeling the lure of the stage and needing an outlet for his unwanted emotions, he came to Broadway. There he met Kit—wooed her and married her—bottling up his abnormal desires inside himself.

Despite the cover copy, Andy Moore is not particularly tortured. Dowd's novel is a realistic look at a forty-three-year-old man with an active homosexual past who rediscovers his passion for men after seven years of being happily married. The novel details his struggle to be true to himself and to discover what he really wants and needs.

Andy's high moral standards are neatly juxtaposed with the actions of his love interest, the much younger Quentin Burke, who is continually dishonest in his dealings with both his male and female sexual partners.

The Night Air is very much a novel of a specific time and place: the New York theater world of the late 1940s. It is filled with small, authentic-sounding detail—lunches at Sardi's, theatrical name-dropping, backstage machinations, cramped hotel rooms on pre-Broadway tryouts. It also provides a clear window into the complexity of how sexuality was viewed in this environment as the lines between straight and gay, butch and nelly, trade and john, are continually blurred. It is also filled with sharp, often funny, glimpses into the newly emerging culture of homosexual parties and bars.

If *The Night Air* is centered around the city—New York in particular, and specifically Forty-second Street and Greenwich Village—it is haunted by the image of the country. At the end of the novel Andy returns to his small hometown in Vermont. Although Andy seems conflicted—should he choose men or marriage?—a specific memory from his childhood gives us a hint as to what his final decision might be. This memory involves a certain "trouble with himself," that is, masturbation:

> When he was nearly ten, his cousin Harold came to help work the farm, and it was then that this trouble with himself ended, for Harold laughed at it and taught him other things, as frightening as they were pleasant, sinful too in a way, but at least not alone. He was no longer shut off by himself in sin; he belonged to someone, he was wanted, he could enjoy and be enjoyed, and together the sin seemed less terrifying, less culpable. Harold was big, with a handsome mouth and dark red hair; he could high dive and swim four times across the river and back; his chest and hair were hard as a colt's.

Harrison Dowd was born in 1897 and died in 1964. He served in the American Expeditionary Forces during World War I and in the twenties and thirties was a major player in the Greenwich Village cultural scene. A noted musician and composer, he set selections of A. E. Housman's *A Shropshire Lad* to music. He was part of the circle of gay friends and artists who were centered around Edna St. Vincent Millay, and he played Pierrot in the premiere of her famed one-act play *Aria da Capo* in 1919. Between 1929 and 1958, Dowd regularly appeared on the Broadway stage and did film and television work as well. He played the Lobster Man in the 1956 film *Carousel* and appeared on Broadway with Alfred Lunt and Lynn Fontanne in Dürrenmatt's *The Visit* in 1958. He was married to writer Frances Park. *The Night Air* has been out of print since the 1950s.

When *The Night Air* begins, talented composer and actor Andy Moore is contentedly but not happily married to Kit. As his career takes off, he becomes increasingly sexually drawn to men and begins a tempestuous affair with the beautiful but shallow Quentin Burke. In these two chapters, which come late in the novel, Andy has separated from Kit, and his depression and drinking are threatening his career, specifically a new part in a successful Broadway show. In the previous chapter he has just been humiliated and dumped by Quentin Burke and seeks refuge in a gay bar, where he meets Mike, a merchant marine, with whom he had tricked earlier.

Chapter 31

The bar was dimly lit and although the storm was subsiding there were only a few customers. Andy wondered if there'd been a raid. For a moment he felt the edge of sobriety and apprehension, but put it aside, leaning on the bar familiarly and ordering a double Scotch. The bartender was short and stout, rather young, with a Punch and Judy face; he seemed good-natured, amused, not watchful or suspicious. Or perhaps he just didn't care.

"Sort of quiet, isn't it?" Andy said.

"Yeah. It's this dirty weather."

Two men stood next to him, sipping brandy; the older one, his back turned, wore a sharkskin suit, rather tight about his figure, which was stout but fairly well proportioned, except for his behind, which sloped out like a cellar door. The other was young, dark, good-looking, and smiled constantly, sometimes, Andy thought, directly at him. But he couldn't be sure; besides, he didn't want to bother with something already attached. A lone wolf looking for another lone wolf, that's me. Further down the bar a man was beckoning the bartender for a beer. Under one arm he held a large package; Andy guessed there were bottles inside. The heavy bass voice was familiar; he looked again and realized that the man was Mike Colsak. Leaning forward slightly so as to see past the other two men, he kept his eyes fixed on Mike until Mike saw him, then smiled and gave a salute with his right hand.

Mike smiled back, surprised, and lifted his glass but made no move to join him. After a moment or two Andy took his drink over.

"Hi, Mike."

"Hello, there."

"Haven't seen you since last fall." Andy pretended to have difficulty remembering. "Where was it? I forget."

"Sure, the cafeteria." Mike looked at him speculatively, a little on guard. "Making lots of dough?" His eyes were on Andy's overcoat, a new one.

"Oh, enough." The question made Andy uncomfortable, remembering that in the past Mike had often bought him drinks, even dinners, out of his merchant seaman's pay. He tried to catch the bartender's eye.

"Saw your name in the paper. Big shot now, huh?"

"Look." Andy took a quick, careful breath. "Let's forget all that. Break's a break. Let's be pals, no questions asked, what?" He looked at Mike's glass. "Buy you a drink."

Mike lifted his beer and finished it. "Sure, I don't mind." He wiped his mouth with the back of his hand. " 'Fraid I only got time for one, though. Expectin' some friends over at my place." He faced Andy, one elbow on the bar, and smiled.

Andy felt a little disappointed. He looked at Mike again, closer. If this wasn't quite what he'd had in mind, at least he was safe, handsome too in spite or even because of his baldness. Big; muscular.

"You still married?" Mike's voice was gentle, almost hesitant.

"No. Well, legally. We called it off."

"No go, huh?"

"No go. Weren't getting anywhere."

"What's the matter, didn't she like it?"

"She liked it." Andy felt embarrassed. Shouldn't discuss such things with strangers at a bar. Only Mike's not a stranger. "Moderately," he said. "Just moderately."

Mike was studying him, still smiling. "You didn't have any trouble, huh?"

"Times. Everybody has times." Andy felt annoyed. "Let's talk about something else, for Christ's sake. Have another."

"Okay. I just wondered when you said you weren't gettin' anywhere how you made out, you know, with a woman."

"I did all right, get that. It was other things weren't getting anywhere, things you wouldn't know about."

"Why, you think I'm so dumb?"

"No. No, I don't think you're dumb. I think you're a damn nice guy. Intelligent. Good-looking, too," he added, after a slight pause.

Mike grinned, came a step nearer, lowering his voice. "Why'd you say that?"

"Never mind. Forget it."

"Go on, say it. Why did you?"

Andy's face burned. "I forgot. Too long ago."

"So what?"

Andy gripped the bar with both hands, looking down. "You wouldn't be interested."

"How do you know?"

Raising his head Andy saw his own face in the mirror; it looked old and frightened. "We're not so pretty anymore," he said, "d'you think?"

"You mean I'm bald, that what's botherin' you?"

"No . . . I like it." The back of Andy's throat felt thick. "I was thinking of myself, more."

"Let's have another drink." Mike beckoned the bartender. "For old times' sake."

"What about your friends?"

"Aw, they can wait."

Andy, elbows on bar, lowered his head again. He suddenly saw himself as about to cry, and thought, why not? I'm drunk enough now. I have a right to, everybody has a right to, what's holding us back? Too smart, too tough. Like Beryl. Oh, to hell with Beryl, to hell with smartness, toughness; besides, it isn't real toughness. She's as scared as the rest of us. Kit's the one who's really tough. A natural; smart, elegant, all there. Scared of nothing, sorry for nobody, the lady boss.

From a long way off he heard Mike say, "Hey, you drunk?"

"No." Andy dropped his hands, straightened. "No. I was just thinking."

"What?"

"Oh, about things, about not getting anywhere. She was always there, know what I mean? Me, I'd always be somewhere else. Singular. Very singular. Singular pair, the Moores. They say they're Lesbians."

"Ha!" Mike shouted, slapping Andy's shoulder. "That's a hot one. I gotta remember that."

"She's so goddamned brave," Andy said with venom. "What makes women so goddamn brave? Brave and noble and oh so bloody correct."

"You could beat her up."

"No. I respect her too much. I wouldn't know how to begin. And I don't hate her enough; you have to hate somebody an awful lot to beat 'em up." Andy stared wisely and profoundly into his whiskey, feeling very sober and concentrated. "It's what she stands for, *noblesse oblige*. Responsibility. The right thing. That I could beat up. I hate the right thing. With people it's different."

Mike finished his beer and stood looking at Andy, nodding. "You and me both," he said. "Take 'em or leave 'em." His eye fell on the clock over the bar. "Where you livin', then?"

Andy looked at his glass. "East side. Uptown."

"Who with? Anybody?"

"Yes."

"Man or woman?"

"Twins from Ansonia," Andy said. "One's dead."

"All right, you don't have to tell me. Only better go easy on the liquor, you got a long way to go. Might end up in a snowbank."

"Wouldn't be bad. They say it's like going to sleep." Andy put his head back and closed his eyes. "Mike."

"Yeh?"

"Why don't you ask me to the party?"

"Okay. I warn you, it's a dump."

"I like dumps." Andy finished his drink; he motioned to the bartender.

Mike said, "Go easy on the liquor."

"Why?"

"People downstairs raise a stink. Besides"—he shook Andy gently, his fingers hard as hooks—"you're no good when you've had too many, you know that."

Andy smiled faintly, feeling pleasantly sick. He paid the bill, leaving the change. "All set?"

Outside he had difficulty with the sidewalk and had to hold on to Mike's arm. There were no cabs; except for an occasional parked car, buried under a foot-high cake of snow, the streets were empty of all traffic. Street and sidewalk were one, a flat white river that rose almost up to the doorknobs of shops and houses. The air was bland and moist, smelling like washed linen; air from nowhere and everywhere, New Jersey, Montana, the North Pole; air as innocent as milk, as new grass, as narcissus.

Andy breathed deep, wanting to sing, lie down, roll over and over in the snow. Once he stopped in front of a café and demanded another drink but Mike dissuaded him.

It was a long way, longer even than the trip to the bank. The streets got smaller and narrower; they were finally walking down the middle of one which seemed never to have been walked on until now; little and white under the great clearing black sky. Pioneers, Andy thought, and laughed out loud.

"What's the joke?" Mike asked.

"The pioneers have hairy ears," Andy sang tunelessly, clinging to Mike's arm. "Have you got hairy ears, Mike?"

"Shouldn't be surprised."

Andy looked. "Very becoming."

"Screwball." Mike grinned.

"You've got sideburns; even more becoming. I knew a motorman had sideburns once. Walt Whitman loved a motorman, maybe that's why?"

"That's why what?"

"Never mind. 'Pioneers! O Pioneers.' That's by Whitman, too."

"Who's he?"

"The good gray grandmother of us all. Me, I'm the new woman."

Andy danced a little, or tried to, and fell down, shrieking in the snow. Mike stood over him, laughing, then dragged him to his feet. "Come on, bitch." They went on, staggering, arm in arm.

"Here it is." Mike drew out his keys. "You go first. Second floor front."

The house was a small three-story brick, lost among warehouses and tiny run-down shops that sold tobacco and candy to sailors from off the boats docked along the river. The stairs smelled of garbage and above the first floor were in complete darkness. Andy tried not to touch the banister or walls as he groped his way up.

Mike opened the door and went in ahead. Andy heard him tug at a light cord; a single bulb in a glass reflector hung swaying above them, showing a long dim room, sparsely furnished and surprisingly clean, partitioned in the middle by a pair of greenish curtains on a wire. The walls were of white plaster, bare of ornament, except for an old calendar that showed a sailor, legs spread, wigwagging. The room was cold. Against the walls Mike's shadow careened upward from the floor in rhythm with the swinging lightbulb; Andy watched it swell, distend, shrink, swell again. He began to tremble.

"This is it," Mike said. He reached up and put his hand on the light to stop its swinging, then faced Andy. "Cold?"

"A little. I could use a drink."

"Wait." Mike went to the cupboard over the sink and came back with a small glass of whiskey. "This is for special guests," he said. "The others can take beer and like it."

Andy drank, smiling up at Mike. "Thanks."

A moment later there was a shout from the street below. Mike went to the window, opened it. "Okay," he said, hardly raising his voice. "Hold yer horses." He went downstairs and came back with two men, both of them rather drunk. "Meet Melvyn and Chris," Mike said. "Andy Moore, famous actor."

"How do you do." The older man's face was like a squeezed pink dishrag, his hand soft and sticky; Andy had a hard time drawing his own away. "Honored, I'm sure."

Chris, the younger one, stood staring at Andy speculatively, his hands deep in the front pockets of his navy denims. He was a good-looking sullen boy of nineteen or twenty whose face needed washing.

"Say sumpin', Chris, where's yer manners?" Mike said.

"Hi." The boy drew a toothpick from his mouth, turned away, and sat on the broken sofa. "Where's all the beer?" he asked. His eyes were slightly thyroid and his mouth hung open.

Mike emptied the bag and opened four cans. "Mr. Moore's in a Broadway show, big hit," he said. "Buddy from way back."

"Really," the older man exclaimed, passing one hand over his hair. "I was in show business myself, once. La Belle Melvyn, impersonator. Maybe you caught my act, Orpheum Circuit."

"I'm afraid I didn't," Andy said. "I . . ."

"You mean it was before your time only you're too polite to say it, I know." The man simpered. "Don't mind me; I'm ageless, simply ageless."

"He can still touch the floor with his palms without bending his knees," Mike said. "Pretty good for sixty."

"Pardon me, sixty-nine," Melvyn said, and shrieked. "Oh, there I go talking dirty." He giggled. "Somebody ought to wash my mouth out with soap. No, I'm really fifty-three. Never think it, would you?"

"No, never." Andy drank his beer thirstily. Mike handed him another. A little later, noticing there were only a few cans left, Andy offered to go out and buy some more.

"I'll go," Mike said. "You can pay for 'em if you like."

As Andy drew out his wallet, he was aware of Chris's eyes watching him from the sofa, and put it back hastily.

"Turn on the radio, I feel like dancing," Melvyn said after Mike had left. His eyes had a black glitter that came from something other than drink. "I started out as a ballet dancer," he explained to Andy, and went into a slightly creaky glissade. "Nearly starved until I got into vaudeville." He continued to dance, talking meanwhile. "Used some of it in the act, but only for comedy. Did a burlesque of Pavlova in the *Swan* that simply slayed 'em, though I'd said I'd never prostitute myself. Only it went over so big I finally got to like it myself. There comes a time when you have to face facts. Know your place, I said to myself. Your business is to make people laugh. So I did."

"Yeah. Made 'em laugh even on Riker's," Chris said from the sofa.

Melvyn stood still, the pink cloth of his face seeming to fade and unravel. He went on dancing, more energetically than before, jumpy little dance steps from the twenties, with a touch of Spanish. His face had turned a pale yellow. "Excuse me," he said, stopping again suddenly, "I have to go to the john." He left the room hurriedly; they could hear his footsteps fading down the outside hall.

Andy rose and went to the table to get another beer. As he stood opening it, his back to the room, he heard Chris rise and come toward him. He turned. Chris drew a packet of cigarettes from his pocket and offered him one.

"No, thanks. I just put one out."

Chris took one for himself, his eyes on Andy, fixed, persistent. "Got a match?"

Andy gave him a matchbook.

"Thanks." Chris blew smoke from his nose, straight down. "Doin' anythin' later?"

Andy went back to his beer. "You better go back and sit down," he said, controlling his voice.

"Ah, don't give me that." Andy could feel the boy's thigh against his hip. "How about it?" Andy moved away; his knees shook.

"You're drunk," he said. "Cut it out."

"Five dollars," the young man said. "Come on, I gotta place over on Bleecker."

"What makes you think—"

"Lis'en, you got dough." Chris edged toward him. "I seen it."

Moron, Andy thought. Criminal. "Look, I'm not interested. Lay off."

Mike entered at that moment, with the package heavy on his arm. Chris stepped back quickly; his hand went to his groin in a protective gesture. "Oh, no, mister," he said. "You got me wrong." His face looked much older, much less stupid.

"What is this?" Mike put the beer on the table and stood looking first at Chris, then at Andy.

"Nothing," Andy said. "He's just tight."

Mike gave a skeptical grin, then knotted his fist under Andy's jaw. "You behave," he said. He looked about. "Where's Melvyn?"

"Down the hall. Look, you don't believe I—"

"You better behave," Mike repeated, "or Melvyn'll scratch yer eyes out."

"But, Mike, I—"

"He made a pass at me," Chris said. "Had his hand right on it."

"Shut up," Andy said. "Shut your dirty lying mouth."

A maniacal rage twisted the boy's face; he came at Andy, his upraised fist clenched. "Nobody calls me a liar, goddamn it." A stream of filth poured from his mouth, which dribbled. Mike seized his arm, twisted it behind his back.

"Shut up or I'll throw you out," he said. "Punk." He let go the boy's arm and shoved him away. "Go on, sit down."

Melvyn stood in the doorway. "What's he done?" He went to Chris, shook him by the shoulder. "You be good," he said. "Hear?"

"Called me a liar. Nobody calls me a liar." Chris flung himself on the sofa and drew a stick of gum from his pocket, which he bit into and chewed with venomous concentration.

"Ah, ferget it." Mike handed out more beer. Andy sat, conscious that Melvyn was eyeing him oddly, but by now he was too drunk to care what the man thought. "Sing sumpin', Andy; you used to sing. Campy stuff, come on, show 'em." Mike sat beside Andy, drawing him into the hollow of his arm, squeezing his shoulder.

"What? I don't remember." Andy looked hard at his beer, wishing he weren't so drowsy. He turned to Melvyn. "You sing."

"Me? No, thank you." Melvyn pursed his lips. He was obviously put out. Andy rose, bored and irritated; all he wanted was to show Mike he was eager to oblige, wanting to please. He felt lonely and afraid, too, for some reason.

"What'll I sing?" he asked, standing there, swaying a little. "Tell me what to sing."

"One about little furnished flat," Mike said. "I forget how it starts."

It was one of his mother's songs. Andy remembered seeing her in some theater in Los Angeles where she had done a week or two of vaudeville before he'd begun to earn money himself, standing in a blue spot, her low-cut velvet dress showing her overblown breasts, bedizened, still handsome.

"Never lose your heart . . ." He stopped. "I need a costume," he said. "Get me a costume."

Mike, laughing, went behind the curtains and came back with a lavender bedspread, quite dirty and ragged, with a frilled edge. He

helped Andy wrap it around himself, leaving the frills at the bottom;
Andy picked up two oranges from the table and stuffed them in the
front, then wound his scarf, an expensive paisley one, about his
head, letting the ends dangle. Melvyn and Chris sat watching silently
all during this, unsmiling.

Andy began to sing, facing Mike, singing only for Mike. He was
his mother, and the leading lady of a touring company of *The Choc-
olate Soldier,* which he had seen when he was twelve; he was Edith
Piaf and Mlle. Griffard; he was Grace Moore and Mary Martin; he
was fascinating, famous, utterly irresistible.

> *Every girl's a dream neath the silver moon,*
> *So you can't depend on that,*
> *And there'll be no moon but a honeymoon*
> *In your little furnished flat.*

Drunk, Mike shouted for an encore, so he did it again. When he
had finished, he bowed gracefully, lost his balance, and fell on the
floor. Mike rose and stood over him, laughing. "No more beer for
you," he said, and helped him to his feet. "You better get to bed."

Andy clung to Mike's shoulder. "I'll go," he said. "You tell me
and I'll go."

"Her master's voice," said Melvyn. "Come on, Chris; we're in
the way." He rose, haughtily. Chris lingered, giving Andy a look of
contempt. "You stink," he said.

"Get out, the two of you." Mike turned on them. "Don't know
an artist when you see one."

"If he's an artist, I'm Eleonora Duse," Melvyn said, and snig-
gered. He went to the door, turned. "I hate creeps," he said. "I'm
a woman and proud of it. As for that one, she's neither one thing
nor the other. Come along, Blue Boy."

Mike slammed the door after them and came back to where Andy
was sitting. "Jealous bitch," he said. "Pay no attention. She's so
hopped up she don't know where she is. Only been off the Island
three days, the two of them." He sat, looking fixedly at Andy. "How
you feel?" he asked.

"Like a drink." Andy sat up; he looked at his costume, took out
an orange, and rolled it across the floor. "Where's the Scotch?"

"Hey." Mike's voice was suddenly harsh. "You had plenty. Go on to bed."

"Where am I?"

"Oh, for God's sake." Mike lifted Andy to his feet and unwound the bedspread; his hands were slow and heavy with drink. As the coverlet fell to the floor, he undid Andy's tie, then his shirt.

"I want a drink."

"Look, you're plastered already. You can't have any more. I told you. What do you think I brought you here for?"

"Well, what?"

"Go on inside," Mike said. "Be in 'n a minute."

In the early morning Andy woke. It was still dark; Mike, fast asleep, was snoring loudly. Andy rose and tiptoed about until he located the bottle on one of the shelves above the sink. The kitchen smelled of old plumbing and he shook so with the cold that the bottle neck rattled against his teeth. From the river came a wild sad hoot like an animal being stabbed; against the ceiling a streetlight fanned away into endless shade, carrying the room with it. The floor tilted, weaving, trying to throw him off-balance; he saw himself rolling and screaming down it into absolute blackness.

Still holding the bottle, in which he had left enough for the morning, Andy went back and sat on the edge of the bed. He didn't feel cold any longer. He looked at Mike's heavy pale face and strong mouth and felt like Miss Clements, like all the withering lonely women in the world, frail, immeasurably pathetic. He was home at last; this was where he belonged. He sighed, contentedly.

"Mike."

Mike grunted, turned away, then half waking, looked back over his shoulder. "Huh?"

"Do me a favor, will you?"

"What's that?"

"Marry me." It seemed not only the most desirable, but the most reasonable request in the world.

"Oh, Jesus." Mike yawned, held out a huge black-haired arm. "Come back to bed and shut up, screwball."

Chapter 32

I'm sorry, Mr. Moore." The stage-doorman stood squarely in front of Andy, blocking his way.

"Listen, I'm all right." Andy clung to the door, one hand on the man's shoulder.

"I tell you the curtain's up, been up a half hour. Mr. Rayburn's all set to go on." Steve shook his head. "I had my orders; I can't do it."

"Look, Steve." Andy fumbled in his pockets and produced a wrinkled five-dollar bill. "Buy yourself a drink; call it square."

"I don't want your money. Now, please, Mr. Moore, be a good guy and go home."

"But I have to go on." Andy gave the man a shove.

"Go on home." It was another voice. Trying to place it, Andy raised his head slowly. Wyatt stood in front of Natalie's dressing room door, his hands dug into his pockets, a cigar in his mouth. "Don't let him up, Steve." He came forward a little, eyeing Andy. "Go on home," he said, "before I get sore."

"Mr. Wyatt—"

Andy felt a hard, jabbing upward pressure under both arms, felt light, unhooked, flying; it was rather pleasant. Then he was on his face in the snow.

He lay there quietly, thinking only, what do I do next? After a while he sat up, took up a handful of snow, and rubbed it on his forehead. Mike had said he would take him back if he stayed sober, but first he'd have to remember where he lived. The cold long room came back, the taste of the early-morning whiskey, and Mike's huge bare arm reaching for him. Then it was noon and he was frying eggs on a gas range, while Mike sat with his feet on the table, scolding him. The sun came in, blinding over snow-covered roofs. Coffee had a peculiar dirty smell and put him to sleep again. Shouldn't do that. The bed was mussed and dirty, the second bottle was empty, it was getting dark, and Mike was trying to sober him up.

Andy knelt in the alley darkness and hugged himself. He had to find Mike somehow; he'd try the bars. They'd know. Mike wouldn't turn him away; he'd have some food and coffee and sober up first.

Mike was the only one left; and there was a great deal to tell him. He'd see this was no act; the other was an act. Trying to be a husband, a hero to somebody. Hero my ass. You knew a good thing when you saw it, you redheaded bastard, you know which side your butt's breaded on. Whore boy, chore boy with a dingle-dangle-o, who's next? Meet all comers. You're worried, am I? Worried who's going to pay next month's rent more likely.

Andy found himself on the downtown corner of Eighth Avenue and Forty-fifth, near the subway entrance. A small man with two teeth and no left ear was talking to him: "Lizzie Graces came to town yestiddy with six poodles on a leash and ast me to sell 'em for her no questions ast can you tie that? She and my kid sister was in stir a coupla months ago fer pickin' up meat along Broadway not botherin' anybuddy an' who comes along but Red-eye Clancy the goddamn dick I'd like to pull his balls off."

"You do that," Andy said, clapping the man's shoulder. "Free enterprise. Fugitives. You and me both. Pawns. There ought to be a law. Let 'em get up a committee, read the minutes of the last meeting, pass a law for us once in a while why don't they?" He gave the man a dollar and moved on.

His hat was gone, but a drink would fix that. No. First eat, hold it down.

The jukebox yawned as though bored with chewing so much plastic, and he put in more nickels hoping "Allah's Holiday" would come up again, but it didn't. Then he was eating a great dish of goulash at a white table and feeling almost sober. Think for a minute. What do you want? Mike. The big arm, the hair, the shoulders. Naturally. Flee as a bird.

In the subway he read the signs backward for amusement to see what the words would spell: ynapmoC tiucsiB lanoitaN: a slippery, entertaining language which he decided to speak exclusively from now on in order to annoy people.

The bar was longer than before and there was a new barman, very young and short, with freckled arms. Andy described Mike, but the boy didn't respond so he stood quiet and steady at the street end, not daring to walk the full length of the room; besides, the floor was hot. He would catch Mike the minute he came in. He had to have one drink to steady his knees.

"Thanks," he said to the barman as he poured the Scotch. "Ynapmoc tiucsib lanoitan." He had memorized it perfectly; it gave him a feeling of poise, sobriety. The barman, however, remained unimpressed.

"Ynapmoc tiucsib lanoitan," Andy repeated, patiently, smiling.

"Look, buddy, I don't get you."

"The voice of America, spelled backwards," Andy said. He put a dollar on the bar. "How old are you?"

"Twenty-two, why?"

"Yet ah that spring should vanish with the rose." Andy's eyes traveled up the white coat to the young man's hair. "It would be," he said, "only more like marmalade."

"Mister, you're soused. Better sleep it off."

" 'Tis bought with sighs a-plenty and sold for endless rue, and I am two and twenty, and oh, 'tis true, 'tis true." Andy gazed at the young man. "Buy you a drink," he said. "Come on."

"Uh-uh. No, thanks."

"Married?"

"No."

Andy studied the round pink face. "You should be," he said. "Good-looking guy like you."

The young man stared at Andy. "Didn't I see you around someplace before?"

"No. I'm a stranger here. Fresno, California." Andy leaned forward. "Busy later on?" he asked.

"Why?" The voice was suddenly on the defensive.

"I thought you might like to go out somewhere, have a drink with me." Andy shut off the sound of his own mind. "I like you," he said. "I like your face." Then, lowering his voice: "Come on, a quick one. I've got money."

"Look, you better beat it." The voice was definitely irritated now. "Naw, I mean it. Get going."

"Why, have I said something . . . ?"

"Plenty."

"I was only . . ."

"I know, I know. I seen your kind before. Find yourself some other guy. I ain't the type."

"You're annoyed."

"Yer goddamn right." Andy's arm was unexpectedly seized; the young man was half dragging, half pushing him to the door. He felt horribly ashamed and frightened: a man was standing near the door, watching, and Andy saw the scene taking place through the man's eyes; he became the man himself, a small shopkeeper named Frank, probably with a large family, a quiet, self-respecting citizen watching somebody being bounced, feeling superior, disgusted, safe. He'd tell his wife about it tonight, sitting in the living room under one of those lamps with square pieces of glass stuck all around, reading *The Journal-American* with the top buttons of his pants undone for his stomach to hang out comfortably, full of frankfurters and sauerkraut. Didn't look like a bum, either, he'd say, sort of a nice-looking guy with no hat, quiet type, swell clothes but no hat, soused to the gills. If he was quiet, why did they throw him out? (Now I'm the wife.) Oh, I dunno, you can't never tell about those guys, some of 'em are artists, pansies, those quiet guys, like to feel you up when you aren't lookin'. Mercy, she'd say, well, takes all kinds to make a world, did you notice milk's gone up again a cent and a half?

Which am I? Andy wondered, feeling the barman's thumb digging into his forearm, Frankfurter Frank here or Mrs. Frank or that nice-looking guy being thrown out on his ear.

"You can't do this," he suddenly shouted. "I'm Andrew Moore, I'm an artist. I'm well-known, you can't—"

"You're well-known, all right. Goddamn fairy."

Andy was out on the sidewalk, flat against a building, with people staring at him.

Bars were too much alike but it was absolutely necessary he should find Mike now, so he went into the first one he came to and there he was at the far end sipping his beer just as he should be. Drunk's luck, never would have happened to me sober.

Mike looked at him. "You fired?"

Andy nodded, lifting himself carefully onto the barstool.

"I knew it." Mike went on looking. "Where's your hat?" Andy

didn't answer. "Well, I did my best." Mike took a swallow of beer. "What you going to do now?"

"Mike, listen." Andy nodded at the bartender, who pointed at the beer with a questioning finger. "I've got to sober up. You're the only one can help me."

"Oh, Christ." Mike rested his cheek on his hand, still studying Andy closely. His eye fell on the beer which the bartender put down. "When do we start?"

"Now. I mean tonight, tomorrow morning."

"Now means now."

"This is to get to sleep on," Andy said. "Don't be too tough just yet, give me time."

"You gimme a pain in the ass. Educated guy like you with a swell job, what you wanta bitch it up for?"

Andy's lips moved but nothing came. "You're sore," he said. "Why?"

"Sure I'm sore. I hate to see anybody turn into a lush." Mike's voice was patient, almost bored. "Look, I ain't no Salvation Army, only fer your own sake whyn't you stay off it." He glanced again at the beer; then, lowering his voice: "You didn't pick me up last night because it was me you wanted to go home with. Anybody else woulda done."

"No, Mike, you're wrong. I . . ."

"Last fall you give me the brush-off; now you want me to believe you like me. You don't like anybody. All you want is to get drunk and to hell with people. Listen, I know what I'm sayin'. You're a lush, period. You didn't give a damn if it was me or Joe Doakes last night. And by the time I was ready for it you was so drunk you didn't even know it was me. I don't like to see people get that way, I don't care who they are, gives me the willies." Mike looked at Andy. "You weren't like that in the old days," he said. "What happened?"

Andy didn't answer.

"You'll end up in the booby hatch, you know that, don'tcha?"

Andy tipped his empty glass. "I guess I was pretty drunk when I ran into you last night," he said. "But I was glad it was you, and I'm glad it's you now because I want to sober up and live with you.

I want to work for you, look after the house, cook. I can cook. Give me a chance. I don't want to be like Melvyn and get run in. I want somebody steady, somebody I can like, and I do like you, Mike. I mean it."

"Yeah, as long as there's a bottle around." Mike drew out some change and put it on the bar.

"I've got plenty of money," Andy said quickly. "I'll pay for everything I drank. I'll pay my share of everything. More. I'll buy you steaks, I'll pay the rent, anything you say."

Mike turned on him. "Look," he said, "I don't hafta sell it, fer steaks or anything else. I pick what I like. Even if I have to buy it myself."

"I only thought you'd like to have somebody . . ."

"You thought enough. I gotta beat it. So long."

Andy got off the stool and held on to Mike's arm. "Wait, Mike, don't go yet. Wait a second."

Mike lit a cigarette and threw the match on the floor. Andy's hand dropped. "I wouldn't have you on a bet." He straightened, buttoning his pea jacket. "You're nuts," he said. "You better get yourself committed before somebody does it for you."

"Mike, listen . . ."

"Oh, drop dead." Mike turned and went out.

The bartender was watching in a way Andy didn't like. He cleared his throat and ordered another beer. To hell with Mike, he said to the beer. Might as well be Kit, or the man at the Juilliard. Superior. Everybody so damn proud of themselves, everybody having minds of their own. Sobriety. Safety. Somebody started the jukebox and almost immediately he felt better; Mike's going didn't matter any longer. As for sobering up, he could do that on his own, anytime. All he needed was to make up his mind.

A hand fell on his shoulder; he looked up. It was Sam North.

"I thought you were acting. Show closed?" Sam's voice was too cheerful.

"No," Andy said, "I had a night off." He turned back to the bar.

Sam sat, heavily. "Have a drink," he said.

"I have one."

"Oh, come off it, be yourself." He gave Andy a thorough once-over. "Who's your rough trade?" he asked.

"None of your goddamn business."

They sat without speaking. Andy couldn't decide whether he wanted Sam to go or stay, whether to talk or be haughtily aloof.

"Seen Beryl?" Sam asked.

"Couple of days ago."

"She's off me. God knows why. Says I have bad taste." Sam chuckled.

"You always did have."

"I certainly did." Sam stared at Andy, hard.

"Shrdlu," Andy said. "Etaoin shrdlu."

"A weakness for the shall we say obvious." Sam went on staring. Andy stared back.

"All right, if you want to play games." Andy stuck out his tongue, then lit a cigarette, which went out. "Whaddo I say now? Ynapmoc tiucsib lan . . . I forget."

"Sing it. Sing me something. Be Mistinguette." Sam's face was drunk and amused. *"Je l'ai tellement dans la peau . . .* go on, you used to be wonderful as Mistinguette. Legs and all."

"You forgot who you're addressing." Andy's voice and eyebrows rose. "I'm a married man."

"You're a no-good faggot, that's what."

"Pardon me, I am the new woman."

"Yeah. You and a couple of million others." The bartender's voice was genial, not nasty; bored if anything. Used to it. Maybe one himself. Andy ignored him, keeping his face turned to Sam's.

"Ah, but I'm unique. I'm both, retaining the best features of each. I am she who sits all day waiting for her man to come home, the little woman. Brave, silent, correct. Dutiful wife. I am also he who comes home, the little man. Also brave, silent, correct. Dutiful husband."

"You've certainly changed."

"What do you want?" Andy asked. His voice went back to normal pitch. "Money?"

"Got any?"

"Yes." Andy felt sober, superior, and utterly alone. He took a fifty-dollar bill from his wallet and stuck it in Sam's pocket. Then he tipped up on his toes, looking down. "I suppose you think I owe it to you, don't you? That and a lot more. Or don't you?"

"You couldn't pay me what you owe me." Sam narrowed his mouth, his heavy chin tensed. He let the bill stay where it was.

"I gave you whatever I had was worth giving."

"Oh my Christ. The great actress again! Bought and Paid For."

Tears rose to Andy's eyes. "So you were the big benefactor. See Europe, study, be a great musician, I'll pay. Sure, you paid. Never let me forget it, either, bitching everything up at school, dragging me off to Capri. You didn't give a bloody fug whether I ever wrote a line of music or not, all you wanted was the business; all right you got it. Settled. Fini."

"My God, listen to him." Sam's head rolled like a top running down. "Passing the buck, as usual. Drunk the first day out and picking up with every queer on the boat, that's how much you cared about music. Born tramp." He added a more graphic word so loudly that the bartender turned sharply.

"Hey, outside with that."

"All right, who taught me?" Andy leaned forward.

"Listen, you were an expert long before I ever knew you. You loved it."

Andy's face was close to Sam's. "Yes, and it was that or else. What about the Spanish girl? You told me she was sick. I could have—"

"What's the matter? Trying to make people think you're a man?"

The feel of Sam's face was strange, like chicken bones in a bag of jelly. Andy seemed to be standing in a ring of flame, tall and growing taller; the ring narrowed to a rising pedestal; he was lifted, whirling, on fire, beating Sam from a great height now, bending down from the ceiling in a heaven of hate, joy, freedom. One for Capri, one for Vienna, two for Paris . . . but it wasn't Sam's face under his fists now, it was the nobody he'd wanted to kill for so long, the thing, the shadow that talked like Andrew Moore. It was also Mr. Nickle and Miss Ballard and an Austrian count who wore high-buttoned shoes and whose name he had forgotten. And oddly enough, it was Mike and Kit and the Juilliard man. Someone was pushing them both to the door, and now Sam was under him in the snow, kicking and slobbering, his teeth slimy with blood, his hands clawing.

Something jerked Andy's arm out of its socket and hooked it behind him. "Okay, you take Stinky there." The voice was Irish and bored. A panorama of faces suddenly appeared, a little on the bias, as if the film had slipped, faces amused, tense, shocked. "Lock 'em both up, whadda ya say?"

"I haven't paid for my last drink, Officer," Andy said.

The man looked at him as though amused. "Yeah? Well, see you do, first thing in the morning." He chuckled; he was young, fairly good-looking. His voice sounded less bored now. "You talk pretty."

"I'm a student," Andy said. "Advanced composition."

"Well, you advance right along to the tank and compose somethin' for the magistrate tomorrow mornin'."

"I've never been in jail. My wife . . ." Andy stopped, confused.

"You married?" The cop looked at him skeptically. Andy nodded.

"Seven years."

"What the hell you doin' in a fairy dump, then?"

"I must have been rather drunk."

"Jesus, Mary, and Joseph." The cop snickered. "That's a good one. Must have been rather drunk. Boy, you're a panic. Hey, Vince," he called out to the other man who was leading Sam. "We got a perfessor here. Married."

The cops argued quietly for a moment. "We gotta run 'em in," the older one said finally. "Disturbin' the peace." He squinted at Andy. "You been around here a long time, haven't you?" he asked.

"Twenty years."

"I know. I remember a face when I see it." He shook his head. "Why don't you get wise to yourself?"

Andy couldn't think of anything to say. He looked at his feet, which were wet. "I think you'd better lock me up." His face was bleeding and he fumbled for a handkerchief but couldn't find one. The older cop handed him his, which was mussed but quite clean, with a brown border. "Thanks, Officer."

Going up the steps of the police station, Andy's cop said, "You can call your wife in the morning, after the magistrate gets through with you."

Andy wanted to ask what the punishment would be but was too weak and frightened. All he said was, "It won't be necessary, Officer. She's out of town."

He felt confused again when it came to giving the night sergeant his address, then gave the Washington Square one. The fingerprinting made him go sick to his stomach.

In the detention cell, a long, brightly lit rectangle of dirty walls, he went to sit by himself, covering his face with his hands. Sam stood with his back to him, staring at the floor. There were eight or ten other men in the tank, some sleeping, some arguing with themselves; one, a thin young man with a large head and no chin, sat and bit his nails, weeping silently, occasionally rolling his eyes until they seemed ready to burst from the lids like plums.

Andy drowsed, and when he woke, it was with the realization that the liquor was dying on him, that the hangover he had been putting off for days was about to begin. He got up and began to walk, but it did no good. He walked faster, and soon there were a dozen very small people stepping on his heels, running up his legs, and tugging at the back of his neck. He turned on them, a scream of rage bottling itself in his throat; his fingers went numb and his mouth felt like cold potato skin.

Sam had turned to watch; Andy tried to avoid his eyes but finally gave up and went over to him.

"Well?" Sam's lip was cut where a tooth had gone through.

"I didn't say anything." Sam glanced about quickly, then dug in his vest pocket and took out a small packet of pills. He gave Andy two, taking two himself.

"What are they?"

"Sleep."

Andy hesitated, then swallowed them gratefully. He sat on the floor next to Sam and waited.

"Sam."

"Yes."

"I'm sorry."

"You should be."

"No, I shouldn't. But I am. That's my whole trouble. Sin, sin, forgive, forgive."

"Oh, shut up."

"Let him talk." A very old man with dirty red and white bristles standing out from a purple skin stood up and waved his hands at Sam. "Jesus hears him, Jesus knows. Oh, boys, listen, I'm a dirty dog, I ask Jesus every day to listen but he won't and I don't blame him. For twenty-seven years I sold boys' clothes at Wanamaker's and here I am and my own sister won't even speak to me. I could have ended up a fine respected citizen and I became a bum instead. Why? Sin, boys, just plain ordinary sin, liquor and fornication, and playing the numbers. I yielded, I took the easy way, but let me tell you boys, the easy way is the hardest in the end. I—"

"Crap," Sam said. "Go sleep it off."

The old man wept and turned away. "God will forgive you," he said. "You've still got time. If you don't believe me, ask Him to."

"I will," Andy said. "Only he's got to ask me to forgive him, first."

The old man turned back staring. "I never thought of it that way before." He smiled, then a look of terror crossed his face; he shook his head: "Oh, no, no. That's terrible, that's the worst of all, that's the sin against the Holy Ghost."

The young man with the plum eyes gave a loud sniffle and threw back his head; a gargling sound came from his throat.

"I think Clarice has a cold," Sam said. He closed his eyes and began to nod.

Andy felt the fingers of the drug closing over the back of his neck. He fought it for a while, then, as a black moon rolled expanding from the ceiling, surrendered gratefully.

Wyatt's face with its cigar poked itself up through the floor of the front parlor at South Pond and his armpits felt the shameful jab as he went flying into the snow. He lay there again, contentedly, but it was still the front parlor and now he saw his mother being brought in and put down on the couch by the west window. It was a wet, sweltering summer day smelling of peonies and she was serving tea to a group of women. Suddenly there was a commotion; the women rose and formed a circle about his mother, who began giving birth to him, even as she sipped her tea. Between the women's skirts he could see himself erupt like a burst grape; his mother seized him between thumb and forefinger, turned him about in the low golden sunlight once or twice, then with a look of triumphant self-satisfaction popped him into her mouth.

LONNIE COLEMAN

Sam

David McKay, 1959

Near the beginning of *Sam* we see Sam Kendrick, a gay man and noted New York publisher, having lunch with his friend Reeve, an older and rather queeny man-about-town.

"Why don't you ever publish a gay book? Just to please me. I know a young writer who's done one I think is terribly good."

"Let me read it and we'll see."

"Your books are always so proper and normal," Reeve began defensively.

"If I saw a good one about homosexuals, I'd publish it. The only ones I see are trashy or sentimental. A dream world of television drama, with the sexes changed a little. They all end with a suicide or a murder."

"So dwamatic." Reeve batted his eyelashes.

"How many of us do you know who've killed themselves, or each other?"

Reeve pondered briefly. "I can name a few I'd buy guns for. Will you read this book?"

Here we have, in 1959, a frank discussion between two gay men about the state of homosexual publishing. Sam, of course, is wrong in his contention there are no "good" books with homosexual characters, but what is significant here is the discussion about the relationship between gay life and its fictional representation.

While *Sam* contains some of the settings and themes of its contemporaries, it is far more frank and open about homosexuality and gay life than almost any other mainstream novel of its time. While novels like Truman Capote's 1958 *Breakfast at Tiffany's* or James Purdy's 1959 *Malcolm* indicated their character's sexual orientation, nothing comes close to Coleman's understated yet detailed look at gay male relationships.

Part of the novel's success is due to its not really being *about* homosexuality. Coleman's theme is the inability of selfish people to love anyone (including themselves) and the harm that they cause those who are capable of love. Sam and the callow Walter (who uses sex to promote his acting career) are juxtaposed with Sam's best friend, Adeline (who is in love with him), and her violent husband, Toby. Coleman takes this complicated quartet of people and puts them through a grueling minuet of betrayals and violence—Walter leaves Sam, Addie loses her baby, Toby's repressed homosexuality erupts in his raping a trick—which finally ends on a contented note after Sam meets a new man and forges what promises to be a healthy, happy relationship. One of the most astonishing aspects of *Sam* is that its title character meets his true love at a bathhouse, and Coleman shows us—and the common reader of 1959—the usually hidden world of gay male cruising. While John Rechy's headline-making *City of Night* was released in 1963, shocking the literary and popular world with its descriptions of gay male sex, Coleman had several years earlier broken similar ground, in a far quieter and more traditional manner.

Coleman published his first novel, *Escape the Thunder,* in 1944 and acquired a reputation as a Southern novelist who dealt with social concerns, particularly race. (His 1948 play, *Hot Spell,* was made into the 1958 film with Shirley Booth and Anthony Quinn.) In 1955, *Ship's Company,* his collection of stories set on the USS *Nellie Crocker* featured two stories with explicit gay content: "The

Theban Warriors" and "Bird of Paradise." Late in his career Coleman became a bestselling author (with a cowriting credit on a television miniseries) with his trilogy about antebellum plantation love and intrigue. In *Beulah Land* (1973), *Look Away, Beulah Land* (1977), and *The Legacy of Beulah Land* (1980), Coleman portrays both homosexual and heterosexual trysts with alacrity, even depicting an interracial, homosexual, incestuous coupling between a slave owner and his slave son. In 1981 Coleman published *Mark*, about a young man discovering his homosexuality in a small Alabama town during the Depression.

William Laurence Coleman was born in 1920 and died in 1982. *Sam* was published in cloth by David McKay, with a paperback edition by Pyramid in 1961. The paperback cover features a man's hand in a flamboyant gesture holding a cigarette holder beneath the copy "A Frank Novel of the Life and Loves in a Strange Twilight World"—an image that is decidedly not reflective of Coleman's tone. *Sam* has been out of print since the mid-1960s, and none of Coleman's fifteen novels are now in print.

These two chapters give us a glimpse of Coleman's complex view of gay male relationships and interactions. In the first, which occurs at the beginning of the novel, we observe the powerful emotional and sexual bond between Sam and his younger lover, Walter, even though there are class, career, and monetary tensions between them. The second chapter begins with Sam, depressed over the stillbirth of Addie's child and the realization that Walter has finally left for good, going out drinking in a desperate attempt to relieve his pain.

Chapter 3

Sam's house was on a quiet block of Greenwich Village near Washington Square. The section had changed, was changing still. Apartment houses filled what had been open sky. Many of the old houses remained, but not in sufficient numbers to stamp the area with their character, as they once had done. The house had belonged to Sam's father, and to Sam's grandfather, whose names were also Samuel Kendrick. Sam's grandfather had founded the publishing house of

Kendrick's and brought it to its first glory. During the father's time the company flourished for a while; for a longer stretch of years it managed merely to hold its own.

When Sam finished his schooling at Columbia in 1942, he went almost immediately into the navy. The war years were prosperous for Kendrick's, but when the war was over and Sam came to work there, he found that what he had long suspected was true: his father was neither a good businessman nor a good editor, and the firm depended to a dangerous degree on its backlist. Sam worked for a year in the sales department. In 1947 he was made an editor. In 1950 his father died of a heart attack. In 1951 Kendrick's had money problems which Sam solved by borrowing from his old friend Reeve Keary. Since then Kendrick's had prospered. Sam's vitality, his love of publishing, and—soon—his knowledge of it matched his grandfather's.

When Sam returned from the war, his father converted the top floor of the Greenwich Village house into an apartment for Sam, keeping the lower floors for himself. On his father's death—his mother had died in 1930—Sam simply moved downstairs. He thought for a while of renting the top floor as an apartment, but he was reluctant to have strangers, or even friends, in the house that had been home to his family for three generations. He decided, instead, to give the apartment to his houseman. M. L. Custer was a gentle, solemn Negro man in his sixties. He had worked most of his life at Kendrick's. When Sam was a little boy and visited his father at the publishing house, Custer played and talked with him. But as he grew older, there were conflicts between Custer and the younger men who worked in the stockroom. They said his ways were fussy and old-fashioned. He thought they were not "particular" enough, and he did not like hearing their dirty stories.

When Sam offered him the job of keeping the house in Greenwich Village, Custer was relieved and happy. He lived on the top floor alone. He had a widowed sister, two nieces, and a nephew living in Harlem, but he was not intimate with them.

As the taxi drew near the house, Walter said, "It's cold!" and dug his hands deeper into his overcoat pockets. The taxi stopped and they stepped out. Sam paid the driver; Walter jumped over the dirty snow packed on the curb and ran up the steps where he waited until Sam joined him. Although he had his own key, he always waited for Sam to unlock the door when they came home together. It was a habit they had never spoken of, growing naturally out of the fact that Walter had been in and out of the house for several months as a guest before he moved in.

"Shall I light the fire?" Walter said in the living room as Sam turned on the lights. The living room ran the length of the house, and Custer always had wood and kindling laid ready in the fireplace.

"I don't know," Sam said indifferently. "It seems warm enough. Will you be up long?"

Walter dropped his overcoat on a chair. "Let's stay up a little."

"You were so eager to leave."

"I wanted to be home with you. Are you really tired?" Sam nodded cautiously. "Oh."

Touched, although he knew where conversation would lead them tonight, Sam said, "Go ahead and light it."

Walter smiled quickly, struck a long match, and touched it to the wadded paper under the kindling. The fire caught, and Walter rubbed his hands together before it. Sam took off his coat and loosened his tie. He turned sharply when he heard Walter's laugh.

"Andrew isn't tired," Walter said.

A full-grown Abyssinian cat entered the room from the stair that led down to the dining room and kitchen. Without a glance at Walter the cat walked over to Sam, his eyes kindling as he went. With a leap he was on the back of the chair, kneading his claws gently into Sam's discarded coat, looking up at Sam. Sam looked down at him without speaking.

"Ah, Andrew, silly old Andrew!" Walter exclaimed jollily, coming between them, rubbing the cat's back fur roughly the wrong way.

The cat leaped to the floor, shook himself, gave two licks to his left shoulder, withdrew a few feet, and turned to stare coldly at Walter.

"You know he doesn't like that," Sam protested.

"Yes, I know!" Walter said happily. "But he looks so goddamn dignified, I have to ruffle him."

"Cats don't like being ruffled."

"You do, don't you?" Walter caught Sam around the waist and

hugged him close a moment. Over Sam's shoulder he saw Andrew's contemptuous stare and thrust Sam away from him, his good humor breaking off into irritability. "That cat, that damn cat. Look at him looking at me."

"Don't be silly," Sam said, going to the fire and poking a log.

"He looks at me like I'm a cretin."

"That's because he thinks you are." Sam laughed, to make a joke of it.

"Custer and Andrew. I'm afraid I'm not their favorite actor."

From the fireplace Sam said, "Don't be a child."

"Do they really like each other, or do they just join forces against me?"

"I've never discussed it with them." Sam yawned, bringing Walter to sudden alertness.

"How about a beer?" Walter suggested.

"Not for me."

"I'd like one," Walter said stubbornly, going toward the stair. "Can I bring you anything?"

"A glass of milk if you're going down," Sam said unwillingly.

Walter disappeared down the stair, and presently Sam heard the refrigerator door open. He turned one of the two large chairs slightly to face the fire and sat down. The cat came out of the shadows and jumped to the arm of the chair, lifting his face into Sam's. Sam wrinkled his lips and nuzzled the cat's neck with his nose. Andrew bowed his back with pleasure, turned, and swept his tail flatteringly under Sam's chin. Sam laughed. "Crazy. Crazy Andrew," he said softly.

The refrigerator door slammed.

"Enough," Sam said, hastily making a slide of his lap and legs and pushing the cat to the floor.

Walter came up the stair with a glass of milk in one hand and a can of beer in the other. He stopped halfway across the room to drink from the hole he had punched in the can. Shifting the other chair to face the fire, he moved a small table between them and set down his beer can.

"Why don't you use a napkin or a coaster?" Sam said.

"Coaster doesn't fit a beer can."

"You'll leave a ring."

"So. Custer can wipe it up."

"He's already cleaned for the party tomorrow."

"Boy, I wish I worked for you," Walter said. "Such consideration." Sam shrugged and dropped his hand along the side of his chair where he knew Andrew was sitting out of Walter's sight. Running his thumb gently along the depression between Andrew's shoulders, he felt that he and the cat were conspirators, and smiled at his fancy.

"I forgot," Walter said, reaching into the breast pocket of his shirt and withdrawing a note. "Custer left this for you in the kitchen."

Sam took the note and read: "I ordered the flowers. Six dozen long-stemmed red roses to be delivered at three o'clock tomorrow. Mr. Keary called and said could you make lunch at one instead of twelve-thirty." Sam wadded the note and tossed it into the fire.

"Where are you lunching with Keary?"

"Plaza," Sam said, and sipped from his glass of milk. Andrew, sitting very quietly, suddenly lifted his face until his whole head was enclosed in Sam's dangling hand.

"Another one," Walter said. "Custer, Andrew—Reeve. I can't get used to calling millionaires by their first names."

"Just takes a little practice."

"I don't remember his encouraging it."

"He likes you all right. You've never seen much of each other." Sam watched Walter sip from the beer can again, saw the malice enter his smile as he set it down.

"It doesn't matter whether Reeve likes me or not. He wouldn't like anybody you shacked up with. He and Addie get on together, though, don't they?"

"I believe so," Sam said, looking back at the fire.

"Well, I don't care. It embarrasses me to be seen in public with him anyway. The way he overdresses. It's a dead giveaway when old faggots become old dandies. His thin Italian shoes and his suits always a little too snug. As if anybody notices what he's trying to show off. Also, the way he talks—about anything he wants to without lowering his voice. It embarrasses me."

"It wouldn't if you thought of Reeve or yourself, instead of what strangers might think."

"You never know who the strangers might be."

"I never wonder."

"Well, it's different with you." Walter sipped again from the beer can, and Sam blinked at the ring already showing on the table. He got up, took a magazine from another table, wiped up the ring with his handkerchief, and slipped the magazine under Walter's beer can. "Sorry I'm such a slob," Walter apologized mockingly. Sam sat down again.

"What time is your lunch date tomorrow?" Sam asked.

"Twelve-thirty."

"What's her name? I don't seem to be able to remember it."

"Jane Frisbie."

"Oh, yes. And she's a reporter. You haven't seen her since I've known you."

"She's been away doing freelance articles. Turkey, Egypt, India. Other places."

"Oh."

"She's very successful. She used to be mad for me."

Sam drank the last of his milk. "I really am tired."

Walter said quickly, "Reeve sort of raised you, didn't he?"

"No," Sam said, "my father did."

"You know what I mean. Showed you—certain ropes. You were his boy."

"I think I always knew where the ropes were, and I was never his boy."

"Not for want of his trying, I bet." Sam did not answer. He got up and set his glass in an empty ashtray on the low table in front of the sofa. "He saved the old firm for you one time, didn't he?"

"I like to think I did that," Sam answered, returning to the fireplace and standing with his back to it. He folded his arms and looked quietly at Walter until Walter's eyes began to shine with anger. "Reeve put money into the business, for which he got shares, the voting power of which belongs to me."

"To do that, he must have liked you."

"We have agreed that Reeve likes me and that I like Reeve. The investment was a good one for him. I knew it would be. The firm was basically sound, it was simply short of ready cash. My father hadn't put aside enough of the money made during the war to take care of slack times. Reeve spends more in a year giving presents to chorus boys and subsidizing 'promising' young painters and writers than he put into Kendrick's. Certainly he knew I wasn't trying to use him."

"You mean the investment didn't involve any—cozy private services."

Sam did not smile. He stared at Walter a long moment, sick at the sight of enjoyment on Walter's face. "No, it didn't involve any private services."

"Still," Walter said quickly, "you love the old firm enough to, don't you?"

"It's never been necessary to put my love of the firm to that kind of test."

Walter laughed outright. "You've had it easy, Sam. You just walked right into it."

"I was born into it. Headfirst. I walked very late. Boy babies often do."

"All right, don't get touchy," Walter said in an overfriendly way that was not friendly at all. He let his glance roam over the solid old furnishings of the room. "It's easy for you rich boys to have scruples."

Sam said deliberately, "You poor boys always say that to let yourselves off the hook. I believe we've come to the point of the conversation. It was a very long buildup. If I'd read it in a book, I'd have suggested the author cut it. I'm tired, as I've said. What is it you wanted to talk to me about? I'm ready."

"It took you long enough," Walter said sulkily. "You don't think I've been having fun, do you?"

Sam's face softened. "No." He sat down again, facing Walter.

"Sam," Walter said, and then paused to take a deep breath, "I'd screw chickens at a carnival if it got me what I wanted."

Sam sighed impatiently. "You know as well as I do New York is white with the bones of actors who thought they could rise to the top by dropping their pants."

"I admit I've had my disappointments." Walter forced himself to smile before letting his face harden. "But not this time. Here's the deal, Sam. Tomorrow night Eloise McKenzie is coming down here. She's going to be looking me over more than she ever did in her office or on television. If she decides I'm all right, she's going to fix a date with Eva Fairchild. We all know about Eva Fairchild. She won't do a play that doesn't have a part in it for a young man like me. That young man is always Eva's escort. He takes her to Sardi's. He takes her driving and to the beach on their days off. When she wants him to, he stays at her apartment all night. That isn't very often, I hear. If I get past McKenzie to Fairchild, I've got to make Fairchild like me. I plan to do just that, Sam."

"You don't have to do that. I've told you I can get you a job in a minute. A decent job."

"With Kendrick's?" Walter said, smiling.

"No, not with Kendrick's. With another publisher as a salesman. You'd make a good salesman."

"I don't want to be a salesman, Sam. I want to be an actor."

"Then be an actor, don't be a whore. You wouldn't have to do such things if—"

"If I were a good actor? Maybe, maybe not. I know you think I'm untalented, but—"

"I think no such thing."

"Yes, you do, Sam."

"I've never seen you in anything that gave you a real chance."

"You've seen me in big parts in summer theaters. *Arms and the Man*—"

"I thought you were fine, that with more experience, if you wanted to, you could—"

"Don't bullshit me, Sam. I know what you think of my acting, and I don't give a damn. What I give a damn about is that this is the way I'm going to make it. Do you think I want to be Sam's boy?"

"You're not. You make your own money."

"I live here rent-free. Have I ever paid for a meal I've had here? Custer knows. Andrew knows. Addie knows. Reeve knows. Every time they look at me, I see they know."

"You're crazy."

"I may be. I'm also sick of it. How do you know I'm not taking you for a ride, Sam?"

Sam reflected. "For one thing, you've never taken any help I've offered."

"Maybe you didn't offer me the right things. Now if you had cultivated the acquaintance of a few producers—and you could have. Maybe put a thousand or two in their rotten shows occasionally—"

"Don't be an ass."

"When I was a slum kid, I thought *ass* was a dirty word, but I've found that all the most cultivated people use it."

"Is that so?"

"That's so, old buddy," Walter sneered. When he spoke again, his voice was thick with self-pity, and maybe pity for Sam, too. "Old buddy-boy. Sam, if you care about me, tell me it's all right. Tell me we can still see each other."

Sam said, "If you go through with this, I never want to see you again."

"Sam!"

"I mean it."

"You really don't give a damn about me, do you? I'm just a—"

"I'm trying hard not to give a damn about you, Walter."

"Sam, I can't live the life anymore! You're strong, and you can do it, but I'm not, and I can't! People are talking about me, and all I've got is my reputation!"

"Your reputation?" Sam was genuinely surprised.

"Before I met you, sure I played around some. I played with boys, and I played with girls. But I never got involved with any of them. Nothing serious ever happened. I was my own man. I joined the club at night and resigned in the morning. That was all right. That I could handle. What I can't handle is making a life of it, knowing everybody knows. Do you know what people think about people like you, Sam? Do you know the words they use to describe you?"

Sam frowned and did not answer.

Walter's face twisted with self-hate, and his voice was calculated to lash both Sam and himself. "Fairy! Queer! Queen! Homo! Mary! Pansy! Sixty-niner!"

"Never mind," Sam interrupted quietly. "I know them all."

"Then how thick is your hide?" Walter demanded, trembling.

"As thick as it has to be to keep out the cold."

"Don't you know that every time they look at you they—"

"They! Who are *they?* Don't be a fool. You're naive to suppose that every time anyone looks at me or talks to me he's speculating on my sex life. Do you, every time you see and talk to someone?"

Walter laughed helplessly. "More often than not."

Sam did not laugh with him, but continued to look at him severely. "When I was younger than you and more emotional about these matters than I am now, I went to my doctor for a routine examination. A little something was wrong—I forget what, it was long ago. But I was so preoccupied with myself and full of guilt for what I was, everything that went wrong with me seemed God's just punishment for my wickedness. I blurted out, 'Doctor, there's something I haven't ever told you that may affect me physically—I'm a homosexual!' I wasn't sure he'd heard. He kept writing on his pad. Finally he looked up, and you know what he said? He said, 'Been getting much lately?' "

"That was a damn silly thing for him to—"

Sam shook his head. "I was grateful. It put me in my place, and it set me to thinking. I realized that I wasn't the only one with my problem, and that my problem wasn't the only problem in the world. Everybody has problems that drive them crazy, and most people never solve them. I asked myself if I really thought my way of life was wrong, or if in thinking so I was merely genuflecting to the ideas of other people. For years I had pretended to myself that I would change. I admitted finally that I was a homosexual, that it wasn't a phase, and it wasn't a disease. I'd been to bed with women and felt nothing at all, although it was possible for me to make love to them if I shut my eyes and thought of a man. *That*, I realized, was wrong, *that* was evil. I swore then I'd be true to myself and not try to be true to the cant of society. Those women I went to bed with, it never really worked, although I 'went through with it,' as they say. But every one of them, without knowing what was wrong, knew something was wrong and felt unsatisfied, inadequate, unhappy. I, of course, felt miserable. Why should I go to bed with a woman and make both of us unhappy when I can go to bed with a man and make both of us happy? I began to go to bed with men without shame or fear. I made them happy, and I made myself happy. I felt whole and healthy for the first time. For the first time I was a man."

"Still," Walter said stubbornly, "you can't buck society, Sam."

"I'm not trying to. But I insist on having my place in it. Not theirs. *Mine.*"

Walter shrugged. "So you've got it solved."

"I've got it solved," Sam said ironically. "Knowing what you feel and following your way is just the beginning. That was enough for a while, but then I wanted permanency. I wanted somebody to love and live with."

"Why don't you get married, Sam?"

"You haven't been listening to me."

"You could do what you wanted on the side. You could find a woman who'd understand."

"I despise men who do that. Have you ever noticed their wives? Tense, watchful women who look at every man they meet with suspicion. Is it worth that to have a child? Not to me. I don't speak lightly. I should like to have a child. I'd like to hold in my arms a—thing whose being was the result of love between me and someone else. But I never shall." He shook his head and repeated a statement that had come into his mind many years ago. "I shall have no child and no child's child to warm my winter years." He frowned. "Of course many married people don't or can't have children. And many people who do have them lose them through death—or hatred. Still, I should have liked being a father."

"Instead—" Walter's voice was edged. "You'll go on seeking—'permanency'!"

"What else can I do? I know it doesn't exist for anyone, but I have to act as if I believe it does." Sam tapped himself on the chest lightly with the tips of his fingers. "I'm a nest builder, not a vagabond. This is my house. My father was born in it. I've lived in it a hundred years. I want to go on living in it with somebody who loves Sam, somebody Sam loves and can expect to stick with him tomorrow and next week and twenty years from now."

"If you'd like to go out now looking, if you'd like me to move my things out tonight—"

"Don't be a fool!"

"You've said that more than once tonight!"

"I'll say it again!" Sam showed real anger for the first time. "You are a fool to throw away what I have to give you! Do you think somebody like me comes along every day?"

Walter shook his head again and again. "I can't do it, Sam. I can't." He threw his hands up, and his voice rose. "I'm glad I can't. I want to be on the other side with the others!"

"All right, Walter," Sam said simply. "I didn't force you into this, did I?"

"No. I didn't make any promises either."

"If you had, what difference would it make, feeling as you feel?"

"I've been honest."

"More with me than with yourself, I think."

Walter stirred restlessly in his chair. Then his troubled face cleared, and he slumped back again. "Well, you've got Addie. Maybe she's your permanence."

"Addie has her own troubles."

"She'll always have them, and you will, too—as long as you feel the way you do about each other."

"Let's not talk about Addie," Sam said quickly.

Walter looked at him mockingly. "That's sacred, is it? It's all right to give me hell for what I do, but what about you and Addie? You can't shut me up, Sam, and don't try to! If it hadn't been for Addie, maybe you and I would have worked out. And if it weren't for you, maybe Addie and Toby could be happy. Have you thought of that?"

"Shut up!"

"Oh, no! Solemn old Sam who has everything figured out! Smug old Sam who knows what's right for everybody to do—except himself, except where his own feelings are involved. You're blind, Sam, for all your big talk!"

"God damn you!"

"Oh ho, oh ho! Sam's mad, because he hates the truth! Easy to put it all off on me, isn't it, Sam? Easy to put Addie's troubles all on Toby, isn't it, Sam? Sam!" Sam had got up from his chair and started for the stairway that led to the bedrooms on the next floor. "Sam!" When Walter ran after him, he stumbled over Andrew. "Have you been there all night?" he demanded angrily of the cat. Andrew backed away from him spitting. When Walter got to the next landing, Sam was in his room, and his door was closed.

Walter ran past his own bedroom, rattled the knob on Sam's door, and found it locked. "Sam!" he shouted, pounding his fists on the door. "Let me in! Let me in, Sam!"

The door opened, and Sam whispered angrily, "Be quiet, you'll wake Custer!"

"I don't give a damn if I wake Custer. Let Custer hear me, let everybody hear me. You're not going to run away from me just because I say something you don't like to hear and won't face!"

"Keep your voice down!"

Walter looked toward the ceiling and shouted, "Custer! Custer, wake up and listen, you sneering bastard!"

Sam slapped Walter hard, and Walter let his knees buckle. He sank to the floor and stretched himself there full length. Presently the telephone on the bedside table began to ring. Sam picked up the receiver.

"Yes? . . . No, I'm all right. Good night, Custer." He put the receiver back on the cradle.

Walter said, "Custer running to the defense of ole Marse Sam." He took a handkerchief from his pocket and blew his nose. Then he got to his feet. They looked at each other with sudden embarrassment.

Walter turned to the door. "Sorry, Sam."

Sam touched his arm.

Walter said, "I didn't mean to hurt you. We both said a lot of things—"

"We said true things," Sam said, "and we meant to hurt each other."

"I guess we succeeded," Walter said.

"Being sorry doesn't change anything."

"No," Walter said with difficulty, "it doesn't." He put his arms around Sam's waist. "Tell me good night, Buddy-boy. Buddy-boy, Sambo." Sam kissed him gently on the lips. Walter tightened his grip. Sam tried to jerk away, but Walter held fast, speaking quickly, imploringly, "No, Sam, no, no. Please, Sam. Once more. I can't face it thinking I'll never hold you like this again. Sam, be good to me, be good. Oh, Sam, I love you!"

Willingly or not, flesh responded to flesh. Sam ceased struggling and put his own arms around Walter. "I know," he said. "That's the hell of it."

Chapter 12

When he left Toby, Sam stopped at a drugstore to make two telephone calls.

Dan was able to tell him a little more. The birth had been in the normal way, but the baby had never breathed. Addie was asleep. She would not be told until next day what had happened.

He called his house and spoke first to Custer, who asked about Addie, and then to Reeve, who did not. Reeve told him the young men had just gone off together and that he and Denis Everett were about to leave.

"I suppose Walter hasn't come in?" Sam said.

"You didn't expect him, did you, Sam?" Reeve's voice was sympathetic.

"He hasn't called, or anything like that?"

"What is 'like that'? No, dear Sam, not a word."

"Good night, Reeve. I'll talk to you tomorrow."

"Don't call early. I don't expect to get to sleep for a while." Sam could hear faintly over the wire a laugh, not Reeve's. He hung up.

He did not go home. He asked the taxi driver to let him out at a bar two blocks from his house in Greenwich Village. It was not an attractive or companionable-looking place. He had passed it a thousand times and never gone into it. He chose it tonight because it was the sort of place to get drunk in, where no one would talk to you or try to make sporting bets or even laugh at the television. There was, in fact, no television set. The bartender was a thin, sourfaced man of middle years; the skin of his bald head was gray and scaly. The other inhabitants were all men. They sat alone without talking, their passive expressions indicating that they were hardly thinking.

It took an hour of rapid drinking for Sam to begin to feel the numbness of brain he desired. When it came, he slowed his drinking, but kept at it steadily. By two o'clock he could think of Addie; he could console himself: she didn't die. He could think of Walter up to a point. He could not think of Walter as he might be at this moment. He tried to and was filled with such rage and resentment he switched his thinking quickly to—no, not Toby; he still couldn't think of Toby.

Two-thirty, three; and the blurry edges gathered in to the center of his thinking. He remembered promising to read a book for Martin Cranch and give him a report on Monday. Poor writer, to be read by Sam at such a time. He would put it off a couple of days. Martin liked the book; he should give it a careful reading. He'd had a party tonight—was it possible? Only tonight, or last night he'd still had Walter.

Go home, Sam.

Who said it? Nobody. There was no one to say it or care whether he went home or to the devil. Home was where all the Kendricks had lived; he could not go there feeling as un-Kendrick as he felt now.

By three Sam was drunker than he had ever been before. He left loose change on the bar, slid off the broken-springed stool, and went out the door. It was very cold. He turned up his overcoat collar and stood looking about him. The street was deserted: no cars except parked ones, no people walking. A taxi came slowly along the street. Its light showed that it was free. The driver brought it to a halt and called, "Cab?"

Sam knew that if he got into it he would not go home. Home was two blocks away, and if he were going there, he would walk. If he took the cab, he would go to the Turkish bath he had heard of but never visited, the one patronized by homosexuals.

"You want a cab, mister?"

Sam stepped to the curb. "Yes."

The attendant at the reception desk offered Sam a strongbox for his watch and wallet, gave him his key on an elastic strap, and directed him to a flight of stairs. The stairs were many and steep, and it took Sam several minutes to maneuver them. He was panting when he reached the top. The corridor he found himself in was narrow and dark. He went along it, passing doors that were closed and doors that were open, until he came to a small lighted room where a sleepy-looking attendant was reading a paperback novel. He held out his key. The man took it, looked at its number, selected a cotton robe and towel, and told Sam to follow him.

There were small red lights along the dark passageway, and men walked to and fro, some quickly, some slowly, like preoccupied inmates of a lunatic asylum. The attendant pulled a cord, lighting Sam's room, and held out his hand. Sam tipped him, and he went away.

He took off his overcoat and hung it on a splintery hanger before sitting on the wobbly straight chair. Examining the room, he took satisfaction in its sordidness. The green paint on the narrow iron cot was chipped. The sheet and pillowcase were clean but did not quite cover the mattress, which was thin, mean, and dirty. There was a spittoon between the chair he sat on and the bed. On the wall was a small, dusty mirror. On the back of the door—the door was not quite closed—a large, obscene drawing had been ineffectually erased. He looked at the smudged lines with wonder. What dreams had been dreamed here, what agonies of desire enacted? This, he remembered, was said to be one of the sinful places of the city. He had never seen a more squalid room in his life.

The door was pushed open by a short, stocky man in a cotton robe. He wore horn-rimmed glasses. "Do you have a cigarette?" he asked, entering the room hesitantly.

"Sure," Sam said, fumbling in his jacket pocket and holding out a package.

"A match?" The man was studying Sam's face. Sam fumbled again and found matches. The man lit a cigarette and gave the matches back to Sam, squeezing his hand.

"Are you leaving or just getting in?" the man said.

"Just got here," Sam said.

The man smiled. "You look all in. You ought to get some sleep." He waved his cigarette in the air. "Thanks," he said, and went out the door, pulling it not quite to behind him.

Sam took off his shoes and socks, then stood and undressed. He lost his balance trying to get his shorts off and fell against the bed just as the door was pushed open by another stranger. "What do you want?" Sam demanded. The man fled.

Sleep, that was what he needed. But first he had to go to the bathroom. He hadn't been during all the time in the bar. He put on the cotton robe and thin slippers, remembered to take his key, and went out the door. It locked when he closed it. He peered at the number over it and wandered down the passageway. He found the bathroom at the end of another passageway beyond a watercooler. The floor was moderately clean. The two urinals were full of discarded cigarettes. As he stood in front of one, the smells of wet tobacco, stale urine, and the sweet perfume of the deodorizer sickened him. A man came and stood beside him at the next urinal. He stared frankly at Sam, and Sam stared at the wall, hiding himself as well as he could with the robe.

He washed his hands with coarse brown soap at a heavy basin. There were no paper towels, and he had not brought the towel from his room, so he dried his hands on the sides of his robe. Trying to find his room, he lost himself. Men were walking, men were standing, men were sitting on window ledges. They stared at him, but none of them spoke. He was surprised to see that many of them were old. Fat men, thin men, tall men, short men, men with gray hair and dark hair and blond hair and no hair. In their robes they looked as sexless and quaint as French schoolchildren in smocks on their way to school. He wandered, not trying to find his room any longer, walking with the other walkers, copying their aimlessness. He felt no desire—he was too tired and unhappy and drunk for that—but he began to feel some of the nervousness that masked the desire of the others. Once he found himself looking through a partly open door at two men beginning to make love. They saw him, and one of them closed the door.

He went on. Stopping to light a cigarette, he was approached by a young man, but after a few words the man saw that Sam was drunk and left him. He turned blindly into a room, and the man there quickly got out of bed, pressed Sam's face against his bare bosom, and implored, "Bite me, bite me hard, daddy!" Sam backed, frightened, out of the room.

He went into another room. The man in the dark there struck a match, ostensibly to light a cigarette, actually to see Sam's face and to show his own. Blowing out the match, he said in a matter-of-fact way, "What do you like to do?"

Sam said, "I wanted to talk."

"I don't," the man said tonelessly. Sam left him.

He went into another larger room that was evenly divided between spectators and actors. He found it as briefly interesting and as quickly boring as watching dogs fornicating in the street.

He came to a group of three very effeminate men chatting and laughing in the passageway, their string belts tied elaborately in the back, like old-fashioned little-girl sashes. They stood out because most of the others there were not effeminate. The three were shunned as much as if they had been women.

Exhausted, he found himself finally in front of his own door. He unlocked it and went in. Without turning on the light he slipped off his robe and slippers and lay down on the narrow bed. From the room next door he heard movement and moaning. He went to sleep quickly, with an erection.

He woke slowly from his deep sleep and did not at first know what was happening. Gradually he became aware that three of the old men he had seen skulking like jackals in the passageway had sneaked in at his unlocked door. They quarreled and fought over his flesh as if it were carrion. Unable to fend them off, or perhaps wanting this final degradation, Sam subsided, whimpering. When they had done, he felt that indeed his body was dead and done, and nothing for it but to shuck it off and get a new one. "Not dead yet!" he protested. They laughed at his craziness, knowing he was drunk and helpless and that they had left nothing. Cackling in self-congratulation, they slipped out the door. Sam turned his face into the pillow and cried exhaustedly.

He woke again. Someone had thrown a robe over him. He raised his head and saw that the door was closed. Then he saw a burning cigarette in the dark and the figure of a man sitting in the chair beside his bed.

"Who are you?" he said.

"It's all right," the man said.

"Is it?" Sam said dully.

"Yes. I knew they'd get you when I saw you earlier. They wait for someone to come in drunk. Do you feel better?"

"I don't know how I feel."

"You slept an hour."

"How do you know?"

"I've been watching you."

"Why did you do that?"

"Would you like some light?" The man left the chair and pulled the string that turned on the bare bulb set into the wall. When he turned, Sam saw that he was near his own age. He was tall and thickly built, but not fat. His brown hair was neatly combed.

"Do you have a cigarette?" Sam asked, moving his arms outside the covering robe. The man gave him a cigarette, lit it for him, and sat down again. "What do you want?" Sam said.

"Nothing."

Sam smoked, examining the man's face. The man let himself be examined without changing his expression. When he was satisfied, Sam said, "What kind of ghouls come here?"

"Ghouls like you and me. You must have wanted them to come in; you left your door open. That's the understanding here. If you leave the door open, it means you don't mind company."

"I didn't know that."

"Is it your first time here?"

"Yes."

"It's not a bad place. It's depressing, but a lot of perfectly nice people come here because there's no other place to go. The queer bars are mostly for the flirts and teases."

"I don't go to the bars."

"What do you do?"

"I've been living with someone," Sam said.

"I did once," the man said.

The man looked around the room. "All kinds of people come here," he said. "Married, single, truck drivers, bankers, punks, and priests. The worst that can be said for them is that they're pathetic, looking for a little love in the dark because they—we—can't bear to try it in the light. Take a good look at the place. You'll be back. And don't sneer. Whatever you find here was in your mind before you came, or you wouldn't have come."

"You don't know why I came."

"You came looking for something worse than you are, so you could forgive yourself."

"You don't know me. I don't have to forgive myself."

"You're lucky."

"Those old men—"

The man nodded. "With grizzled hair on their bodies as dry as dead flowers on a grave. What else can they do?"

"Who are you?"

"It's not a place to give names."

"My first name is Sam."

The man stood again. "Get up and dress and go home. I'll help you if you like. Or leave."

"Stay, please. What time is it?"

"After five."

"Is there a shower?" Sam asked.

"Downstairs. I'll show you."

Sam put on his robe and slippers, found his key, and followed the man out of the room. On the basement floor they went into the steam room for a quarter of an hour and then took cold showers. Sam's head cleared. He felt tired, but himself again. The attendant helped them dry themselves, and they went upstairs. Sam unlocked his door, went into his room, and pulled the light cord. When he turned, the man was gone.

Sam began to dress. It was quiet. In one of the far rooms he heard snoring, the only sound. He began to feel lonely and slowed the process of dressing. As he tied his tie, the man's face appeared over his shoulder in the dusty mirror. Sam turned with quick relief. "Hello."

The man was fully dressed, wearing an overcoat and hat. "Hello," he said, and smiled for the first time.

"You came back," Sam said cheerfully, putting on his jacket.

"Yes," the man answered.

"What is your name?"

The man hesitated. "My first name is Richard."

"Mine is Sam."

He smiled again. "You told me."

Sam put on his overcoat. "I'm ready," he said.

They went downstairs and checked out at the desk. The attendant gave them their wallets and watches, and they went down to the street together.

"Would you like to come to my place?" Sam said.

"No," Richard said. "You need sleep, and I do, too."

"Will I see you?" Sam asked.

"What's your telephone number?" Richard asked, taking a pen and piece of paper from his jacket pocket.

Sam gave his number. "That's my house, not my office number. You can get me there most evenings around six."

Richard looked at the number he had written down. "I'll call you sometime. Not soon, though."

"Why not?"

"Because I think you're in a mess and ought to get out of it by yourself. I don't enjoy holding people's hands through crises."

"You did tonight," Sam said.

"I didn't enjoy it."

"Thanks for doing it."

"Sam?"

"Yes?"

"Don't go back there."

"I won't," Sam said.

Richard took a deep breath. "I'm going to walk a bit before I get a cab. Good night."

They shook hands, and Sam held Richard's. "You will call, won't you?" he said.

Richard smiled and took his hand back. "I'll let you worry about that, if you want to." He turned and crossed the street. Sam watched him stride along until he came to a corner, turned it, and disappeared.

PART TWO

The New Gay Novel: Happier Homos and Happier Endings

Beginning in the early thirties, some alternative publishing houses specialized in books with characters and content marketed specifically to a homosexual audience. To avoid censorship and legal prosecution, they were often circumspect in their advertising and marketing. They represent the beginnings of what we now call the gay press movement and the independent gay presses of today.

The histories of these alternative presses are complex, as they were routinely beset with economic difficulties as well as legal harassment and prosecution. In spite of these difficulties, they managed to bring to an eager public books that would have found no other publishers. In their forty-year history they revolutionized what kinds of erotic writing could make it into print and radically changed the publishing industry. There is no continuous history of one company throughout this time line, but rather a series of publishers (and types of publishing) that ultimately ensured the kinds of "free speech" and "freedom of expression" we now take for granted.

In his remarkable social history, *Bookleggers and Smuthounds: The Trade in Erotica, 1920–1940*, Jay A. Gertzman charts the enormous changes in the publishing industry between the wars. In the twenties, New York was home to an incredibly active subindustry of printing and selling erotica. From the reprinting of "classics" such as *Fanny Hill* to mass-produced sexually explicit comic books (commonly called Tijuana Bibles), small, independently run companies produced an enormous amount of "smut." Because such material was illegal, these companies were often fly-by-night enterprises, operating only one step ahead of the law. Their relationship with the larger, more respectable publishing industry was tenuous, as the mainstream firms generally wanted nothing to do with them.

Most of the erotica industry was run by Jewish immigrants who had found a profitable, if not very secure, niche in the underground publishing world. Private entrepreneurship was, of course, a traditional way for immigrants to move into the culture of mainstream American business. From the mid-teens to the forties the "smut" business was commonly seen and referred to as a "Jewish" phenomenon. During this same time, many Jewish editors and publishers also began their own far more respectable publishing companies (such as Alfred and Blanche Knopf). Because these publishers took an interest in new, often provocative European and British literature, they also found themselves under attack by the censors. The censors were as eager to go after the first American edition of D. H. Lawrence's *Women in Love* as they were an obviously illegal edition of badly reprinted Victorian porn. To complicate these already fraught social dynamics, the main arbiter and enforcer of censorship was John Saxton Sumner, Anthony Comstock's handpicked successor at the New York Society for the Suppression of Vice, a group that received solid financial and political support from the Catholic Church. The image of the Jewish pornographer had such currency in popular culture that, as late as 1944, Bishop Fulton J. Sheen could write in *Love One Another* that Jews must not accuse "Christians of being anti-Semitic" because the "Christian deplores that a particular Jew publishes filthy books disruptive of morality."

What this suggests is that books with daring, erotic, or socially challenging content were published because people who were already outside the accepted social and "moral" framework took enormous risks. The bravery of these small, often felonious presses, along with the courage and intellectual and literary acumen of the larger presses, established a firm base in the United States for publishing materials that would be considered obscene: Margaret Sanger's books about family planning, Radclyffe Hall's *The Well of Loneliness*, Gustave Flaubert's *November*, James Branch Cabell's ribald fantasy *Jurgen*, and almost any book with homosexual content. Because of lawsuits brought by these publishers, the complex array of American censorship laws and other ancillary prohibitions were eventually broken down by the mid-sixties.

One of the most notorious "alternative" publishers of the thirties was Panurge Press, a mail-order company that specialized in limited editions of erotica. Founded by Esar Levine, it published an assortment of titles ranging from Frank Harris's *My Life and Loves* to dubious sociological works such as Gaston Dubois-DeSalulle's *Bestiality: An Encyclopedia of the Carnal Relations Between Human Beings and Animals*. It also published Georges Eekhoud's late-nineteenth-century novel of homosexual love, *A Strange Love*. Levine was arrested several times and once spent six months in prison waiting for trial because bail was not granted.

Greenberg Publishers was a small, not highly respected, but established New York house that published a wide range of titles; it recognized that there was a small but lucrative market for homosexual-themed books. In 1931 they published André Tellier's *Twilight Men*, and in 1932 a two-volume, abridged translation by Whittaker Chambers from the German of Anna Elisabet Weirauch's 1919 three-volume lesbian novel, *Scorpion*. In 1933 they published Richard Meeker's *Better Angel*, a sympathetic novel of a young man's coming out and finding love. (Under his given name, Forman Brown, Meeker had a career as a popular songwriter and puppeteer in the forties and fifties and wrote gay-themed children's books in the 1990s.) In 1949 Greenberg published Nial Kent's *The Divided Path*, and in 1950 James Barr's now classic *Quatrefoil* (as well as his collection of short stories, *Derricks*, in 1951). Most important, Greenberg published Donald Webster Cory's groundbreaking work, *The Homosexual in America* (1951), the first serious, nonexploitative, insider look at the subject. Greenberg was repeatedly harassed for publishing homosexual titles and in 1953 was taken to federal court, fined $3,000, and enjoined from reissuing any of them.

Greenberg's experience showed there was a "gay market" for these titles. In "Selling Gay Literature Before Stonewall," David Bergman shows how Brandt Aymar, the general manager and vice president at Greenberg, started, in conjunction with Donald Webster Cory, the Cory Book Service. Taking the names and addresses of people who had written to Greenberg after the publication of *The*

Homosexual in America, Aymar and Cory built a substantial list of between two to three thousand subscribers for their book club. Unfortunately the club did not last. Bergman suggests that there were too few available titles for the Cory Book Service to continue (although close to fifty gay-male-themed books were published by mainstream presses between 1949 and 1954). In addition, how large a gay subscription society or book club could grow in the early fifties was limited, given the obvious dangers of placing one's name on a mailing list or soliciting gay materials through the mail.

In 1952, H. Lynn Womack, a former headmaster of a boys' school and professor of philosophy at George Washington University, took over Guild Press and within a few years turned it into the world's premier publisher and distributor of gay male erotica and literature. Womack published nearly a dozen "physical culture" magazines, ran a large pen-pal service, published overtly sexual porn paperbacks, and set up effective distribution networks through bookstores. His battle against the censoring of physique magazines resulted in the groundbreaking Supreme Court decision in *Manual vs. Day* (1962). In addition to securing the legal right to publish such magazines, the decision was important because, as scholar Jackie Hatton states, "It asserted that there was such a thing as a homosexual identity, and that homosexuals had the right (within the limits of censorship laws) to express that sexual identity." Historian John D'Emilio claims that Womack was selling 40,000 copies of his magazines per month when the post office seized them in 1960. In 1965 he was selling 750,000 a month.

Womack instigated another revolution in gay publishing. In 1964 he began the Guild Book Service, which offered subscribers a wide array of titles. Guild Press published five hardcover books for the club, including Phil Andros's *STUD,* Gillian Freeman's *The Leather Boys,* and Hugh Ross Williamson's quirky mystery *A Wicked Pack of Cards.* The Guild Book Service also offered nearly eighty other titles of interest to gay men, including cloth editions of works previously released by mainstream publishers, such as John Rae's *The Custard Boys,* John Selby's *Madam,* John Bowen's *The Birdcage,* Flannery O'Connor's *The Violent Bear It Away,* Richard Meeker's *Better Angel* (under the title *Torment*), and Gerald Tesch's *Never the Same Again.* Along with this was an assortment of pulps such as Orrie Hitt's *Male Lover,* and the humorous *The Gay Coloring Book.* Reading through the Guild Book Service catalog from 1965–66, it is possible to get a sense of the wide range of books gay men were reading in the years before Stonewall.

Censorship laws were falling away by the midsixties as mainstream publishers, such as Grove Press, fought for the right to publish titles like *Tropic of Cancer* and *Naked Lunch.* This encouraged smaller, gay-oriented presses to begin publishing novels and nonfiction of interest to gay men. Argyle Books, Pageant Press, Sherbourn Press, and Oliver Lytton Press all started operation during this time, and while none of them lasted for long, they were a crucial link in building a gay readership as well as fostering gay writers. While mainstream novels about homosexuals were part of a broad public discussion about sexuality and masculinity (and by extension heterosexuality, marriage, and the family), novels aimed at a more narrowly defined homosexual audience were more likely to be a celebration of gay male sexuality and community. The fantasy of the socially outcast queer getting the high school hunk in *Maybe—Tomorrow* would never have made it into print with a mainstream publisher.

These two selections are representative of what was published by this alternative publishing industry. "Spur Piece" is from James Barr's collection *Derricks,* published by Greenberg in 1951. *Maybe—Tomorrow* was released in 1952 by Pageant Books, another small New York–based publisher.

JAMES BARR

"Spur Piece"

from Derricks

Greenberg, 1951

In 1950, James Barr made a name for himself with the homosexual
military novel *Quatrefoil*. Published by Greenberg two years after
Gore Vidal's *The City and the Pillar,* it tells the story of two lovers
whose nearly attained happiness is thwarted by a calamitous accident. Despite its tragic ending, Barr made it clear that the men loved
one another with honesty, grace, and integrity: "He had gambled
with life for happiness, and miraculously enough had won. But as
he put his hand out to receive the award, it had vanished. Life and
the game, both were a dream." That Vidal's novel ends in man-
made tragedy—the murder of the beloved in the original; his rape
in the 1965 revised edition—is the logical outcome of the author's
ideas about how men are destroyed by the military and the strictures
of maleness. Barr takes a far more generous view of human nature;
in his world, traditional maleness is compatible with same-sex erotic
desire.

After the success of *Quatrefoil,* Barr published *Derricks,* a collection of seven short stories that range in style from Sherwood An-

derson–like descriptions of small-town life to a James M. Cain–inspired tale of violent adultery and homosexual seduction. Barr struggled to create an authentic American narrative—his prose is reminiscent of such wildly diverse sources as Willa Cather, James Farrell, Fannie Hurst, and Zane Grey—that includes same-sex love and passion.

"Spur Piece," the penultimate story in *Derricks,* is a fascinating variation on the subject of love between homosexual men and boys. Gerald Tesch's 1956 *Never the Same Again* deals with similar material, but his characters are trapped in a violent, nonunderstanding world. Here Barr situates repression as a matter of individual psychology: it is the uptight, overly scrupled Tom who cannot see the love and maturity that he is being offered. While other novelists were playing with, and into, the idea that homosexual men "corrupted" youths, Barr presents us with a story in which the protagonist's moral failing is his refusal to love a younger man.

Barr's vision and work did not occur in a vacuum. In 1950, Tennessee Williams published *The Roman Spring of Mrs. Stone* and Patricia Highsmith's *Strangers on a Train* was released. In 1951, Carson McCullers's *The Ballad of the Sad Café* and Paul Goodman's *Parents' Day* were published. All of these books dealt with some of the same themes Barr has in *Derricks,* and while their styles and structures are, for the most part, more dazzling than Barr's, it is his frankness and candor about the homosexual content that makes him unique.

Little is known about Barr's life and career. He was born in 1922 and died in 1995. The dust jacket of *Game of Fools,* his 1955 play, published under his real name James Fugaté, states that he earned his living as an oil-field roustabout. He obviously had some contact with the homophile movement since *Game of Fools* was published by One Inc. *Quatrefoil* went through many printings in the Greenberg cloth edition; the British edition of *The Occasional Man* states that one hundred thousand copies of *Quatrefoil* were sold. Barr wrote a brief introduction to the 1966 paper release (which included many pages of line drawings), and this was rereleased in a Gold Star edition in 1971 under the title *Other than a Man.* In 1966 he published *The Occasional Man* as a paperback original by Paperback Library. In 1982, Alyson Publications reissued *Quatrefoil* with a new epilogue by Barr. *Derricks,* published in 1951, did not have a paper edition. A cloth edition was released in Great Britain by Rodney Books in 1966. All of Barr's work is now out of print.

Spur Piece

Tom first saw him the year the lad was fifteen, the same age as Lucy, Tom's orphaned niece. It was the summer before the two children entered high school. That was in 1946, just after his discharge from the Navy, and Tom was spending the summer as he would spend most of his others in the future—the first two weeks in his parents' home while he took over his father's duties in the wheat harvest, then two months at the university in Chicago toward his doctorate, and the remainder of the vacation back in his hometown with his family again until he returned to teach at State. Tom always made a point of giving his family as much time as he could spare, partly for Lucy's sake, partly for his parents'. It would have been a simple matter to turn the wheat harvest and planting of the family farms over to an overseer, but because it pleased his father for him to do so, Tom always did it himself. He came home late in May and again in early September and saw that the crops were as secure as man could make them. His mother always enjoyed having him home and looked forward to the year when the doctorate would be won, the chair of literature at State secured, and her son could spend his entire vacation in the three-storied white house that occupied a quarter block of the town's nicest, elm-edged section. Not that she resented Tom's long, arduous education or his chosen field of endeavor, but there were times when she and Mr. Kennedy would look at one another and sigh over their children.

Their daughter Belle had died at such an early age and so suddenly. They remembered a carefree girl waving from the open car beside her husband. "Take care of the brat, darlings," she had said, "and we'll pick her up about five. Now you behave with your grandparents, Lucy." But perhaps Belle was not really gone, Mrs. Kennedy often tried to console herself. Certainly there were no drunks driving heedlessly from intersections where she was now. Belle was still away on a short trip. If only the old lady might really convince herself of that, life would be so much easier. But it was impossible to do so for long, for Lucy was quite the young lady of fifteen now, and piling worry on worry for the aged Kennedys. It did seem a heartless thing for even Fate to do, giving them the precious responsibility of a granddaughter after they had reared their own children so carefully. But their generation knew how to bear their burdens with dignity and fortitude.

Tom had arrived on this earth only in the nick of time, for Mrs. Kennedy was then in her forty-fourth year. Such a solemn infant he'd been, never bothering to cry. "He's too busy thinking," Mr. Kennedy would say, and he'd chuckle softly over the wide-eyed baby staring at the top of his bassinet like a pink little man worrying over the world's problems.

Mrs. Kennedy had worried at first, too, that something was wrong with the baby, that it had not been wise of her to have borne him at such an advanced age, but the child had walked and talked long before he was expected to do so and he read at the age of four. Of course, Belle had taught him to do that as a joke. But the joke had been on them for too early he was in school, too soon his marks were excellent, too often his teachers came to Mrs. Kennedy privately to say, "There's really no point in holding Tom [never Tommy, even in those days] back in the coming grade all next year, Mrs. Kennedy. I'm sure he could do very well in the grade following, so if it's all right with you, I think I'll ask the principal to let him skip the second grade." And the fourth and the seventh, until he was graduating from high school before his fifteenth birthday. It was so absurd, his wanting to go on to the university the very next year, but somehow he had persuaded them to allow it. And yet, the boy had never been spoiled or pretentious about his unusual ability. He was so grown-up, even in his humor.

"He won't take spoiling," his father had said one day with a frown. "He's too much a man for his age."

"Why, Mr. Kennedy, whatevah do you mean!" Mrs. Kennedy's soft voice cajoled and reproved her husband at once. "All children take to spoilin' like a duck takes to watah!"

"Tom doesn't. I offered him a brand-new wheel if he'd help out on the farms this summer. He said his old one would do him fine for several more years. But he said he'd work on the farms for nothing. It just isn't natural."

"Didn't he want anything?" his wife asked in her gentle way.

"Books," Mr. Kennedy replied absently. "Something or other about the classics. Knew I wouldn't recollect 'em once I was ten minutes away so I had him write 'em down." He handed her a slip of paper.

"The Hahvahd Classics," Mrs. Kennedy read. "Ah declahe, Mr. Kennedy, if that boy hasn't outsmahted you right propah. These books will cost you at least a hundred dollahs whereas you could have bought a new wheel for thirty."

"Well, I'll be danged!" Mr. Kennedy said, his smile growing to cover his face. "Now ain't he the case!"

"*Isn't*, Mr. Kennedy," his wife admonished softly. "*Ain't* isn't propah!"

But even if his parents hadn't delighted him, Tom would have returned home each year for yet another reason—his niece, Lucy. Being reared by her grandparents was no cinch for the girl, he knew. There were too many gaps that only he could bridge for her. The older couple, while giving their granddaughter the sound principles to live her life wisely, did not always make the necessary allowances for the changing fashions and manners of a changing world. Situations arose that only Tom could mediate.

"I don't think Lucy needs to wear long underwear this winter, Mother. You've said yourself that the winters are growing milder."

"But we're so fah north, Tom, and her skirts are so short."

"But she's a young lady now, Mother, and beginning to attract attention here and there."

"Oh, Tom!"

"What were you doing at the same age, Mamma?"

"Well, girls married youngah in mah day," his mother said coyly.

"Even so, I think if you wrapped Lucy up well and had Mr. Suggs drive and fetch her to school on the worst days, she'd be all right."

"We'll see, Tom, we'll see."

Or perhaps it was Lucy herself who began: "Tom, if I came up to the university next week would you drive me into the city and go with me to buy a new dress? I hate to ask Gramma. She tires so easily these days."

Their eyes met and laughed together.

"Going to spruce up, eh?" he said wisely. "Okay, but no bare backs or black satin trains for another four years, you hear?"

"No bare backs and satin trains, I promise. And, Tom, don't you think I could stand another five bucks a month on my allowance?"

"I think you might stand ten, if it's dollars instead of bucks, but you'd better rely on it from me, not your gramma."

And still later: "But, Dad, the boy only called to see if Lucy would like to go to the movies with him. I can't quite believe he deserved such a questioning as Lucy tells me he got. You might scare him away permanently. And after all, you've known his parents and grandparents all your life. Tell you what, why don't you have Lucy ask him out for lunch after church tomorrow. That would please her, and later, if they want to go to the movies in the afternoon, tell them it's all right. Lucy has a head. She won't make many mistakes."

And not much later, it was: "Tom, when do you suppose I can have a car of my own?"

"I don't know, baby, but when you learn to drive you can wreck mine a couple of times first."

"Really, Tom, you aren't kidding me?"

"When did I ever kid you about anything important, Lucy?"

"Tom, it's no wonder folks up at the university fight to get in your classes!"

The summer of 1946 was one of serene happiness for the Kennedys. For the trio in the white house it meant that Tom was home after four years of agonized waiting, and for Tom a period of ugliness was over and he was returning to a world of literature, culture, and teaching. Life was pretty topnotch all around.

Wheat harvest was in full swing when he got off the train, and he barely had time to say hello to the family before he was grinding over the hot, dust-choked roads from the farms to the elevators where the Kennedy trucks joined a never-ending line of others waiting to be weighed in and unloaded. The little town hummed with its yearly importance and the branch line of the Santa Fe was a shifting, shuddering ribbon of dual-engined trains that bore hurriedly into the heart of America's wheat belt like hungry snakes and then crept away like politically protected looters with their easily plundered burdens. On the smaller farms neighbor women were regimented to cook for the extra hands that had appeared overnight with the fleets of combines. Buffet meals moved from kitchens to the shade of the elm trees outside where grimy men rolled up their sleeves and lined up grinning before the spread of home cooking. At night they slept in barns, barbershops, or the high school gymnasium in their own bedrolls. Sometimes, usually just before they moved on, there would be dances and ice cream socials, and then the churches, which hadn't bothered to sound their bells for the past fortnight, would take in within a few hours more money than would grace the collection plate in the next three months and the preachers would smile, thinking of the largesse that had been and the imminent exodus of the ungodly.

But this was only the first day, Tom thought irritably as he leaped from his light truck and rushed toward the weighing offices of the local elevator, his tally book in his hand.

"Mr. Jansel, Mr. Jansel," he called to the harassed man behind the desk, "your weigher has made a mistake in the grade of this last wheat! Kennedy farms have never produced anything near this low!"

"Weights all right, Tom?" Mr. Jansel asked over his spectacles. "Mighty glad to see you home again, son."

"Yes, yes, the weights are fine, and thank you, sir, good to be home, but the grade of this wheat. I've looked at that wheat myself, every load of it. It's the best in years."

"We'll take a look, Tom. Where's one of your trucks?"

"Thank you, sir, there are three or four in line. You can check all of them."

"One of them's all that's necessary, Tom. I'll just take a look before I speak to the grader. New man, just breakin' in. Regular feller's at dinner right now. Be back in ten minutes. They do better if they get hot meals. 'S'why I let 'em go. This here's one of your trucks, ain't it?" Mr. Jansel indicated a squat, short-cabbed monster.

"Yes, sir, and the next one in line is, too."

Tom looked down the waiting line to locate others. His eyes caught and held on a truck behind one of his own.

"Just one's all I need," he heard Mr. Jansel say from a long distance away. "Just one."

The driver of the truck that Tom had noticed was just a kid. He'd gotten down to examine his tires. There was nothing unusual in the boy's youth, for during harvest everyone—men, women, and children—turned out to drive the trucks that kept the combines moving. Nor was there anything strange about his clothes: denim shirt, jeans, and loafers. He looked like the average youngster of the village, but he reminded Tom of someone or something he'd known very well all his life. Was it an abstract fancy, or was it himself at the same age? The fair curly hair, the broad white brow, the same slender gracefulness of the body that fell so naturally into the picturesque attitudes of the painted saints and peasants of the old masters.

The boy, about to climb back into the cab of his truck, was looking at him, his head tilted slightly as if to question the man's interest in him. And at the smile that came slowly to the boy's face, Tom fell in love.

"You're right, Tom," Mr. Jansel called, "there's a mistake all right. Come on in and I'll fix it up for you right now."

Tom turned reluctantly and said, "Coming, Mr. Jansel." He looked back and found to his joy that the lad had not moved. Now the smile asked, "Do I know you? You seem to have the advantage, I'm sorry to say."

At that moment one of his own drivers approached lugging a thermos jug of water in either hand.

"Hey, Tom, want a drink? I got some cold water here."

"Yeah. Yeah, I sure do." He looked back to the youthful driver. "Want a drink, kid?" The boy nodded and came to them. Tom unscrewed the lid and poured cool water into it. "Here," he said, handing the cup over, "drink first. You may have to move in a hurry."

The boy bent his head and put his bright lips into the clear water. Reflections of the sun ringed his face, revealing the clearness of his skin, the deep pure color of his eyes, and the fine promise of regularity in his features.

He drained the cup and gave it back smiling. "No more," he said in a voice that was sharp and delicate. The line of trucks had started to move, so he turned and ran, shouting over his shoulder, "Thanks a lot, Mr. Kennedy. That was swell!"

Tom felt as if he had had a touch of sun. He drank quickly and went inside. Mr. Jansel had his tally books ready for him. It was with effort he got into his truck and finished the day.

That night in his room before he retired Tom turned the incident over in his mind a long while and came up with several startling facts. For the first time in his wanderings through the ages of literature he understood man's passionate love for extreme youth. How often he had encountered it and what beauties it had called forth from the pens of the initiate, yet how cold the idea had always left him. To him, youth had seemed the period of sexless charm, devoid of personality, individuality, and attraction to the adult taste. This he still believed, but now more than anything else he wished he might have touched the lad's shining lips, held that youth to feel it respond to his urgings.

He went to his bureau and took out an envelope of signed photographs and thumbed through them slowly. Such a galaxy there was—his first affair, a recent captain, a boatswain, a college athlete, twins, a man from his hometown now in New York, a professor of geology, a fellow now in Panama, a young New York detective he'd met in France, a violinist, and so on. He hadn't realized there had been so many. At last he found the one he sought. Clipped to the back of the handsome smiling face, Tom found a letter he'd written several years ago. He'd kept it because it had been the last he'd written to the man. He read:

Dear Carson,

I was not pleased at all with some of the things you told me in your last letter; in fact, I was horrified. I refer to the incident of the high school student. I am going to speak very frankly, Carson, and if I have one less friend at the end of this letter, then that is the price of honesty.

In the first place I cannot understand your state of mind when you allowed yourself to become enamored of a youngster of sixteen. Where is the source of this attraction that seems so ruthlessly powerful? I have known very few high school students (presuming they are of less than legal age) whom I would consider capable of taking a mature role in an adult emotional relationship, and I am aware that many marriages are contracted in the teens and do last many years, but delicate as the marriage situation is, it has the sanction of society to sustain its young members until they have reached the emotional maturity necessary to begin living by their own ideas. Homosexuality between the very young and the adult is criminal, not only legally but, I should think particularly in your case with your background and intelligence, personally. Youth is a period for protection, not exploitation. The youth of any country should be given every right and opportunity to become normal adults. If, when maturity is reached and the individual then learns he is homosexual, and he is willing to work out his own problems, then there is all the difference in the world in your starting point. Your sin is in your motive to influence one, who society says is as yet incapable of making up his own mind, into a state of being that exists very badly as a sexual perversion, a mental sickness. That is society's opinion and society is greater than the single desires of its members. I am glad to hear that the young man has rejected all your overtures. I daresay he will learn soon enough, if he is about to enter the Armed Forces, that men care for other men, and from sources that will mold him in a more normal way of thinking—

There was more in the same vein. Tom did not read it, he could not bring himself to do so. How disgustingly smug he had been in his ignorance. It was understandable now, his loss of Carson's friendship, yet he had condemned him so brutally at the time. Idly Tom looked through the many photographs again. How alike all the faces seemed now, all possessing to a varying degree those same characteristics he had found in the important one. Here was the same pattern in himself that he had so often observed in others of his stamp—the one perfect relationship and then the years spent in search of a duplicate in the many to follow. How much man pays for his fear of the new. And how different all these men had been from the inspiration of his present feelings. Was this a sign of progress—no, not progress—rather change? He should be ashamed of himself, he decided, but when he remembered the questioning smile, he smiled too. Had the boy guessed what was in his mind? No, he had not guessed. Instinctively he had known, Tom was as sure of that as he was of life. He wondered who the boy was. Surely he must be new in town or Tom would have noticed him before now.

For a while Tom played with the desire to bring into being a relationship that would be perfect, one that a scornful world could never attack. A scornful world? Yes, there was such a thing, he reminded himself, and he'd made his peace with it long ago. The treaty he'd accepted held harsh terms, but fair ones, and by those very terms he knew that he was violating his agreement in even planning to see the delightful youngster again, for the first term said he was never to degrade, or use his influence to degrade others. And to influence one as young as this was unheard of. Only among those of his own kind might he seek companionship and remain within his rights. That was the inflexible law, Tom knew, and he accepted it again with an old feeling of philosophic loneliness. But in doing so, his personality remained intact. That was the important thing.

He did see the boy again, however, the next day and every day during harvest. Sometimes he spoke, but usually he was able to prevent it by moving away in another direction. Once, sitting in a café for fifteen minutes, he observed the lad without discovery. The world could not complain of his behavior for he was locked away from it in the fastness of his own mind. There the boy might come whenever he chose, might stay as long as he liked, and ask and give whatever he desired. This was the one weapon (or was it, after all, only an unguent) society could not prevent his using.

The first morning after harvest, the day he was to leave for Chicago, Tom was awakened by a soft tap on his door. He looked up to find Lucy grinning at him through the half-open door like an imp from the forest outside Athens.

"Hey, lazybones, how about some tennis before anyone else gets down to the courts?"

"Okay," Tom agreed, stretching luxuriously, "if you can find my racquet and gear after all these years."

"They're in your closet, restrung and new, so crawl out and shower. I'll be ready in ten minutes. Don't keep me waiting."

The door closed and Tom got up. A quarter of an hour later they reached the courts, where Lucy groaned, "Oh, Tom, there's a set already."

"But there are three other courts."

"But I wanted just us here, alone, like old times."

"Then you should have called me earlier, lazybones." He grinned.

They went inside the fenced area and Tom glanced at the players for the first time. The one in the far court was the youngster who had caused him so much thought lately. The boy waved and Lucy waved back.

"Friends of yours?" Tom asked. No need to make an ass of himself before anyone, Lucy least of all.

"Yes. Want to wait a minute and say hello?"

"Sure." He had always shown interest in her friends.

They waited for the ball to hit the net and the two boys to come to greet Lucy. With the first boy Tom remembered vaguely from other years, he shook hands and said it was good to see how much he'd grown during the war. With the newcomer he remembered too vividly he shook hands and said, "I don't know your name, but I do know you drive a truck. How are you?"

"Just fine, sir."

Darn it all! Why did the kid look up at him as if he were a minor god? And why did the lad have to look more like god bait each time Tom saw him?

"His name is Chris, Tom. He's new in town, and he plays a swell game of tennis. Almost in your bracket," Lucy said.

"Well, if we don't get some of my kinks ironed out, he'll be above my bracket," Tom said. "Let's get started."

Halfway through their set the two boys came to watch them and Tom was conscious of a slight shoddiness in the remainder of his game.

"How about some doubles," the boy named Chris suggested at the end of the set.

"I'm afraid not this morning, unless Lucy wants to take you on. I've got packing to do." He went to pick up his sweater. Lucy explained she would have to go, too.

"Going swimming today, Lucy?" Chris persisted.

"Maybe later. We're driving Tom to the train—'less you'd like to take the later train, Tom, and come swimming too."

"I'm sorry, honey, but I've got reservations out of the city."

Chris came forward and put out his hand. "I'm glad to have met you, Mr. Kennedy. I hope I'll see you again sometime."

"Thank you, Chris." Tom grinned, and added treacherously, "I imagine you will. I'll be back awhile in September."

"Until then, sir."

Tom got in the car and let Lucy light his trembling cigarette.

"Didn't realize tennis was so strenuous." He laughed.

"He's awfully polite, isn't he?" Lucy said. "Gramma says he's the only young gentleman I know. She says he reminds her of you in ways."

"Chris? Oh, very polite. Is he your particular boyfriend?"

"Oh no," Lucy replied almost scornfully. "Wait until you see Harold. He plays football this year."

Tom smiled. "That rather cuts poor Chris out of it, doesn't it?"

"I guess so, but he doesn't care. He doesn't go with girls steady like the other fellows. He's a brain, like you. Straight A average all through grade school. Already knows what he's going to be—an engineer-physicist."

"He must be a brain," Tom agreed, feeling better with the courts behind them. And he asked, "Where will he go to school? Does he know that too, already?"

"Oh yes; State. He's going to win a scholarship, since his folks don't have too much money. He'll probably ask you all about the setup at State the first time he has a chance."

Perhaps there was something in Greek fatalism, Tom thought. Then he remembered his treaty, but it wasn't going to be easy.

The summer in Chicago passed. He signed up for an unusually heavy schedule, since he too wanted to end these doctorate sessions and spend his summers at home. There was the usual round of studying, hard work, perplexing problems, nights out on the town, parties, and casual affairs. He found his preference running to broad brows, light curly hair, the slight and extremely youthful in appearance. He could only laugh at himself, but he could not believe his laughter.

Soon after he returned home in the fall and planting seemed to be well under control, the superintendent of schools rang him up one morning, "I say, Tom, we're in a bit of a jam up here at the high school. Our term's just starting, you know, and our new English teacher is still ill with mumps. She can't be with us for another week and it just occurred to me and Lucy that since you've a couple of weeks free before your classes begin at State, well, I was just wondering if—"

Into Tom's mind flashed an image of bright lips, the head of Ganymede to one side, a questioning smile.

"Why," Tom said, "I think I can help you out, sir."

"Fine, Tom, I knew I could count on you. We'll get our English classes off to a flying start this year."

He had four classes a day. He taught for one student, more particularly for the one face that eagerly drank up every word, every gesture, every expression he was willing to put forth. He was aware of the rendezvous every morning at ten o'clock when the class convened, and because of it, he lectured with all the brilliance he could command. He outlined the entire high school course for the boy in five lectures, drawing upon a store of English and American literature for the amusing, the colorful, the macabre, the fascinating—in short, the seductive. It was his one opportunity in the presence of the world that ruled him to influence and yet remain legitimate. He told stories, and revealed the pageantry of letters from two rich sources. Across his admirer's fresh imagination he sketched with bold but subtle strokes history, humanities, manners, the events and beliefs from *Beowulf* to Shaw, Cotton Mather, to Steinbeck. He was deliberate, he was wary. He was lost. Society had given him five hours. He had turned it into five years.

The superintendent dropped in for the second lecture and returned to hear the rest of them.

"You're a great teacher, Tom," he said later. "I've often thought it wise to bring these subjects to life for the students. So few can these days. By stirring the imagination at this stage, one generates the eagerness to go deeper. How is it you do it so well? What is your secret, Tom?"

"Why, the obvious one, sir." Tom smiled. "Love—of one's subject."

"Ah yes, of course, how true."

In 1947 Tom found it harder to keep his behavior impeccable in the presence of Chris, who availed himself of any opportunity to seek the professor out in the few brief weeks at home.

By 1948 Tom had convinced himself that the boy was heading in one direction, that he was heading there without anyone's benefit, certainly not Tom's. And when he happened to see Chris with a football player in the balcony of the local movie house in a state of more than scholarly camaraderie, Tom was delighted in spite of his sudden jealousy. Opportunities to dominate the boy he found a dozen times a week, and always he discarded them. But who was to say his influence would not do as much good as harm? He spent hours pleading his case, and always smiled at the end of the long harangue and pointed out his first agreement with the world, not to use his influence to degrade, for Tom knew too well that a man must believe in himself, in his own integrity, before he can even pretend to live.

In 1949 he found it easier to keep away from the boy since Chris seemed to be spending all his time with his own age group. Tom refused to ask Lucy about him, yet always he seemed to be in the possession of a complete dossier of fact and gossip. He knew when the boy had his first basketball triumph, his first girl, his first drink of hard liquor and its amusingly related effect. And with philosophic sadness he saw Chris gradually draw further away from him. It had to be so.

In dealing with the variant, Tom knew, one can never rely on any reasonable sequence of behavior or expect any guaranty of result from the actions of the subject, for the dealer is always motivated in such cases by instinct and emotion, yet never has one to be more cautious of that deplorable pair. It was as if Tom knew he might reasonably trust himself one time in a hundred with no way of knowing when the one time would turn up. Chris was much too risky. He might stand too near the norm.

Conceivably he could help the boy, not only financially—and perhaps that is the least help anyone can give in an ultimate sense, certainly if one is dealing with intellect—but paternally and professionally. With what patterns he might tool that green, pliant mind, what tattered edges of thought he might trim away to neaten all future functions. Tom was satisfied from every indication he had observed in Chris that there was but one future for him—the future of the sexual invert. Would he not be doing the boy, himself, and the world a favor if he took him over at this stage to mold him instead of at a later one, after he had picked a bitter, battered personality from some evil-crawling barroom or the ruins of a barely begun family life? Would he not be saving everyone concerned ugliness, pain, anguish? But Tom had been ridden by Reason too long to feel the spur of anything so nervous as Desire. Reason had taught him that fact must first be actuality, and that any other state is doubt. He knew he saw the situation through a veil of emotion, and the obvious to others might remain obscure to him. On what did he base his supposition that the boy was headed for inversion? Instinct. On what did he base his interest and desire to help him? Primarily, love. Too many other influences could lead the boy to normalcy, Reason said, and as Tom agreed, he resigned himself yet again to waiting.

Thus the years passed and Tom made no aggressive move. The eyes of the boy, when he rarely saw them, continued to hold admiration and invitation, and a half-known desire. Tom had learned again the old lessons, had accepted the old controls anew, but for the first time with a great measure of calmness in his resignation. And he began to feel that the years of investing in the demands of this world were paying off in concrete, if small, dividends. The position he had purchased for himself, though as yet unsecured, was removed, safe, soothing, and comfortable. There, he knew, the years before him would not be so desolate, for a part of him had already decided that Chris was not a part of his destiny.

Chris graduated from high school in the spring of 1950 with the highest scholastic record since the one Tom had achieved years before him. The boy faced possible induction into the Armed Forces in the midst of his college years. Tom went back to Chicago for his last term and received his doctorate. That summer his parents took Lucy to England and France before sending her East to the school she had selected.

It had been a most eventful summer for all of them, they decided at a dinner one night a week after Tom's return from the North. It was an ordinary family affair, at which Chris was a guest as he had been frequently in recent years, for the boy was liked by every member of the Kennedy household. To Tom's parents, Chris was a younger Tom; to Lucy, he had become a brother, a sharer of ambitions, a Tom of her own age.

As they left the table where they had lingered until the maid had literally driven them away, Chris turned to Tom.

"May I talk to you for a moment, Tom?" He had adopted the familiarity the previous summer and Tom had noticed with amusement he seemed to grow with pride each time he uttered it. But the careful urgency in the boy's tone made Tom glance at the expression in the maturing face before he said, "Of course, Chris, I was just going upstairs."

In Tom's study Chris crossed to the window, where the blend of summer heat and autumn magic came in from the darkness outside, and turned to look about the room.

In the years Tom had known him, Chris had lost much of his blank youthfulness, but to a very good advantage. At nineteen Chris was not yet a man, nor was he still an adolescent. As he had grown older his face had formed and set along more mature patterns, the body's frame had enlarged and filled out more solidly. It would be hard to describe the boy now, Tom decided, without slipping off into sentimentality or terms that would proclaim his personal interest quite as boldly.

"Lucy's very lucky," Chris said a bit wistfully, "living in this house—with you. I often tell her she doesn't appreciate the advantage of being with you so much. If it were mine—" His voice broke suddenly and he looked uncomfortable.

"Lucy is growing up in one direction, Chris. You are in another." Tom smiled.

"Tom, will there ever be a time between us when you will treat me as an equal—not as a child?"

Tom was startled at both the words and the vehemence with which they were spoken. "Why, yes, of course there will be, Chris. But it will come gradually. Some of it is here now. Have you really doubted it?"

"I do doubt it now," Christ replied tightly. "For four years— since the first day I saw you at the grain elevator—I've felt that, well, maybe you thought that I was kind of special, as I've always thought you were. But each time I try to come close to that special feeling you seem to push me back into the category of Lucy's friends."

"But you can come to me and talk as you want at any time, Chris."

"No. I can't. Every time I try to get close to you, I just can't."

"Chris, what do you want of me," Tom asked, growing uneasy at the lad's boldness and becoming more determined to stop it at once.

"I don't know. I can't say. I can't seem to put it into words—except in my own thoughts and they don't sound right when I want to say them to you somehow. But when I think of you, when I am with you, talking to you, I just want to say or do something to make myself sure that you are, well, *my* particular friend more than anyone else's. Please don't be angry with me, but there comes a time in every fellow's life when, if he wants to get close to his ideal, well, he just has to take matters into his own hands!"

Tom studied the tense face, trying to decide what lay behind this sudden desperation, trying to guess what had happened. At last he said, "Chris, Lucy is very dear to me, in the way of kith and kin. You are important to me in yet another way, an even more compelling way perhaps."

"How is it more compelling?" Chris asked with ill-suppressed eagerness.

"I can't say, Chris, not right now."

Visibly, the boy's hopes died. After a pause he said bitterly, "I've enlisted in the Navy, Tom. I leave next month."

"But your scholarship!" Tom was as surprised as he knew Chris had wanted him to be. "You've planned toward this fall a long time. Your grades will easily get you a deferment."

"I know what I must do now," Chris replied solemnly. "I can go to college after the war."

"Of course." Tom felt suddenly tired and dull.

"But if I'm old enough to fight in wars," Chris said purposefully, "to vote, am I not old enough to be treated as an equal by you?"

"On some levels, yes," Tom forced himself to answer. "On others involving experience and significance, no, Chris, not yet."

And then, with the air of playing his last card, the boy took a small book from his coat pocket and held it out on a hand that shook.

"Tom, do you know this book?"

It lay in the boy's outstretched hand, suddenly making Tom think of a scorpion or some other poisonous creature as he recognized the title. Yet he took the book and pretended to glance through the pages for a moment.

"Yes. I know it, Chris. Why?"

"Is it true—what it says?"

Tom knew what he meant. What could he say? How could he answer with both honesty and wisdom? The book was a classic, written by a man who had since won a Nobel Prize for literature, but written three decades ago, in another country, another society, another world, another century—and certainly never for the eyes of a boy such as Chris. Yet Tom knew if he were not careful Chris would force and crystallize an issue between them by his youthful interpretation of this work. He began to grasp the desperate plan that lay in the boy's mind. His enlistment in the Navy, and now this.

"No," Tom said evenly, "it is not true, anymore."

"Then is it not honest?"

"Once it was considered to be." Tom made the lie stronger, but to relieve his guilt added, "Even though there was a great outcry against it."

"But is it honest now?"

"Chris, there are things you should not know at your age, or if you do know them you should beware of them until you can understand them fully. There are different times for the understanding of different elements in our lives."

"But I understand this," Chris protested quickly.

"A little perhaps, but not with the objectivity you need to examine it with safety. To accept this book as an actuality at this time would be to sway you before you should be even influenced on such a subject. One day this book will mean something entirely different to you. Novels are to be read for enjoyment or relaxation, not instruction, Chris. That is why you study from textbooks in school.

The art of fiction is an art of reflection, not of shaping. You are undoubtedly unaware of this fact."

"But what is told here in this story could happen again today," Chris persisted.

"Perhaps. But, Chris, one does not deliberately build such situations as the ones described in this book—unless one is a kind of monster."

"Were those people in the book monsters?"

"I suppose not. But the times have changed drastically since that book was written. The subject was then a taboo. The author sought to bring it out of the wrong ranks into the light where it might be studied and understood. What I must make you comprehend now is that it is wrong for any person to contract alliances with other people until he fully understands the complete significance of those contracts and alliances. If a man gives his word on anything he must be ready to carry out his intentions in the face of every condition that might arise. You are still much too young to be expected to commit yourself in any way. One day you will be an adult in this world and if you have acted wisely, your foundation will be intact, solid. Then you will know what you want—and you will be glad you have not made any wrong decisions."

From the boy's face he knew how pathetically inadequate his words were, how confused he appeared to one who was even more confused than he might suppose, how stubborn and selfish he seemed before his admirer. Yet there was nothing he could say to clarify the situation without plunging himself into a morass he had fought valiantly to free himself of for four years. He watched the boy's mouth grow bitter as he said, "So once more you've pushed me back into the ranks of Lucy's friends."

"I'm sorry, Chris. One day you will be glad for it."

Tom supposed he deserved everything he felt at this moment seeing himself in Chris's expression; but then did he deserve it? Was being decent, fair, and noble worth the unhappiness he had caused them both in the past minute or so? And Tom, remembering the sanctuary he had built against this very time, told himself again that by his standards being what he was, was worth any price. He hoped he was right.

As he handed the small book back to its owner, it slipped from the boy's fingers and fell. As he bent to retrieve it, a billfold slipped from Chris's breast pocket and dropped open near the book. Tom, to his complete amazement, saw that the picture the boy carried was a snapshot of himself and Chris, one that Lucy had taken three summers ago on the tennis courts. Tom's arm rested carelessly across the boy's shoulders. They were both smiling. It was a good likeness of them both.

Tom had completely forgotten the particular afternoon, and then into his mind, for no apparent reason, there suddenly flashed the image of an envelope of photographs among his own effects. The parallel was startling for it was so simple, so obvious. But, of course, this was the only picture the boy had of him. It meant as much to Chris now as each of Tom's possessions had once meant to him. In thinking of and treating Chris as something less than an adult, Tom realized that perhaps he had been failing to grant the possibility of the boy's being sincere in his affectionate attachment.

Tom saw the last escape from his four-year prison of frustrated desires close before his eyes and the new years of bondage stretch before him cold and melancholy, filled with the uncertainty and doubt from which he thought he had just freed himself. He had honestly tried to break his own heart by breaking Chris's bonds of hero worship. Unwittingly he had been as cruel to that one he honored above all others as he had ever been with anyone in his life, and all in order to gain society's approval and his own peace of mind. But even with its approval he saw how clearly society would still be scornful of him, and his peace of mind would be more a result of pain than of wisdom. Tom was surprised at his own lack of perspective in expecting to ignore the boy completely until he had broken forth into the safe realm of maturity.

Now the forgotten snapshot made him realize that perhaps he was committing a graver error in giving the boy no hope than he would be by an actual declaration of his feelings; that sending him away with a clean break might actually do the boy more harm than good; that the resulting rebuff might cause Chris to turn for healing to the first opportune person and to suffer an even greater wound than his own qualified commitment might inflict. He remembered the assortment of personalities one must encounter in the services—

the crudely attractive with so little workable knowledge, so few moral standards, and he thought of Chris, hurt and seeking. The boy desperately wanted a norm at this time, a criterion by which he might judge others, the all-important sense of belonging to that one he admired above the rest. Tom, in bowing before a society that scorned him, was sacrificing too much. Now the risk ran in another direction. And he knew that he could not ignore it now that he recognized it as it actually existed.

Yet he understood the dangers therein too, the waiting tantalizing years: Chris in service, the letters written from the very depths of longing, the unconscious drawing closer from that singular purpose of their separate natures, a new, maturing Chris in uniform, the brief days of leave and the guard between them that would grow weaker each time they met. And at last the inevitable uniting when the boy would not be put off any longer because of his lack of experience. There was a tremendous risk, and a tremendous involvement. And deep in Tom the moral ache of battle revived and came into its own aching fury once more.

He watched the boy's embarrassed efforts as he tried to conceal the picture as quickly and nonchalantly as possible within his pocket. At last Tom smiled.

"Wouldn't you like me to autograph it for you, Chris?"

The boy's eyes brightened uncertainly but he remained silent as he took the picture from its case and handed it over.

Tom took it to his desk and sat down. He studied the bit of glossy paper for a long while, seeing it as Chris had seen it all these years, and would see it in the years to come.

"I think I've some clearer ones you might like to have, Chris," he said, calling forth the boy's radiant smile at such unexpected good fortune. "I'll find them tomorrow." And turning the picture over he took a pen from its holder and wrote across the back in bold strokes, "For Chris, with love, Tom."

JAY LITTLE

Maybe—Tomorrow

Pageant Press, 1952

Mainstream presses of the fifties had to be relatively circumspect in their marketing of novels about homosexuality; smaller, gay-oriented presses were not bound by the same rules. Here is the dust-jacket copy on the cloth edition of *Maybe—Tomorrow*, which details the coming out and eventual blossoming of its hero, Gaylord Le Claire, a young queen in a small Texas town:

> As we first meet Gaylord, he doesn't realize why he is unlike anyone else he knows; why he has longings to be near a high school friend, Bob Blake; why he wishes he were a girl. His unhappiness is intensified by the cruelty of his high school friends, who realize before he does what he is and what it means.
>
> Bob seems to "want" him, but at the same time doesn't satisfy Gay mentally nor seem to be true to him. It is only after Gay has been on a trip to New Orleans, where he has met others like himself, that Bob, torn and twisted by the jealousy he feels for people Gay has met while away, admits to Gay that he loves him, and that he wishes them to be together.

Two conclusions are to be drawn from this jacket copy: First, the publishing house knows who its readers are and is doing its best to attract them. Second, the liner notes must have been written by Jay Little himself, for they are in the same twisted, convoluted, and tortured prose that runs rampant through *Maybe—Tomorrow* and Little's second novel, the 1956 *Somewhere Between the Two*. Little's prose is as frenzied (and sometimes incoherent) as it is sincere. It is impossible not to be moved by it. And not unlike the prose of Jacqueline Susann, it is compulsively readable; you have the feeling that this is a story he had to tell and it is not surprising that for more than fifteen years both *Maybe—Tomorrow* and *Somewhere Between the Two* went through multiple printings in cloth and paper. The paper edition of *Somewhere Between the Two* claims that the books were read by hundreds of thousands. This may be an exaggeration, but the distribution of pulp paperbacks in the 1950s and 1960s was extraordinarily pervasive, and they could be bought in train stations, drugstores, card shops, bus depots, luncheonettes, department stores, and five-and-dimes, as well as bookstores. If his actual sales figures were even half of what the cover copy claims, Little's books probably had both a gay and straight readership.

On one level *Maybe—Tomorrow* is the classic gay fantasy: High school hunk and heartthrob Bob Blake actually can't get enough of Gaylord Le Claire, and at the novel's end, they end up moving to New Orleans. So much for the tragic ending of the 1950s queer. There are none of the emotional or psychological complications here that we find in the work of James Barr, Lonnie Coleman, or Fritz Peters, but the power of *Maybe—Tomorrow* comes from Jay Little's insistence that we take this fantasy—this alternative world—seriously. When Gaylord goes to New Orleans, he meets gay men who are immersed in the city's exuberant gay culture. Little's descriptions of their language, their bars, their apartments, and their clothing is wonderful documentation of Southern gay male life in the 1950s.

Jay Little is the pseudonym of Clarence Lewis Miller. He was born in Texas in 1917. The dust-jacket copy of *Maybe—Tomorrow* notes that he "entered the entertainment world after his graduation from high school. He sang over radio station KTIC in Houston and had a fifteen-minute program once a week for more than two years. His theatrical ventures have included work in Hollywood, San Francisco, Miami, New Orleans, Baltimore, and New York." He worked at the Pasadena Playhouse and—according to the dust jacket on *Somewhere Between the Two*—"went into the florist business in Beverly Hills."

Maybe—Tomorrow was published by Pageant Press in 1952. *Somewhere Between the Two* was published by Pageant in 1957. Both titles were released in Paperback Library editions in 1965 and went through many printings. They are both out of print.

This early chapter describes the torment that Gaylord experiences from his peers, and his meeting of the handsome and masculine Bob Blake.

Chapter 4

The next morning Gaylord awoke with a jump. He had been dreaming and his mind was still trapped between the dream and the early-morning light coming through the blinds. He tried to remember, tried to recall the dream that had left his heart pounding, his body quivering, but he couldn't. It had vanished like the darkness. It took him several seconds to come to himself and to the reality of his surroundings. Had he really been dreaming of Blake? There had been many dreams in his life lately, and the ones about Robert Blake were so real, that even on awakening he could have sworn they had actually happened.

He ran a hand over his jaw feeling the few bristles that had sprouted in the past few days; rubbed his drowsy eyes with both hands; yawned and stretched for the ceiling. He started to worry, folded his hands under his head and stared at the visions playing tricks with him. The violent and disconnected happenings of the past evening lulled within him, and as he came to full wakefulness he felt a subtle alteration in the atmosphere of the room. Was this really his room? His storehouse of earthly possessions? His eyes gazed about the room as his fingers groped around his groin. Had that really happened or was it only a lost dream? Surely, no other boy had ever been called a girl before.

The dance, the slim vocalist, the music, even Robert Blake, became a blur of nothingness, but the drunkard was vivid in his mind. He felt of his cheek. It was true, for the cheek was slightly swollen.

Why, puzzled Gaylord, had the drunk chosen him to dance with? Amazing.

Shaking himself out of his self-absorption, he glanced at his watch. "Darn, it's only ten to seven," he mused. "Oh, well . . ." He yawned again and a little smile crept across his face. Delicate laughing lines formed under his eyes. He had been mistaken for a girl. All his life he had viewed the thought with wonderment: a boy who should have been a girl. For a long time that had been a dream but last night it had almost happened.

". . . you beautiful doll." The words were clear and real this time.

His eyes closed and blinked open again. It was amusing now and he felt complimented by the mistake. He was different, separated from masculinity more than ever. The words came back, served to remind him of his secret longing, and remained.

Gaylord tossed on the bed, wondering if Blake would like him if he had been a girl, recalled how always there had been something dreamlike about Robert Blake. But then, so many things seemed like dreams to him. That man at the dance last night. Surely that had been a dream. The way that woman pawed over Max . . . a dream. Thelma White. That also seemed like a dream now . . . like something that had not actually happened. That just couldn't happen to him. It was dream stuff. Or was it all real and true and was it that he, Gaylord, was the dreamer?

Well, he'd find out when he saw her again. If she smiled at him in that ugly way of hers he'd know if it was really a dream or not.

Thelma White . . .

Gaylord wanted to forget that name. He didn't want to ever hear it again. She had tricked him . . . had even mentioned something about Robert Blake . . . what had she said about Blake?

Robert Blake . . . Bob.

Good-looking, honorable, and strong. He knew his own mind. He'd never go with a girl like Thelma White . . . she had lied about him. He'd never make fun of anyone or even allow someone to say ugly things about his friends . . . not Bob . . . not Bob. Yes, Bob was good. He would be so proud to have him for a friend. But he thought of Joy.

Joy . . .

Where did he and Joy go last night?

They had probably gone for a ride after the dance . . . a long ride, looking for some secluded place to park . . . a place where they could be alone.

Fiercely he wished he were a girl, so that Joy could never have him. In the next breath he prayed, "Oh, God, why wasn't I a girl. I'd never complain again if I was a girl . . ."

He kicked off the sheet and sprang from his tumbled bed. He wore pajama pants but no coat, and was apparently warm, for under his nose were drops of perspiration. He ran across the room, stood in front of a mirrored door. "I haven't changed," he said, facing it. "I still look the same . . . my face and chest do." His hand moved over his chest, against his warm flesh. He brushed back curls from his forehead, pressed them in place. Lazily, he looked at his reflection and his movements were slow and easy as if with the drug of vanity. He noticed the red spot on his cheek. "Son of a bitch," he murmured. "It is true . . . it did happen."

With a sharp jerk he untied his pajamas. They fell breaking about his ankles like hungry ocean waves. He stepped out of them and stood naked before the mirror. "It's still there," he said. "I wish it weren't." He pulled at the coiling growth. What he saw only dissipated the clarity of reality. He tightened the smooth and developed muscles of his buttocks, watched his thighs grow firm and hard. Looked at himself a long time, trying to discover some invisible part upon his flesh.

"I wish I were built like Bob," he cried. "I'm too white. I've got to get a tan . . . Damn . . . life's so complicated." How could life ever be happy for him?

He went to the bathroom and stepped under the shower. The tingling sensation of the water hitting his body felt good. He turned on more hot water, his skin reddened, and he uttered a cry and bit his lips. This wouldn't give him bronze skin. How silly could you be? He looked down at his body again, rubbed a delicately scented soap over it, looked at the growthlike shadows around his groin. He hadn't changed. In fact, he seemed to have grown.

Oh, Bob . . . Bob, he thought, and the blood in his veins hardened and grew warm. He tightened his palm, and out of the pounding motions, came; I shouldn't do this . . . I'll feel tired afterwards . . . I'll . . . he closed his eyes and wished he had never begun this evil vice but already he had capitulated to his lust, which was a depraved way for sex, he told himself. He wasn't so damn different. He was just like the rest . . . just as bad as any other fellow. But all boys did this . . . it came with growing up. Even men, he was told, found in this act the keenest pleasure for pent-up emotions seeking release. It was simple . . . so easy to do . . . with a girl it took time . . . many dates and time. With a girl you had to take your time. With some girls you didn't. He remembered his first terrifying experience . . . remembered where and just how it had happened. He never wanted to go through that again . . . never.

Gaylord had often wondered why boys carried pictures of naked men and women with them. He had a couple of them locked in his dresser but he wouldn't think of carrying them on his person or showing them to anyone. But every once in a while he would take them out of his dresser drawer and look at them. Especially the one of a naked man about to mount a girl reclining on a divan. The man in the picture did have a handsome body. Not fat and ugly like most of the pictures he had seen. But he was always afraid his mother or father would find them. He would certainly have been ashamed . . . sex had never been mentioned in his family and he was glad that his father had never told him the facts of life. But he had learned . . . learned through the boys at school.

He walked from the shower and settled his naked body back peacefully on his bed. He felt relaxed but he was sorry he had been too weak of character to stop before it was too late. That first time he had done this had been terrifying, painful. But after the pain it did relax your mind . . . still afterwards he hated himself for his weakness, making promises it would never happen again. But it had continued . . . his resistance had been beaten again and again, unable to cope with the burning inside. Still it was better than with a girl . . . God, yes . . . that one and only time with that girl was awful . . . terrible . . .

"I wonder if Bob does," he mumbled. "Wonder if he does that more than with girls . . . bet he's had lot of girls . . . anyone he wants . . . they all like him . . . I wish he liked me."

To his disgust, Gaylord found that the morning school bell had rung. He walked down the hall thinking, "I could go back home, but I might just as well go on in and face them . . . guess they'll crack some smart remark about my being late . . . I wish I didn't feel like a stranger walking into that darn room. I wish I was at my desk. I'll go home . . . no . . . I'd better not," he thought suddenly. "If I go home I won't see Bob . . . I've just got to see him . . . wonder if he saw me last night . . . wonder what he thinks if he did . . ."

He opened the door and walked to his desk.

"Gaylord, let's try and be on time," the teacher said before he had a chance to sit down.

"I'm sorry, Miss Grey," he answered. "My watch must be slow." As he looked down at his watch, he heard several giggles.

"Let's leave just a little earlier from now on."

"Yes, ma'am."

He did not look about him. He was much too preoccupied with his books. He wondered if his teacher knew what had happened this morning . . . could the others read his mind? Was she at the dance last night? How many in this room were? "I hope they didn't see me," he prayed. "Oh, God, I hope they didn't."

"Morning, Gay," whispered a feminine voice from behind him.

He turned his head slightly. "Morning, Joy," he answered shyly.

Wonder if she saw me? He didn't mind so much if she had. She wouldn't tell anyone or even let him know she had. But suppose one of the boys had heard the drunk. Nothing could be worse than that. Bet Bob wouldn't say anything. He didn't go around hurting people's feelings. There sure was something appealing about him. Anything he did was all right with everyone. Well, after all, why not? Wasn't he the star football player?

He thought of the time Blake's car battery had been dead and how he had asked for a push. He remembered Blake saying, "Gay, could you give me a push . . . Go easy so that your bumper doesn't get scratched . . ." What difference if it did. Blake was worth more than an old bumper to him. He was so glad that Blake had asked him, he didn't care about a few scratches . . .

The sun was up and beautiful over the school, and the small open windows between the wings caught its rays and sent them inside the cool classroom. In a corner a spider was already busy weaving a larger web. It looked all silvered with dew hanging there from sky hooks. From the spider Gaylord's gaze fell on a new face seated across the aisle opposite him. He wondered why he had not noticed him before. Obviously he had been there all the time.

Gaylord's heart jumped. He was a handsome boy sitting there behind the desk. And when he smiled, deep dimples formed in his cheeks. His hair was neatly plastered down and his clothes were very clean.

Gaylord pushed at his books, knocking a pencil to the floor. He didn't see it fall and was surprised when the boy handed it to him saying. "You dropped this."

"Oh, thanks . . . I didn't know I dropped it."

"You're welcome."

Gaylord wanted to say something else, but when words wouldn't come, he smiled. He felt the blood creeping into his cheeks and silently cursed himself. There was something warmly companionable about this boy. "I need someone," thought Gaylord desperately. "I need someone and I believe he needs someone too. I'm young, maybe, only seventeen. But I'm older than my years in some things. But there is no one to understand . . ." Maybe he would understand . . . maybe . . .

The gym director waited for them. He stood there, one foot on a folded chair. Instead of looking at them, he seemed to be watching his feet. He was a short, bushy man with green eyes and deep red hair. For a while he watched his foot on the cement floor. Then he looked at them and stood on both feet. "Everybody here? Get yourselves stripped and dressed in a hurry, men," he yelled. "We've got lots to do today." He shifted his stare over the class. Then noticing Gaylord, who had just come through the swinging doors, his ugly mouth opened again. "Did ya hear what I said, Le Claire? Get the load outa your butt and today I want you back here on time." His screaming crossed the room.

"Yes, sir." And Gaylord walked to his locker and began undressing.

He wondered if it would ever be possible, in this world, that he would one day hold his face up to his gym teacher and they would look directly into each other's eyes. I'd sure like to tell him to go to hell, he thought. And someday I'm going to.

He tugged at the buttons on his shirt and slowly uncovered his chest. He strove against his warm-fleshed nudity as he pulled off his underwear. He felt eyes watching him standing there naked and he was glad he wasn't short and fat like some of the others. He grabbed his blue gym trunks and quickly slid his slender legs through them.

He stood there with the others, arms folded, waiting for the instructor to speak. He looked at the tangled hair, the blotted pinkish chest of his teacher and the dirty red trunks around the flabby waist. You ugly thing, he thought. You filthy person. At least you could have your trunks washed.

He squirmed, wishing they'd start, shifting his weight from one foot to the other. He hated the class and, after the first trying week, was on the verge of quitting, but decided against it. He was determined to have a good physique, and the exercises would do that for him. He had worked hard all year but it had been worth it. He had developed handsomely. Even his hatred for his teacher had subsided at times—other times his hatred had deepened.

There was a mad scramble of naked legs and arms when the instructor yelled, "That's it for today, fellows. Hit the showers!"

Gaylord stepped aside to let a running boy pass. Another stuck out his foot and tripped the would-be Mercury . . . then laughed. They all laughed at the sprawled-out body on the floor, all except Gaylord. To him, it wasn't funny . . . why, the fall could have broken a leg.

Yells of delight filled the room and echoed in the huge beams overhead.

Gaylord slowly walked to his locker. He was anxious for the others to shower and leave. He wanted to be alone when he took off his trunks. Wanted to be alone when he stood under the long line of showers.

He opened his locker and ran his hands through his pants' pockets . . . trying to locate something . . . anything to take up time. Then he hung them back, glanced around the almost deserted room. I guess I've taken long enough, he thought. I'm glad some don't take showers. They sure must smell.

He took off his trunks and walked rapidly toward the swinging doors.

A husky boy wildly pushed it open and came running toward him. His naked body and flying hair dripped with water and his face gleamed with excitement. Right behind were two others running after him. One had a filled sponge which he threw but missed, and the other a dripping towel he kept snapping at the boy's buttocks in front of him.

"Look out, Gay," screamed the water-soaked individual, running past, his arms flying through the air, his face filled with wild excitement and laughter. He quickly turned his head to see how far behind his pursuers were.

Gaylord tried a faint smile, watched him. It was not until he turned that he discovered the boy with the towel had stopped beside him. He saw the big feet and hairy legs standing in front of him. He cringed, expecting to feel the wet cloth fall across his own bottom.

"Hey, fellows," the boy bellowed, squinting his devilish eyes. "Come back here. I want you to see something." He pushed back the dripping hair from his forehead.

Gaylord heard the scuffling of returning footsteps. He didn't know what was going to happen, but he was sure it wasn't going to be anything pleasant. How can I get away, he pondered quickly . . . I've got to get away.

"Whataya want, Pete?" asked one, looking at the boy with the moving towel.

"Look." He laughed, pointing at Gaylord. "Look at the tool this sissy's got."

Gaylord's legs began to tremble.

Pete continued, "Shit, I thought you had the biggest one in school, Stud, but Pretty Boy here's got you bested by a couple of inches."

Gaylord put both hands over his groin. They followed as he walked.

Stud went on, "What's the matter, Pretty Boy? Don't you want to show it off? You ought to be proud of that honker."

Gaylord tried to grin. "It's nothing to show off."

"Ain't it?"

"No."

"Does it make the gals squeal, Pretty Boy?"

"Hell, even I get a grunt out of them when I poke this in them."
Stud grinned. "With a jock like that you ought to make them yell,
Daddy." He held out his own. "Let's measure. Let's see how much
longer it is than mine."

"I've got to take a shower, Stud."

"Hell, you ain't dirty, Pretty Boy. What's your hurry? You didn't
answer my question."

Gaylord sputtered, "What question?"

"Does it make the gals squeal?"

"Shit, Stud . . . he ain't ever had a piece of ass, have you,
dearie?"

I certainly have, Gaylord wanted to shout but he only walked on.

Stud grabbed him by the arm . . . said, "Come on, let's measure."

"Let's get it hard, first." Pete giggled, and reached between Gaylord's legs.

"Don't, Pete," Gaylord pleaded with disgust. "Please don't."

"Please don't," Pete sarcastically mocked him. "Mama's baby
don't want the rough boys playing with his peter, does he?"

Gaylord slapped the hand on his flesh and demanded, "Leave me
alone." He continued walking slowly. They followed too close.

One whistled and laughed. "Fellows . . . look at that pretty ass
. . . how'd you like a crack at that, Stud? Bet it'd be better than that
whore you've been screwing." He slapped the naked cheeks and the
sound echoed.

He wanted to run but was afraid they'd trip him. He had to use
his head. He wouldn't let them get the best of him . . . but what
could he do?

"Look how soft and shaky it is too." Pete laughed. He shook the
flesh and followed it with a lightning-quick slap.

Gaylord's buttocks burned and so did his mind. "I said I've got
to take a shower . . . leave me alone, damn it, and I mean it."

"Why, Gaylord, you said a nasty word." Stud put his hand on
his naked chest. "Shame . . . shame. Don't you like flattery. All the
girls think your face is so pretty. Well . . . we like your cute butt."
He giggled. "Don't we, fellows?"

"Sure we like it . . . in fact we like it so much let's all have a crack at it, huh?"

"Sounds good to me. I ain't ever corn-holed anybody before, but I'll try anything once."

Gaylord took another step, then tried to run. It was like a horrible dream when you tried to scream but no sound came. He couldn't escape now. They had circled him, and, quick as a cat, one had thrown one arm about Gaylord's neck and pressed hard. He put his other arm around his waist and Gaylord felt parts of their bodies touch.

"Come on, dearie . . . I'm hotter than a bitch dog . . . ain't had a piece in two days. Ain't ever been up the back door." He laughed.

Gaylord's waist hurt from the tight gripping. "Don't," he cried. He broke away from the boy.

"Aw . . . come on." He picked up a piece of soap from the floor and massaged it in his wet hands. It lathered freely and with these hands he grabbed Gaylord. "Come on . . . I'll fix you up."

"And you said you ain't been up the back door before, Pete."

"That's what I said, but I'm a damn liar."

"That's what I thought." Stud laughed.

"I'll show you how it's done." Pete grinned. "I'll be first."

"Like hell you will," snapped Stud, and grabbed Gaylord. His bareness touched Gaylord's leg. The leg jerked as though a live flame had been put to it. His legs came out of the paralysis then and he kicked and struggled. At that, Stud pressed his body closer to his, pinning Gaylord against him.

Gaylord was crying inside his head. They can't do this to me. Why should they always pick on me? I've never hurt them. Around his waist the wet hands tightened and a swish of wet cloth circled his knees. He turned and stared at the exposed part of Stud's body in paralyzed horror. It was wormy white contrasted with the ugly sallowness of his face and hands. He felt the same kind of nausea he had once felt when he had gone out with Thelma White, but this was worse. He saw the cruel, tense look in the smoky eyes. And now he felt hard flesh against him. While his head rocked, he tried with his legs to free himself. With his elbows he tried to jab Stud's sides. "Let me go," he sobbed. Squirming and kicking he tried again to be free.

"Let's carry him to the can."

"Yeah. No one's there now. Grab his legs."

"Yeah, grab his legs," repeated Pete.

The naked body pressed closer against his back and skinny strong arms went around his chest. Two more hands grabbed for his kicking legs, holding one firmly in a viselike grip. Gaylord twisted, screamed, and kicked backwards with his free leg. He was without fear now. Through a drunken blur that filmed his eyes, he fought back the best he could. The kick brought results. It struck Stud in his groin.

"God damn you son of a bitch," Stud yelled in pain. He let go for a second then tightened his arms around Gaylord again. His stiff naked body drew closer. "I'll give it to you right here if you don't stop that kicking . . . you damn jackass."

And now they were all around him. He couldn't run. He couldn't even kick anymore. Please, God, he prayed, let someone come along. He was cornered. Trapped. Already his feet were off the floor, there was no way to free himself . . . he was helpless . . . please . . . he prayed again . . . don't let them do this to me . . . please . . . don't let them . . .

Robert Blake carelessly walked toward the school gym and stood barefooted on the top level watching two little girls playing jacks. One of the children grinned, showing a large gap.

"What happened to those two pretty teeth you had the other day, Marion?" he asked.

"They fell out, Bob, but the rabbit gave me two nickels for them."

"That so?" He grinned and patted her head playfully. "Now you'll get two new teeth, won't you, and you'll have two nickels too."

"I sure will." She smiled. She liked Robert Blake. He had bought her ice cream several times, but that wasn't the real reason. He was so pretty and always spoke to her. He always took time out to say something to her. Had even played jacks with her. She looked up at him and asked, "Want to play jacks with us?"

"Not now, honey . . . I've got to take a shower."

Innocently, she looked at his naked chest and legs. "Did you lose your shoes?"

"Uh-huh," he teased. "Can I wear yours?"

"They wouldn't fit, silly." She looked at his big feet.

"Don't think so, huh," he chuckled. "No . . . I don't guess they would."

What was that? Sounded like a scream from the gym . . . Blake perked his head and listened . . . Yes, there it was again, faint but real. Someone was in trouble. He'd better hurry.

He raced towards the gym door, caught the handle in his large hand. It grated noisily on its hinges and swung open. It was warm in the gym and the smell of sweat caught in his nostrils.

He saw the group of boys and thought it was a fight. Then he saw Gaylord, his face streaked with fear, being carried helplessly towards the toilets. Blake felt a trembling inside him, seeing Gaylord make a pathetic gesture as though to lift his tormentors. He saw the lips moving, shaping cries, but they were low and tired. Blake rubbed his knuckles together angrily. He was on his heels.

Gaylord heard the sound, looked up, and saw Blake running towards him. He was running madly and his yells were loud and demanding, filling the deserted gymnasium with a resounding echo.

"What the hell's going on in here?" he demanded.

The eyes of the three boys, their hands loosening their deathlike grip, watched the tall, glistening figure running towards them. Saw the long masculine legs, shadowed by curly hair sprinkled even and thickly, continuing over the expanding chest. Dark olive skin that started on the broad forehead, covered the large biceps of both arms, and ran below the knees to the tensely drawn thighs. The hair was short and glistening. Strands fell over the frowning forehead and the white gymnasium trunks made the waist look even smaller. They met his glare with a sheepish grin; their hearts pounded faster, this time from fright.

Stud's lip curled back to show a broken tooth, said, "Hi, Bob."

Blake's entire body was wracked with anger. The tears he saw squeezing through Gaylord's eyes were held tightly back as though he were ashamed of them, but the illness inside his own heart was the worst he had ever experienced. Three of them, he thought angrily. Three of them against one . . . chickenshit bastards. "Put him down!" he demanded. His voice was a loud explosion and his dark eyes a cold stare. The three boys still held their prize. "I said put him down!" and Blake grabbed Stud by the arm fiercely. His big hands were tight and cruel. Stud did as he was bid and the others followed. Gaylord was free.

He said nothing, only stood there limp. He wanted to cry, but couldn't. The Greek god standing there wouldn't want him to cry. And he wouldn't. He held his teeth together hard. He felt his fear leaving him and recognized in this bronze body everything he himself didn't have. He wasn't jealous, only admiring.

Stud twisted his lips after Blake's release. "Look what we found, Bob. A Venus." He giggled nervously.

"Yeah, a Venus with a penis." Pete laughed, twisting the towel he still held. "A Venus with a penis," he repeated. "That's good, ain't it?"

The three boys tried to laugh.

Blake stood there and his muscles looked and were strong and powerful. "Fine thing," he finally said and his eyes were mean. "I'm surprised at you guys. Trying to be tough, huh. Why don't you call some more so you can really get him down? There's only three of you . . . That's chicken, all right. Damn shame I call it when three grown men jump on one. Damn shame . . ." He turned to Gaylord. "Are you all right, Gay?" He grabbed Gaylord's hand.

The hand felt good. "I'm all right," Gaylord said, but he could still feel what had touched his body. He felt like the skin would be eaten away there.

"I'm surprised at you, Stud. Picking on someone smaller than you." Blake looked at the big-eared boy.

"He's bigger than Stud in places, Bob. Look." He pointed, and Gaylord grew crimson.

Blake did look and Gaylord had an impulse to run, but the hand on his shoulder was enough to stifle that impulse completely. He could not leave Blake. He looked up at him and there was no youth in his eyes now, no tenderness, no gaiety. Blake stared at the three boys with burning gravity, his whole expression that of a man mad enough to kill and powerful enough to do so.

"Shut up . . . God damn you," Blake shot at them.

The three shrank back.

"Hell, Bob," one whined, "you don't have to get so red ass. We were just having a little fun . . . weren't going to hurt him." He tried to grin. "Can't a fellow have a little fun?"

"Not when it means hurting someone. Not as long as I'm around, no one's going to have fun at someone else's expense. Now get out, get out—and if I ever catch you doing this again I'll forget I'm a gentleman."

"We weren't going to do anything . . . Hell—"

"I said scram . . . Get out of here before I kick the shit out of the whole damn bunch of you," Blake yelled between clinched teeth.

And each boy thought he would do just that. They sneered but backed away.

"Come on, Gay." Blake grinned and put an arm around Gaylord's shoulder. "Let's take a shower. Maybe that'll get rid of this stink around here."

They walked toward the shower, Blake with his arm still around Gaylord. One of the boys yelled at them, "Be careful he don't knock you up, Pretty Boy." Then, all three hurriedly ran from the gym.

"Bastards," Blake muttered without even looking back.

"Thank you, Bob," said Gaylord gratefully. "I don't know what I would have done if you hadn't come along."

"Forget it, Gay. We'll both feel better after a shower."

Gaylord thanked him again. They walked through the swinging doors together and crossed the shower's tile floor.

They stood in front of the showers and Gaylord watched Blake's thick fingers strip off his trunks, pull them down over his hips. Then they fell of their own accord to his feet, a circle of white, whiter than the sudden exposed buttocks. He watched Blake scratch his ribs and was surprised that he wasn't embarrassed.

"Damn . . . water's cold." Blake grinned under the heavy spray. "Come here, Gay . . . this will make you feel good."

Gaylord caught the extended hand and stumbled after Blake under the cool water. He flung his arms around Blake's waist. He didn't care if his hair got wet. He pressed his face against the bronze hairy chest and cried. He didn't want to, but he could no longer restrain himself.

Blake's arms encircled him, held him tenderly, and pulled him closer. Their wet bodies rubbed against each other and the fragrance, waterborne, scented the air. It felt comforting to be in Blake's embrace.

"Don't cry, Gay." His fingers moved across the forehead, smoothed the curled hair, mussed there, brushed them back. "They're not worth one single tear . . . don't cry . . . please don't . . ."

"Oh . . . I can't help it . . . I'm such a baby," Gaylord sobbed. "No wonder they pick on me . . . no wonder they . . . why am I so . . . so . . . I wish I were like them . . ."

"Now you know you wouldn't want to be like them . . ." Blake raised the dripping head with both hands. "I like you just as you are . . . what's wrong with you . . . there's nothing wrong with you . . . Gay."

Oh, yes, there is, Gaylord wanted to shout . . . I'm a sissy . . . that's why they make fun of me. I like to wear girls' clothes . . . powder . . . rouge . . . perfume . . . I don't want to like it, but I do . . . I'm a sissy and I can't change . . . I want to be a girl . . . was taken for a girl last night . . . I wish I were a girl so I could love you . . . I'd love you so much. He stood there in Blake's arms, crying softly. His breath caught occasionally in his throat and made him gasp. He looked up into Blake's eyes and hugged him tight, clung there voiceless . . .

"You know, Gay," Blake breathed softly, "you . . . you do remind me of a . . . of Venus."

He kissed the upturned lips and the spraying water formed a glass curtain of protection around them . . .

PART THREE

Truly Pulp:
"Gay" Life in the Shadows

There is no precise definition of the term *pulp novel*. It is used loosely and often refers more to a book's cover art than to its written content. In the fifties, many fine novels were thought of as "pulp novels" simply because they were marketed with eye-catching, erotically suggestive covers. (Samuel Butler's *The Way of All Flesh*, even with heaving bosoms and prettily gartered legs, is still *The Way of All Flesh*.) But there are two qualities a pulp novel should have: melodrama and an emphasis on the sensational. In pulp novels, emotions run high and realistic narrative often runs out.

This idea of the pulp novel—emotionally overwrought and slightly out of control—came to fruition in the fifties. It was an extreme manifestation of the growing importance of Freudian psychoanalysis in mainstream American culture, particularly in regard to sexuality. Freud's theories had been introduced to American audiences in the early part of the century, and by the twenties he had became popular in avant-garde circles. By the thirties his ideas were firmly embedded in popular thought, particularly through the practice of psychoanalysis. Psychoanalysis promised to uncover a whole new world of dreams, hidden needs, primal secrets, and only half-understood longings. In the world of fiction, it brought readers closer to characters' inner lives, helping to explain their exciting, tempting, and titillating fantasies and desires. Not surprisingly, psychoanalytic thought and interpretation—usually of the most vulgar variety—met its perfect narrative expression in novels about the "twilight" world of homosexuality.

In the twenties and thirties homosexuality was generally understood in medical terms as "inversion"—the opposite sex in the "wrong" body. Psychoanalytic theory transformed that medical diagnosis into a psychological one. It was welcomed by both medical professionals and laymen alike since it "explained" homosexuality to a nation that was desperately trying to understand the changes occurring around sexuality and gender in the postwar period. The impact of Freudian thought on pulp fiction of the period is explicitly evidenced in Harlan Cozad McIntosh's novel *This Finer Shadow* (1941), a strange story that revolves around a butch sailor named Martin and his various relationships with shipmate Rio, Mr. Roberts (a gay man who falls in love with him), Deane Idara (a woman), and Carol Stevens (a gay man). The book is a mad, dizzying meditation on the possibilities of gender bending and bi- or polysexualities, and its climax features a drag ball during which the already confusing names, genders, and identities become even more confounded. McIntosh is not subtle in his elucidation of his characters' psyches:

Carol did not sleep well that night. He had dreams of strong masculine things; but they felt good. Early in the morning his child-mind was tired. His fantasies and adult body had exhausted him. He awoke and turned over to be spanked. His father had always spanked him when he was bad. But now he did not feel his father's callused hand against him, nor could he see his father's frown and long, unshaven jaw. Carol turned over again, realizing vaguely where he was. . . . His father was dead. He was not being spanked. Something had been taken away from him and his mouth trembled. . . . The strong nostalgia made him sick. He wanted to be bad, and then feel the hard hand and weep happily as his father struck him.

The narrative's psychoanalytic orientation is made even clearer in this passage:

In his room Martin laid his head upon his desk. He wondered about Roberts, his magnificence at the drag, the mad poem intended for himself. Confused by these thoughts, he fell asleep. He dreamed that he was in the bow of a shining canoe, spinning down a great, white length of rapids. In the stern of the boat two men were fighting. Rio, and the giant with the white, rain-soaked shirt were striking each other fiercely. Above them hovered the spirit of Freud, smiling at both of them and holding a battered text in one hand and a setscrew in the other which were apparently to be awarded to the victor. Roberts, however, in the form of mist, obstructed the blows of the fighters until the two gladiators became entangled and suddenly dissolved. The spirit of Freud withdrew hastily, while the adviser, with a faint smile at Martin, sat down in the boat as it rotated toward destruction.

This Finer Shadow is a remarkable mess: conflating the thirties concept of the "invert" with the psychoanalytic motifs of the forties, the novel is an attempt to make sense of the ever-changing ideologies surrounding homosexuality. John Cowper Powys's introduction conveys the swoony ambivalence voiced by most critics of the novel. After announcing that the "book is a terrible tragedy, and one that certainly in the fullest classical sense *purges our passions*," he asserts:

> Men and women who make the pathetic mistake of thinking themselves what is called "normal" ought all to read this tragic tale, so that they shall be *shamed,* not into human sympathy, but into philosophical insight; whereas those of us who make no such claim, and are confessedly engaged in the hard struggle to get ourselves in order, will find in Harlan McIntosh's book just what we have been seeking in vain: a stark, authentic, unmitigated rendering of what it is like *really to be* what these complacently detached investigators analyze from so safe a distance!

While McIntosh's use of psychoanalytic themes is rudimentary, even laughable, other novels of the forties and fifties used them with more grace and precision. Carson McCullers's *Reflections in a Golden Eye,* though published the same year as *This Finer Shadow,* is far more psychologically adept with equally baroque material. Ten years later, Fritz Peters (the pseudonym of Arthur A. Peters) brought a deft psychoanalytic touch to the now classic *Finistère* (1951). His psychological acumen was no surprise since his first novel, the 1949 *The World Next Door,* was a bravura performance, charting a (clearly repressed gay male) war veteran's recovery from a nervous breakdown.

The jacket copy of Stuart Engstrand's 1947 *The Sling and the Arrow* notes auspiciously that its author was inspired to write this novel "last year when he was rereading Stekel's writings on abnormal psychology." A curious, disturbing work—about what we would now call transgenderism—the book uses psychoanalytic terminology and concepts to express its core ideas. Herbert Dawes, a dress designer who insists on dressing his own wife in boyish clothing and has a difficult relationship with his domineering mother, becomes obsessed with the attractive Coast Guardsman who visits his next-door neighbors. When it appears that Dawes is having a nervous breakdown, his wife and friends speak to a professional. Dr. Kahn (almost all psychiatrists in novels of the forties and fifties are Jewish) interprets one of Dawes's recurring dreams. In the dream Dawes is sitting in a doctor's office with his mother. The doctor explains that he has a cancer growing within him, but the word is pronounced *cuncer.* No one wants to believe Kahn's interpretation: that Dawes has an inner desire to be a woman. The plot careers recklessly on until Dawes murders his wife (after urging her to have an affair with the man with whom he is obsessed).

Henry Morton Robinson's 1947 *The Great Snow* also deals with a "weak," artistic son and his problematic relationship with an aggressive, tyrannizing father. Robinson was a highly acclaimed poet and novelist noted for his psychological insight. In *The Nation,* Diana Trilling praised his ability to "use psychoanalysis as an instrument of health" by "translating clinical information into novelistic terms." In one of the most remarkable passages in the novel, the father, Russell Cobb, sits at his fourteen-year-old son's bedside waiting to see if he will pull through a serous illness.

"There's something else, Father." Rod's fevered brain was losing direction now. "When the muskrats frightened me, the boys at school laughed and called me a name. Name of a flower." A wondering gaze. "Pansy."

As if dodging a gun barrel pointed straight at his eye, Cobb tried to avoid the tormenting vision summoned up by that name. In clairvoyant detail he saw the scenario of his son's life as a homosexual. If Roddy lived and was fortunate among his kind, he would become one of those exquisite creatures, parasitic as mistletoe, that flowered most brilliantly in the airs of decline. The rooms through which his son would pass, the voices of Roddy's friends and lovers, the murmured fidelities, the screaming jealousies of the disdained and the clipped cruelties of the disdainers, the special tones and language of these parody courtships—Cobb heard, saw them all. Had his son been born for this? Should such a life be valued, preserved? Everything in Cobb's experience and training, his masculine vanity, his contempt, pity, and fear of homosexuals, whispered a bitter "No."

Roddy dies—in part because his parents are too busy with their own extramarital affairs to even notice he is sick—and his grief-stricken father realizes too late how his own "masculine vanity" has led to the tragedy.

While the novels excerpted here certainly are emblematic of a fifties pulp sensibility, they are also the product of the culture's new fascination with psychoanalysis. Drawing upon the work of analysts such as Irving Bieber and Edmund Bergler (particularly *Homosexuality: Disease or Way of Life?*), psychoanalysis was increasingly used to "explain" the pathology of homosexuality. Very often pulp novels, such as Michael De Forrest's *The Gay Year*, would draw on psychoanalytic ideas to demonstrate that homosexuality was an emotionally unsatisfying illness. Vin Packer consciously uses psychiatry as a straightforward narrative device in *Whisper His Sin*, but ironically undercuts it by exposing the real emotions and feelings that the doctor misses. Ben Travis's *The Strange Ones*, James Colton's *Lost on Twilight Road*, and (in a much cruder way) *The Memoirs of Jeff X* all rely on mainstream psychoanalytic concepts that were completely familiar to the common reader.

MICHAEL DE FORREST

The Gay Year

Woodford Press, 1949

There may be a broken heart for every light on Broadway, but that doesn't mean it isn't still the gay white way. *The Gay Year*'s Joe Harris comes to New York to be a star and ends up being kept by the wealthy, older, "unhandsome" Reginald Hartley. This leads to a secret life of picking up men in playgrounds and thoughts of suicide. Joe throws himself into the ocean off Cape Cod, but is saved by a heterosexual woman minding her children on the beach. And then he has a revelation:

> The truth is, Joe began, I'm not really "gay," I'm not soft and yielding as I thought myself to be with Roger, though I may have something of it in my makeup. And I'm not the lone wolf I've lived like since summer. I never was that at all.
>
> Joe stopped to question himself. Was he, he asked, indulging in rationalization even now? Was he still trying to explain away circumstances? If there was ever a time to be truthful with myself, he thought, it is now. I've got to face Joe Harris as he really is.
>
> "I'm not really 'gay,' " Joe repeated, "I've never really been

a homo. I've only been lonely." It was as simple as that. He knew now what it was that made him want Roger so hotly that first time at the theater. He wanted someone to admire him. He had wanted a friend. Such a friend as Roger Stuart could become, wise, schooled in the theater, respected and admired as an actor. One little compliment from Roger and he had been ecstatic. And Roger had provided another gratification and Joe promptly decided that it had all been ordained.

In its plot, *The Gay Year* is similar to *The Night Air*, featuring a protagonist who must sort out his various sexual desires while struggling in the New York theater scene. But while Dowd's novel is a nuanced, probing examination of complex emotions, De Forrest's world is a flattened-out vision of these same concerns. While it never exploits its subject matter—in the way that Lew Levenson's raucous and tawdry *Butterfly Man* does—*The Gay Year* is essentially pulp in its sensibilities. That is, it mistakes sentimentality for emotions, hysteria for drama, and is happy to entertain us with preconceived images and ideas, but never challenges us to move beyond them. Joe's heterosexual redemption at novel's end is unearned and unfelt; he simply hasn't displayed the psychological depth to make us believe that there really is a Joe Harris.

When he is not descending to women's magazine clichés—"Central Park wore a haze of yellow green, like the frothy veils that graced the Easter hats in the store windows"—De Forrest has a good eye for material detail: what people wear, how they talk, how they move. His description of the Sweeneys, down-on-their-luck drunken bar owners who decide to turn their lower Second Avenue gin mill into a posh gay bar called the Club des Arts, is witty and insightful.

The original cloth edition of *The Gay Year* claims that Michael De Forrest "attended college in his native Missouri until a chance to act in summer theaters lured him eastwards. New York was the logical spot after that, and he's been a resident of the Empire State ever since. . . . He is now at work on another novel in his Greenwich Village studio, which is now home to him and his wife."

The Gay Year was first published by Woodford Press in 1949. It went through multiple printings. In the fifties it was reprinted by Castle Books, probably in a pirated edition, its authorship now ascribed to "M De F." A Lancer paperback of this edition was released in 1965, and the language of its cover copy is pure pulp: "*The Gay Year* is perhaps the most famous novel ever written about the homosexual fraternity. It reveals its hidden shame, its secret signals, and its strange passions. Some may find it shocking, some may find it sensational—but no one who reads it will ever forget it." *The Gay Year* is now out of print.

The Gay Year traces the journey, over one year, of Joe Harris as he moves from questioning his sexuality to becoming a gay kept boy with a promiscuous secret life to deciding he is really heterosexual. He is never terribly unhappy during this time but realizes in the end "how little gaiety that 'gay' year had really brought him." Instead of regretting it, he accepts it as a time that brought him to a new beginning. This chapter, occurring in the book's third section, depicts a meeting between the self-loathing Harold (who has recently had a casual encounter with a woman who picked him up in the park) and the less conflicted Joe.

Chapter 4

The fountain bubbled, and in the flower beds squat red and white geraniums took the cooling, moist breezes sturdily. Harold watched the gray-clad men clearing out the rectangular pools for the summer lilies. He saw the checkerboards of light going on and off in the offices that towered above him. He recalled the night he'd met her, and it seemed long ago. He wondered if she'd come walking up to him tonight, as he had hoped every night since the first time. He'd never seen her again. He'd spent one night with her, and had dreamed himself through many others. She had left him early the next morning, with no name, no phone number, no identification except a burning memory, and that, too, became part of his dream. He wondered now if it had all been a dream. Maybe there never was a girl. He wasn't feeling too well tonight. He'd been having some kind of hallucinations; perhaps the girl was only a memory mirage. A mirage with soft full breasts and thick black hair. He looked at the golden figure in the fountain and reviewed his conversation with the girl. Harold wondered how many men had read her penciled note in the locket since the night he'd stared questioning and amazed at its scrawled "It won't cost you anything—you're so cute."

He remembered with painful clarity the intense sensations of the night with her. His first affair with a woman. He couldn't have been very satisfactory, he told himself, or she would have come back to him. He must have disappointed her. How many evenings he'd stood here, gazing half-seeing at the fountain, waiting and wondering if she would come. He remembered the revealing tissue-thinness of her dress. It was summer now, and he could imagine her sitting near a wide-opened window, could almost smell her humid body. Maybe the husband had found out about her and killed her or something. What if he'd followed her one night and taken her with some young lover and killed them both? Perhaps things had gone wrong with her pregnancy and she had died. He must have been terrible that time with her. That was it, he thought, she just hadn't liked him.

A taxi, headed downtown, sat at the corner waiting for the go-ahead light. A blast from the horn stopped him, and he looked up. Joe was waving out the window and calling him.

"Joe, well, it's been a long time. What on earth happened to you?"

"I'm moving some things into my apartment. You've never even been down there, have you? Come along with me, it's a nice ride, and you can give me a hand with the clothes, if you don't mind." Joe was glad to meet Harold. He'd not seen any of the boys since he'd moved into Hartley's apartment; now he was moving out, and it felt good picking up the pieces of his old life again. Then, too, he admitted he'd been lonely this week in town, lonely, but too busy getting settled to call any of his friends. Now here was Harold. How nice, Joe thought. He had been glad their paths had never crossed during the Hartley period, when he'd avoided their company to avoid having to make embarrassing explanations.

"How is everybody?" Joe asked. He told Harold about his leaving Malumet, saying he'd found the company unbearable, and the management had failed to live up to its agreement. He didn't go into the personal angle.

"Fine. Wally's working, you know, at the Club des Arts. He says they're doing awfully well in spite of the heat, and he's picked up quite a following."

"Wonderful. Say, let's go hear him, could we? Maybe later this evening. We can go down to my place and I'll dispose of this crap and then go get some dinner and hear Wally—OK?"

"Sure, if you want to. I usually stop in there once or twice a week. The Sweeneys—they own the place—are swell to Wally, and most of the time his friends' drinks are on the house."

"And Charles, how is Charles; still the great seducer?" Joe laughed.

"Oh, he's tamed down a little. He had a kind of a big thing with one of the accompanists at a ballet studio, but he seems to have slipped from that secure unemotional perch of his, because he's been spending more time in his room working out, and he's been getting home earlier than usual. In the show, they're thinking of sending him out with the touring company as one of the solo dancers. Oh, and he also refused an offer to go to Hollywood because the agent wouldn't lay and wouldn't pay, to coin a phrase. Charles said he would have gone all right if the salary had been better, or if the guy had been cuter. I'll hate to see him go out on tour, but it'll be a break for him."

Joe thought of Charles and his sparkling dancing. This was one of his friends he knew would get there. Charles could sleep his way to a good start, but he had the talent to go on from there.

"You knew Lou and Nella got married, didn't you, Joe?"

"No—when?"

"Early spring—they're going to have a baby, too. Lou said he called the bookstore but they told him you weren't working there anymore. I supposed he sent you a note or something. But you were making yourself so scarce, it serves you right if you get all the news late."

"That's wonderful about Lou and Nella. They're happy, aren't they? They haven't been having any trouble about—"

"You mean about Nella's color? No more than they have about Lou's being white. Oh, once in a while Nella says one of the store-keepers decides he ought to snub her, or one of the women in the neighborhood tries to be snooty, but she doesn't let that get her down."

"Nella's a lovely girl. I bet they have a smart kid, don't you?"

"He stands a good chance of being perfect, if parents have anything to do with it. Honestly, Joe, have you ever known such wonderful people as they are?"

"I've known one who was that way, yes." Joe thought of Katherine. He saw her doing a million little housewifely things, and all the while talking so kindly and wisely. He could only envy and hope to emulate her.

Often Joe had found himself thinking of Katherine. Sometimes he wondered if he'd given up too much for Roger. As a person, he didn't think half as much of Roger as he did of Katherine. But he was "gay," and it was silly to pretend he could ever have had the woman who'd saved his miserable little life. She'd given it to him, and he was glad. He was going to have Roger now, the way he'd wanted. He was going to live and work and study and play and make love with the man he'd always wanted so terribly from their first moments together. He was going to belong to Roger and Roger would be his, and they would be together, forever.

"Here?" The driver stopped and pointed to the blue-doored house.

"That's right, could you pull in a little closer? There's a lot of stuff to carry in." Joe fumbled in his pocket for money. It was a ride he'd taken many times, up to see Hartley, home to check for mail when he'd been living with Reggie. This was the last. Tomorrow he would send the door-key back to Reggie in a sealed letter. In the fall, Reggie would find another "Treasure" and give him the key and store his newest "Jewel" away in the blue and white chest, and forget all about him.

"*C'est la vie.*" Joe shrugged as they clambered up the stairs to the apartment.

"What, Joe?"

"Nothing, just being calmly philosophical in the tritest way."

"It's nice, Joe." Harold surveyed the apartment enthusiastically.

"It isn't a patch on your place."

"Well, maybe, but then you don't have to put up with two room-mates underfoot all the time."

"They're beginning to wear on your nerves? I thought you hated the thought of Charles going on tour."

"Yes, I do. But I would be very glad if both Charles and Wally moved out. Joe, do you mind if I unload myself a little? I've always liked you, Joe. I confess I felt mostly just sorry for you, but you always looked a bit pathetic pining over Roger Stuart, but anyhow, I've felt you to be a friend, and I'd like to exploit that friendship and spread my woes, if you don't mind. It helps to talk it out with someone sympathetic. I want a chance to say everything once and for all, and hear myself saying it."

Joe could see the veins in Harold's forehead standing out, blue and trembling. Harold had become very tense.

"Sure, Harold, sit down. Shall I make us some drinks? I bought a bottle of Scotch yesterday as a sort of homecoming present to myself. Soda? Water?"

Returning from the kitchen with their highballs, Joe found Harold sitting slumped on the couch, a cigarette in his mouth. "Now, tell Mr. Anthony all about it." He offered Harold a glass, and took a long sip from his own.

"Joe, I think I'm losing my mind." The statement was flat and unemotional. It was evidently something Harold had tried to say, had rehearsed and said to himself, millions of times, but now that it was spoken, it lacked feeling.

"You'll never know what I've been going through these last few months. Joe, I'm on the verge of a nervous collapse, and I don't know what to do about it. I've been to the doctor. He says I'm all right, but too thin. I need to eat more, but, Joe, I stuff myself, and I still don't gain weight. I'm nervous and fidgety and I bite my nails—I never used to."

Harold eyed his unevenly chewed fingernails. Joe glanced asha-medly down at his own. He'd bitten one off just that morning.

"That's nothing, Harold, I bite mine, too. I try to file them down and even them up, but I keep chewing away at them. I don't think that's anything so terrible."

"Wally has beautiful fingernails—did you ever notice his nails?"

"But what's that got to do with—" and then Joe saw that it did have something to do with Harold's trouble. "Harold, have you thought of seeing a psychiatrist?"

"Who hasn't? So have you, I bet. You'd love to go see one and get cured of being 'gay' and so would I and so would just about everyone else you could name. Of course I've thought of going to a psychiatrist. I'd go tomorrow if someone would tell me where to get the money for it."

"Have you tried to find one—maybe they're not as expensive as you think. I knew someone who paid off his treatments at ten a week," Joe lied. He'd never known anyone who'd gone to a psychiatrist, but he wanted to encourage Harold. "Now surely you could spare that much. Ten dollars a week—you'd have to give up theaters and snacks for a while, but I bet you could pay him off that way."

"God, Joe, it would be worth it, though ten dollars a week is a lot to pay—"

"Ten dollars a week is dirt cheap if it buys your peace of mind." Joe was arguing with such conviction, he almost convinced himself to take ten dollars and go for the first treatment.

Suddenly, Joe saw Harold fall into the pillows and bury his head. "Hell, Joe, I'll never go for treatments—none of us ever will. I'd be afraid of what he might tell me—besides I don't really want to help myself. I'm just weak and stupid and dumb and queer—that's all. Weak and stupid and dumb and queer. I'm supposed to be an artist, only I can't paint anymore, because I've got the shakes every time I take hold of the brushes; and I get headaches if I force myself to work; and I think maybe I need glasses, only the doctor says I don't really—Joe, I've never been so desperate in my whole life."

Joe sat beside the boy on the sofa. He pulled the sobbing head out of the pillows and slapped Harold's face smartly.

"Hey, now, get ahold of yourself. Here, drink something, for God's sake, control yourself. You don't help things any by letting yourself go that way."

Harold was tracing the spot where Joe had slapped him.

"They said they didn't allow any queers to walk down their street." He spoke from beyond a dazed and dreamy face. His eyes didn't focus.

"What? Harold, who didn't allow what?"

"They tried to kick me off the street. I was just walking home, and they tried to kill me. They hate me because I'm queer."

"Nobody hates you. My Lord, Harold, talk sense!"

"She said I was awfully cute. She really did go home with me. I slept with a woman. I had a woman. I guess that makes me not such a big queer, doesn't it? She said I was cute. I think she really did come home to bed with me. It was the day I fainted in the restaurant. I really did faint. I fainted because Wally was dancing in my glass of water, and I didn't like the way he takes over everything that's mine. He's even taken over my own heart, I don't have a single thing that's mine anymore, except my mind, and that's still mine because in my mind I know that I don't really love Wally at all. Honestly, I really hate him. I think he's horrible. He's the one who's swishy. He's the one those guys should have beaten up and tried to kill. He's really queer. I hate the goddamned fairy. I think I really hate him. Do I really hate him? Joe, for God's sake, do I really hate him? Joe, do I? Do I really want to kill him? Joe, am I going crazy?"

Joe stared at his friend. The tears were flowing down his cheeks. His speech had been stuttering at times and saliva trickled down the corners of his mouth. Joe looked in horror at the boy whose talents he had admired and in which he knew Lou put great faith. Some woman had borne this child and raised him and educated him and had hoped for his success, and somewhere along the line, things had happened to him that reduced him to near madness. Poor Harold, Joe thought, as he listened to these chaotic thoughts in that halting voice. Harold had started out so bright and cheerful in the taxi. Now, scarcely an hour later, and the boy had run the gamut almost to insanity. Joe was frightened as he sat looking into Harold's tear-swollen face.

"Come on, Harold, why not stretch out here, and catch a little rest?"

"I'm acting like a fool—I'm just a crazy fool. You see, I am crazy, Joe. I really am crazy. If I weren't so crazy I'd be able to paint now. I could do lots of things now, only I'm losing my mind and that makes it hard for me to concentrate, you understand, don't you? Joe, you're sweet. Joe, Joe, kiss me, Joe. For God's sake, Joe, someone must love me. I may be insane, but someone must love me. Tell me you love me, Joe. Lie to me and tell me you love me. I can't stand not being loved a little bit. Lie to me, Joe. Lie to me and tell me you love me. Lie to me and tell me I'm all right. Lie to me and tell me Wally is good and kind and everything I know he isn't. Lie to me and kiss me and tell me you love me!"

Harold passed into another fit of crying. Joe felt thoroughly afraid now. He didn't know what to do. He wished he'd never seen Harold. He wished he hadn't told the taxi driver to honk. He couldn't take this sort of thing. He was confused enough by his own troubles. He didn't see why he had to go through this with someone else. Hell, he could pull the same lines with different names—he had done that very thing when he'd tried to kill himself.

Then it came to him. Joe knew why he'd called Harold and why Harold had broken down in front of him this evening. He was being a glimpse of himself. Harold's troubles were his own troubles. Harold's hysteria could be his own. They were wading the same deep emotional waters, only it certainly looked as if Harold was in over his head now. Joe knew he had been lucky. Katherine had saved him, and now Roger would teach him to swim, but what could he do for this distraught boy who wept furiously and shook, as he lay stretched out on the bed.

"I must go, Joe." Harold sat up quickly. He rushed to the door.

"Here, I'll let you out. Would you like me to see you home? Maybe I'd better."

"No—noooo. Don't bother, Joe. I'm all right. I'm crazy as sin, but I'll get myself home under my own power." Harold staggered out of the door and Joe hurried to the railing to see that he made the stairs safely. The boy lurched as if he were drunk, yet he'd scarcely touched the drink Joe had given him.

Joe leaned back against the door after he'd closed it. He felt a shiver go through him. It was warmly dark in the room with only a small lamp on. Joe finished his drink and emptied Harold's glass into his own, polishing that off, too. He felt better. God, but this life is a bitch, Joe sighed, as he hurried into the bathroom.

VIN PACKER (MARIJANE MEAKER)

Whisper His Sin

Fawcett Gold Medal Books, 1954

This is one of the most shocking novels we have ever published.

It deals with a strange way of life that has become all too prevalent, and is still spreading.

The book begins in the tormented mind of a boy and ends in the tormented murder of his parents.

Between this beginning and this end, there is a frightening picture of how the blight of sexual distortion spreads, corrupts, and finally destroys those around it.

We also believe that this is one of the most morally enlightening books you will ever read.

The jacket copy on the back of Vin Packer's *Whisper His Sin* sums up the essence of pulp sensibility: titillating, alarming, dangerous, yet ultimately redemptive. Redemptive, that is, for the "normal" reader. But the trick of a great pulp novel is that, while it faithfully adheres to these conditions and standards, it also allows—even invites—an alternative reading.

Whisper His Sin tells the story of Paul Lasher, a psychotic college student who manipulates the younger, insecure, and wealthy freshman Ferris Sullivan into murdering the latter's parents with cyanidespiked champagne. A précis of its plot touches on a plethora of national fantasies about homosexuality—seduction, murder, wealth, insanity, deception. In other hands, this material might simply reinforce already existing stereotypes, but Packer introduces a subversive undercurrent that radically alters the novel. Rather than being antihomosexual in its tone—as the cover would surely suggest—*Whisper His Sin* is a novel about queer hatred. By constantly drawing our attention to the world in which Sullivan and Lasher exist—the queer baiting at school, Sullivan's parents' fear that he will end up a suicide, the repeated chants on the campus of the school song, "I want to be a Jackson man / 'Cause a Jackson man's a goddamn fine man"—Packer conjures up the terror and fear under which Ferris Sullivan was forced to live.

The idea of using the homosexual criminal as a way to critique "normal" society is a constant theme in writing about homosexuality. Patricia Highsmith's *Strangers on a Train* (1950) and *The Talented Mr. Ripley* (1955) are obvious examples, as is Meyer Levin's *Compulsion* (1956). But while Highsmith seems eager to overthrow all moral norms, Packer is more specific in her social complaints, critiquing traditional maleness, family malfunction, and presumed heterosexuality.

By 1954, Packer was no stranger to pulps. Her 1952 *Spring Fire* was one of the first lesbian pulps, and she had published *Look Back to Love* and *Come Destroy Me* in the two years in between. Her 1958 *The Evil Friendship*, about two lesbian murderers, was based loosely on the noted Parker-Hulme case in New Zealand (the basis for the 1994 film *Heavenly Creatures*). Along with Ann Bannon, Paula Christian, and Valerie Taylor, Packer (who also wrote as Ann Aldrich) is ranked as one of the classic lesbian pulp writers. Under her real name, Marijane Meaker, she wrote *Shockproof Sydney Skate* (1972), about a teenaged boy raised by a lesbian mother. She has also written numerous books about gay and lesbian teens under the name M. E. Kerr and has been called "one of the pioneers in realistic fiction for teenagers." She lives in the Hamptons.

Whisper His Sin, which has been out of print since the 1950s, is based on the celebrated Fraden-Wepman cyanide-cocktail case of the early 1950s in which a young r   :d his parents. But Packer takes this basic material and spins it into a psychological thriller of a young man caught between his sexual desires, a lethal friendship, and his hateful family. This chapter—reminiscent of scenes between Tom Ripley and Dicky Greenleaf in *The Talented Mr. Ripley*—occurs halfway through the novel and charts a turning point, during semester break, in Paul Lasher's seduction of Ferris Sullivan. But even as Paul begins to lead him into the shadowy gay world, we can see that the greater danger lies in the expectations and the demands of the heterosexual family, who will be the true cause of Ferris's downfall.

Chapter 10

> Q. What did you say?
> A. I said we were *straight!*
> Q. Straight?
> A. It's just an expression. It means normal.
>   *—From the psychiatric interview with Paul Lasher*

The roomette Sullivan had reserved on the train going back to New York was small. Lasher sat next to him, beside the window, and Sullivan leaned far over in the seat hugging the other side of the compartment. They had been that way since Washington, where Lasher had bought a pint of cheap whiskey, which they were both drinking, Lasher avidly, Sullivan gingerly.

The train whizzed by open, cold-looking country with signs of frost on the ground under a gray afternoon sky. They were due in New York at 7:30 P.M.; it was a little after four.

For the most part, Lasher had been doing the talking. Sullivan listened silently, unused to friendliness with Lasher, and peculiarly embarrassed by it now that it was settled that they were friends. Lasher talked about his ambitions for the future, about his yearnings to be a songwriter or an entertainer of some sort, something in which he could use "this," and he'd bend over and pat his guitar case. Sullivan would look at Lasher's long, tapering fingers and nod his head, and then think about how he was going to get the money for Lasher.

Lasher was drinking his whiskey straight, but Sullivan had added water to his own, and a lump of sugar to sweeten it. It still tasted bitter and medicinal to him, but it went down easier now, and made him more relaxed.

"What's the matter, Sul?" Lasher said eventually, noticing for the first time that Ferris was quiet.

"Nothing. I'm fine."

"Sort of getting used to *us*, hmm?" Lasher put his hand on Sullivan's knee. It made Sullivan jump.

"You aren't still afraid of me, are you, Sul?"

"Of course not, Paul."

"Well, then, relax, Sul." Lasher rubbed his hand across Sullivan's dark trousers. "If it's Fry you're worried about, don't let him get you. We'll think of a way."

"I'd quit Jackson," Sullivan said, "if it didn't mean my mother mocking me, telling me I couldn't get along *anywhere*. That's what she'd say, too."

"You don't get along with her?"

"I hate her!" Sullivan said harshly.

"Well, don't quit Jackson, Sul! You know, Sul," Lasher said, bringing his hand up to the flesh of Sullivan's wrist, "I'm fonder of you than anyone. At *Jackson*," he added.

Sullivan's face flushed. "We ought to be there in a few hours," he said, changing the subject.

At five-fifteen the pint was half-gone. Lasher had drunk most of it. He had his shoes off, and his suit coat hung on a hook at the side of the compartment. His stocking feet were boosted up on the windowsill, and he leaned toward Sullivan. It was getting dark outside the train windows, and streetlights bobbed by as the train sped through little Eastern towns.

Lasher said, "You read a lot, Sul, don't you?"

"Yes."

"I wonder, did you ever read a book—what was the title? Ah— I think it was called *Day into Night*."

"Who wrote it?"

"I don't know, Sul. Can't remember."

"Is it a modern novel?"

"No, it was written way back in the forties."

"Well, then it's *modern*," Sullivan said.

"Sure. I meant that it was modern. It's modern. *Day into Night*. You never read it, hmmm?"

"No," Sullivan said. "What's it about?"

"Somebody lent it to me when I was in the Army. You know, you'll read anything in the Army. It was a funny damn book, all right."

"A humorous book?"

"No, a serious novel. A serious modern novel."

"What was the theme?"

"Oh, I don't know. If you haven't read it . . . It was about two guys, or something. . . . About the stuff Fryman's always yapping around."

"Oh," Sullivan said.

The train whistle shrieked when the train went through the tunnel in New Jersey around six o'clock. Lasher had been playing his guitar and singing, and he set it aside then and looked over at Sullivan, who was grinning. Sullivan really didn't know how to grin. A smile looked almost painful on his solemn face, but his eyes shone a little from the liquor and his expression was as happy as it ever got. Happier, maybe.

"That's a nice song, Paul," he said.

"It's an old one from the southern Appalachian Mountains. It's a folk song, but it's more like blues, really. You know that part in it, in the chorus—" He began to sing the part; "True love, don't weep, true love, don't mourn, I'm going away. . . ." He stopped and smiled at Sullivan. "That's like blues. It's sad. You feel it when you sing it."

"I never liked songs like that before," Sullivan said. "It's strange. . . ."

"What, Sul?"

"Nothing," Sullivan said.

"You never have much to say, do you, Sul?"

"What is there *to* say?" Sullivan answered.

Before they pulled into Grand Central, Lasher held up the nearly empty pint of whiskey.

"We might as well finish it. No sense wasting it."

"I don't think I can take another," Sullivan told him.

"You can, Sul!" He handed the paper cup half-filled to Ferris. "Split it with me."

Sullivan forced it down.

"Good?"

"Yes."

"Anyone meeting you, Sul?"

"No."

"No one's meeting me, either. It's early yet, too."

Sullivan looked out the window at the black nothingness for a while. Then he said, "I have twenty-five dollars."

"Save it," Lasher said.

"I thought we could—have dinner someplace."

"It's swell of you, Sul," Lasher said. "But I can't spend your money. We're in enough of a jam. Sure wish we could, though."

"We *could,*" Sullivan said.

Lasher didn't answer him right away, but as the conductor shouted, "Grrrr-and Central!" Lasher said, "I heard about this place on Fifty-sixth Street—they serve food and everything. Course, I don't know much about it. Some guy told me once. Some guy said it was a different sort of place."

The 46 Club *was* a different sort of place. Outside it didn't look too different from any of the little combined cafés and bars between Fifth and Sixth in the Fifties. It was a little darker, and there was a heavyset fellow sitting near the window looking out suspiciously, but it had the usual green awning in front, the menu posted behind glass to the side of the door, and the hatcheck girl visible from the outside, leaning on a counter to the left of the bar, reading a historical novel borrowed from a rental library.

Nothing about it seemed different until Sullivan and Lasher got inside, in the plush, red-walled back room, where a moon-faced colored boy tinkled "Mad About the Boy" on the piano, and a smiling waiter pointed to "Frogs' Legs Provençal" on the menu with his wiggling little finger and cooed ecstatically that they were "simply deevine." Then, as they sat there, sipping highballs and looking around at the other patrons, they saw the difference.

All of the habitués of the 46 Club were men. They were a handsome group, each one appeared wonderfully healthy, and they all, with the exception of a few short and stout ones, seemed tall and broad and strong. They were magnificently tailored, and as Paul and Ferris listened to snatches of their conversation, they revealed themselves as gifted, intelligent, distinguished, if occasionally somewhat affected, men.

One of them, a titanic-looking blond boy, was between planes for Hollywood. He was sitting to the left of Ferris and Paul, with a dignified silver-haired gentleman who was discussing a novel he had just completed. To the right of them, a lively fellow with a hearty laugh and a loud, resonant voice had just come back from Acapulco, where he had photographed Mexican dancing girls. His companion had a thick accent, a diamond ring on his thumb, and a copy of *Cue* spread before him. They were looking in the movie column to see if one of Jean Cocteau's old movies was playing anywhere. A sad-looking young boy in the corner near the piano requested "These Foolish Things Remind Me of You" over and over; a very drunken pair of advertising men argued about a client's memo on Zip soap; a somber trio tasted their wine while the waiter waited to see if it met with their approval; and three or four unostentatious couples quietly ate their dinners and talked.

Lasher was the first to speak. "Looks like we really ran into something, hmm, Sul?"

"All men!" Sullivan said.

"I guess it's pretty *obvious*, hmmm?"

Sullivan took a sip of his whiskey and ginger ale. It tasted all right now. The ginger ale made the difference. He said, "I've never been in a place like this."

"Do you think *I* have? It's new to me too, Sul."

"I've heard about places like this, of course, but I thought they were all in Greenwich Village."

"If you're uncomfortable," Lasher said, "we'll just clear out. Right now."

"I'm not *uncomfortable.* I'm just . . ."

"What?"

"Surprised."

"Maybe we ought to get out, Sul."

"They don't look unhappy."

"We don't have to stay."

"They don't look like—*sissies,* either."

"We can just tell the waiter we don't like the place."

"I've lived in New York all my life and I never—"

"We can eat the soup and go."

"I wonder if they're *all*—that way. Some of them don't look—"

"Do you want to stay?" Lasher said.

"Look at the one by the piano. He looks a little like Dooley."

"Shall we stay, then, Sul?"

After the mock turtle soup, they had the frogs' legs Provençal, half a bottle of *vin rosé,* garlic bread, garlic salad, creamed spinach, *baba au rhum,* and coffee.

It was a quarter to eleven when they took their coats from the hatcheck girl and bent over to pick up their luggage.

"Lasher!" a voice said from behind them. "Well, Paul Lasher!"

Lasher turned and faced a big fellow with a large, roundish face, a ruddy, sunburned complexion, ox eyes, and a flat nose that looked as if it had been squashed down on his face. He was with two other boys who had already gone out the door, and he stood with his hat in his hand, staring at Paul with a pleasant, surprised smile.

Lasher said, "Hello, Wayne."

"Well, my God!"

"Wayne, this is Ferris Sullivan," Lasher said, stepping aside while Sullivan shook hands with the man. "Wayne Saunders."

"*How've* you been, Paul? You still going to that place down in Virginia? The last time I heard from Vic—"

"Yes," Lasher said. "I'll finish up this year."

"Well, that's swell, Paul." He slapped Lasher across the back. "That's swell!"

Lasher said, "What are you doing now?"

"I've been in Iran. Oil company. I just got back about a month ago."

"And your wife?" Lasher said.

"Margie? We're sort of on the splits, Paul. Margie's with her folks in St. Louis. To tell you the truth, we haven't lived together in over a year now."

"That's too bad," Lasher said.

Sullivan was a little drunk. As he stood there he sort of weaved from side to side, his hand catching the wall every now and then, his eyes bleary.

"Say, Paul, there's a party tomorrow night, over at Rug Cain's studio. You'd like Rug. He's an artist, a damn good one, too. Drop in if you can. I'd like to talk to you. Here," he said, pulling out a notebook and a stubby yellow pencil. "I'll give you his address. Nothing special—just a get-together."

As he wrote, Paul picked up his suitcase. "I don't know," he said. "I'm staying with the Osbornes at the Plaza. I don't know what they'll have in mind for tomorrow."

"Trudy?"

"Yes."

"Well, I'll be damned." Wayne Saunders grinned. "Still seeing her, eh?"

"If I can make it, Wayne, I'll—"

"Try!" Saunders said. "Hell, come after your date. You were always double-gaited." He laughed uproariously and slapped Lasher's shoulder again. Then, before pushing his way out the door, he nodded at Sullivan and said to Paul, "And bring your friend, Paul, by all means."

Outside, at the curb, Lasher hailed a cab.

"The Plaza," he told the driver, "and leave your flag down. You'll be going uptown from there."

Sullivan sat beside him without talking.

"We had a good time, didn't we, Sul?" Lasher said.

"Who's Vic, Paul?"

"Vic? He's the fellow that told me about that place. A guy I used to know in the Army."

"Oh."

"Well, don't sound so glum, Sully boy. Lord, this is the beginning of our vacation."

"I'm not glum. Particularly."

Lasher looked over at Sullivan, sitting in the shadows of the taxi, his long legs crossed, the cashmere scarf knotted around his neck and flung loosely over his shoulder.

"Sully?"

"What?"

"Is something wrong? You acted like you were having a good time during dinner."

"I was. During *dinner.*"

"Well, what the devil?"

"You know full well, Paul."

"I know *what?*"

"You could at least explain it to me."

"Sully, you're talking in circles. What's up?"

"How is it that you know someone in—that place?"

"I've known Wayne for years."

"Are you going to that party?"

"I don't know, Sul," Lasher said. "Why?"

"No reason."

The cab sped up Fifth Avenue and spun around at Fifty-ninth, waiting for the light. The hansom cabs were lined up along the Park, and the large pine tree in the middle of the square was trimmed with lights and colored Christmas balls, a blinking star at its top.

"When I get home tonight," Sullivan said, "I'll write out the check for four hundred dollars. I'll send it to you in care of Osborne. I'll get the rest—somehow."

Lasher looked at him, surprised. "What's all this about? Good Lord, Sul, we'll be seeing each other over the holidays, won't we? Why suddenly spoil the evening by bringing that subject up?"

"I don't know what your plans are," Sullivan answered.

"Well, I expect to see *you,* Sul! Good Lord!"

"How would *I* know?"

"Is something biting you, Sully?"

"No."

"Something *is.* Was it Wayne? Was it because we met Wayne?"

"I just don't want to bother you," Sullivan said. "You have your own life—things to do. You know people."

The taxi pulled to a stop at the Fifth Avenue entrance to the Plaza. A doorman hurried to open the cab door.

Lasher grabbed his suitcase, then he looked at Sullivan.

"Sul? If I *do* go to that party tomorrow night, want to come?"

Sullivan hesitated, not facing Lasher. "Yes," he said.

"Are you *sure*, Sul?"

"I said yes," Sullivan said.

The bedroom was dark. A tongue of light cut across the darkness as Mildred Brody Sullivan opened the door, slipped in, and shut it behind her quietly. Feeling her way across to the table between the two beds, she snapped on the small lamp and called in a whisper, "Earl! *Earl!*"

She had a yellow, quilted robe over her flannel nightgown, and her hair was pinched to her scalp in tight curls, fastened with bobby pins. She leaned over and shook her husband's shoulder. He came awake slowly, opening one eye, squinting toward the light.

"Matter?"

"Ferris just got in, Earl! It's *midnight.*"

Dr. Sullivan rolled over and pulled the sheet up to his neck, his hands fumbling for the blankets. He said sleepily, "Miss his train?"

"No! Earl, wait until you hear *this!*" Mildred Sullivan grabbed a cigarette, her hands struggling nervously with a match folder. She lit the cigarette and exhaled the smoke in a vast cloud that blew toward the doctor's nose.

"Is he all right? There isn't anything wrong?"

"Wait until I tell you!" She began pacing up and down between the beds, holding the cigarette and speaking in a low voice as though she were telling a secret. "I sat up waiting for him after you came in to bed. I was worried. I thought maybe something *had* happened. Well, heavens, I haven't seen him for months. So of course I sat up for him! *Waiting* for him. I finished reading that serial in the magazine, the one I was telling you about, and—"

"Get on with the story, Mil!" Dr. Sullivan sat up in bed and rubbed his eyes.

"Well, I *am*. I finished the serial, and then I had something to eat, and I was just rinsing the dishes in the kitchen when I heard steps in the hall. I'd know his steps anywhere! I could feel him coming, and it made me so excited, Earl. I haven't seen him in months! So I just felt like bursting, but I walked into the living room as calm as you please, and when the door opened he walked in, I said, 'Welcome home, Son.' And I just stood there. I said, 'You're late.' Earl, I wasn't criticizing him or anything, I was stating a fact. All I said was 'You're late.' He gave me the funniest look then, Earl. Honest, I never saw him look like that. I don't know—as if he was looking clear through me. Not like the way Ferris usually looks, sort of hangdog, you know, but—different. And do you know what he said then? He said, 'I'm also intoxicated!' and he picked his suitcase up and marched back to his room. Not another *word*, Earl! Not—another—word!"

Dr. Sullivan sighed and sank back under the covers. "I don't know," he said, "what gets into a boy, drinking at his age. I don't know. . . . I'm sorry, Mil. I know you looked forward to seeing him and—"

"You're *sorry!*" she said. "Earl, what's the matter with you? Don't you see what this means?"

"*Means,* Mil?"

"It means that he's got enough spunk to go out and whoop it up! He probably went with a whole gang from the university! *You* know how they do. A whole bunch of boys out on a binge! Devil-may-care! Gentlemen songsters off on a spree!"

She was laughing now, pulling down the covers of her bed, singing to herself: "To the tables down at Morrey's, to the place where Louie dwells . . ."

Dr. Sullivan stared at her out of his small myopic eyes, a puzzled frown on his face as he said, "But, Mil, he was rude to you. He didn't even—"

"I don't care! Don't you see?" she said, turning to her husband with a triumphant smile. "He's a man! At last he's a man, Earl!"

She switched the light off, still humming to herself a little as she lay with her hands behind her head.

BEN TRAVIS

The Strange Ones

Beacon Book, 1959

Could a Woman Cure This Man's Desires?

Ray was no twisted homosexual driven by unnatural desires. He was a perfectly normal young man, and a handsome one. But he was also broke and hungry—making it an easy matter for him to be picked up and seduced by as skilled a thrill seeker as Bruce Carton.

The affair left Ray in an agony of doubt and guilt. He got his revenge by replacing Bruce as the escort of the wealthy Amelia, a woman glad to pay the bills for her thrills. But the doubt—the guilt—persisted. To prove his manhood, Ray started having an affair with a beautiful young actress. . . .

Amelia would stand for male competition maybe, but not rival females. Ray had to make his choice—give up other girls and live like a gigolo . . . or become a plaything for unnatural men.

The back cover copy on *The Strange Ones* replays a theme that runs through many pulp novels: The young, innocent, down-on-his-luck normal guy needs a few bucks and a bed for the night. Against his better judgment (and his "nature"), he is dragged down into an unnatural, twilight world from which he may never be able to extricate himself. But what you see on the alluring covers of these novels is not always what you get.

For *The Strange Ones* is really more about gold-digging and sexual exploitation than homosexuality itself. In its own minor (and admittedly not very well-written) terms, it is an updated *Les Liaisons Dangereuses* crossed with Budd Schulberg's *What Makes Sammy Run?* Ray, Bruce, and Amelia are selfish and mean-spirited people who form various alliances with one another for their own pleasure. *The Strange Ones* is far less concerned with Ray's sexuality—"Ray Dobson's dilemma was terrifying to him!" screams the front cover—than with the morality of simply using people for sex. If there is any "loving" sexual activity in the novel at all, it is between Bruce and Ray:

> Ray's eyes opened automatically, and he could see nothing but Bruce, standing before him. But he felt no negative emotion now. He only felt fascination for Bruce's body and a quick stirring of excitement that made his heart and pulse beat furiously. Abruptly, Bruce knelt on the bed, and for a minute their eyes met but neither said anything. Ray was incapable of speaking. The awakening had come over him fully, and he felt awed. He was no longer afraid; instead he was relieved and filled with desire. This was a beginning.
>
> He reached up his arms and pulled Bruce down, deliberately hard against his body, and put his arms around him. Then their lips crushed.
>
> "Oh, God," Bruce said. "How can they say this is wrong?"
>
> "Don't talk," Ray said. "Just love me the way I want to love you."

While *The Strange Ones* was content to rely on advertising themes that demonize homosexuality, it is important to remember not only that cover art and copy often obfuscated the actual content of many novels, but that the content of paperback originals varied enormously. Like their more literary counterparts, they functioned as a public forum for discussing larger cultural issues. By the mid-fifties there was a growing critique of the American ethos of placing economic and social success above everything else; of grasping for "the best of everything" and finding nothing. Granted, *The Strange Ones* is a lot closer to Rona Jaffe's popular potboilers than Herbert Marcuse's *One Dimensional Man,* but they all make the same point.

The Strange Ones has been out of print since the mid-1960s. In this early chapter Ray meets Bruce Carton, who, for all of his urbane sophistication—liking progressive jazz is a dead giveaway in pulp novels that a character is less than normal—is really a nice guy. Their frank, nonjudgmental, matter-of-fact discussions of sex, rare for a pulp novel, give *The Strange Ones* a slight air of impertinence and self-knowledge.

Chapter 3

Ray arrived in New York just after 9:30 A.M. As he walked out of the bus terminal to Eighth Avenue, he realized there was a heat wave in the city too, but at least there was a breeze, and the humidity didn't seem so great.

He went into the first restaurant he saw, sat at the counter, ordered a large breakfast, and collected his thoughts while he ate. He wanted to get a room in a large, air-conditioned hotel where he could stay until he could find a nice apartment in a residential area; but he ruled this out of his mind almost immediately. He had less than $600 in his wallet, and he would use this up quickly if he went to an expensive hotel. He had no idea how long it might take him to find the kind of apartment he wanted or how much he would have to pay in advance for it, and in the meantime he had to eat. He would have to look for a job after a while, but he didn't want to think about that yet. Actually, he dreamed of getting along somehow without a regular job. All his life he had dreamed of finding the pot of gold at the end of the rainbow, and he would have been delighted at this moment to discover some way to achieve it without any particular effort. But at the present he decided to be a little conservative and check into a cheap, ugly hotel just off Times Square where he had often stayed on his leaves when in the Navy.

He was assigned by the elderly, cross desk clerk to a room on the third floor, for which he had to pay $35 in advance for a week, plus a fifty-cent tip to a plump, effeminate-looking young man who showed him to the room and asked him if he would like to go to an exciting party that night. He refused the bellhop and told him plainly that he just wanted to be left to himself. He was sure the boy was queer, so he told him that he would report him to the manager if he ever spoke to him again. The bellhop departed quickly without another word, and Ray was at last completely alone in the world the way he had dreamed about.

He stripped off all his clothes, pulled the top sheet back, and fell into bed. He closed his eyes and tried to lose consciousness, but he was too tired to sleep at once, but this didn't matter because he could sleep forever if he chose to.

That was why Ray had come to New York—in a very large city he could have absolute privacy and complete independence; the city and its millions of people would not disturb him. He could drift and nobody would care what happened to him, and that was exactly the way he wanted it. He was sick of being forced to live, and now that he was completely free and on his own he felt the cooling waves of relief and contentment that soon lulled him into a deep, dreamless sleep from which he did not awaken until just before nightfall.

He felt dull as he opened his eyes. The room was stuffy and bathed in the gloom of a cloudy twilight which depressed him, so he got out of bed and went directly into the bathroom where he stood under a cold shower for five minutes. He felt refreshed after that, and he let the air dry his skin as he shaved; then he dressed in his only suit, which was dark blue and tight-fitting, and went out of the hotel to get supper.

The streets were less crowded at this time of the early evening, and he decided to walk for a while and look at the city before he went into a restaurant. Soon he found himself on upper Fifth Avenue at Central Park, and obeying an impulse, he entered the lobby of one of the expensive hotels. He was aware of the grandeur around him more than anything else. It was, true, a faded grandeur of drooping palms in chipped pots and ornate, lavish furniture, but Ray appreciated it and it delighted him. He couldn't quite explain why— except perhaps that being poor made him more conscious of any degree of richness. He decided to have a drink.

He went to the bar, sat down on a stool, and ordered a Scotch and water from the very important-looking bartender. He was served silently and quickly.

Sipping his drink slowly to avoid for a while being asked by the bartender to have another drink if he were going to sit there, Ray was suddenly aware of somebody watching him. There was a sparkling clean mirror behind the bar in which Ray could see most of the large room behind him, and as he turned his head away from the bartender, darting his eyes over the other customers, Ray saw who was staring at him. It was a young man whom he judged quickly to be around his own age—twenty-two—sitting at the bar two stools away from him, drinking Scotch also. The young man was ruggedly handsome, with a square jaw and wiry, blond hair, and Ray noticed something in his eyes when he met them in the mirror that he couldn't understand. They stared at one another for a long time, and then Ray looked away and picked up his drink. He took a long swallow of the liquor because he hated to be stared at, but he was still conscious of the young man watching him, so he turned from the reflection in the mirror to face him. The young man said, "Hello."

"Hello," Ray said. "You know, you've been staring at me."

"Yes, and excuse me. But do you know me?"

"Should I? Why?"

"Because I've been thinking that I have seen you somewhere before. Yes, I'm sure now I have. Do you by any chance have the same feeling?"

"Possibly. Your face might look familiar if I could remember faces, but I can't."

"But you were in the Navy a couple of years ago."

"Yes. I've just been discharged four months."

"Then I do know you. If I'm right, you were on my ship during the last few weeks I was in the service. Your name is, I think, Ray."

"You have a good memory. I don't know your name."

"Sure. I'm Bruce Carton. We had quarters next to one another, and we were together on several night watches. Don't you remember me?"

"Yes. I do now."

"Gosh, but it's wonderful running into you again after such a long time. Let me buy you a drink."

"All right."

Bruce caught the attention of the bartender, ordered the drinks, and moved over to the stool beside Ray. "Are you staying at this hotel on a visit here?" he asked.

"No. I couldn't afford a place like this. I'm staying at a small hotel just off Times Square, but only until I can find an apartment. I'm going to live in New York permanently now."

"Hey, that's terrific. And I can tell you right now you'll love the city. There's no other place quite like New York. I've been living here myself, with my aunt, since I got out of the Navy, and I never want to think of leaving here. I hope we can see a lot of each other."

"Maybe you could help me find a job."

"Well, I'll try. But let's not talk about that tonight. This meeting one another again is certainly a must for a celebration. How about it? Will you have dinner on me?"

"Sure. That would be fine."

"Great. Finish your Scotch. We'll have dinner here, and later we'll think of something interesting to fill the evening. Unless you want to suggest some other restaurant. Do you?"

"Anyplace you say is okay."

Ray stood up and finished his drink while Bruce paid the bar check, and then followed him back to a side door, and down a short hall directly to the hotel dining room where the headwaiter showed them to a table in the back of the room against a dark mahogany-paneled wall, and placed a menu before each of them. Bruce picked up his menu immediately and studied it until the waiter had left, and then he laid it aside and smiled at Ray, who was looking only at the expensive prices.

"Please don't let the prices worry you," Bruce said. "I have plenty of money, but I'll sign the check, so my aunt will really be buying this dinner. Don't hesitate to order anything you want."

"Then I'd like another Scotch, and the large shrimp cocktail to start with."

"I think I'll have the same."

"Would you care if I had a double?"

"Of course not."

Ray looked across the table at Bruce while he ordered for both of them, feeling already that it was going to be a very fine evening indeed; and since Bruce had hinted to him pleasantly that he was wealthy, Ray felt not a qualm for drinking the most expensive Scotch and ordering a large, fine dinner to satisfy his terrible hunger. He even decided firmly that he would take every advantage to cultivate Bruce's fondness for him if Bruce continued to display such generosity. After all, Ray thought delightedly, it was much pleasanter having a rich friend to make his life easier than having a poor friend only to dream with about comfort and avoiding work.

"What do you want to do now?" Bruce asked when they had finished.

"I don't care. You name it—it's your party."

"Well, I could probably still get us a couple of tickets for a musical—or we could visit some of the bars around town I know."

"It's up to you."

"Then let's go up to my aunt's apartment. It's just down the block from here, and there's a great supply of liquor and air-conditioning. We won't have to go out in the heat between drinks."

The apartment where Bruce lived was a large and elegant duplex penthouse on Central Park South. The decor was contemporary modern. The comfortable, low furniture in the living room was of foam rubber with expensive silk covers, and the room was dominated by a lavish curving staircase at the far corner that rose to a small balcony and two doors which were the doors to the bedrooms. Tucked under the stairs was a tiny bar that Bruce went to directly and mixed both of them drinks. Everything here to Ray was beautiful, as his eyes admired every detail of the vast room and his heart ached with envy.

"Do you like?" Bruce asked, handing him another Scotch and water.

"It's magnificent. Your uncle must make a lot of money."

"He did, and after he died my aunt invested very wisely. I think she's about the tenth wealthiest widow in New York."

"I'd like to meet her."

"Well, she's out of town for a few days now. The music I put on the hi-fi is by Fritz Elliott. Do you like it?"

"Great—I like progressive jazz."

"Then we have something else in common besides our mutual taste for Scotch. I have a complete collection of Elliott's recordings."

They sat down in chairs facing each other across a great square marble cocktail table, drank and listened in silence to the records. Then suddenly it was after one o'clock the next morning. It still seemed early to Ray, but Bruce was yawning frequently and this made Ray feel uncomfortable. He said that he was sleepy too, and that he would leave. Bruce objected.

"Why don't you spend the night here?" he said.

"I couldn't do that."

"I wouldn't know why not. When you can sleep in air-conditioned comfort, why get overheated walking back fourteen blocks to a cheap, noisy oven?"

Ray chuckled. "You've made your point. I accept your offer."

"Then we can go upstairs now."

They took fresh drinks with them and walked up the wide stairs to Bruce's bedroom, which was large and square with big windows that looked out on Central Park. The room was walled with a dark-grained, smooth wood, and the rug and bedspread and draperies, which were the deepest color of blue, had a dull red edging of thick fringe to accent the subdued, gloomy richness. The whole grandeur of the room nearly took Ray's breath away.

He finished his drink, set his empty glass down on a tiled table, and stripped to his shorts immediately. He fell limply back across the big, low double bed, spreading his legs and arms wide on the cool satin sheets and sinking his head into the soft, oversized pillow.

Bruce came back into the room, wearing only his monogrammed white silk shorts. Ray looked at him dully and, for lack of anything else, asked, "How do you manage to keep your figure in the city?"

"That's easy enough. I belong to a health club. Maybe you'd like to go there with me sometimes as my guest and work out."

"Thanks. I'd like to very much. I want to keep in shape, and I know I couldn't afford to join."

Bruce flicked out the lights and crawled in beside Ray. The bed was plenty wide for both of them, but Ray was suddenly aware that Bruce had lain down much closer to him than was necessary, and his breathing seemed heavy and unnatural in the coolness of the room. Ray said nothing and did not shift his position. Instead, he thought about the feeling of their arms and sides and legs touching lightly together, and he began to wonder, but soon he was conscious of recognition.

Bruce stirred slightly and rested his arm on Ray's thigh and leg, gently. And he knew what Bruce was when his hand moved slowly— but Ray only relaxed now, making his mind a blank and his body an offering, as Bruce's searching lips first touched his neck and finally his closed mouth, which he opened quickly.

After a while, Bruce lay back and stretched out on his own side of the bed to rest. Immediately Ray got out of bed and went into the bathroom. He turned on the light over the black-and-white tile counter and gazed at his own reflection in the mirror.

You are a bastard, he said to himself, to let yourself be had by a queer.

But the experience wasn't, after all, without a certain enjoyment. He felt sexually satisfied now, for one thing, and at least he hadn't been pawed and slobbered over by some female slob with a high voice and a plump body. He would never let such a person touch him. He was making the comparison in his mind, and this was the thing that most surprised Ray—Bruce was definitely the handsome athletic type, and he had never associated masculinity with abnormality until tonight. The revelation left him a bit shaken and strangely awed, but he did not think disgusted.

His body was sticky all over, so he decided to take a shower. He stood under the icy water and let it penetrate his body until he began to feel numb. Then he switched off the water and stepped out into the bathroom, but he wasn't startled because he half expected what he saw. Bruce, sitting on a stool and watching him, tossed him a thick, clean towel, which Ray caught with one hand. He started to dry his hair. Neither of them spoke at once, but their eyes met and they remained staring all the while Ray dried himself. He wondered casually if he ought to feel self-conscious about someone like Bruce watching him, but he decided that he didn't particularly mind. After all, Bruce knew his body very well now, and Ray had no reason to be ashamed of his build, which was perfectly formed, lean and muscular. If Bruce got some sort of enjoyment out of looking at him that wasn't a crime. At last, they talked.

"I hope I didn't shock or scare you," said Bruce.

"Don't worry, you didn't. I take all things in my stride."

"I'm grateful, too. Perhaps I should have given you some warning, but I suppose I was afraid of that. I don't know what I would have done if you had gotten up and dressed and left. Probably nothing, but I wanted you very much, so I might have tried to force you. I'm homosexual, of course. But you're not."

"No, I'm not," said Ray, knowing this was the truth, and knowing that Bruce knew it, too, but wanting to impress it upon him with the firmness in his voice.

"But you are trade. That means that you let me seduce you."

"Don't kid yourself, friend. I'm normal."

"Of course you are. This is just to satisfy my own curiosity. Why did you prostitute yourself?"

"I suppose because I figured you were entitled to something in return for spending all that money on me earlier tonight."

"Then you trade for money. Well, I think that's the best and nicest exchange. Have you done it before? I mean for money—forget the usual experiments with childhood friends."

Ray looked at him, amused at his clinical-sounding probing.

"No," he said flatly. "Frankly, this sort of thing has never happened to me before."

"Would you do it again for money?"

"With you?"

"Oh, I'm speaking generally now. There must be a thousand young men in New York, as masculine as I am, and would gladly pay you to sleep with them. I am just wondering if you would do it."

"I don't know. Do we have to talk this way?"

"Of course not. I was merely interested in some of your reactions to a thing like this."

"Look, let's get something straight. I don't consider myself having a single tendency in your direction just because I'm here with you tonight. I'm doing this only because I gained personally by it. I won't do anything unless I am benefited in some way that pleases me."

Bruce looked at him, startled. "That's an intriguing philosophy.

You are saying that you look on sex simply as something pleasurable for which either homosexual or heterosexual release is perfectly all right."

"That's right. It makes no difference in the dark if it's a man or a woman, and I don't care that much to go looking for it and give it away."

"I understand. Shall we go back to bed now?"

"Look, I'm tired. I would like to get some sleep."

"We can both sleep later. But perhaps you will be willing to remain awake longer if you'll go and look in your shirt pocket."

"That depends," said Ray, going back to the bedroom.

His shirt was folded neatly over the chair where he had hastily draped his clothes. He reached into the pocket and pulled out some crisp, new bills. He counted them, and there were five of them—$500. Bruce was standing beside him now, his arm around Ray's waist.

So what the hell, Ray thought, how else could I make this much money in one night so painlessly?

He tucked the bills back into his pocket and tossed the shirt across the chair.

"Let's go to bed," he said.

JAMES COLTON (JOSEPH HANSEN)

Lost on Twilight Road

National Library, 1964

While in many cases "pulp" is a sensibility, it is also a style of marketing. James Colton's *Lost on Twilight Road* is a sensitive, well-written novel about a young man's coming of age in Southern California in the 1950s. Yet the drawing on the cover on this 1964 National Library Books paperback original—the only edition ever printed—shows a mature young man being sexually assaulted by a topless, full-breasted woman. The cover copy reads: "The lemonade was spiked. The woman was near naked. It was taking unfair advantage of Lonny, because he hadn't wanted her advances. But it was another of the many episodes which caused him to be lost on twilight road." The back of the cover is quick to appeal to our sympathies: "With any heart at all in your bosom, you can't help but feel a kindred sorrow for this boy, as well as some sort of dislike for the people whose tolerance of the unfortunate goes no deeper than the first layer of skin on their bodies."

This is a good—if badly written—description of the tone of *Lost on Twilight Road*. Colton's prose is precise, his eye exact, and his pitch empathetic. Although it is his first published novel—he was forty-one at the time—it is clear that he is a serious writer. Because publishers needed a constant flow of new titles, the field was open for new, inexperienced, and unpublished authors to prove themselves.

Colton's deep empathy with his characters is notable; so, too, is his enormous sensitivity in dealing with racial issues. Lonny's affair with Pablo, as well as the scenes set in the Chicano neighborhood, are highly unusual in homosexual pulp writing of the time. While more mainstream novels will frequently use racial "passing" as a metaphor for closeted sexuality—Lonnie Coleman's 1958 *The Southern Lady* is a fine example—it is rare in mainstream or pulp novels to see interracial love affairs or sympathetic portrayals of nonwhite communities.

Like many pulp writers of the period, Colton had little control over much of the publication of his work. His original title for this novel was "Valley Boy," and he felt that the publisher's title was sentimental. He also wanted to publish under his own name, Joseph Hansen, but since he had already published stories as "James Colton" in *ONE* (which had a strict policy of only using pseudonyms), he continued using the name for his early novels. Reading *Lost on Twilight Road* is to see not only the beginnings of Hansen's career, but the gestation of what we now call gay literature. Hansen was an editor of *ONE*, the first homophile publication, from 1962 until 1965. He left after an "angry schism" and then founded another homophile magazine, *Tangents,* where he wrote reviews, articles, stories, and a news column. The magazine folded in 1970. In 1969 he produced a radio show, *Homosexuality Today,* on KPFK-FM, Los Angeles. Between 1964 and 1971, Hansen wrote eight novels and a collection of stories for various publishers, including Argyle Books, Greenleaf Classics, and Olympia Press. His 1971 novel, *Todd,* was inspired by and set in the Los Angeles Gay Liberation Movement. In 1970 he wrote *Fadeout,* his first Dave Brandstetter novel, which was to secure him fame.

Joseph Hansen was born in Aberdeen, South Dakota, in 1923. He married Jane Bancroft in 1943 (she worked with him on *Tangents,* writing an advice column). As Joseph Hansen he is the author of seventeen novels and eight volumes of stories. He has also written two novels under the name Rose Brock. Almost all of Joseph Hansen's books remain in print. None of the books he wrote as James Colton are in print.

Lost on Twilight Road tells the story of Lonny, a poor young man who is attempting to find both himself and a purpose in life. He has struck up a close friendship with Gene Styles, the local newspaper editor, who has hired him to work in the office. Earlier Lonny has discovered the closeted Gene in bed with a male lover. Styles worries that this will damage Lonny and has no idea that his younger helper has his own secret life.

Chapter 7

If theirs was a friendship at all, if that was the term for it, it was almost a wordless one. They needed nothing of each other but what they gave, the naked warmth and hunger of their bodies. If Pablo's face, smooth, high-cheekboned, was cold as a fine piece of Aztec pottery, there was nothing cold about the quick, smooth-muscled litheness of him. This was warm and wonderful to hold.

In the dim light that filtered into Lonny's room—where they went only after nine, when Mrs. White had darkened her part of the house and gone to bed—in the dim light, in silence, the fairness of his own nakedness, contrasting with the brownness of the Mexican boy's coloring, made the only pattern Lonny felt any need of now. Gene Styles had lent him books of paintings and sculpture, feasts for the eyes and the emotions. The books lay untouched on the coffee table.

That Friday night, when the editor sat in the room where Lonny had made love in the dark to Pablo, where now the bright light burned, where the editor's voice seemed loud, where they drank their accustomed coffee, Lonny felt annoyance and constraint. His need for Pablo had become, already, in three nights, compulsive. He was impatient for Styles to leave—a feeling he'd never had before—so that he could go out and find the boy and bring him here.

For Pablo wouldn't come alone. Lonny always had to go seek him. He might be anywhere in the little town, alone at the café, or with twenty others outside the bowling alley, or with a smaller bunch in the half-dark, tar-marked school yard of Santa Teresa, the

Catholic church, maybe swinging by his knees from a steel bar. Under an arc light in a street of scabby wooden buildings that bore Spanish signs, he might lazily toss a baseball with three or four other boys, or maybe take turns straddling some luckier kid's greasy motorcycle, racketing it down the empty block and back. Or he might loaf on the seat of a dismantled car and drink beer from a can, beside the huge, cavelike garage where the hot-rodders met.

The boys he chose to hang around with were dirty and sullen-faced, the girls loud, overlipsticked, and black-mascaraed. Lonny wanted nothing to do with them, a thing Pablo understood without explanations, understood and accepted. When he saw Lonny approach, stand off at the edge of the school grounds, or on the oil-stained sidewalk in front of the garage, or under a streetlamp across from the bowling alley, he simply walked away from the gang and came wordlessly to Lonny, and they went home to Lonny's place, together. . . .

"Lonny," Gene Styles was saying, "I asked, do you recognize this painting? It's the one I showed you in the folder that book club sent to the office."

Blinking, pretending interest, Lonny leaned over the art book on the table. "Which one?"

Styles sighed and pointed.

"Oh, sure, Gene." Lonny looked alertly at the editor. "Michelangelo. *The Sistine Chapel.*"

"Wrong. It's Raphael, *The School of Athens.* In the Vatican." He shook his head, discouraged. "Lonny, you're not paying attention. You're nowhere near here tonight." He closed the heavy book and leaned back in his chair. His gaze was level. "It's what happened at my house Tuesday, isn't it? That's what's on your mind."

"No," Lonny said. "No, Gene, honest. Of course not. That's—well, none of my business." He stuttered and felt color rise in his face. "I'd forgotten—all about it." He didn't want to talk about it now. With the advent of Pablo, the pressing need was over.

"Don't lie, Lonny. You've been acting strange all week." Styles's face was set. "Don't try to tell me what you saw wasn't a shock—of course it was. And don't tell me you know what it's all about, either, because you don't, do you?" It was a challenge.

"Well, I—guess some people just—"

"No, you don't," Styles concluded glumly.

"But I don't care," Lonny cried. "Forget it, Gene."

"I would, if I thought you could," Styles said. He set down his empty cup. "But from the way you've been acting, you're obviously preoccupied with it. I know damn well you haven't read one word this week. And you look as if you needed sleep. What've you been doing—lying here trying to figure out what—what homosexuality's all about?"

"No." Lonny rose quickly and bent to pick up the cups. "I haven't. Wait a minute. I'll get more coffee."

He dreaded to go back, and delayed as long as he could in Mrs. White's gleaming yellow kitchen, pouring coffee from the shiny glass maker. Still, he could figure out no way to avoid Styles's explanations and apologies—all so embarrassingly needless now. However, when he edged back into the room, going carefully to avoid spilling from the steaming cups, the editor had changed his mind. He turned from staring out the window.

"You're right," he said. "The thing to do is exactly what you said—just forget about it. You're how old—seventeen, eighteen? I have no business talking to you about these things. If you want to know more about the matter, I suggest you go to a doctor or a minister, because what I think is only a minority opinion. And we do live in a society, Lonny. We're not laws unto ourselves. Anybody who says he doesn't care what society thinks is a fool. So get somebody else's informed opinion on this subject—not mine."

He sat down, leaned forward, and opened the art book again. "Now, then, look at this painting. Recognize that face, the bright coloring, the yellows and greens?"

"Van Gogh," Lonny answered, relieved.

"A Dutchman." Styles nodded. "A member of a family of Amsterdam art dealers. But he left his family to paint in France, where all the excitement was. Spent most of his life there. He was half-crazy, a wild man. You can see the wildness in the power of his paintings. What he was became part of what he did with pigment on canvas. That's the way with all good artists, whether they paint, or write, or compose . . ."

The old excitement of teaching took hold of Styles. His voice and manner warmed to his subject. The strange uneasiness and tension vanished. He moved on from van Gogh to Gauguin, another painter of wild colors, who ran from civilization to bury himself on a South Sea island; to Monet, who painted the colors of sunlight; to Cézanne, who saw behind the shapes of things to their essential meanings.

And Lonny listened, with almost a complete return of the old wonder and delight Styles's talk had always generated in him. There were more cups of coffee. The time was—almost—forgotten. Then, finally, Styles looked at his watch, closed the book, and drove off through the chill night. Lonny watched him go, almost with his old fondness. Almost as before, his mind was dizzied with ideas, images, and colors.

But there was a difference tonight. For tonight another picture overlay the remembrance of all those he had looked at in the bright book—the image of Pablo's dark, young body and his own commingled naked in the nighttime. He grabbed his jacket, shrugged into it, and hurried from the house. . . .

In the next month, he worked alongside Gene and slept his nights with Pablo, and was absorbed constantly in one activity or the other. Styles's Friday-night visits continued. Nothing appeared to be wrong. The presence of Pablo, the fact of Pablo—the unsmiling Pablo, who seldom had a word to say, who smoked sweet Mexican cigarets in the dark when they lay beside each other, tired out, blissfully spent—the presence of Pablo made it easy for Lonny to overlook the change in Gene Styles.

He did see it, yet it happened so gradually that even someone not preoccupied might have missed it. The editor, always lean, began to look gaunt. Lines appeared in his forehead. Those beside his mouth deepened. The fine mouth itself became a thin line. He was a man who'd joked a lot. But his sense of humor seemed to dry up during the gray month after Christmas.

He'd been mild, good-natured always, since Lonny had come to work for him. Now he lost his temper when mistakes cropped up, or when subscribers, advertisers, or contributors of news items crossed him. He bawled out Matt Prior for typographical errors. He even snarled at Lonny sometimes, though he always apologized when he'd cooled off.

Pablo's house, a lath and board shanty he lived in with his chubby, brown mother and six small, black-eyed brothers and sisters, stood near Lordsburg's railroad tracks. Lonny often walked there with Pablo late in the night, at midnight or even after. They passed, on their way, through the darkened, tree-shadowed square. And one night Lonny noticed, as they emerged from the park, that a light burned in the *Standard* office across Main Street. And inside sat Gene Styles—alone, but doing nothing, only staring ahead of himself, sightless. The troubled and depressed look on the editor's face reached Lonny even through his armor of selfish happiness.

He wanted to say something to him the next day, and the next. But he was always driving off on business through the February rains. Lonny saw little of him when they weren't both too busy for talk—the paper demanded more and more of their time. Then, on Friday night, Styles seemed a different person, almost his old self, filled with enthusiasms, wry humor, the drive to talk and teach. Several times Lonny came close to mentioning the late nights of grim brooding in the office. But he always shied away at the last minute.

Then, on a night when rain poured down with a steady, sweet drumming on the roof of his darkened room, and he and Pablo grappled in the urgent, hungry struggle of their lovemaking, Lonny heard a car door slam, heard footfalls run up the cement walk, the noise of shoes on the steps outside his door. He sat up sharply. So did Pablo. Knuckles rapped the door.

"*Dios!*" the Mexican boy whispered. His black eyes glittered with alarm. He swung his feet to the floor.

"It's my boss," Lonny said. Gene Styles used that knock Friday nights. Only this was Wednesday. And it was late, eleven-thirty. But that only meant he couldn't pretend he wasn't home. Besides, where would he go in the rain? He had to answer the door. The knock repeated itself, a little louder. Lonny said, "Get your clothes and go to the bathroom, Pablo. I'll come get you when he's gone."

Pajamas hung in his closet, though he hadn't worn any for

weeks—not since Pablo had come. He pulled them on, looked to be sure Pablo had gone, then snapped on the lamp and pulled open the door, blinking as if he'd been asleep.

Styles burst in. He wore no raincoat and no hat. His hair and the shoulders of his jacket were soaked. He mopped his wet face with a handkerchief.

"Listen, Lonny, I've got to talk to you. I—" He broke off, squinting. "Oh, hell, did I get you out of bed? I'm sorry. I—don't even know what time it is. Is it late?"

"Doesn't matter," Lonny said. "Here, you'd better get out of that wet coat." He moved to Styles to help him with it and caught a strong whiff of alcohol. It shocked him; he'd seldom known Styles to drink. Lonny still associated the smell with that part of his life he wanted to forget—his mother and the trailer. He hated it. The editor was clumsy in his movements, pulling off the jacket, and unsteady walking to the armchair. He dropped into it heavily. Lonny hung up the jacket and pulled a bath towel from a drawer. He handed it to Styles.

"Better dry your hair," he said. "What's up, Gene? Something wrong at the paper?"

"No," Styles said sharply. "Why should there be? Is that all the hell you think there is in my life—that damned paper?"

"Well, no," Lonny said, "no, Gene. It's just—well, I happened to notice you've been working there late these nights and—"

"Oh, you did, did you?" Styles was heavily sarcastic. "You just happened to notice. Spying on me again, is that it?"

It was no use arguing with a drunk, Lonny knew. All the same, he had to choke back his anger. And it hurt him to see Styles snarling and ugly.

"No," he said softly, "I've never spied on you."

Styles grimaced and turned aside. "No, no. I didn't mean that. Excuse me, Lonny. I'm—well, why be devious about it—I'm drunk. My life's in a hell of a mess, and I've gotten stoned, and I've routed you out of bed to weep on your shoulders. Why you? You're only the kid that works for me. Well, I'll tell you why—because you're the only person in the world who knows about Max and me—about what we are and what we do together, see?"

"Yes, Gene," Lonny said, and held his hand out for the wet towel.

Styles stopped mopping his hair and gave him the towel. He carried it to the hamper in the closet. When he turned back, Styles had stopped in the midst of combing his hair to frown.

"What's that?"

He pointed with his comb. In the blue ashtray on the coffee table lay a burned cigaret. One of Pablo's. Its smoke, sweet and sharp-smelling, hung in the damp air of the room. Beside the ashtray lay Pablo's cigaret package. Gene Styles leaned forward and picked it up, examined it curiously, then looked inquiringly at Lonny.

"Thought you didn't smoke."

Confused, tongue-tied, Lonny turned his eyes from the editor's—turned them, he realized, too late, the wrong way, turned them to the rumpled bed, which he suddenly saw was too much disordered to be accounted for by the presence of a single sleeping boy. He did no more than glimpse the bed; he realized his mistake so quickly. But he turned back to find a red-faced and acutely embarrassed Gene Styles struggling up out of his chair.

"Oh, hell," he said. "Oh, Lord, Lonny, you've got some girl here, haven't you? And I burst in like a—oh, Christ, kid, I'm sorry. How stupid can I get? Where's my jacket? I'll leave right now. Good God, what did you do with her, the poor kid?"

Yanking down the jacket, he sent flying the wire hanger Lonny had hung it on. He lurched, confused and apologetic, toward the outside door.

"Forgive me, will you? I promise, it won't happen again. I just—" He hauled the door open. "I just had to talk to somebody and you're the only—friend— No, never mind." He fled into the rain.

In the watery glimmer of the streetlamp, Lonny saw him struggle with the car door and half fall inside. Then he could hold back no longer. Forgetting that he wore only the thin pajamas, he ran barefoot down the steps and out onto the puddled walk. Styles was fishing the car keys out of his pocket. Lonny yanked open the door and got in beside him. He caught the editor's arm.

"Wait," he said. "Gene, wait. You're wrong."

The editor laughed dully. "Don't be childish. You don't need to lie to me." He started the engine, released the hand brake.

"I know that," Lonny told him. "That's why I'm going to tell you the truth. It's not a girl, Gene."

Styles looked at him sharply, suddenly no longer drunk. "What're you talking about?"

"It's a boy," Lonny said. "Understand? A boy that was in there with me."

"Oh, my God," Gene Styles said. He switched off the engine, turned on the seat, and gripped Lonny roughly by the shoulders. "Not on account of me, Lonny? Not because of what you saw between Max and me that day. This is not hero-worship, surely? I know imitation is the sincerest form of flattery, but if I'd ever thought— Now, listen to me, Lonny, and try to understand. A boy your age is often mixed up about these things. You don't want to start forming relationships that—"

"No," Lonny broke in. "You're wrong, Gene. It's not that. I knew somebody like that once." (He meant Hal Willard.) "And that's not me. I—well, I mean, it's really the way I am. And—" He blurted out what he'd tried to say and held back for too long, blurted it defiantly and in a rush of compassion. "And there's nothing to be ashamed of about it. So quit acting ashamed, Gene. You don't have to, not for me. I'm ignorant and you're smart, and for a long time I've wanted you to tell me this. But I'm telling you, instead. It's all right. If that's the way you are, it's all right. It's good. Isn't it, Gene? Isn't it?" He had to stop to catch his breath.

The editor stared at him, long and gravely and without speech. Then he turned away and gripped the steering wheel and leaned his forehead against it, shutting his eyes. It seemed a long time before he sighed and straightened up and looked again at Lonny's anxious face.

"You'd better get back in the house," he said hoarsely. "He'll be wondering what happened to you."

"But it is all right, isn't it, Gene?" Lonny begged.

"I don't know," Styles sighed wearily. "It's complicated, Lonny. But even if I believed it were all right, I don't think I'd tell you. A decent man has obligations—especially to younger men who trust him and look up to him. No, I'm not making any recommendations tonight, Lonny." He started the engine again. "Go on, now. Get out. I'll—see you tomorrow."

Baffled and hurt, Lonny pushed open the door, slammed it behind him, and ran, scowling, back through the rain to the house. But his anger disappeared when he found Pablo patiently waiting for him, brown and naked as a savage, in the delicate lavender coloring, the delicate lavender soap scent of old Mrs. White's bathroom. He sat on the closed toilet fixture, elbows on his knees, and flicked open and shut with a practiced thumb his prize plaything, a glittering switchblade knife.

Lonny peeled off his soaked pajamas, and Pablo, pushing the knife away into a pocket of his clothes that hung over the rim of the claw-footed bathtub, stood up and took the towel from Lonny's hands and dried him. He said nothing at all. Neither did Lonny. They switched off the bathroom light and walked noiselessly, naked, down the shadowy hallway. In the room, Pablo lit another cigaret and laid it in the ashtray.

And they went back to bed.

Memoirs of Jeff X

Zil, 1968

I was never coming home. Not after the school principal had notified my parents how I had been caught in the basement under the locker room of the school gymnasium in very embarrassing circumstances with another boy.

It had happened after school hours. That particular place, that sort of basement, was seldom visited by anyone in school, whether student or faculty member. It was used as a storage room for athletic equipment not in use during the time, such as barbells etc. . . .

To us, it seemed to be the safest place in the world. Nevertheless, we were caught there, by the principal himself! And to add even more weight to our sudden disgrace, they had fallen upon us the precise moments when our purpose was more evident; therefore our guilt was shameful and undeniable. I was found over a discarded exercise bench with my pants out. My legs were sprawled over the other boy's shoulders as I had completely abandoned myself to his ministrations, enjoying all the thousand needles of pleasure piercing my senses into an ecstatic thrill.

This is the beginning of Jeff X's memoir, and it is hard not to be charmed by what is either the complete lack of any talent for writing or what is perhaps the most unique voice in pulp writing. Jeff—X?—has an almost eighteenth-century cadence to his prose that would not seem out of place in *Pamela* or *Tom Jones*. There is also the curious phasing—what does "with my pants out" actually mean? He is even reticent about the sexual details. His "dear reader" style becomes all the more charming and teasing as he exploits every rhetorical circumlocution possible to postpone the salient sexual facts.

Many gay pulps of the sixties have idiosyncratic voices, in part because the smaller, less industry-based firms didn't really edit the books. Large firms such as Gold Medal were highly professional, but smaller ones like Zil Inc.—the publisher of *Memoirs of Jeff X*—were happy to have content to fit between two covers. This becomes even more evident at the close of the decade, when the publishing of sexually explicit books became extraordinarily profitable, and editors had to produce dozens of titles a month for their various series.

Memoirs of Jeff X has been out of print since the late sixties. The following scene, which occurs halfway through the book, begins with Jeff having a moment of doubt about living in New York: "But I was afraid, as usual. It was always this way! Always afraid, always nervous, always as usual. It was always this way! Always afraid, nervous, always hungry and looking for a place to sleep. Was this the gay life?" He soon meets a strange, older man, with a "guttural Baltic type of accent" who "smells of salt and fish," who invites Jeff to his dingy tenement room. Here he begins to give him boots and a black leather jacket to put on.

My eyes opened wide at what he held. They were a pair of glittering jet-black leather boots, complete with leather laces from the vamp all the way up to the calf portion. They were polished as smooth as black silk. Just looking at them got me all excited.

"Hey, those are real sharp!" I said, delighted. I'd seen other hustlers wear boots and always thought if I could raise the money, I'd get a pair. Gave me a butch look, too.

"You take." He pushed them out.

"Gosh ... I mean ..." I felt gratified and wondered what his whole game was.

"Take this, too."

Now I received another shocker. The next item was a black leather motorcycle jacket, reaching down to below the hips. It was real leather, with all sorts of buttons, buckles, and gleaming nail-heads or something. If I put those things on, I'd be a real mean one! I thought.

"Nice, real nice." I looked at him. He was smiling that same gold-toothed grin. "You want me to keep these?" I said hopefully.

He shook his head. "*Ja, ja* ... put on."

There it was! The usual request! Just an excuse to get me in my birthday suit. Okay, if that was it ...

"Want me to change right here?" Despite the fact that a few dozen men had used my body, slept with me, performed all sorts of queer acts with me, even made me do a few things while they watched, I was still a little shy about undressing before someone.

"*Ja, ja* ... I watch ..." Then he took off his old-fashioned blue pin-stripe jacket, hung it up on a nail attached to a pole of some sort.

I kicked off my loafers, squirmed out of my socks. Then I yanked my shirt off. Naked except for my skin-tight jeans, I knew I looked like a real nice blond muscle boy. Others said it and I was vain enough to feel excited about it.

For his benefit, I put on a little more of a show. I bent over, pretended to fumble with the tight rivets of my jeans, worked on my zipper, letting my hair fall downward to give my face this wild angel expression which always worked so well with my clients.

It worked.

He grinned and said, "Nice hair—smooth like a girl's." He reached over, stroked my hair, then ran his chafed and blistered palm over my bulging biceps, caressing my chest. "Nice boy—nice muscles. Not like these skinny ones from Forty-second Street."

Again, I continued my show, sucking in air and deepening my chest, even bending my arms in a physique pose, letting my biceps now as thick as billiard balls roll around.

"Like what you see?" I asked.

He jerked his head in approval. "Take off your pants ..." He was quick ...

I slithered out of them, letting them drop around my ankles, kicking them away like a blue jean puddle, if you know what I mean. Naked, I let the full beam of the kerosene lamp light up my pink skin, catching the hidden crevices and shadowy nooks of my body. I knew a few tricks. I knew I had a sexy masculine body, an innocent boyish face, and that combination drove the queens wild. I never omitted to accentuate all these physical advantages of mine.

Yes, the man seemed wild, over me.

"Come here." He was still seated, his arms held out, reaching for my thighs, then cupping my firm hard buttocks. He pulled them apart and, only as I yelped as a shock of pain tore through my hips, did he go gentle.

"Easy, easy man," I kept imploring him.

He found the rest of my body. His work-worn hands were like sandpaper as he gripped me hard, squeezed and pulled while he kept grinning up at me to watch my reactions.

"Go ahead," I urged, anxious to get it done with. "Do what you like."

He appeared to be too casual—the exact opposite of my anxiety. It was not unusual and I should have been used to it by now. They were always slow—as if wanting to enjoy it bit by bit, right down to the last drop; while I was always anxious to get it done with.

Later on . . . I would change . . .

He used both hands to stroke and caress, making me shiver, feel spasms tearing through my insides. The sharp sandpaper effect on my taut sensitivity was driving me wild with excitement. I didn't know this man could make me feel so much with all his apparent awkwardness and his lack of gentleness.

"Put on boots—and jacket. You look nice in black leather with your yellow hair, boy . . ." It was just about the longest speech he had thus far made.

"Okay, mister." I almost said "pops" and was glad I did not let it slip through. Once you're naked, you better watch it. They can really get mad at you and make you feel it!

I turned my back, feeling his hot breath as he came closer, still sitting but arching his body forward. Now I felt his rough beard (he badly needed a shave) as he kissed me while I bent over to put on the boots.

He even reached between my thighs and fondled me, sometimes too hard. If I flinched, he relaxed but then became just as hard and demanding.

Stepping into the boots made me feel something real big. And I do mean BIG! My feet were naked in the boots and the contact of my soles in the leather prison sent shock waves of power throughout my whole body. The way I felt, I could have had a dozen johns and all of them would have been satisfied.

He was kissing me in the worst way, his lips and tongue just about everywhere, driving me wild.

"Put on the jacket," he directed when I turned around, his callused hands still gripping my thighs, now going upward. "Nice . . . blond . . . soft . . ."

I felt a bolt of fire down at the bottom of my stomach. "Hey, man, what're you doin'? Want a sample—go on top, here." I pointed to my blond head. "Okay?"

He wrinkled his furrowed brow and appeared not to understand. "Put on jacket." But he stopped yanking my soft hair down from where it really hurt. What weirdies some of those creeps could be! The whole place was weird, too.

The motorcycle jacket came just down to my thighs. If I could see myself in a mirror, I would have laughed at the way the bottoms of my buttocks peeped from beneath the black leather; the creases dividing the two firm mounds from my strong thighs now looked very naked and sexy. That's probably what drove those queenies real wild.

"Like?" It was about the only word he could comprehend. So I repeated it quite often.

He nodded shortly. "No button up."

Obviously, if I buttoned, I'd cover up what he wanted most. Now, with my heavy black boots stomping on the rotted floorboards, my gleaming black jacket covering me from shoulders down to pelvic bones, I came toward him again.

He acted real wild. For a rough-looking old salt of the sea, he could sure act like a queer. Just shows you that you can never tell by the appearances.

He was fondling, stroking, pulling, and doing all sorts of things to me. As for myself, I shoved both of my fists into my leather jacket pockets, rocked on my heels, and let him do what he wanted.

I shifted my body, let him cup my buttocks in the palm of his hands, while he was really kissing me all over. Slowly, I maneuvered to get the most of his caresses. I felt the flicking flames beginning to burn me. It was a wonderful feeling, despite my reaction of guilt and shame. It was the next best thing to really going to town with a girl. But how would I know? I never had a girl, never really wanted one. What did I want? I wish I could find out before it would be too late.

My muscles were strained and the guttural sounds that filled the musty room made me feel deeply ashamed. I almost tottered in my leather-booted legs, but this seaman really held me tight, digging his fingernails into the firm flesh of my muscled buttocks. It hurted . . .

Everything seemed to be happening at once. I felt the familiar fire that surged through my loins. My muscles grew tight, like knotted ropes, and I had to suck in my breath. I could hardly control the shivering—this was it—

Suddenly, it broke through. I almost screamed from the released tensions as it gushed forth. The leather jacket clung to me like a second skin. I was bathed in an alternately hot and then cold sweat.

Again and again it happened. This man was really anxious. He couldn't get enough of it.

The awful sounds he emitted were so sickening that I almost felt my stomach heave up. What was wrong with me? Since when was I getting so sentimental? This man was using me—okay—call me a male whore—but he was getting his fill and he had to pay up. So what's the big fuss?

I felt everything being drained out of me. I also had the same fleeting reaction that someone had encircled me with a red-hot live wire—gripping me where a man is real delicate. I could hardly stop shaking back and forth.

Something happened then.

It was quick.

Too quick.

What I felt next was a heavy clout across my face.

"Hey—what're doin' to me?" I was released, naked except for

the black jacket and boots, feeling ashamed and humiliated at the way I was floundering.

The foreign seaman's face was a mask of hatred. He looked like a maniac. It must have been the leather jacket and the boots. This kind of paraphernalia always did things to the queenies. His fists felt like thick iron balls. He let one loose, smashed me across my jaw. I fell back as sharp pain ripped through my head.

"Cut that out . . . what'd I do?" I was half-sobbing as he smashed his fists into my naked vulnerable stomach, then he became cruel—real cruel as one foot lashed out, tripped me, and I fell backward, my head slamming on the floor.

He gripped me so hard that a knife stuck in my groin would not have hurt so bad. Oh, man, did that hurt! I felt like dying . . .

"Please . . . please . . . no . . . no . . . NOOOOO!"

He was infuriated, moved by a rage gushing forth from unknown abysses of his being. I was really frightened. I didn't know I would fall in such hands. The man hadn't seemed to belong to that kind at first sight.

I tried to squirm free but the more I did it, the more he squeezed until I felt waves of blackness engulfing me. My efforts grew more and more feeble and I kept thinking, as if in a haze, Oh, no . . . don't let it end that way . . . Not this way. Please . . . oh, God . . . please . . .

. . . I had to stop writing the details in this diary. Know why? The very thought of what happened made me sick. You can imagine how bad it was when I had to go through it.

Now, as I sit and write this down in my diary, I have fortified myself with a double dose of brandy—straight. It's the only way I can really bring myself to going over the ugly mess.

It was a mess, believe me.

Where did I leave off? Oh, yes . . .

That horrible sadist—and he had turned out to be a real perverted sadist in every sense of the word—did a foul thing as he tortured me, letting me writhe around on the floor like an impaled slave who was turned into the plaything for cruel captors.

Then he yanked off my jacket, but let me wear the boots.

"I punish you . . ."

These were the first words I heard when I began to revive. A splash of ice-cold water drenched me and also awakened me.

"Please," I started to plead, struggling to sit up. But sharp, knife-like pains ripped through the bottom of my stomach; I had to lie, sprawled out like that, naked except for my laced-up black leather boots that gleamed in the flickering light of the kerosene lamp. "Don't . . . let me go . . . please . . ."

"I think you nice boy." He spat on me, hurling a large tin can to the far side of the dingy room, where it fell with a clatter. Now, I was dripping wet, my silky blond hair plastered to my head, my sharp blue eyes registering fear.

He was saying, agitated by this strange unknown rage, "You not nice . . . you're queer . . ."

"No, no, you've got it all wrong, mister." I tried again to sit up and felt the splinters of the floorboards as they cut my bare thighs and buttocks.

A salty taste ran down my mouth; I licked at it and knew it was blood. There were more salty rivers and there were tears, real warm tears coursing down my cheeks. In all my life, I don't think I ever felt as alone and helpless as I did at that moment. Naked on the floor, at the mercy of a depraved foreigner—and he could be cruel—as I would soon find out.

Just how was I going to get out of this scrape? It was a real trap. This guy could kill me. I felt a pang of fear stab through my guts as if someone really sliced into me with a switchblade. Man, this was real rough!

My body was a mass of aches and pains. Each movement sent a shower of needle-sharp pains and spasms through my arms and legs. But this was just the start of what would happen to me.

"No," he barred my path—even though I was still on all fours, feeling helpless and naked because there was no telling what he could do in his frenzied perversion.

"What do you mean, no? Just lemme go, mister . . . let's just end the scene, okay?" I tried to act tough but my voice was squeaky and registered fear as naked as I was.

I struggled and tried to hoist myself upward even though I was so filled with aches, I almost collapsed—when this weird one's fist shoots out and smashes against my ear.

I felt as if someone set off a rocket right in my head. The dark room swerved and I thought blood was gushing out of my nose.

Maybe it was. I fell down again, screaming when I really hit a sore spot. "Hey—you off your rocker, or something?" I sniffled and knew I was crying—like some silly kid. "Lemme go," I pleaded again.

"You be punished . . . Boy is bad, get punished."

Again, I felt an ice-cold shudder race through my body, then an uncontrollable sweating. I was in a real bind. I felt the tears come out and really pour. Okay, okay, so call me a kid—a little kid who's scared. That's exactly how I felt. Only I had no one to protect me. I knew that even if I screamed good and loud, all it'd get me would be a sore throat. We were at the waterfront, in an abandoned building in a neighborhood where even cats were a rarity.

I could have fought him—but he was like a brick wall, work-hardened and tough. Worse than that—he was mad. He could have killed me and left the scene and vanished somewhere on the seven seas and nobody would ever find him. I had heard of so many blood-chilling stories about people like him. Only, I thought this kind of thing never really happened . . . Now, I was learning better . . . the painful and bitter way.

"Please." I tried to work on his emotion, following his stiff gait as he went over to the trunk, dug deep and started taking out some objects. "Please, can't you just skip it . . ."

He was coming back, his sunburned face a dark mask of horror. His eyes looked cruel. His mouth was twisted in a grim line. He held some ship ropes in his brawny hands. His sleeves were rolled up, showing thick, gnarled, and rope-veined forearms.

He looked powerful. Like a ship's mainmast. You couldn't break him.

"You scream—I make it worse. You be punished—you bad boy and bad boys are punished . . ."

I was so terrified I could have died right there on the spot. The dust clouded up as I struggled, feeling lancing pains shoot through my body. "No—no—keep away from me!"

Stupidly, I tried to fight him off by rocking on my hips, kicking at him with my heavy leather boots. I hit him all right, but the blows just grazed.

"You bad boy . . . bad . . . like other American boys . . . too wild . . . punish you . . . make you scream . . ."

The words screamed at me in recurring echoes. "Make me scream!" Oh, no—oh, God, don't let this happen to me! If I've been wrong, punish me another way—but don't let it be that way—with some wild maniac who wants to torture me . . .

I floundered around like a wet fish. I tried to kick as he planted both of his feet on either side of me, hurled me over facedown, then gasped as he worked to swing the ropes around my wrists. Yes, he was going to bind me up in those chafing ropes.

"Get away . . . get away . . ." My screams were half sobs and I was now hysterical with terror. The screams bounced back at me and then echoed throughout the whole house. It was so eerie, it was almost like a nightmare. I kept hoping that I would wake up and find it all to have been a horrible bad dream and nothing more.

The wild maniac seized my hair, yanked my whole head upward, almost ripping my prized blond locks from my skull. "Nice hair . . . like a girl . . . only you pretend to be tough boy . . . But I tame you . . . like a girl . . ."

My head felt as if it were going to be ripped from my shoulders, the way he had a tight grip on my hair and was pulling my entire head in all directions. The blood rushed to my nostrils, through my ears. Everything turned red.

I was sniffling and sobbing, having lost whatever little masculinity I had left. "Noooo"—in between choking sobs—"don't . . . don't . . . please, mister . . ."

"You deserve . . . you turn into a good boy . . . when I finish . . ."

The thick ropes were knotted around my wrists, secured to a beam. They were so tight, they might have been chain manacles. They forced my palms to face one another. My arms were stretched far above my head—I was stretched out flat, incidentally, facedown. So, try to picture this grisly scene—it has become a mental scar for me.

The maniac was muttering as he bound my wrists to the beam, then he looped a thick knotted rope around my booted ankles—yanked hard until I was spread-eagled.

Just how it was done, I never did find out; neither did I want to know the details.

I felt them!

The ropes were secured, forcing me in a spread-eagled position, faced down on the splintered floor that bruised me real good.

"What . . . what are you . . . ?" I twisted my head, struggling against the thick knotted ropes that held my wrists together and also imprisoned my legs—parted to the breaking point—to some unseen beam.

Now I saw what he had carried out of that old-fashioned sea chest or trunk. I felt a shock of horror down to the pit of my stomach.

It was a black, coiled leather whip—gleaming like a snake, and as vicious looking—the tip was split into what looked like three little tails. It was a foreign thing. Something to . . . whip . . .

"NOOOOO!" I screamed until my lungs felt raw and bleeding. I struggled, my body muscles becoming rock-ridged and stiff.

That was when it began!

Here in a deserted house on the waterfront, just a few minutes from civilization, I was held a slave—bound in a spread-eagled humiliating posture, naked except for my leather boots—at the mercy of a horrible maniac who was now raising the evil-looking black leather whip for the first lash.

The whoosh of the whip was like the roar of an angry beast. The lash sliced across my shoulders. It was like a hot wire searing into my muscles. I screamed from the shock of the pain.

"Scream—scream—you bad boy—you queer . . ."

The maniac raised the gleaming black leather whip and it whooshed down again, a little bit lower on my back. Again, I felt the red-hot lancer of pain as if a hot sword were sliced into my muscles. I could feel the shock tear through my body, burning me. Again I screamed and sobbed, horrified at what was happening to me.

The more I struggled, the tighter the rope bonds became around my wrists. I felt the white-hot flame sear my back again and again, descending lower and lower until it reached my buttocks. Here the whip stopped.

I was sobbing like a beaten girl, completely dominated. The whipping had squelched whatever pride in my manhood was left. I had no human dignity. I was nothing but a humble slave, "Ppppp-llllleasssse . . . ," pleading for mercy.

Now I felt something else. It was a thick leather belt—doubled over—whacking at my buttocks. This crazed maniac was spanking me! He was really spanking me. The leather belt let loose with a series of thick whacks until I felt so raw and bruised, I knew I'd not be able to sit down for a month. My whole bottom must have been crisscrossed with thick red welts. It is fantastic how much pain a person can take without falling unconscious. It would have been a blessing for me to have fainted. But, no, I remained perfectly conscious, feeling to the tiniest fiber of my being the red searing pain the sadist was inflicting on me.

"Spank . . . like a bad boy . . ."

Again and again, the leather belt punished me until I was a raw mass of punishment. Now I was so spent, so exhausted from the weeping, that I could hardly gasp for air. I could not even cry.

All I wanted to do was die . . .

Somehow, the spanking stopped. I did not know what next to expect. It couldn't be as horrible as what had happened already!

Foolish me!

It was going to be much worse!

The crazed maniac was breathing heavily; his sweat-stained body gave off a fetid odor as he grunted while walking around the creaky room. "Bad boy," he kept muttering to himself. "Gonna get it . . . never be bad again."

There was a rustle and the belt clattered to the floor. Next, the sound of clothes being moved—or removed.

The maniac planted both feet on either side of me, then dropped down to his knees. When the contact was made, it was obvious that he was naked—or he had removed his pants. I was so mixed up, my body burning with pain, I could hardly think straight.

Now I knew—with a shock—what he was going to do to me. This was the worst! It was something I always dreaded—something most hustlers fear—and would kill before they let themselves be used.

"Nice boy—soft with muscles . . ." His hands reached beneath, gripped me hard, and did things to make me come alive. "Smooth skin . . . nice hips . . ." His strong hands gripped my buttocks and pulled . . .

"NOOOOO! Ohh, no . . . don't . . . please . . . you can do anything . . . not that . . ."

"I make you feel like a girl—not a tough boy . . ."

It started slowly. I tried to fight but with my wrists and ankles shackled, helpless, at his mercy, there was nothing I could do but endure the punishment.

A battering ram . . . that's what he was.

In a crazed haze, I thought an enormous mallet was being hammered into me. Deeper and deeper it went, ripping me apart, filling me until I thought I would burst.

Any other torture would be mild compared to this. It was a physical and mental torture. He was humiliating me, ruining me, using me . . . not like a girl as he pretended . . . girls have comfortable organs for this kind of thing . . . but like an animal, or I don't know . . . like a queer . . . that's it . . . like a queer.

The livid shaft of pain penetrated until I was so impaled I could scarcely whimper. I suffered even greater punishment when this sex maniac pinched my buttocks, forcing me to wiggle, which only added to his perverted pleasure and my agonized torment.

His body was like a living mallet as he heaved and undulated. It took a while before he reached the high peak. Considering his age, that shouldn't be much of a surprise.

When it happened, every nerve fiber in my being was alive, raw and naked.

It was the most agonizing hell that I would ever know.

Much, much later, he got up, dressed himself. He grunted about my being punished and that it "teached" me a lesson or something like that. I was in the throes of such agony that I could scarcely muster enough breath, let alone to try to reason things out.

"Lemme go," I whimpered, unable to cry anymore because it was all taken out of me. Each move sent a wave of knife-sharp pain ripping into my hips.

"If you be good . . ."

"Yes . . . oh, yes . . . I'll be good." I was willing to promise him anything if only he'd release me.

He untied me, kicked me viciously in my buttocks, and sent me sprawling in a dark corner. Here, I could watch him through my bloodshot eyes as he dressed himself, picked up a suitcase and then turned to me.

"You remember now . . . be good . . ."

Then he was gone—

Yes, now as I look back, I see that it was so bizarre it could only happen in a nightmare . . . but it did happen . . . exactly like in the wildest of those stories I had read with disbelief.

Just how I managed to get out of that house of hell is still a mystery. But I washed up my wounds in the foul-smelling sink, put on my clothes, feeling every little movement through unbearable pain searing through my tortured body. I don't know how I managed to stagger out of this place. I probably had to crawl out. I remember that I did not even bother to bolt the door. Who cared about that? The only thing I wanted was to be as far away as possible, never to see this hellish place again.

Oh, yes, I did receive one little reward—a pair of black leather boots and English-style leather motorcycle jacket. These things would help me, later on.

I was wearing them when I staggered outside. The cool night air washed my lungs and sent a little energy into my beaten, tortured body.

Then, somewhere near the waterfront, I blacked out.

PART FOUR

Out of the Twilight World: The Sexual Revolution Goes Lavender

The emergence of the overtly sexual gay male pulp novel did not occur in a vacuum. Not only had the radical change in censorship laws allowed the publication, and, what was just as important, the distribution, of books such as *Gay Whore* or *Hollywood Homo,* but gay male consumer patterns had also changed: There were now more men who were out and unafraid to purchase books with frankly homosexual themes from the racks in drugstores, bus stations, and in the newly emerging venue of the "adult bookstore."

But other cultural changes as well encouraged—in the broadest sense—the evolution of this genre. Commonly enough in the 1950s, gay male themes were accepted as part of mainstream literature. Heterosexuals could read about, and learn about, the gay male world in books such as Harrison Dowd's *The Night Air* or Michael De Forrest's *The Gay Year*. These books were, to a large degree, marketed to a heterosexual readership. And straight readers were curious and often eager to read about the "shadow world" of homosexuality. Some of this curiosity may have been prurient, but much of it was probably honest interest. Heterosexuals have always been curious about the lives of gay men and lesbians, and novels that dealt with gay characters and gay themes were the best, and the easiest, means of satisfying that curiosity.

But it was not only novels that illuminated the lavender shadows for heterosexuals. From the 1950s on, nonfiction works also shed light on this mysterious world. Perhaps not surprisingly many of these nonfiction books were not as literary, sophisticated, or nonjudgmental as the novels of the same period. Often, these books took the tone of a exposé that would guide the heterosexual reader through the terrifying "secret world" of the homosexual. The most famous of these was the *Confidential* series by Jack Lait and Lee Mortimer. The authors, newspaper columnists on the theater beat, covered the sleazy underworlds of New York, Washington, and Chicago in bestsellers that titillated as they informed. Chapter 15 in *Washington Confidential* (1951) is titled "Garden of Pansies" and begins: "If you're wondering where your semi-boy is tonight, he's probably in Washington." Writing in semi-tough-guy tabloidese, Lait and Mortimer spell it out for their readers:

> The only way to get authoritative data on fairies is from other fairies. They recognize each other with a fifth sense immediately, and they are intensely gregarious. One cannot snoop at every desk and count people who appear queer. Some are deceptive to the uninitiated. But they all know one another and have a grapevine of intercommunication as swift and sure as that in a girls' boarding school. They have their own hangouts, visit one another, and cling together in a tight union of interests and behaviors.

And where are these hangouts? Lait and Mortimer mince no words:

> Their chief meeting place is in leafy Lafayette Square, across Pennsylvania Avenue from the White House.... They also gather in Franklin Park, a few blocks away, in the center of the business district.
> Many cocktail lounges and restaurants cater to irregulars. Most of them are near the Mayflower Hotel. The most popular resort is the Jewel Box, near Sixteenth and I, NW, formally known as the Maystat. It is a cocktail lounge with entertainment by a piano player, who sings semirisqué lyrics. The waiters are obviously fairies. Most customers seem to fit into that pattern. The night we went there, a police car with siren screaming pulled up. We figured it was a pinch. After the cops

threw out two customers, a waiter told us that everything was okay.

"Those boys got fresh," he said. "They tried to flirt with those two women sitting there. We don't tolerate flirting—anyway not with women." Then he minced off, hand on hip.

This breathless, hard-boiled style—half James M. Cain, half Hedda Hopper—is vintage fifties. It is also a long way from the empathetic nuance of *The Night Air* or Lonnie Coleman's *Sam*.

As a more distinct market for paperback originals—pulps—emerged, it also changed the way that heterosexuals were able, and willing, to learn about gay male lives. Men and women who might eagerly have bought a mainstream novel with homosexual themes would be far less likely to pick up a copy of Richard Amory's *Song of the Loon* or Carl Corley's *My Purple Winter*. It wasn't just that these books were slightly more explicit about the anatomical details of gay male sexual activity—heterosexual readers had little trouble contemplating John Rechy's 1963 *City of Night*—but that they were written from the inside of a gay consciousness; they were written with a gay readership in mind. To be sure, a plethora of new, mostly literary gay novels were published in the 1960s that found a secure heterosexual readership: James Baldwin's *Another Country* (1962), Charles Wright's *The Messenger* (1963), Gore Vidal's *Myra Breckinridge* (1968). And homosexuals turned to these books as well. But gay readers also devoured the new wave of gay pulps.

One of the most curious, eccentric aspects of this new gay pulp writing was that while it ranged from the lurid *(The Boys of Muscle Beach)* to the more literary *(Song of the Loon)*, its essential sensibility was sensationalism. Part of this was because *any* discussion of the gay world was going to be, by its nature, an exposé: What had been hidden was now visible. But it is notable how often the sensationalistic nonfiction of the 1960s written by heterosexuals easily dovetailed with the language, style, and sentiment of the gay pulps written by and for gay men.

Here is a short excerpt from Jesse Stearn's 1961 *The Sixth Man*, a journalistic look at homosexual culture in New York:

In some gyms, particularly on Manhattan's more effete East Side, there are so many homosexual muscle men that the ordinary male interested in keeping fit gets the feeling of being surrounded. In one health center, well-known as a mecca for the gay set, they virtually monopolize the exercise room—and, in the security of superior numbers, "let their hair down." Some waltz in with Capezios, instead of the customary sneakers. Others fancy ballet slippers. Nearly all sport bikini-tight shorts, which leave little to the imagination. And their shirts, when they wear them, run the spectrum from shocking pink to deep purple.

They smile at one another as they mince, swagger, or toddle through their calisthenics, revealing an inclination to work in teams. Intimate physical contact between partners is common. They find it almost routine to touch one another, often caressingly, but usually unobtrusively, as though the contact was incidental. "They pass weighty barbells and dumbbells to one another with endearing smiles," an observer said, "and when help is needed for the precise performance of a difficult calisthenic, they often make it a labor of love rather than an exercise. Instead of holding down a companion's knees with one hand so he can do a sit-up without bending the knee, they sit down and straddle one another's legs, facing each other, smiling as though this was the most natural thing in the world."

In style and even substance there is not much difference between Stearn's prose and that of *The Boys of Muscle Beach* or *Gay Whore*. Indeed, it raises the question, did he learn to write from gay pulps, or did gay pulp writers learn to write from reading Stearn?

The urgency and luridness of the *Confidential* series is *echt* fifties pulp writing. Its insistence on detail is a betrayal of its fascination and obsession with the topic; even its condemnatory stance is alluring. Stearn is less excited but cannot avoid the details that have captivated his imagination: the ballet slippers, the colors of shirts, the smiles on men's faces as they work out together. In many of the paperback books on gay life (supposedly intended for heterosexual readers), there seems to be little difference between sociology and porn.

If gay pulps were pedagogical for homosexual readers, then these nonfiction works were equally so for the heterosexual audiences. They learned about gay life; they may have been turned on a little. Many of the nonfiction books contained fairly detailed descriptions of gay and lesbian sexual activities. They may even have learned a few things about sex that they had not thought of—or not given themselves permission to think about—and considered incorporating them into their own actual or fantasy sex life. But more than this, heterosexual readers had their own lives validated. By reading descriptions of homosexuality's deviant nature, they were made to feel secure in their heterosexuality, to have confidence in its "naturalness." Just as gay male readers had their own concepts of what was "natural" bolstered by *Song of the Loon.*

The sixties were a time of widespread sexual inquiry and experimentation for everyone, heterosexuals as well as homosexuals. For the first time in history, heterosexual intercourse could be decisively separated from reproduction. Looser censorship laws and new technologies made sexually explicit material available to larger populations of people. Sex became a big business; adult bookstores and theaters thrived in even the smallest of cities. In this context the increased production and popularity of these nonfiction books is easily understandable, as is the rise in more overtly sexual gay male pulps. They gave straight readers an entrée into a world that was once considered "shadowy" and dangerous, but now appeared much more enticing: They were safe gay porn for heterosexuals, just as gay male pulps were "educational" for the millions of gay men who read them.

The Boys of Muscle Beach

Guild Press, 1969 (reprint from the 1950s)

Sam Sturbridge is one of those real bastards who help destroy the Hollywood image with a simple promise—a promise of "I'll put you in the movies and make you a star!" And all the young man has to do in return is give his sex and mind to Sam anytime, anywhere, and in any manner the prominent director wishes.

Gerry realizes that beautiful muscle boys come cheap. In Sam's life sex is cheap, and he gets whatever he wants. Gerry is then made to compete with the other muscle boys to keep his position in the house, and he does this by his sexual prowess, his willingness to do what he has never done before, and Gerry gradually grows to respect his role and enjoy his sexual contacts—not so much for money, but for personal enjoyment.

Although it is at first not evident, the cover copy on the 1969 *The Boys of Muscle Beach* represents a decisive break from the usual moralistic tone exploited by pulps. The plot is the same—a young boy is attracted to show business and money and meets the wrong people—but here his fate is not a devastating Miltonian fall, but a redemption by and to erotic pleasure.

Up until the mid-to-late 1960s, paperback originals (and some cloth editions) with homosexual content were published by more mainstream houses such as Fawcett and Paperback Library, or smaller and alternative companies such as Argyle and Pageant. Often these books did have "happy endings," but were always fairly circumspect in their sexual detail. Censorship laws were still enforced so stringently (often state by state) that overt sexual descriptions were almost always avoided. A series of Supreme Court decisions in the sixties facilitated the publication of *Fanny Hill, Tropic of Cancer,* and *Naked Lunch* and allowed publishers the freedom to print explicitly sexual material. This led, quickly, to an outpouring of gay books that had been deemed unpublishable a few years earlier. These books almost always presented gay sex as horny, happy, and healthy. The "shadows" had disappeared, and gay sex was now as bright and as clear as day.

Perhaps more than any other publisher of the period, the Guild Press helped readers secure legal access to homosexual erotica. Aside from the Guild Book Service, a book club that offered more than eighty titles of interest to its forty-four thousand members, Guild Press also published "physique" magazines and novels. *The Boys of Muscle Beach* was published as part of a series called the Classics of the Homosexual Underground. These were three-by-six-inch books, stapled rather than bound, and designed to resemble Olympia Press's Traveller's Companion Series. Guild claimed that they were reprints of legendary "underground" gay porn stories. Because even possessing a copy of these stories in the 1950s could lead to arrest, they were mimeographed and passed from person to person in nondescript envelopes or stored in bus station lockers, the keys to which were surreptitiously left with bartenders in gay bars. Guild published more than a dozen of these "classics." The titles were evocative—*San Diego Sailor, Gang Bang, Seven in a Barn, Men's Lake*—and the writing generally crude, explicit, and very active.

While it was now possible to publish *The Boys of Muscle Beach* with impunity, H. Lynn Womack of Guild had started publishing written erotica three years earlier with a cloth edition of Phil Andros's *STUD* (1966). Not as overt in sexual detail as Womack's later books, *STUD* was the work of Samuel M. Steward, former college professor, tattoo artist, and man of letters who took the pseudonym Phil Andros because in Greek it translated as "lover of men." Steward had published some of his Phil Andros stories in European gay magazines such as the Danish *Amigo* and the Swiss *Der Kreis* (The Circle). He wrote, "My philosophy, if I had one, would be pretty simple. The taste of a pizza with a Coke, the sight of a well-made body, the feel of a mouth where it does the most good, the hearing of a piece of music I like, the smell of oil and leather and armpits." The dust-jacket copy of *STUD* notes that in European and Scandinavian countries Andros is "called the American Jean Genet" and that "you will not find in this book any trace of the sad-sick-sorry self-pity of the 'gay' boy for his plight."

Next to the raucous, if amateurishly written, *The Boys of Muscle Beach*, *STUD* is a polished work of literature, but Womack's defense of gay male porn covers them both: "The publication of works such as these is a joyous occasion for all who love freedom and want America to be a society in which the rights of the minorities as well as the rights for a literature of the erotic are upheld."

None of the Classics of the Homosexual Underground are in print today. Steward wrote six other story collections under the name Phil Andros that were published by California-based firms such as Greenleaf, Parisian Press, and Frenchy's Gay line. Under his own name, Steward wrote a memoir and a collection of letters documenting his friendship with Gertrude Stein and Alice B. Toklas, several mystery novels (featuring the famed duo as detectives), as well as books on the history of male hustling and the significance of tattoos and masculinity.

Chapter 6

Sam finally appeared the next afternoon, his wrinkled face beaming. He told Gerry that the film had made a great hit with some of his friends, and he had given them copies of it. Yes, he would show it to him later that night; but, in the meantime, he had other plans for him. A few of his friends would be coming, he told the boy, to meet him.

"But . . . the film test . . . when?"

"We can't rush a thing like that, Gerry," replied Sam. "I thought you trusted me."

"I do . . . but, you promised . . ."

"Well, if that's the way you feel, we might as well forget about the whole thing!"

"I . . . I . . . want to do as you say, Sam."

"Then put yourself in my hands. After all, making a star is not an easy thing to do. There are many handsome young men around Hollywood who would give anything to be in your place."

"I know! . . . I only thought . . ."

"You promised to obey me, Gerry. I insist on that. You might as well face the facts right now that if you want to be a star, you have to pay the price."

"Sure . . . I know . . . I heard that."

"Then, let's not quibble anymore. I mean what I'm saying. It makes me nervous. Now, about tonight."

"But, Sam, couldn't you even give me some idea about the test?"

"Don't get me angry, Gerry! I'll give you the test when I feel you are ready! UNDERSTAND?" he shouted.

"But—all this—sex!"

"Am I hearing a complaint? Evidently you are not satisfied with the way I work. Well, we can always remedy that! I'll have the chauffeur take you back to that dingy house where you were living, and maybe you can do better with some other producer or director!"

"Please . . . I didn't mean to get you angry . . ."

"Then—STOP IT! Here I am going out of my way trying to help you establish yourself, and all I get from you are questions! I'm not used it it!

"Please, Sam . . . I didn't mean . . ."

"You should be punished! That's what you need!"

"Please, Sam . . . I . . ."

"YOU HEARD ME! I want to put an end to all this bickering! Either you do as I say—or GET OUT! And, to prove my point to you, I want you to return to your room this instant and wait there for me!"

He entered his bedroom and laid down on his bed, wondering what Sam was planning to do.

When Sam did enter the room, he showed another side of his personality. His eyes blazed with anger as he approached the bed.

"Strip! I'm going to make clear to you that when I speak I mean business. I refuse your questioning me, and from now on you will do exactly what I say. Strip, I say! All of it! As naked as you were last night! That's better! Now, you lay down on that damn bed and turn over on your stomach and spread your legs apart. YOU HEARD ME, DAMMIT! I'm going to give you the type of spanking your father should have given you long, long ago."

What followed was a further degradation of young Gerry. Sam had a small streak of sadism in him and liked nothing better than to bend people under his will. And, when he first saw the handsome Gerry on Muscle Beach, and saw how vain he was, and the low mentality the boy possessed, he felt sure he would have a willing subject in his hands.

The first blow of the man's opened palm against the quivering globe gave Gerry a start. He was amazed that Sam had so much power in his hand.

The second blow on the other cheek stung him to the quick. He didn't cry out. He braced himself for the blows that would follow. Then a strange sensation entered the boy's body. Coupled with what he had gone through before—being tied down like a slave and used at the discretion of the man—and now subjecting himself to this corporal punishment as if he were a child and had done something bad—Gerry's whole being took on a new change. The hard smacking of the hand against the reddening cheeks of his ass sent strange erotic feelings through him. It was a feeling that he could not comprehend. He wanted to cry out in pain, but something held him in check.

Sam continued the spanking, completely lost in what he was doing. The sight of that handsome and well-proportioned body quivering from the blows he was delivering sent his head into a spin. It didn't matter to him that he also felt the smarting on his hand.

The sight of that flesh turning red, and seeing the twin globes shake, more than made up for the discomfort he felt. The slight whimpering that now came out of the handsome boy added to his pleasure. And Sam was no fool! He knew what was happening!

The erotic feeling that swept through Gerry mounted higher and higher, and he wanted in the worst way to thrash the bed with his body and beg Sam to continue . . . harder and faster! But, he hardly moved, not knowing what would be expected of him. He lay there, a perfect picture of a slave, allowing one of his last defenses to be torn down.

Sam delivered at least twenty stinging blows before he stopped. He stood there, panting as hard as the boy, his eyes never leaving the perfect nakedness that was sprawled out in front of him. Then, without a word, he left the room.

Gerry had a dejected look on his face when he joined Sam for dinner that night. Sam was all smiles. He had been told by the servant to wear a toga, which he did. He ate silently, listening to the flow of words from Sam.

"Muscle Beach!" Sam said. "What a haven for beauty! I saw one boy there that is really an Adonis! Unlike you, he was just strutting around that beach like a real peacock—jet-black hair and all—showing to everyone that he was most unique."

"I wonder if I should approach him like I did you, and see if he is willing to become one of my pupils?"

Gerry didn't want to believe what Sam was suggesting. He had gone too far to be left out. His eyes looked beseechingly at the man sitting across from him.

"You wouldn't like that, would you, Gerry? Finding yourself out in the cold and with someone new taking your place? No, I'm sure you wouldn't like it. But, it's a thought. Of course, I can't see why I cannot groom two boys as well as one. What do you think, Gerry? Should I approach him and invite him here?"

"I'll . . . I'll do as you say, Sam."

"Of course you will! But he was beautiful!"

Gerry went to bed that evening with fear in him. Would he be replaced? Was Sam only threatening him? Was he serious about the new boy?

Gerry found himself shaking the boy's hand, and looking at that almost unbelievable and handsome face. The boy's name was Gil, who was not more than twenty. He stood as tall as Gerry with a build almost identical. He was wearing a tight T-shirt, and faded jeans that clung to his body like a second skin. His bronzed skin added to the aura of his beauty, and the snow-white teeth blazed like pearls.

"What a place!" Gil cried. "Boy, I'm going to enjoy living here after that dump!"

As if to create jealousy between the two boys, Sam placed his hand on Gil's shoulder and cried: "A man from my own heart."

"I'm an all-around guy, Sam" Gil volunteered. "I've been around and know all the ropes. So long as I stay here, you can use whatever I have. Isn't that right, Gerry? We'll make a good pair the both of us. We'll be real buddies, eh? Real ass-hole buddies! Ha-ha!"

"Gerry asks too many questions, Gil," Sam said, now serious. "Maybe you can help me to train him properly."

"Sure! Gerry and I are going to be real pals. Say! That pool down there looks damn inviting. Come on, Gerry, let's go in for a swim, the both of us."

Gil, standing next to Gerry at the poolside, was appraising his body as he eyed him very closely. Gerry was doing the same thing.

"A real nice build," Gil said, feeling Gerry's chest. "And that cock of yours looks like a real piece of meat! What a handful! Go on, feel mine! I'm no midget, either. This thing of mine has been around, boy! It's been in every known hole you can think of. And I like nothing better than to use it. Isn't that right, Sam? This is what you are buying, isn't it? Well, it's yours to do as you will. We'll work for our keep, won't we, Gerry? Anything that Sam's little heart desires, right?"

Gerry had never met a fellow as open as Gil before. But, the charm of the boy fascinated him, and he was rapidly falling under his spell.

Later that evening, Gil insisted that he sleep with Gerry.

Sam readily agreed, much to both the boys' amazement.

Gil jumped on the bed, laughing. He sat on the pillow, hugging his knees to his chest.

"This is the nuts, Gerry! What a lucky bastard you've been!"

"It's not all that easy."

"What do you mean?"

Gerry rattled the entire story out to Gil, then told him: "There's all kind of things," he said. "Movies, then he brings people in to watch while you get fucked; and last night he gave me quite a licking on my bare ass, and I know he got a kick out of that."

"Really!"

"That's right!"

"And how did you like it?"

"Like it?"

"Yeah? Did it give you hot nuts?"

"What do you mean?"

"Come on, you can tell me! I know everything, feller! I'll bet it gave you a great big hard-on, eh? And you liked it?"

Gerry's speechlessness made Gil laugh.

"I can tell," he cried. "I've been through that many times! I get a kick by doing it myself! It doesn't matter if I'm spanked, or someone is spanking me! I mean it! It never fails to work up a stiff prick on me!"

"You mean it?"

"Baby, you are sort of green around the cock circles, aren't you?"

"Well . . ."

"Come on," Gil encouraged, "I want to see that cock of yours as hard as a rock. I haven't sucked on a big, thick, heavy prick for the past four days. You and I are going to have a nice *sixty-nine!*"

Gerry was all for it. Gil's beauty, his strange manner, all fascinated him, and when they lay down next to each other, he saw that Gil already sported a stiff, long, thick erection.

It was quite a cock, he admitted. It was as big as his own. They began licking each other, rolling over on top of each other, feeling each other's balls, and getting to know each other's secret charms.

Gil moved Gerry beneath him and now was lying on top with his knees on each side of his chest, while he held Gerry's cock straight up and was using several inches in and out of his mouth. He kept moving his ass up and down, fucking Gerry's mouth.

It was then that Sam entered the room.

The sight did not surprise him too much. Gil's head was facing the door, and when he saw Sam enter, he pulled his mouth off Gerry's cock and held it straight up, shaking it.

Sam advanced toward the bed, a look of slight anger in his eyes.

"Hope you don't mind, Sam" said Gil, holding his cock deep in Gerry's throat, "I wanted to taste it. It's a beaut!"

"I don't want any sex around here unless I am here to watch it," Sam growled. "That's why I brought you here."

"Whatever you say, Sam," said Gil, ready to remove himself.

"No—don't stop," said Sam. "Keep up what you were doing. I can get a good view from here, but I don't want you to shoot in Gerry's mouth yet. Suck him off, and then fuck his face!"

Gil resumed his position, happy to have Sam watching him so closely.

Sam sat on the bed and spread Gerry's legs further so he would have the full picture of his groin.

Gerry looked down at Gil and saw the pleading in the azure eyes, yet he needed no additional urging. Preliminaries were not necessary here.

Gil held on to the base of the stiff prick with one hand and molded the balls in the other.

Gil's mouth opened and came cascading down, hot and passionate, on the rigid cock of Gerry's.

Gil moaned.

Gerry writhed in ecstasy.

Gil adjusted himself and began to furiously work the thick, throbbing cock deep into his throat, while at the same time pushing his hot lance deep into Gerry's mouth.

Together a rhythm was begun. Together they worked their flesh deep into the other's mouth. Thrusting gently in short, spastic hunches, the entire length of hardening flesh drove deeper, and deeper and still deeper until gasping sounds could be heard, muffled by the huge hunks of meat being swallowed.

A plaintive whimper of raw animal lust quavered from both of the boys. Their eyes were clenched tight in the glory of the moment, and they wriggled their greedy asses hungrily against the pressing weight of each other's loins. Backs and bellies arched and pushed viciously upward and downward until great veins beat in each other's neck. They fought for breath, and wet gasping, sucking, muffled sounds tumbled from their lips.

Cocks drove deeper . . . Pricks into mouths . . . Sucking! Hurting! . . . Enjoying . . . and fucking, fucking, fucking!

Flesh into flesh.

The fullness of Gil's cock gave evidence to Gerry that he was about to reach his climax. Hurriedly, Gerry worked furiously to bring himself closer to having a climax with Gil.

Gil withdrew temporarily, displaying a bright, wet, red-with-fire-like cock and pummeled the thick shaft back into Gerry's waiting, eager mouth, thrusting with great gusto.

Gerry closed his eyes and squirmed his ass up to meet the on-slaught of Gil's hot lips. His hands clutched the rounded cheeks of Gil's ass and pulled him deeper . . . penetrating deeper than anything Gerry had ever known.

Both had reached the point of no return.

Gil heard Gerry moan deep in his throat. Then Gil began raging like a soul in torment, flailing about, wrapping his arms tighter around Gerry's buttocks and legs while his body flipped and fought like a landed fish.

A moment later Gil heard a gurgling sound come from Gerry's mouth as he dropped his hot, thick, white, pearl-like come into the boy's waiting and receptive mouth.

Almost at the same time, Gerry shot Gil's mouth full of hot, heavy sperm as the two labored furiously together, each draining the other's cock of all the liquid substance rolling free from the tight balls that had held it back for so long.

Sam was going out of his mind watching the spectacle before him. He could see both pricks, red, wet from hot come that had been poured through thick veins and released into the boys' mouths.

When the convulsions had subsided, both boys were still swallowing the thick loads shot into each other's mouth until both had swallowed the very last drop of the precious liquid.

As an exhibitionist, Gil was ready to prove to Sam the mettle he was made of. He pulled his body up, reached for a large pillow, and without pulling his wet cock out of Gerry's mouth, he stuffed the pillow under the nape of his neck. Then, kneeling on each side of Gerry's head, he placed his hands on each side of the face and started to fuck Gerry's mouth.

Gerry, still sprawled on the back as he was, was exposed to Sam's hands. He was molding the softening prick, the balls, and rubbing the soft flesh in his groin. He knew he would get Gerry to harden again real fast, and when the prick commenced to fill with hot blood, he held it up.

Gil continued to fuck Gerry's mouth, his eyes glued to the connection. Sam also watched the connection, but his hands now frigged Gerry's prick with short strokes. He could see the trembling in Gil's groin and knew he wasn't far from his climax.

Gil gave a moan as the juice began to spurt out of him, and he dug his prick as far in Gerry's mouth as he possibly could while he once again emptied his balls.

He fell back on his heels, his face the look of satisfaction written all over it. Gerry remained on his back, gathering his breath, while Sam continued to frig his cock slowly.

Chapter 7

Well," said Sam, his look of anger still on his face, "I didn't think you boys would be at each other's cocks so fast. As I told you, I don't want anything underhanded around here. I don't like it. You are here to do as I say—and nothing else."

"Gee, Sam!" cried Gil. "You are right, of course, but I wanted to see how the bastard tasted."

"As I have already proven to Gerry, obedience is the rule here. In order to see that this doesn't happen again, I have to punish the both of you."

"Gee, you're right, Sam," again cried Gil, getting off the bed. "You do what you feel you have to do—Gerry and I will take our punishment. We have it coming."

He stood in front of Sam, his head hung low. He knew that all this was part of the act, and he was all for it. His cock hung down all red and swollen. Sam remained sitting on the edge of the bed. He told him to turn around and place his right foot on top of the bed, on the other side of Gerry, while he kept the other foot on the floor.

Gil followed the directions and had to hold himself up by placing his hands on each side of Gerry's still prone body. That left his ass sticking out, and his balls could be seen hanging loosely in their bag.

Part of Gil's body was held suspended over Gerry's with the faces only a foot apart.

Sam began to belabor Gil's ass, slapping one firm cheek after the other. At each slap, Gil's body jerked forward. Sam had released Gerry's hard cock, and now he reached down between the opened legs of Gil and took a firm hold of the hanging balls. He held them tight as he continued spanking the two cheeks in front of him.

Gil began to cry out.

"Oh! . . . Oh! . . . Oh, Sam! . . . Please! . . . I won't do it again! . . . I promise! . . . Ohhhh! . . . You're burning me up! . . . Oh, my poor fucking ass! . . . My fucking poor ass! . . . Oh, you're squeezing my balls too tight . . . too tight! . . . Oh! . . ."

In his position, Gerry looked at the expression on Gil's face that was suspended over his. A thrill ran through his body as he heard the words from the boy's lips, the way his body shook, and he could see his cock getting harder and harder. Now, Sam let go of the balls and reached further to grab the hard cock. He held it in a firm grip, pointing straight down, pulling against Gil's groin, while his hand continued the hard and furious spanking. His hand began to work up and down the stiff prick as he continued to send blow after blow to the hard, red cheeks.

"Oh! . . . My poor ass! . . . Oh! . . . Please, Sam! . . . I promise I won't do it again! . . . My cock! . . . FUCK! FUCK! FUCK! . . . You're jerking too hard! . . . Too tight! . . . You're gonna make me shoot, Sam! . . . Please stop! . . . Oh, my poor fucking ass! . . . Please! . . . Too hard, Sam!"

Sam stopped the spanking abruptly. Now he had a firm hold of the prick from between his legs, and still held it pointing down. His hand worked up and down the column as fast as he could make it. Gil was now moaning, shaking all over, and almost collapsed as the juice was forced out of his prick and onto Gerry's body below him. He did collapse. As soon as Sam got the last drops out, his body fell forward and dropped against Gerry.

"Now, let that be a lesson to you, Gil," cried Sam.

"Yes . . . Yes . . ."

"And now it's your turn, Gerry!"

Gerry's body was aflame from what he had just witnessed. Now he looked forward to being treated in the same manner. Gil had been right! It was the pleasure and not the pain that counted. As Gil removed himself from atop of the boy, Gerry remained silent and motionless, awaiting Sam's directives.

Sam's hand was red from the strong castigation he had given to Gil, and he was not about to pain himself any further by doing the same thing to Gerry. Therefore, he ordered Gil to do it for him.

"Sure, Sam . . . how do you want him?"

"In front of the mirror—standing up."

Gerry obeyed. He stood several feet in front of the mirror, sideways, and Sam ordered him to keep his eyes on the mirror so he could see what was being done to him. Gil stood in back of him at an angle and bent over so he could deliver the blows better. Sam knelt in front of him, also at an angle, so he could attack his front.

Gil proved the statement he had made—that he was an "all-around guy." His spanking of Gerry's ass was professional, showing that he had done this many times and knew how to bring out the heat in a body. At each slap of his strong hand, Gerry's front was sent lurching forward. Sam had a firm hold on his prick, frigging it, and saying, "You'll be spanked until you shoot your juice!" But Sam was not frigging the cock too hard or too fast. He wanted this to last.

The scene continued unabated, with Gil forgetting the spanking he had received, and losing himself completely in the one he was giving Gerry.

Gerry cried out as Gil had done earlier, which helped to raise the lust in Gil. In no time, his own prick was hardening—giving a jerk at every swing of his arm. This, after the two fast orgasms he had already experienced, showed Sam the sexual strength of the youthful Gil.

Gerry's cock was as hard as an iron rod. Every vein stood out on it prominently. It felt like a hot piece of steel in Sam's grip, as he continued stroking it. The cries and pleas of Gerry worked on him like magic.

Sam then had his mouth on it, sucking hard and deeply, still frigging the base of the thick, solid cock, causing more pain to the boy as the strength was drawn out of him.

Gil had stopped the spanking and watched with bleary eyes as

Sam devoured the boy's cock. Gerry's legs buckled from under him and Sam stopped just in time before he collapsed on the floor.

Gil stood there, breathing hard, his cock hard and pointing upwards. Sam remained on the floor and now faced him.

"Jerk!" he cried.

And Gil was doing it. He stood there, legs apart, his mid-section thrust forward, and his right hand tightly riding his cock at a terrific speed. Sam's head was only inches away, his eyes watching the fast movements of the hand. In the state he was in, it didn't take long for Gil to reach his third orgasm. Seeing this, Sam wrenched his hand away and finished him off, with the head of his prick buried deep in his mouth.

Tongues of fire seared through Gil's loins. He threw his head back and began to mumble incoherent words as the strength was pulled out of him. Sam was like a vulture, wanting the full payment. He stopped only when Gil was on the point of collapse.

Sam got up and left the room without another word.

Gil and Gerry were soon fast asleep.

RICHARD AMORY

Song of the Loon

Greenleaf Classics, 1966

It is conceivable that Richard Amory's 1966 bestseller, *Song of the Loon,* and its two sequels *(Song of Aaron* and *Listen, the Loon Sings . . .)* were the most widely read gay fiction of the sixties and seventies. Published by Greenleaf Classics, they went through multiple printings and, within a few years, attained the status of classics. (Tom Norman, in his invaluable reference work, *American Gay Erotic Paperbacks: A Bibliography,* estimates that thirty percent of gay men in the United States had purchased a copy of *Song of the Loon.*) It was certainly popular enough to generate a 1970 porno film and even to spawn a parody sequel, *Fruit of the Loon* by "Ricardo Armory" (which was not written by Richard Amory, but was published by Greenleaf).

The cover copy on the first volume of the *Song of the Loon* trilogy framed the novel as part of a distinct literary tradition: "[It's] a mystical blend of elements from Hudson's *Green Mansions,* J. F. Cooper's *Leatherstocking Tales,* and the works of Jean Genet. What evolves is unique and inimitable . . . an unforgettable fantasy. It will leave no reader unstirred, for every man knows, secretly, that he can indeed hear the haunting cry that is the . . . Song of the Loon."

Amory's writing is a heady cross between a lush poetic epic verging on parody, a boys' adventure story, and Victorian porn: "In the agony of pleasure, his loins tensed and thrust upward; his body arched, belly hair glinting in the sunlight, chest muscles knotted, then broke and fell with a wrenching moan." It seems, too, to be a wonderful example of critic Leslie Fiedler's contention that early American literature is specifically homoerotic in nature, a constant retelling of an erotic love between a white man and a man of color.

> The sunlight turned the man's hair to new copper; shirtless, his deeply-muscled shoulders stretched and tightened as he paddled, formed knots and hollows across his back. His chest hair gleamed with sweat, and the thin line of hair down his belly, widening below the navel, was flattened against his undulating muscles. He paused. The jays returned, still screaming.
>
> Another sound reached him, from upstream, a thin sound, and hollow; then it stopped, and began again. He started paddling, silently gliding across the still pools near the bank. At the bend in the river he paused again.
>
> Perhaps fifty yards upstream was an Indian, leaning carelessly against a fallen tree, playing a wooden flute. He was also shirtless, and his black hair, unbound, fell past his shoulders. Broad, smooth chest: lithe, narrow waist, as supple as a willow tree.

In *Love and Death in the American Novel,* Fiedler uses couples such as Huck and Jim, Ishmael and Queequeg, and Natty Bumppo and Chingachgook to illustrate his argument, and Amory is clearly continuing this tradition with Ephraim MacIver and Singing Heron. Was Amory consciously drawing on Fiedler? (Amory was aware of his literary antecedents; his intro states that the Native American characters are taken from "very European characters from the novels of Jorge de Montemayor and Gaspar Gil Polo," and "painted with a gay aesthetic red and transplanted to . . . the American wilderness.") *Loon* draws upon an old tradition in American writing that combines the themes of the innocent pastoral with that of men fleeing into the wilderness to escape the constraints of civilization. For the gay reader in the late sixties, this was a back-to-the-woods hippie fantasy as well as a reconfirmation of the naturalness of homosexuality.

But it wasn't simply the insistence on the "naturalness" of homosexuality that earned the *Loon* books their tremendous popularity, but rather that they read like literature. The comparisons to Cooper and Hudson on the cover copy, the Walt Whitmanesque poetry scattered throughout the book, and even the subtitle ("A gay pastoral in five books and an interlude") signaled that this was a sincere, if not serious, piece of writing. While no one mistook the *Loon* books for *great* literature, they were recognized as good, solid writing. Through wit and imagination they transformed the traditional western—the most masculine of American literary traditions—into the setting for a gay love story.

But Amory's novel was not just a simple feat of inversion—turning traditional cowboys and Indians into Romeos and Juliets—for at its heart the *Loon* series is about a spiritual quest. The *song* of the loon is an inner calling. At the end of the story the protagonist has a transfiguration of Whitmanesque transcendence that has as much to do with democracy as with sex, as much to do with being at one with all people as with appreciating nature.

The betrayal of American democracy was something homosexuals understood all too well. Stonewall was still three years away, and the progressive movements sweeping through the nation—feminism, civil rights, youth movements—stirred the idea of homosexual liberation, but did not do much to deliver it. Raids of gay bars were common, electroshock therapy was routinely prescribed, and simply being gay or lesbian could get you fired, arrested, or imprisoned. The larger implications of the *Loon* series spoke to all of that.

The *Loon* books were a significant event in gay publishing and culture. They set a standard of ambition for gay erotic and porn writing that few other writers ever met. Richard Amory was the pseudonym of Richard Love. He published five other novels between 1968 and 1971 with Greenleaf Classics and with the Olympia Press Traveler's Companion series. They are all now out of print.

Song of the Loon tells the story of how the white European hunter Ephraim MacIver learns to love himself and other men though the tutelage of Native Americans and their culture. The narrative is a picaresque, rambling from one situation to the next. In this chapter Ephraim, who has been the lover of Singing Heron, meets Tlasohkah, who introduces him to traditional Native American homoerotic activity before they become lovers for a short time.

Book Three

For the rest of that afternoon and the following day, Ephraim paddled slowly but steadily up the increasingly narrow, increasingly rapid river. It was becoming obvious that soon he would have to leave the canoe and travel overland to the cave of Bear-who-dreams; the directions given by the old Indian at Astoria had been specific enough, but Ephraim was concerned now lest he lose his way. Ixtlil Cuauhtli had said he would have no trouble finding a guide when he left the river, but none had appeared. Ephraim had assumed that Eagle Camp, mentioned by both Singing Heron and Cyrus, could be easily found, but now he wasn't sure. Perhaps he would miss it altogether.

He dismissed the thought from his mind, and began to think instead of Amatus Sum. He felt warmly pleased with himself, knowing that he would meet the Indian again, and that their next meeting would be one of pure, frenetic lovemaking. He smiled to himself, thinking of it, remembering the dark, lithe body, the intense, darkly handsome face, the almost constantly erect penis. There will be time for everything, he thought. We will do everything. We will roll on the grass for hours, coming, and coming again, until we are exhausted.

On the morning of the third day he decided to leave the canoe, having spent several hours in fruitless battle against rocks, shallows, and rapids. Actually, his progress had been very slow for over a day, but he had continued upriver simply because he enjoyed the struggle, enjoyed the new strength in his arms and shoulders. It was pleasant to realize that the month or more of river travel had toughened him, made him harder and more powerful. He could feel the difference in his shoulders and in his belly: the muscles were larger, like knots, and tireless. He welcomed every new test of his strength, meeting each challenge to his endurance with a new confidence and with a cheerful sense of mastery.

Nevertheless, he had to stop. He hid the canoe in a thick stand of lodgepole pines, out of sight from the river, and made up a pack which he strapped across his shoulders—blankets, a knife, an axe, a tinderbox. His breeches were worn through at the knees, and thin in the seat; his shirt was in tatters. He seriously considered leaving his boots, for each had a small hole in the sole, and they wouldn't last until he could get moccasins. But he wore them anyway.

Away from the river, the land rose sharply in broken, rocky sweeps; the earth and sky seemed vertical, and unending. His vision traveled far, over patches of dark green that shaded the lower slopes of the mountains, over lighter green far in the distance, and earth-brown, and the reddish yellow of hard, bare rock. To the southeast was the mountain he was looking for. Tall, peaked, pointing to the sky; at the foot of this mountain was the painted cave. An eagle soared in the distance; a grasshoppper whirred before his feet. He started to walk among the oaks, firs, madrones, and willows of the riverbed, straining his ears for the sound of the falls he knew to be ahead.

At midday he was hungry, but decided to wait until reaching the falls before allowing himself to think of food. It was too early in the season for fruit or berries; perhaps he could catch a fish, he thought, and regretted not having brought more food. But he quickly forgot about it, not caring in the slightest for his stomach.

He saw the falls before he heard them—saw them perhaps a half-hour's distance away. The riverbank sloped sharply upward, even here, and he started to climb, clinging at times to roots and saplings, trying to keep the falls in view. At the top, finally, he lay down to rest under a Douglas fir, and the feeling grew inside him that Eagle Camp must be close by. Perhaps an unexpected noise, or the faint trace of a trail, or perhaps a thin odor of smoke—

He stood up to study the land more carefully, and saw the Indian before the Indian saw him, and leaned against the fir to watch him. The man was tall, slender, graceful; his hair hung in two braids down his bare shoulders. His breechclout was narrow and beaded, and hung halfway down his thighs following the movements of his legs as he stepped. His face was angular, with jutting cheekbones and chin, deep-set eyes, wide mouth with thin, sensitive lips. He was picking flowers, and had loaded one arm with the same lavender daisies Ephraim had picked for Cyrus. Ephraim judged him to be somewhat older than Cyrus—perhaps thirty-five, perhaps forty. The muscles of his buttocks flexed softly as he walked; in back, the breech cloth covered only the cleft and a bit more. Narrow waist, slender hips—

Ephraim moved, and the Indian looked up. They gazed at each other in silence, and Ephraim smiled slowly in greeting. The Indian raised his hand, and the faint trace of an answering smile crossed his face; an eyebrow wavered upward. He came toward Ephraim, not taking his eyes from Ephraim's face. Ephraim continued to smile in as open a manner as possible, but his glance flicked momentarily down to the Indian's long, wiry body.

The Indian lowered his hand. "Hello," he said softly.

"Hello," said Ephraim, but his throat caught. "Hello," he repeated more clearly.

"I was hoping you would come today," the Indian said pleasantly. Tiny, expressive quivers played about his lips and eyebrows.

"Have you been expecting me?" Ephraim asked.

"Ah, yes. Someone from downriver raised a smoke signal several days ago to tell of your coming, and of the fact that Mr. Calvin and his strange companion had passed without causing difficulties. Either I or one of my companions has been waiting for you here since yesterday." His voice was very soft, with a melodious lilt.

"This is Eagle Camp, then," Ephraim said.

"Close by, yes. Would you like to come with me?"

"Yes, thank you," Ephraim said. "Actually, I was beginning to be afraid of missing the camp; I see now that I had nothing to fear."

"Nothing at all." The Indian smiled and turned, leading Ephraim to a trail through the woods. Ephraim contemplated the Indian's back, his legs; he was a small-boned man, with slender ankles and knees, yet the muscles of his calves and thighs swelled sharply and softly, as he walked. And again the gentle flexing of his buttocks— Ephraim's heart began to beat faster.

"May I ask you your name?" Ephraim said.

The Indian turned and gazed levelly at Ephraim. "My name is Tlasohkah; I am sorry that I didn't tell you before."

Ephraim smiled. "My name is Ephraim, which you undoubtedly knew already."

"Yes," Tlasohkah said. Then he turned and continued to glide along the trail.

They were joined at length by a younger Indian, possibly eighteen, who greeted Ephraim with a happy yelp and then conversed with Tlasohkah in an Indian tongue that Ephraim couldn't understand. He caught his own name once or twice at the beginning, and then they must have proceeded to another subject, for he didn't hear his name again.

Ephraim felt a bit slighted, but decided not to worry about it for the time being. All the while, the young man punctuated and emphasized his conversation by touching Tlasohkah in one way or another—on the back, on his shoulder, or by taking his hand momentarily—casually, but knowingly. At times he glanced and smiled at Ephraim. There was an adolescent smoothness to his body that Ephraim found uninteresting, but perhaps, all the same, he and Tlasohkah were lovers. Ephraim didn't like this idea at all.

Suddenly, the young man ran off, disappearing down the trail. Tlasohkah turned to Ephraim and explained, "We were discussing the plans for the evening's games and entertainment. Very few of the young men now at Eagle Camp speak English; I hope you didn't feel left out."

"Not at all," Ephraim lied, and the lie showed on his face. "I think it is up to me to learn your language, and not the other way around."

Tlasohkah smiled, almost gravely. "Possibly so. But it is a very difficult language; only one white man has learned to speak it well, and that man is Cyrus Wheelwright."

"I didn't know that Cyrus spoke Indian—" Ephraim mused.

"He does. I taught him. He is a very intelligent man, and was able to learn our tongue in a very short time. But after all, there are other ways of communicating than by means of words—" He touched Ephraim lightly on the shoulder.

"Quite so," Ephraim replied, smiling, and touched the Indian's back in return. Perhaps, he thought, the young man was not Tlasohkah's lover.

The path led out of the forest and twisted sharply around a low, rocky hill; on the other side was a flat, open meadow, studded with pines. Among the trees were a scattering of tents, and in the center, a permanent wooden council chamber. The sides and roof were formed of carefully hewn slabs of cedar, carved and painted with designs reminiscent of the Indian blankets Ephraim had seen in Astoria. There were a handful of young men in the camp, many of them the same age as the adolescent Ephraim had seen earlier. They had been playing a type of hoop-and-stick game when Tlasohkah and Ephraim appeared, but they quickly dropped the game and stared eagerly at Ephraim, chattering among themselves and to Tlasohkah in their own tongue. Ephraim smiled in greeting, and the young men smiled shyly in return. Several of them were strikingly handsome; all were gracefully muscular.

Tlasohkah led Ephraim into the council hall, and the young men continued their game; their calls and shouts floated in, contrasting sharply with the peaceful darkness inside. "You may sleep here if you wish," Tlasohkah said. "And I thought that perhaps you would like to exchange your clothing for what the Indians wear."

"Yes, I would," Ephraim said. "I would particularly like some moccasins; my boots are falling apart."

Tlasohkah stooped and opened a wooden chest in one corner of the dark chamber; from this he pulled out a pair of moccasins, Indian-style leggings, a sleeveless deerskin jacket, and a beaded breechclout. He handed them to Ephraim. "Try these on," he said.

Ephraim pulled off his boots and shirt; Tlasohkah was watching him closely. But as he started to unbutton his breeches, the Indian turned and walked out of the hall, leaving him alone. Ephraim was slightly disappointed. *Perhaps,* he thought, *he's not at all curious—*

He pulled the breeches off quickly and reached for the breech clout. But he detected the soft sound of approaching footsteps, and delayed putting it on, pretending to examine the beaded design.

It was Tlasohkah, standing in the doorway, regarding him with interest. Ephraim felt the blood rushing into his cock, and quickly tied on the cloth in confused embarrassment. *He is interested,* he thought.

Tlasohkah brought a bowl filled with a warm stew, and offered it to Ephraim wordlessly, but Ephraim noted a pulsation in the vein at the Indian's temple. "Thank you," he said. "I haven't eaten." He sat down and began to eat, sipping the liquid and eating the rest with his fingers.

Tlasohkah still carried the flowers he had picked when Ephraim had first seen him; he sat down opposite Ephraim and began braiding them into chaplets, exactly as Ephraim had done for Cyrus. "How odd," Ephraim said. "I made one exactly as you are doing several days ago."

"Sometimes," the Indian said, "people with similar thoughts will do or say similar things. But it is a strange coincidence. Would you like to help?"

"Yes, certainly," Ephraim replied, and they divided the pile of flowers. From time to time Ephraim glanced at the Indian's breech cloth, but could learn nothing. They worked in silence until they had made chaplets from all the flowers.

Rising, Tlasohkah placed one about Ephraim's neck and one about his own, smiling his grave, almost sad half-smile as he did so. Ephraim thanked him with his eyes. "If there is going to be an entertainment tonight," he said softly, "I think I should sleep this afternoon."

"Yes," Tlasohkah answered. "You can sleep in here, where you won't be disturbed."

"Thank you," Ephraim breathed, and touched the Indian lightly on the chin. Tlasohkah's eyelids quivered, then he turned and left.

Ephraim spread his blankets in a dark corner, took off his breech cloth and lay down. He was asleep immediately.

The sound of drums awoke him—gay hoots and laughter coming from the outside. Sitting up suddenly, he discovered a bowl of the same stew by his blankets, and ate it gratefully, knowing that Tlasohkah had placed it there.

He began to think about, to consider this Tlasohkah. The thought was exciting. Tlasohkah was extremely attractive, with his long, slender, pliant body; the pliability of a steel spring, the suggestion of steel, of steely grace—and yet willing, receptive; soft, perhaps soft to the touch, yet hard. The body of a long-distance runner. Ephraim wondered, fascinated, *What does he look like naked?* and found himself thinking of the softly flexing buttocks, the cock, the belly hair, then the buttocks again. Nevertheless—had Tlasohkah shown any particular interest in him? No—and yes. He couldn't decide.

He rose, stretched, put on the breech cloth, chaplet, and moccasins, drew a blanket around his shoulders, and peeked out the door. The moccasins were wonderfully comfortable. He wriggled his toes, and ran his fingers through his hair.

A short distance away was a campfire; a group of Indians sat about it in an open clearing. Noticing a trickling stream nearby, Ephraim first splashed the sleep from his face with icy water, drank, then walked over to the fire, holding the blanket tightly wrapped around his body.

Tlasohkah was off to one side with a drum between his legs, beating the leather head with his long fingers. Ephraim sat beside him; Tlasohkah stopped drumming and smiled at him. Ephraim said, "Good evening."

"Ah, good evening," Tlasohkah replied softly, melodiously. "Did you sleep well?"

"Yes," Ephraim answered, "and thank you for the food."

"You knew it was I who left it there?" He began drumming again, a new rhythm, practicing, limbering up his fingers.

Ephraim didn't feel like answering right away, but Tlasohkah's eyes were upon him, expecting a reply. "I felt it was you," he said finally. "My feelings know."

Tlasohkah smiled broadly for the first time, showing a row of beautifully white, even teeth. The long lines on either side of his lean cheeks deepened with the smile. He was pleased, and turned to watch the group of young men, evidently considering the conversation fulfilled.

Ephraim too turned to watch the young men about the fire, some were watching him, also; others were still eating, but most were simply playing around aimlessly, chattering and laughing. He turned back to Tlasohkah's drumming, watching his fingers, trying to catch the rhythm of his beating, but it changed from one rhythm to another just as he thought he had learned it. Tlasohkah noted his frowning concentration, and called out an order; one of the young men ran off and returned shortly with another drum. He placed it on the ground before Ephraim. Ephraim thanked the young man, and was given a happy smile in return; then, turning his attention back to Tlasohkah's drumming, he began, tentatively and lightly at first, to imitate the rhythm. Tlasohkah nodded as he became surer, then stopped his own drumming, allowing Ephraim to continue alone. It was a simple beat, but strong, and moving. They continued with new beats until Ephraim had learned several easy ones, and one that was a bit more difficult.

A jangle of bells and rattles at his side made Ephraim look up startled. Someone had dropped what looked like deer antlers by his side, and thongs having many small metal bells attached to them. He looked at Tlasohkah in puzzlement, then he saw the others, and began to understand. They were fitting the antlers on their heads, tying the bell cords around their calves and arms. Tlasohkah started the first rhythm, the one Ephraim had learned first. "Watch this dance, and learn how to do it. When you think you know how, you should join them. It is called the Elk Dance, but I think it is as much a game as a dance; or perhaps there is no difference."

The dancers slowly began to organize themselves in a row. Ephraim counted fifteen of them. The drumbeat continued; louder now, and steady; some of the dancers began the step, then all fell in. Ephraim watched their feet. Some were singing, but not all.

The step seemed to be simple; Ephraim was sure he could do it, and was putting on his antlers when one dancer, with a bound, detached himself from the group and turned to face them. Ephraim stopped to watch.

The single dancer pawed the ground with his feet, lowered his antlers, and charged, still in step with the others, around in a circle. A jeering went up from the row of dancers; the soloist bellowed challenges. He leaped, pawed, and charged until another dancer leaped out to meet him.

They faced each other pawing and snorting, circling, charging past each other. Then, with precision, they locked antlers and circled, still in step, first one way, then the other. Ephraim saw that it wasn't a game of strength, but of skill; the first dancer was leading, changing direction rapidly; the challenger was trying to follow. Then the challenger was thrown out of step by a swift right-left maneuver. They straightened up, laughing, and the line of dancers hooted. The loser retired to his place in line, and another took his place to try his skill.

Ephraim finished fastening his antlers and bells and fell in line, still wrapped in his blanket, holding a pair of gourd rattles. He caught the step rapidly, and concentrated both on his own feet and on the maneuvers of the mock-fighters. As new challengers won or were defeated, he noted that losing was merely a question sometimes of being forced to dance one step or even a half step too many on the same foot; the dancers' timing had to be perfect in order to follow the fast, surprising changes of direction.

After half an hour of continuously dancing the jogging, hopping step, Ephraim felt warmed up and limber enough to issue a challenge. A brief spell came when nobody wanted to solo, so Ephraim leaped out with a cry, throwing his blanket aside.

A delighted roar filled his ears. He pawed the ground and snorted, enjoying himself, laughing at the jeers. Almost immediately an Indian leaped out before him to take up the challenge. It was a man Ephraim had noticed before—somewhat older than the rest, broadly muscular, with black, shining eyes. He laughed at Ephraim, pawed, charged, leaped, and snorted. When Ephraim was ready, he lowered his head and they locked horns, circling in place to the right. It was more difficult than Ephraim had expected, for the circle was very tight, and the dancing was performed in a bent-over position, but he managed it well enough. Then he switched to a leftward circling, and his challenger followed him easily; Ephraim began to admire the other man's skill. Thereafter Ephraim tried every trick he dared in order to throw his challenger off-balance, but none of them worked; the Indian followed him effortlessly.

After many minutes of fruitless circling back and forth, a murmuring grew in the line of dancers, some laughing calls, and Ephraim knew he should give up; his dancing had been equaled. He backed off and straightened up, smiling broadly, and threw his arm about the Indian's shoulders. The Indian smiled back in surprise.

"You are a very good dancer," Ephraim said, and retired back to the line. The Indian didn't understand, and looked to Tlasohkah in puzzlement. Tlasohkah called out a translation, and all the dancers cheered, laughing and shaking their rattles.

The drumming stopped, and the dancers dispersed. Ephraim picked up his blanket, walked over to Tlasohkah, and sat down. Someone had brought a kettle filled with liquid; a young man served Tlasohkah and Ephraim in a hollow gourd. Ephraim tasted; it was mildly fermented, somewhat like beer, but white in color, and with a greenish taste.

"*Newketle,*" Tlasohkah said, and took a sip. "For festival occasions."

"It's strange," Ephraim said.

Tlasohkah shifted his position on the ground. "What you said to Ya-nah was unexpected, and was very pleasing to everybody," he said. "It is not necessarily the custom to compliment one's challenger, especially one who has defeated you—"

"But it was true—he was very good. Perhaps after I've had some practice, I will be able to defeat him, but certainly not now."

"And something else that perhaps you didn't realize," Tlasohkah added. "If he accepts your challenge, that means usually that he is interested in you. In this case, I am sure that he is."

"Really? I didn't know that."

"And now you do know." Tlasohkah tapped on the drum, staring into the fire. "Ya-nah is eagerly sought after by many young men. Are you interested in him?"

Ephraim considered his reply very carefully. Finally he said, "I don't think so."

Tlasohkah, expressionless, glanced at him levelly, then turned to his drum, beginning the first measures of a new dance. Ephraim went off to get more *newketle.*

CARL CORLEY

My Purple Winter

PEC *French Line*, 1966

The gay pulp industry did not encourage originality, texture, or innovation. Writers were usually paid no more than $250 a book, and there were no royalties; this was contract labor. (It is estimated that Richard Amory made no more than $2,500 on the *Loon* trilogy.) By 1967, when it was clear that a great deal of money was to be made on both homosexual and heterosexual pulps, publishing houses were happy to buy salable product and place it on the market as quickly as possible. Writers were encouraged to write quickly; those who made it their living had to.

This situation, however, also had its benefits. Aside from certain set rules and formulas regarding length of manuscript, chapter length, and degree of sexual explicitness, writers were free to do as they wished. Editing was minimal. If an author had a vision, a style, or even a quirky way of expressing himself, the chances were good that it would have a place in the final project. Carl Corley's talents were suited to such an environment.

Carl Corley wrote twenty-two novels for various publishers between 1966 and 1971, the majority of them published by PEC's French Line. (He also did the artwork for many of his novels.) Almost all of his novels take place in the South—often in his home state of Mississippi—and many describe actual places, towns, and settings. Some of the books take place in the 1920s or 1930s. His themes range from sexual identity to family drama to moral questions of what it means to live responsibly in a chosen community. *Sky Eyes* (1967) is a historical novel that takes place in early nineteenth-century Mississippi and details a relationship between a Choctaw Indian and a white solider of Swedish descent. Here, Corley exploits the same motifs that Amory did in the *Loon* books, but his vision is far less pastoral and more violent, churning with racial and sexual tension. If Amory imagined that nonwhiteness was simple erotic salvation for Europeans, Corley's racializations are more complex, blackness or foreignness often signifying a complex mixture of degradation and redemption, often in religious tones reminiscent of Genet, or even Flannery O'Connor. The 1968 *Black Angel* is an odd, allegorical tale of a wealthy man, the black angel, who spends twelve days being visited by young men from a male whorehouse. Each episode ends in varying degrees of sexual distress until in the end the black angel dies and becomes the object of a cult. While the story's eroticism is sexually explicit, the use of the black-angel image is mystifying. Corley's prose is idiosyncratic and compelling. Often an odd mixture of Erskine Caldwell (without the humor) and a naïve but startling folk style, all of the novels read unlike any other pulps of their time. While the family drama fits clearly into the acceptable Freudian model—Corley's mothers exhibit a near Victorian goodness; his fathers are terrifying in a Faulknerian manner—he always manages to rise above the stereotype and produce authentic protagonists.

Corley worked for years at the Mississippi State Highway Department and later as an artist and model builder for the Louisiana Department of Transportation. Corley is also an artist and has painted and designed the covers for several of his books. He now lives in Mississippi. Historian John Howard has written extensively on Carl Corley and his work in *Men like That: A Southern Queer History.*

My Purple Winter, published in 1966, is the first book in a trilogy that includes *A Fool's Advice* and *The Scarlet Lantern.* All of Carl Corley's books are out of print.

My Purple Winter tells the story of Brut Toro, a fifteen-year-old who falls in love with Dany Buck, a half-French, half-Creole laborer on his father's Louisiana farm. After the brutish father discovers them, Brut is sent to New Orleans to live with a repulsive relative. He soon leaves and drifts into hustling before attempting to save himself by going home to be rescued by Dany. This is the opening chapter.

Chapter 1

My name is Brut Toro—a name of which I will always be proud—yet it is a name which but poorly perceives my nature, for I am neither brutish (nor brave), nor, yet, am I Spanish. My name is like my mother, who gave it to me in the violence of the stormy night on which I was born—and I am like her, too—wild and passionate and strange . . .

A dark gypsy woman, my mother, and she bore me out of some sort of strange and bitter rebellion; bore me despite her hate for her marriage and the bonds of her settled life. Hers was an identical passion against both these aversions . . . the same hate which roused in her at anything ugly or unclean. My mother was a rover and she was born for the gypsy's life; the joy and sorrow of the wanderer; the wealth of a world which is new around each curve of the long, long road. Caught, caged, prisoned by her marriage and its house, her spirit could not soar and had no outlet for its emotions and, so, turned dumb within her.

The owl may fly; the mockingbird may sing his raucous song, but my mother owned neither flight nor song. Yet, like the mockingbird, there was the store of golden music in her heart and, like the toneless owl, she knew in her heart the intoxication, the joy of a fancied flight on an endless May morning.

All the wonderful things my mother felt for and in nature—and could not express as she wanted—all the stored honey, the black hatreds, the deep, never-ending homesickness for the unfenced wild—these my mother gave me. The whole meaning of her wayward heartbeat flowed into my own, softly beating heart, as though she passionately threw a life she did not want and could not give a value, into my own outstretched arms.

When I was at the age of fifteen, she was fled like the leaves and the winged creatures of departed summers, but her deep love for me was so strong, so imposing, so overwhelming—like a dark room filled with the smother of a strong perfume—that, when I reached puberty, I had turned from the attitudes of a normal existence and had given myself to love of my own sex. My admiration was for the male—which I considered the more colorful, the more glamorous of the two.

In the fabric of my life, that this should happen was only natural. My mother's love for me was consuming and overwhelming, and to feel affection for another woman would have been an impossibility. I could never have but one mother. The soft wings of her love, trembling about me, shutting out the light, the wind, the smell of the world outside, drowned and filled me to the exclusion of all other females forever. To have offered affection to one would have been an affront to the love my mother spun around me like a cocoon.

At that callow age, approaching the threshold to young manhood, the sap of my loins full-blossomed and ripe for harvest, I had never known the father's love I so sorely needed. I was sick on affection. I wanted something stronger, something freer, more violent, cleaner—something to counterbalance the cloying, stifling cloud of her love which locked me, sightless, speechless, deaf, within the soft but unbreakable barriers of her world.

There was no way I could look but to the male. Here was the perfect proxy to the flowery rooms, the velvet-draped windows, the wine-colored shadows—even at highest noon—together with the wax roses within their cages of glass, the white lace curtains which cascaded down the windows to throw their fantastic patterns of light and shadow on the thick carpets, the endless tapestries, the interminable evenings alone with her while the haunting strings of her harp invaded my senses. The discords within her found their way to expression, not through words, but through the delicate fingers as they caressed the strings of the vibrating instrument until I felt as though those same strings were looped about my throat and would strangle me with their soft, unrelentless pressure.

It was my mother who was to blame for my strange, my deeply dark passions, even at that age of inexperience—and yet, my heart feels pain at even attaching the thought of blame to her, so little did she deserve it. Where was she to turn? Where could she give her love? She and my father were so indifferent to each other as to make me think one did not know of the existence of the other. They were as indifferent to each other as day and night, with no blending of twilight or dawn to establish the reality of their diverse identities.

They did not hate each other. It was not that. Their own deep, silent passions took opposite directions and contrary forms. My mother steeped herself in playing the harp, in her embroidery, in her overwhelming love for me. My father engrossed himself in his passion for the fields, his collection of coins, and his warped and blind hatred and distrust of anything which was beautiful. Here only did conflict between them emerge—he hated beauty because she loved it. He hated me, for the same, punishing reason. There was nothing wifely about her nor parental about my father, and in all the time I can remember them, not once do I recall ever having seen any evidence of affection between them.

I think my father always hated me. It was his defense against her, to spoil for her anything which brought her joy. He called me "runt"—which, I suppose, I was—and often scornfully remarked that I should have been "thrown back" at my birth. I am small, just barely over five feet high, and my burden on the scales comes to barely a hundred and twenty pounds. Yet, I was hearty as we who are small must be in order to survive existence among the giants. I possessed robust health and, according to my mother's admiring description, strikingly good looks and a perfectly proportioned body. These attributes came from my Greek heritage. In school I never entered into the athletics or games and did little to enhance my miniature, but muscular, physique.

Like the Greeks (my grandfather had come to Rankin County, Mississippi, from Athens) I loved the out-of-doors . . . the rich blackness of the soil, the thick of nature's own smells strong in my nostrils. My growing years were spent in the midst of these, riding horses, plowing, doing numerous chores on my father's farm—all helping to make the bud of my youth burgeon, rich, and full and compelling. From the constant life in the open, my skin was as dark

as an acorn and was smooth and radiant with health. I was proud
of it and of the riot of black curls which crowned my head and
tumbled into my eyes, coming to a clean point at the back of my
neck. My eyes were those of my mother—strange, fawn-colored eyes
like water with tawny flecks floating in their large, clear irises. In
their shy honesty, her eyes (and mine) were akin to those of a fox
or other wild thing and in all my characteristics of stance and motion I was patterned after her—graceful and covert as any wild creature's.

My life, up fifteen years, would have been a lonely one had it not
been for my mother's undivided concentration of her love on me.
The excessive warmth and doting on me did not, happily, damage
my vigor because I often felt my manhood pulse and I fought against
the smothering affection of my mother just as I resisted the corrod-
ing hatred my father turned on me.

Mother never learned the rudiments of music—was never a master of the harp—but there was within her that native and natural
ability to draw music from whatever was designed to create it. On
long, rainy evenings when Papa was away and just the two of us
stayed snug under the dry roof, her fingers would leap and search
and agitate the harp strings and the passionate despair and the de-
spairing passion of her gypsy's soul would fill the room, seemingly
to bursting. So wildly did she play—so great was her forlorn aban-
don in the music she made—the freshly cut flowers would tremble
with their vases and the dark living room would shudder with the
vibrations.

"It's the angels answering," she would whisper, in awe, when the
walls would creak under the pulsing agitation of the harp's strings.
"It's the flutter of their wings as they hover to listen!"

Whether it was the angels listening, I will never know, but there
were times when her heart and her soul and her fingers were caught
up in something mystic and paralyzing and compelling—something
outside herself, conjured up by the fire and heartbreak and agony
of her music—which reached into the dark places of her soul, the
places where genius and madness lurk and contained the darkly
flashing stream of her existence as it poured out in sound. On these
occasions, when it was time to go to my bed, I did so in wonder,
expecting in the dark some manifestation of the unnameable and

indescribable something which swept out into this world through my mother's frenzied and possessed fingers.

At yet other times she would be obsessed with her embroidery and her nimble fingers would make the glinting needle fly over the enormous cloths, trapped and stretched taut in the frame. Her back arched (I can never recall my mother sitting in a chair with even her shoulders touching the back of it), her eyes gathering to her mind the myriad colors with which she worked her magic.

"Come, Bru," she would whisper when she had finished with a tapestry. "Feel the softness of the silk thread; feel the colors; see the picture I have painted with these many strands . . ." And I would run my fingertips over the gleaming surface she had created, following her fingers, gazing as she drank in the spectacle. "It is like the lawn of a fairy's castle," she would whisper softly . . .

To this day, when I am in the stores of New Orleans, and encounter the huge tapestries which abound in the shops on Royal Street, I need only pause to see a surface with my fingertips and the texture lures me back to my mother and my memories of her. And my eyes never fail to flood with scalding tears in my sorrow for the loss of her. Within me beats the somber pain of ignorance. I do not know where she is—I know not if she is alive—my poor, brave, unhappy mother . . . the substance of my youth and the fashioner of my existence.

When I was very small, she would point things out for me, call to my attention the teeming activity of the nature all about us. The budding plants, the tadpoles in the pond, to the caterpillars (calling them "butterflies-to-be"), to wasps building their houses of mud and to the bees, busily coming and going across the clean, white boards which provided the way to and from the neat, white hives Papa built and set in rows down the orchard. No bud was too small—none too drab in color—not to deserve her pointing it to my attention. In the early spring, our feet would wander through the damp woodlands, noting the newly blossoming dogwood—"the cross of Jesus" she called the flowers—rolling May balls until they were purple, picking up shells and sharks' teeth in an old stone quarry. To my round-eyed amazement she explained that, once upon a time, this was the bottom of the sea. Sometimes, we'd pick cowslips, which she described as "keys to heaven." In those wondrous days and years with her, neither the woods nor the water looked darksome in the fine Southern spring, with the bursting of the new leaves and buds the color of corn in the birch tops. Only in our own, deep oak woods was there ever a look of the back end of the year, the young leaves looking so brown, and I would always instinctively take her hand when we wandered through the dimness of its depths.

It was always a thing of pleasure to sit with her in the meadows and look up into the far hills. The larches spired up in their quick green; the cowslip gold seemed to steal into your fabric and even the pond seemed but a blue mist in a yellow fog of birch tops. Over it all was the flavor of a dream—the whole place was caught and held in it with a quiet and serenity which shattered with a jar at no more tumultuous a passing than the hum of a wild bee. Even this small furor brought me up with a start, so deep was the unreality.

I wish God would give me such calm, such serene experience of time a-stop, now. How I hunger to clamber back through the years to relive those precious, golden sensations. There was little sense of time, only of great happiness and peace which I have forever lost . . . happiness with no aftermath of pain nor terror nor tomorrow . . . pure, crystal, exquisite. I steep in remorse for not knowing, then, how infinitely precious, how magnificently valuable was the treasure I held in the warmth and security of her great love. Now that I have lost her, forever, the emptiness is like a cold weight within me, heightened by the unwelcome light through the treetops when a great trunk has been severed by the woodsman and the felled giant leaves the gap of his departure in the dappled structure of the roof overhead. The sky leaks into the empty place and sorrow dances with fear along the high-tossed branches.

I remember all she ever told me, but one thing she said will always stand clear in my memory, because it was so much herself. It was early spring and we were venturing through the apple orchard. The bees whined about our heads, then joined in the long, black threads of their speedy flights. My mother was showing me the pink apple blossoms, or buds, for they had not, as yet, frothed.

"They are little babies' hands," she had said, smiling as she bent a limb down so that I could see them closely. "Little pink fists closed over tiny pieces of gold."

Greedily, after the manner of all children, I pulled one of the wee buds apart, searching in vain for the tiny, precious store but no little gold coin was there. The petals fell, absently, from my trembling, eager hands.

"There's nothing in them," I said, disappointment showing in my eyes.

"But you do not see them with your eyes," she explained, "you see them with your heart."

In that one phrase she caught the reality of her life.

One comment of my father's, too, has stuck with its barbed sense in my memory. The words and the action are greatly responsible, I am certain, for setting my course toward my kind of passion. It was when I was very small and he was seated at the living room table, busy in examining his collection of coins. There was one of them which had always caught my eye and drawn my curiosity and I was so filled with the urge to examine it in detail, I'd tremble each time I saw it. It was a huge coin, of gold, brought to these lands by my grandfather from Greece. The gleam of its surface contained, in exquisite detail, a relief of a naked god, a youth molded and formed with muscles and conformation of a striking beauty. To see it there, under the lamplight, always sent my emotions into a state near ecstasy.

On this occasion, my desire and determination combined to make me reach out and slide the coin from the table into my hands. My father, busily poring over a book on coin collection, failed to notice my action immediately. It gave me a moment in which to study the figure and in that brief time I memorized every last detail. The figure was totally naked and I trembled at the clarity of the clear manifestation of his male sex. As I gazed, I began to tremble in some mysterious longing and, becoming faint, must have gasped for breath.

My father turned abruptly and, seeing the coin in my hands, slapped me smartly across the mouth almost in the same motion snatching the coin from my child-size fingers.

"It is forbidden!" he shouted, putting the coin back among the others. That one word has echoed through the years in my mind. Linked with the beauty of the naked god on the coin, the "forbidden!" has dominated my dreams and, ultimately, my actions, never failing to leave me with a sense of dark, continuing guilt in my sexual encounters with boys. The word "forbidden!" has made it all the more daring a thing, the more mysterious, the more darkly secretive.

It drove me like a whip—yet, at the same time, it pulled me backward as though I were reined by invisible threads. It was this thing which drove me ceaselessly—drove me to Dany Buck and beyond. That one word, despite all my father's stern discipline and the heavy tax of prohibition which he laid upon my life, made futile any effort to sway body or mind from this same path of desperate and consuming desire.

Had my father ever shown the slightest affection or regard for me; had he even represented himself as an ideal—an elevated pattern to offer me a challenge—I know my desires would have followed the channels dictated by my masculine conformation in normal fashion. But not once did he ever manifest anything to or for me. When I sought for love among my own sex, it was the love my father denied me. Beyond those gloriously happy days with Dany Buck, as I searched deeper and further into the dark concrete caverns of New Orleans; searched in that jungle sans inhibitions, the French Quarter; searched Royal and Bourbon and St. Charles Streets and their bars, taverns, and dance halls; searched in the crumbling apartments crammed back of the walled courtyards; I was, blindly and mindlessly as a child, still seeking that which was forever lost to me— that love my father had refused to give. The compulsion which kept me on this doomed search for something out of my youth, I recognized was futile, but resisting it was something which, inside me, was every bit as impossible as ignoring the taboo my father shouted across the naked, golden god at me.

I later knew my father never loved anyone or anything, even the farm, over which his eyes ran so longingly. As he devoured the acres with his hungry gaze, it was not from love of the land or of the home but only in crass speculation on what it could be made to yield up to his grasping, insensible hands.

His farm lay upon a rise amid numerous other hills crowned with dark sable pine and cedar—as my mother described it: half in faery and half out—and it glowed a deep emerald, a gemlike luster in a setting of gray and violet clover. Mississippi country is never colorless. It still holds, when every blossom is withered, in its great, mysterious expanses, a bloom which is like the spirit of the departed blossoms. Against the subdued surrounding of the fields and slopes, acre on acre, the homestead's barns and stacks held and refracted each ray of sunlight, especially at sunset. The house itself was built of find, mellow old sandstone of a weatherworn and muted red which takes on a beauty all its own under the direct rays of sunrise and sunset, almost as though itself was radiating the light which reflected from it. It was, to me, beautiful and to my mother likewise, and we loved it dearly. With the chicken houses, the silos, the smokehouse, and the various other essential structures, it was to me, in the days of my childhood and youth, a kingdom.

Below the hill stood the cottage where Dany Buck and his parents lived; the three of them hired by my father to work the land, to tend the stock and whatever other chores were necessary to keep the farm in order and as productive as my father's grasping mind and hands could make it.

I was aged fifteen at the time existence crested in the anarchy of my nature and Dany was but four years older. The years had been friendly to Dany in the matter of his good looks and his physical perfection. His hair was almost the color of wine, dark, and it lay smoothly over his head, so alive and shiny and clean it was as though he took a brush to it daily. The gold-tipped strands matched the color of his skin, which was utterly smooth without blemish or scar and radiantly bronzed from the hot Southern sun, the winds, and the ministrations of the out-of-doors. His eyes were a deep brown, the shiny brown of leaves at the bottom of a quiet forest pool, and somehow, Dany always looked at you from the depths of them, never the surface. When he looked, you melted, for his eyes were like his heart, deepened and saddened a little by a lifetime of servitude to hard tasks and long hours and wages of mere existence—but there was also the mellow quality of consideration and an overflow of understanding in them. Dany was as pure as homemade bread, as clean as hill spring water, as simple as a breath, and he possessed no hint of the guile, the cunning, and the deceit so common among my schoolmates. All things he was, I was not, and recognized this as truth. You could—which I never did—tell him the most impossible lie and he would believe it. In the simplicity of his uncomplex nature, he was, in all truth, monumentally gullible—but in Dany it was no fault. His gullibility helped me win him for my own.

My father may have bought his hands and his never-tiring servitude, but his body and his heart, I know, belonged to me.

When I watched Dany pitch hay, milk, or do any manual chore with his lithe savage's body stripped darkly to the waist, it was like a kind of music humming in my blood. His tight blue jeans revealing, like a second skin, the play of each magnificent muscle in his thighs and buttocks as he worked, the light glistening on his bare torso, wet with sweat. He had the swarthy, rakish look of a pirate about him, wearing—as he always did—cuffed rain-boots for his work. Filling my eyes and my consciousness with the picture of him, I would tremble as one in the throes of a seizure. As he lifted the powerfully muscled arms to toss forkfuls of hay onto the thatch, I would get glimpses of those dark patches of hair beneath his armpits and this would release in me, like imps and devils of desire, the frantic longing to see the other dark patch of hair I knew must decorate the fork of his magnificent thighs.

Like the coin, the bright, magnetic image on the coin, I thirsted and I suffered to see him in detail . . . every detail . . . and to know what crowned that dark area I could see, yet could not see, where the tight jeans bulged and swelled at the crotch. The agitation which visited this mysterious place of my fever, when Dany's muscles were bulging and straining at heavy tasks, would leave me without breath, my heart pounding like the heavy sledge his huge hands wielded as easily as a toy.

Because I was younger than he (or perhaps it was because he worked for my father and felt, thus, obligated to do my bidding), I do not know, but he was ever good to me, dropping his work to do this or do that at my whim. Then, sometimes it would be necessary for him to work into the dark to catch up with the chores he had abandoned for me. Those favors he accorded were like holy relics to me, adding with each, another medal to my collection in the daring, silent passion of love for him which possessed me and consumed me. When, by chance, his hand, hot in the exertion of labor, would brush mine as I worked beside him, shock would jolt through me, leaving in its aftermath a weakening limpness which threatened to collapse me.

One afternoon, working at a remote haystack, the flash of black beneath Dany's arms roused me to new heights of yearning desire and the imps the sight freed within me set me to tormenting him at every turn. Often we laughed and teased each other with word and gesture but this day my fever led me to new areas of daring and, laughing excitedly, I pushed him backward into the haystack. Caught off-balance, Dany fell, spread-eagled and laughing at being thus tripped up. Quick as a cat, though, he was back on his feet, a hand darting like a striking snake to imprison an ankle and snatch me, head over heels, into the soft, warm, fragrant cushion. Sputtering and fighting for breath, I made for him and locked my arms around the supple, slippery waist as though to wrestle him off his feet. With a deep chuckle, Dany's hands took my hips like a pair of velvet vises, turned me end for end, and dropped me back in the hay. Before I could regain my feet, he was upon me, laughing and teasing.

"We wrestle, ha?" he asked as my breathing stopped for a pace and his hot body descended on my own. Somehow I knew I must continue to struggle to keep the stricture of the hard-muscled arms and the heat of the smooth, sweaty skin against mine. Ecstasy roared through me as I writhed and turned as one possessed and my manhood rose and beat against its tight confinement as the unequal struggle went on. Finally, the end came, all too soon, yet almost too thick with ecstasy to bear. Dany, laughing in triumph, pinned my body, flat, beneath his and I felt the rigid press of his crotch against mine, the pain almost too much to bear but too bittersweetly marvelous to resist. With teeth clenched, I arched my small, rigid body against the fulcrum of my mingled agony and delight as Dany, with my arms pinioned above my threshing head, held me supine and helpless. Slowly the smile faded from his shining face, gleaming with the sweat of his exertions as he knew the direction of my desire.

"Ah, Bru, the sap is risen," he said, quietly, slowly freeing the crush of his crotch on mine and sinking back on his haunches. I sat up, shaking, eyes finding the huge displacement of his bulging jeans as my hand sought my pants in an attempt to ease the constriction of my garment. Dany came to his feet and extended a hand to me, to bring me upright. I felt as though all my father's bees were buzzing in the fevered throbbing of my body and I gasped for breath as my eyes, still bound to the sight of Dany's swollen crotch, fought to stay open against the pull of the heavy lids . . .

From that moment, the memory of his hard-muscled limbs and the torturous ecstasy of the moment plunged and struggled within me, both in dreams and in daylight. Where once my desire had been a yearning for an unknown thing, one full-moonlit night I dropped off into fitful, twisting sleep and the dream of Dany returned. As, in my fancy, I once more struggled in the precious mystery of his crushing limbs, I collapsed, paralyzed, in the grip of an ecstasy which drained me and frightened me and left me in thrall to the mighty wonder of it. From that night onward, my want for Dany was as simple as my hunger for bread, my thirst for water, and my need for rest. I wanted him with the thwarted rage of fifteen and I followed him about the farm, constantly, his shadow and his tempter—though I did not then realize it—leading him, his body, and his emotions into a cage which would make him prisoner . . . my prisoner . . . for life.

Not that I am, basically, ruinous. I was desperately lonely, without brother or sister to share my existence; desperate to escape the woolen, suffocating affection of my mother (tragic for one at that time of life); starving for a relief from my loneliness and for love denied me by my father.

JACK LOVE

Gay Whore

PEC French Line, 1967

Beautiful.

That's Randy Nelson.

Homosexual . . .

That's Randy Nelson.

A good lay—that's Randy Nelson!

A specialist in pleasing men—that's Randy Nelson.

The most educated and experienced lips and tongue in town—that's Randy Nelson!

Randy Nelson is one of the beautiful people, but there's nothing unique in that in Hollywood; it's jammed with beautiful people—male, female, and some whose sexual identity is in question.

Hollywood is the tree society—everybody swings. But few swing like Randy Nelson!

Randy stopped at the corner, waiting for the light to change. He let his eye wander over the crowd. Several men glanced in his direction, and he, in turn, glanced in theirs. It was the code of recognition: the quick appraisal, the look, the smile, and invitation—the ritual.

It was there for the asking. Asking, hell—it was there for the slight smile, or even a raised quizzical eyebrow.

This is the opening page from *Hollywood Homo,* a 1967 novel by Michael Starr, published in Publisher's Export Company's (PEC) French Line and reprinted two years later. This company published about eighty gay-porn pulps from 1966 to 1971, including *Gay Whore.* While the novels of Carl Corley are unique, literary works, the bulk of novels published by French Line were merely competent, although they did evidence occasional wit and every now and then an above-ordinary sense of eroticism. But even without reaching high literary standards they are at the high end of the industry standards for the time and evocative of the manners, morals, fantasies, and concerns of gay men of the period. Their plots are fairly predictable: *Hollywood Homo* has a sex-and-blackmail plot, but really revolves around Randy's immorality and self-involvement; *Glory Hole* is about a vice cop who gets too into his work; *Gay Stud's Trip* (mixing two genres) is about surfers and LSD.

Gay Whore, set on Fire Island, details the emotionally rocky relationship between two men, Jack and Benton, the former struggling with the implications of remaining "one of the highest-paid whores in Mother Martin's whorehouse." While many other novels focus solely on the lives of individuals, *Gay Whore* repeatedly talks about a gay community: " 'Here's another surprise for you.' Benton winked. 'I own a house on Fire Island where we'll be spending most of our weekends this summer, in a mostly gay community.' " The idea of a "community" is rare in pulps and porn novels from the mid-1960s, since so much of the action and tension relied on the characters being isolated, lonely, and eventually finding someone but not a community. *Gay Whore* also gives us a fascinating fictional look at Fire Island life in the 1960s: the meat rack, beach cruising, and the "opera party."

Jack Love is probably a pseudonym. *Gay Whore,* as well as *Flesh Trap* and *Silent Siren,* the three novels published under this name, are out of print.

In Chapter 8, Jack has met a trick named Bob, who is introducing him to the world of gay whoring.

Chapter 8

The trip back to the city took about three and a half hours, but to Jack it was the longest journey he had ever taken. They had waited almost an hour before the train came in, and it was almost two hours more before they reached Pennsylvania Station. It seemed as if they had been traveling for days.

Bob didn't say two words to him throughout the entire time and this made it all the more tedious and depressing. He couldn't think how to start a conversation that wasn't merely idle and silly chitchat and so he had no choice but to let the silence hang heavy in the air.

Jack was dead certain Bob realized he didn't want to be alone with his thoughts, and he simply couldn't understand Bob's silence, except to think that maybe he was naturally closemouthed and even petulant generally, after the first warm, cordial overtones to friendship had been made. And there was a chance, too, that Bob had found him attractive last night through a beer haze and now regretted striking up any conversation at all.

Jack stared at him. They were in the taxi now, inching along in the heavy traffic.

"Do you know, this silence between us is driving me nuts," he said.

"Oh—I'm sorry." Bob grinned. "Did you want to talk about something?"

"Well—I thought we might talk—about anything."

"Look, Jack, there's no point in discussing the past now that you've made a clean break. And our future hasn't begun yet."

"Is that the only reason you've been so silent?"

"Of course."

"Oh." Jack looked out the cab window; he had lost contact with their position in the city. "Where are we going?"

"To the place where I live."

"Well—where is that?"

"Just a few more blocks up this street."

"Oh. Do you live alone?"

"No."

"Oh! I thought—"

"Don't think," Bob said flatly. "If you really want a new and different kind of experience from anything before, don't think. Just let me lead you to it. You are game for anything, aren't you?"

"Sure. What can I lose?"

And Bob said, "Stop here, driver."

They were in front of an elegant-looking town house on a street that Jack couldn't associate with. They got out of the taxi and Bob paid their fare; Jack followed him into the foyer and stared.

"Good afternoon, Bobbie," the obese man said.

Looking at him, Jack was instantly reminded of a grotesque fat-man that he had seen once in a circus sideshow. He was a grossly obese man whose swollen body with its squat height gave him a definitely womanish appearance. And he was dressed in the most outlandish suit that Jack had ever seen. It was royal purple silk, and it fitted him in such a snug way that the excess fat on his neck, breasts (for you couldn't call it a chest), and hips rolled; his voice was raspy and high-pitched, contributing to the almost total impression of femininity.

Bob said, "This is my friend, Jack Barstow. Jack, this is Mother Martin."

"So happy to make your acquaintance." Mother grinned.

"Yes, yes. How—how are you?" Jack was flustered by this man, and mostly by his odd name. Who was he, really? And what on earth could Bob possibly have to do with him?

"You did quite well, Bobbie," Mother said. "I'm proud of you."

"Are you?" Bob asked sheepishly.

"Yes, I am. He is simply gorgeous. I've not seen anything so perfectly admirable in a long time."

"I'm happy you're pleased."

"Delighted!" Mother exclaimed. "You're a good boy, Bobbie, and you have a superb eye for perfection."

They were talking in absolute riddles as far as Jack was concerned, and while this didn't particularly disturb him, some sixth sense did seem to give him pause. It wasn't anything special that he could put his finger on though, and he even thought that maybe he was allowing himself to become excessively emotional and wary simply over the odd appearance of Mother Martin, and so he tried to shrug the whole thing off. In fact, he had already decided to give any experience a try, no matter how bad it proved to be, and he chided his mind for attempting to disturb him.

Bob said, "We'll go on up to my room now."

"I shall see you this evening, Jackie," Mother said. "Bobbie will extend our invitation to you and explain its necessary details. I trust that you will be comfortable and happy here."

"Thank you very much," Jack said perplexedly.

He didn't know what to make of Mother's words, but it was of no real importance in his present state of mind. And he wasn't going to ask questions, either; he was just going to go along and let things happen as they happened. So he silently followed Bob upstairs. He didn't comment immediately on Bob's beautiful room. He just remained speechless in the stance he took in the middle of the room, until Bob closed the door and walked over, looking at him amicably.

"All the furnishings are priceless antiques, Jack," he said. "I'm especially proud of my double bed. It's genuine Empire and worth thousands."

"This is all magnificent," Jack said.

"Yes, isn't it," Bob continued, "and I'm happy and proud to be one of the chosen dozen."

"Chosen dozen?" Jack blinked.

"There are twelve of us boys who work and live here in fabulous bedrooms, just like this one."

"Well—frankly," Jack said, "I don't get any of this."

Bob laughed. "Of course you don't. Please sit down, Jack."

He hesitated and then sat down slowly in a chair; Bob went to another chair and sat down too. They faced each other across three feet of a marble coffee table.

"Jack—I'm one of the twelve highest-paid gay male whores in the city of New York."

He said it so very quietly and offhandedly that nearly nothing of his enormous statement of confession registered with Jack, at first. He simply stared. And then he suddenly sat rigidly erect in the chair as the thunderous shock and surprise bolted into his mind, but he was absolutely speechless. His breathing stopped.

"Let me explain everything," Bob went on. "This town house, probably the most beautiful and elaborate of its kind in the world, is a whorehouse for the wealthiest and most prominent gay men on earth. They are men who can afford everything but one thing—letting it become known they are gay. So, they visit here when they come to New York, and they come from all over the world. They shell out one hundred and fifty bucks to bed down for the night with me or one of the other boys. In that bed right there, Jack, I've made love with men such as a top movie star, the president of an oil company that encompasses the globe, and an honest-to-goodness king."

"Oh," was all that Jack could say. He was still catching his breath.

"It goes without saying that the address of this house is probably the best-kept nongovernment secret in the world," Bob continued. "Mother Martin is our male madame, naturally, and we boys are treated like gods by him. We have the best of everything, and we live like princes. I've been here over three years now, and I couldn't be happier. Now what do you say about that?"

"I'm—I'm flabbergasted!" Jack exclaimed. "I never knew that such a place existed, anywhere. And I still can't quite believe it."

"That's understandable. I told you, we're a well-kept secret."

"Well, how on earth did you hear of this place, and get this—this job?"

"Just lucky." Bob winked. "Actually, I was touring Europe for thirty days. The trip was a high school graduation present from my one rich aunt. And I met Mother Martin at a gay party in Rome. I'd gone there with a famous Italian movie star who picked me up in the lobby of my hotel. We talked and so I came right here when I got back, straight from the boat."

Jack shook his head. "Gosh—"

"Aren't you impressed?"

"I certainly am, Bob! And I'm also pretty stumped. I mean, how come you were allowed to bring me here, and tell me these secrets? I'm not worth a hill of beans. So why am I so special?"

Bob chuckled. "Can't you venture a guess?"

"No. No, not at all!"

"All right. Let's go back to last night, for a minute."

"Yes! What were you doing out on Fire Island?"

"Why, Mother sent me on a mission," Bob said. "In the summertime, the Island attracts the cream of the gay crop from all over, and I was delegated to go out there yesterday to look for a recruit to replace one of our boys who left last week."

"I guess you didn't find anyone, did you?" Jack said.

"On the contrary, I met a simply splendid boy!"

"You did?"

"That's right. I met you, Jack!"

Jack sat bolt upright in the chair. "*What!*" His eyes were wide. He flushed, then tried to smile. "You're kidding!"

"No. You're extraordinarily perfect for the purposes here. I saw it at once when you came into the bar. And didn't you see how delighted Mother was with you, a few minutes ago? You've already got the job, Jack, if you want it."

Jack stared. "That's why you were so friendly last night! You deliberately trapped me!"

"I had a job to do."

"And all that talk about becoming good friends, and wanting me—that was all a lie! You were tricking me all the time!"

"I had a job to do."

"The only thing I don't understand," Jack said, "is why you tried to make me patch it up with Benton. I don't think that was very smart of you. I might have done it, and stayed with him."

"Never. Not with the psychology I used on you. I manipulated you like a puppet on a string, until you made a clean break with Benton, that's exactly what I planned."

Jack stood up, his legs planted apart, and glowered furiously at Bob.

"You son of a bitch!" he roared.

"Now wait a minute—"

"Wait a minute, hell! I ought to beat the shit out of you!"

Jack braced himself and waited for Bob to stand up before he charged him, swinging. But Bob remained motionless in his chair.

"It doesn't have to be like this, Jack," he said quietly. "It doesn't have to be bad at all. And I don't want it to be that way, believe me."

"Explain yourself," Jack panted. "And be quick about it, before I beat the hell out of you. Explain!"

"When I met you last night, you were already looking for an out with Benton. Why else do you think you were so susceptible to my flattery and tricks? So you used me just as much as I used you, really. You wanted to exchange your easy life for an easier way of life that would let you play the field. Aren't we offering you all that, right here?"

"I don't know!" Jack yelled. "I mean, I hate being tricked like some dumb bastard!"

"But you can forgive and forget that, if you really want all the sex experiences with men that you can get. This is the easiest way I know how, they come here to you!"

Jack's fists were still clenched.

"The thing I hate most," he said, "is that you and I can't make it."

"I don't know what you're talking about. We—"

"Oh, you don't know what I'm talking about!" Jack said sarcastically. "I'm talking about *us!* Are we ever going to bed down together, now?"

"Of course we are! That's what I'm trying to tell you, if you'll give me the chance. Tonight is going to be our night—all night!"

"Thanks for the small favors. But no, thanks!"

"Oh, stop acting like an ass!" Bob exploded. "You only really want to make the scene with me once, period. Then on to someone else; you want variety. Isn't that the real truth?"

Jack stared at him. Bob had hit the nail squarely on its head all right, he thought, although it was kind of painful to admit to himself that he wanted precisely that; he might desire a man, and then have him, and afterward, the next morning or even the same night, feel it impossible to ever want that particular man again. Well, he'd just have to accept it because he realized the admission was coupled with his growing belief that he must go along even blindly and let the chips fall where they might. And suddenly, his angry ego simmered down a little and he was aware of the stirring of excitement.

"Is everything really a ball here?" he asked.

"It's great," Bob said. "Will you stay, then?"

"Perhaps," he said. "Let's see how tonight goes."

Chapter 9

After a short nap and a long shower in Bob's private bathroom, Jack was still undecided about whether or not he wanted to stay. They had just finished dressing when a young French houseboy wheeled a large portable serving table into the bedroom loaded with a buffet of roast beef, turkey, shrimp, lobster, assorted salads, and all the trimmings. Jack conceded that Mother Martin definitely knew how to put the pressure on a prospective recruit.

It was a few minutes after 9 P.M. when they walked downstairs and into the foyer. Mother Martin joined them; greeting Jack with a smile, he said, "I hope you are having a pleasant time here, young man."

"Well—dinner was certainly outstanding," Jack replied.

"I'm most happy to hear you enjoyed it. I personally taught our chef everything he knows. I was, at one time, considered one of the world's leading authorities on culinary arts."

The best Jack could think of in reply to that little bit of information was, "Oh."

Mother stood looking at him, smiling, and Jack's feeling of uneasiness began to grow, partly because he knew that he was inadequate at making polite small talk, but mostly because Mother's geniality seemed somehow excessive and therefore suspect.

"I must go now," Bob said. "Mother is going to look after you for a while, Jack."

"Oh—"

Jack's uneasiness leaped in growth now. There had simply been no warning at all that he was to be left alone with Mother Martin, and it was impossible to believe that he was capable of diminishing his nervousness around this odd, obese man. Damn Bob! He had turned and left the foyer abruptly.

"What—what does Bob have to do?" he said.

"He must go change," Mother replied, "for you."

"For—me?"

"Yes. You'll soon see, Jackie. Please follow me."

Mother led him silently through a door at the rear of the foyer, and they went down a short hallway, which had several closed doors opening off it. Jack went through a doorway, which Mother held open for him, into a small room that contained two plush easy chairs and a bar cart, stocked with liquor bottles, sparkling clean glasses, and a container of ice cubes. Jack noticed that the chairs faced a large, undraped, floor-to-ceiling picture window, which overlooked a single enormous two-story room that seemed to be theatrically lit by dim, concealed lights, recessed somehow in the walls or ceiling.

"That is The Arena out there," Mother explained. "There are twelve tiny rooms, exactly like this one, surrounding The Arena. You can't see them because these picture windows are actually one-way mirrors, installed to protect the privacy of one client from another."

"What goes on in The Arena?" Jack asked.

"The initial entertainment of the evening," Mother said. "When a client first arrives, he is shown directly to one of these rooms where he is made as comfortable as possible. Which reminds me, would you like a drink?"

"Yes."

"I thought so. You seem a little nervous."

"I—I'm just excited," Jack answered, knowing it was at least partially a lie.

"Scotch?"

"That's swell, on the rocks, please."

"Certainly." Mother poured the drink, continuing, "Anyway, in about five minutes, my dozen boys will parade into The Arena where they will perform an ancient ritual that you will surely find stimulating. But I'll let you see that for yourself. Telling you about it would only lessen your surprise and certain appreciation."

"And then—"

"After the entertainment, each client selects the boy that he wishes to spend the entire night with. Naturally, I have already conceded Bobbie to you, this evening." Mother reached out and touched his cheek, and his eyes glistened with overt lust, Jack thought. "I wish you a night to always remember. Now, if you will excuse me, I must speak to other clients. Bobbie will come up for you, after the performance in The Arena. Meanwhile, please help yourself to any quantity of the Scotch you desire—and enjoy yourself to the fullest measure."

"Thanks," Jack said.

Mother moved toward him suddenly and took him by the shoulders and kissed him on the mouth with a hardness and roughness that nauseated him, and then he released him and went out quickly, and Jack gulped his drink and hastily poured another, swallowing it rapidly, in an attempt to make the liquor dull his disgust. Then he fixed still another Scotch and sat down in one of the chairs facing The Arena, which suddenly glowed in a stronger white light. Music began to play from hidden speakers and the effect was at once intimate, and sensuous.

The Arena opened, and twelve boys walked slowly into the middle of the room. They were, including Bob, the most beautiful young men that Jack had ever seen in his life, and he immediately felt vulnerable to every single one of them, which seemed to prove the diversity of his desire because there were not two of a type among them. The only thing they had in common were exquisitely beautiful faces. The rare faces of timeless beauty haunted him first, then Jack felt an excited awareness of the extraordinary and entirely perfect bodies, which were stripped completely naked except for tiny posing pouches that left little to the imagination. Examining them so, with the thought of bedding down with every one of them, he began to feel a stirring of desire, and he laid an ice cube on his tongue to cool his lips and mouth. But the burning sensation of passion continued to grow in the pit of his stomach and he sat rigidly erect in his chair, in excited anticipation.

He took a deep shaky breath and blinked his eyes; following the brief blink, his eyes focused again to note that they had ripped off their posing pouches. Jack stared, and then his eyes darted from one to another, until they returned to concentrate upon Bob.

Jack closed his eyes and visualized kissing Bob tenderly, his lips and hands moving lightly over Bob's body. He opened his eyes again, after a moment which became almost frantic, and he gasped; Bob, as well as the eleven others down in The Arena, had come together in twos and threes with a single purpose that wasn't going to take them very long to reach now. He riveted his attention upon

Bob, who was taking the initiative with an incredibly well-hung blond boy, and a generously endowed, black-haired Italian too; all the while they were kissing Bob's mouth and eyelids and ears, and then their lips and tongues found his flat belly, while his own hands continued to move, and move again, and still once more until he shifted his position carefully.

The music was mounting in a wild frenzy that matched the dozen bodies slapping together in jarring contact down in The Arena, and Jack was so aroused that his right hand moved instinctively and sought the zipper of his trousers. He slumped, throwing his head from side to side, almost senseless with desire, and then he thrashed about in the chair, his mouth opened wide; his whole body shuddered frantically in tune to primitive, savage movements before his eyes.

Jack was totally collapsed in the chair. He chewed his lower lip and watched the lights dim out slowly in The Arena, which was now empty again, but the music continued to play while he sat there recovering and waiting. He didn't have to wait very long; sixty, ninety seconds later Bob's strong hands were on his shoulders from behind him.

"If you're ready," he said, "we'll go back upstairs now. I want you, Jack."

They walked side by side without speaking until they reached Bob's room, and Jack reached out for the buttons of Bob's shirt. "Please, let's hurry," he said.

"Patience," Bob replied. "I have to take a shower first."

"I—I guess I should, too. Can we both shower at once?"

"You know, I was just going to suggest that. It can be fun."

Jack moved his hands on Bob and gave him a gentle squeeze.

"Let me undress you," he said.

They smiled languidly, facing each other, and their hands began to remove one another's clothing until finally they stood naked under the spouting shower nozzle, their arms around each other's waist, while the water splashed upon them like sensuous, soothing fingers.

Bob reached out for a bar of soap and lathered his hands behind Jack's back, still holding him in their embrace with his elbows against Jack's sides, and then his soapy hands began to caress Jack's buttocks and back with slippery ease.

"How does that feel?"

"Great!" Jack answered and picked up the bar of soap. "Let me show you."

He lathered his own hands and let them slide quickly over Bob's arms and chest, down to his hips. Bob in turn, while washing Jack's back, allowed his hands to explore further, and Jack spread his legs apart to give him freer access.

"WOW!" Bob grinned. "You are an eager number!"

"Yeah!" Jack nodded. "Let's get this shower over! I want to get to bed!"

"Me too," Bob whispered, shutting off the faucets after they had rinsed off. He turned to Jack, saying: "And then?"

Jack frowned and repeated, "And then—what?"

"Well, tonight won't go on forever. So what do you think now? Isn't this place pretty perfect for you?"

"At least, it's an entirely different world," replied Jack, stepping out of the tub onto a thick bath mat.

"That's just it!" said Bob, scrambling out after him. "This is a world, full and complete within the wall of this town house. You'll feel safe here, Jack, and never have a care or worry again. You'll drift far above the maddening outside world."

He started to dry Jack with a large towel, allowing his hands to run over his body, making detours to fondle the parts he enjoyed touching the most.

He didn't particularly want to think anything through right now, it just wasn't exactly the right time. All he really cared about now was getting into bed with Bob, Jack thought as he lay back on the bed.

Bob began a slow, thorough journey with his tongue over Jack's body, finally focusing his attentions on the jutting, throbbing flesh that thrust up from between his legs.

Jack moaned aloud at the sensation Bob's hot mouth provoked. As his sighs of pleasure increased in fervor, Bob accelerated his actions and suddenly there was a violent outpouring of Jack's passion. Bob pressed his own hardness down upon Jack's flesh, letting his own energy spill out.

———

The two lay side by side savoring their cigarettes, in a relaxed and contented mood.

And as always, when he had a minute to think, Jack started going back over things in his mind, and he wondered to himself if this was another of Bob's tricks?

Well, here I am acting just like a baby again, he thought; an experience in The Arena surely isn't going to kill me. Commitment to a crime is one thing, and commitment to evil is another, but The Arena wasn't really evil; it was completely within the realm of human experience.

Jack came to the conclusion that he couldn't possibly judge anything totally evil until he had experienced it for himself, and he was perfectly willing to do precisely that. So there! He was no longer at loose ends, now that it was suddenly clear to him what he had to do. He had to experience life in The Arena. He had to taste every experience that it offered him. That was the only way that he could ever mature; he had to live, so live, the good with the bad. Then he could choose again, with a clear conscience that wouldn't leave him wondering in dissatisfaction about anything at all.

He sat up, leaned over, and kissed Bob hotly on the mouth.

Bob looked up, his eyes sparkling. "Does that mean that you're going to stay?"

"YES! A thousand times, yes!" Jack replied, as his hands began to move.

Bob closed his eyes. "You're getting me excited . . . !" He moaned.

"I hope so!" Jack murmured.

"Easy!" Bob whispered. "I want this one to last and last, and last!"

And Jack replied, "It's going to—all night!"

"Then let me—"

Jack didn't object when, without finishing his sentence, Bob shifted his position and rearranged his body on the bed. He was curious, was all. Well, after all, this was the very first time he had been to bed with a professional GAY BOY and his mind was naturally aroused and curious about the procedures of professional gay sex. And he suddenly thought to himself: I must learn how to do this too!

Bob had turned about on the bed, seeking out Jack's trembling flesh, now pointing out at him strongly. As he shifted into position, he felt Jack reaching for him in a like manner, and soon they were engaged—one on the other, their joint actions becoming more feverish by the second.

Jack began to gasp with the urgency of his release—causing Bob to draw away at once.

"Please! PLEASE! I'm going mad!" Jack shrieked.

"Adjust! You can stand it!" Bob replied, fighting to control his own passion.

"No. No!"

"Yes, you can. Take it easy. There's a long way to go yet."

Jack thought that he would surely burst right then and there, but he held himself rigid, not moving even the slightest, fearing it would certainly be all over for him if he did, and he positively did not want it to happen that way, without pleasing Bob.

They were dutifully considerate of one another for a while, waiting apprehensively for a lessening of their mutual desire, and with the passing of time it was possible to achieve a quieter feeling down there, which they seemed to recognize instinctively in each other.

They began at the exact same time, and now they knew no holding back. Their lips crushed together, then hands sought flesh, mouths sought flesh, flesh sought flesh, and they were sweating, gasping, and slamming together and finally moaning until their throats burst into shrieks of shattering ecstasy.

Then they lay back, breathing heavily, limp. They cuddled together, holding one another without embarrassment, and it seemed obvious to Jack that he had never felt so satisfied before in all his life. Not only had Bob thrilled him; he also made him feel exalted, and so Jack was completely on cloud nine. Well, almost completely. Because he suddenly had an irrational thought, right out of the blue.

He wondered where Benton was at this moment. Benton, Benton, Benton.

And the name and the mental image of him persisted until Bob's arms went around him again, and the joy of his body drove everything else out of his mind again.

CHRIS DAVIDSON

A Different Drum

Ember Library/Greenleaf Classics, 1967

Publishers of porn have frequently tried to give their literature an aura of respectability by claiming that they serve a higher social purpose. Perhaps it was to this end that Ember Library Books and Phenix Companion Books (both divisions of Greenleaf Classics) included such strange flyleaf copy in all of their books.

A good example would be Chris Davidson's *A Different Drum*, a 1967 novel set during the American Civil War. The cover art features two handsome Union soldiers—an older, bearded man, and a younger, late-teenaged boy—getting undressed for bed. The cover copy reads: "They Heard—and Answered—The Compelling Call of—A Different Drum." The flyleaf copy details the dramatic tension of the story, but then places it in a context that can only be called odd for a porn novel:

> Major James Joshua Winfield Turner has a real problem. He has the necessary leadership to handle his troops in war, but has he the ability to resist their charms as individuals?
>
> Alex Comfort, in *Sex and Society*, points out that: "Forms of behavior have to be considered in light of what is known

about their unconscious origins, in the light of what is customary or tolerated within a given culture, in the light of the part they play in the individual's mental economy—of why he does what and when and where. It is disproportionate, if we are interested in the social effects, to lay much emphasis on the kind of physical variation or deviation in behavior—such object deviations are of great biological and psychoanalytic interest because of the light they may throw on the way in which sexual 'releasers' operate."

Similarly, Davidson's 1967 *Caves of Iron* is introduced with a strange reference to Paul Goodman:

Tommy might have done well, before he turned twenty, to read Paul Goodman's *Growing Up Absurd*. Had he a slightly better insight into the way that the world turns, he might not have found himself in prison—and the wildest time of his life. For, as Mr. Goodman states: "A boy of ten or eleven has a few great sexual adventures—he thinks they're great—but then he has the bad luck of getting caught and in trouble. They try to persuade him by punishment and other explanations that some different behavior is better, but he knows by the evidence of his senses that nothing could be better."

Were these quotations from "respectable sources" meant to ward off legal prosecution? It seems unlikely, since by 1967 the battle against censorship had fundamentally been won. Were they a remnant of the "white coat" mentality—the name given to sex films of the fifties that were introduced by a "doctor" explaining why the movie was "educational"? Clearly some time and thought went into choosing these passages—other books quote esteemed psychoanalyst Clara Thompson, Frankfurt School theoretician Herbert Marcuse, and even the author of *The Mass Psychology of Fascism*, Wilhelm Reich.

A logical explanation for these editorial decisions might be that these quotes were a form of camp, poking fun at the old restraints that publishers had had to abide by to make their books "legal." But there is an alternative reading. While at first glance they might seem witty, they may also be intended seriously, as extracurricular suggestions for the readers. It is not a stretch to see that *Caves of Iron* is, in its own way, a fine illustration of Goodman's theories about adolescent male sexuality. The Guild Book Services offered *Growing Up Absurd* in their catalog, as well as Edgar Z. Friedenberg's classic *The Vanishing Adolescent*.

Chris Davidson published fifteen novels between 1967 and 1969, all of them through various divisions of Greenleaf Classics, Inc. Some of them have historical settings and characters *(Song of Alexander)* or feature "exotic" locales *(The Gay Gods)*. *Go Down, Aaron* is daringly set in a concentration camp, its Jewish hero forced to have sex with Nazi officers. Although its cover copy is exploitative, the novel itself, while problematic, is far more nuanced. Davidson also wrote about gay men in a college campus setting *(Buffy and the Holy Quest* and *Buffy Rides Again)*, as well as a novel about gay politics, entitled *Coming Out*.

A Different Drum is the story of Major James Joshua Winfield Turner, of the Union Army, who goes through a traumatic series of relationships during a battle to recapture New Orleans from Confederate troops. The older Josh falls in love with one of his enlisted men, Derek, who has been separated from his own lover, Tommy, during the war. After Derek pulls away emotionally from Josh, the older man finds himself attracted to Lucien, the slightly effeminate son of Etienne, on whose plantation they are staying. Davidson is not afraid to let his characters have complicated emotions or (at least for porn) have complex sexual desires. In most writing of the period it would be unheard of for the butch, older Josh to be a bottom to the younger Lucien. Davidson is also willing to trust his readers with narrative complexity as well. In this chapter the four men pair off into two couples as Josh tries to come to terms with Derek's rejection.

Chapter 6

The lights from the wharves and warehouses sprinkled their reflections on the slow-moving water, and from where they stood on the planquette, Etienne and Derek could see the dark hulk of a river scow as it floated sluggishly down the water causeway.

They watched for a moment the darkly silhouetted outline of the long line of trees on the other side of the river, and then moved down the walk to the saloon. As they walked through the door a burst of sound from a battered old player piano, mixed with lusty male laughter and the clinking of glasses, hit their ears.

The saloon was filled with lots of blue uniforms of the Yankee troops stationed here, and an occasional civilian suit of white or buff of one of the Southerners who didn't mind associating with the conquerors.

Derek and Etienne nodded and smiled as they made their way to the back of the room, as someone or other would wave a greeting. They found a place at the end of the bar and Derek ordered rye, Etienne bourbon.

"You know, on the whole," Etienne commented, looking the crowd over with a practiced eye, "you Yankees are a fine-looking bunch of young men."

It was true. Now that the war was in its third year, most of the common soldiers were young men, men that had been conscripted and shoved into the ranks. The ages of these men ran from as young as fifteen years to somewhere in the midtwenties.

They were a lusty and rowdy lot, filled with the glory of their newly found manhood and the rousing excitement of war.

Derek smiled and even tingled a little at the sight of so much virile young maleness. Since he had come to be with Josh, Derek needed and demanded a great deal of love and pleasure. Before, scarcely a twelve-hour period would go by without their making love, and even though it had only been the night before that they had last made love, even now Derek could feel the need and desire of it begin to course and flow through his loins.

He knew that Lucien and Josh had begun something between them, and even though he had prepared himself for their separation as soon as he had realized that Josh's affection for him was steadily becoming more intense, the physical shock of his absence was now beginning to make itself felt. He smiled nervously at Etienne's remark and they both noticed that his hands shook a little when he raised his glass to his lips.

"My son and Josh seemed to have established the beginnings of a close and firm friendship, don't you think?" Etienne asked, watching Derek's face closely for a reaction.

"Hmm? What? Oh! Yes, they seem to have hit it off very well," he said.

"It's no wonder they were tired. I mean, spending the whole day together like that . . . ," Etienne commented, wanting to know just how much Derek suspected or knew.

"Yes, from what I saw of it, your plantation is quite a large one." Derek was not quite sure exactly what the relationship was between Etienne and his son. Nor was he able or even ready to reveal himself completely to Etienne. He knew that the man was a homosexual like himself, but that, and the fact that Etienne knew about him, still didn't help their relationship.

It would be wiser, Derek felt, to allow Etienne to take the first step in creating a cause-and-effect relationship between them.

"It's so large that it would take an entire day to look at it."

"But Josh said that they hadn't seen it all . . . ," Derek mused.

"Yes, well, perhaps they took their time. They probably stopped for lunch somewhere. My son's servant always takes care to pack plenty of food when Lucien goes out on a surveying trip. For a servant he's very conscientious."

"You mean Louis?"

"Yes. I bought him the day my son was born. He's only two years older than Lucien, and they're very close."

"Oh?" Derek drained his glass and sat it down on the bar, indicating with a nod of his head that he was ready for another one.

"Yes . . . exceedingly close." Etienne was waiting and watching Derek closely for any reaction, no matter how slight. He, like Derek, was waiting for the other man to make the first move, but unlike Derek, he didn't mind throwing out comments to create, or try to create, reactions.

"They mentioned the oak grove, didn't they?" Etienne commented, bringing the conversation back to the original subject of Josh and Lucien.

"Perhaps they stopped for lunch there. It's a beautiful spot, dark and green and private."

Behind them, and just out of view of the main room, a small table sat in the darkness, and at it, two young men of the Union Army.

Even though there was room enough for three or perhaps even four people, the two men were sitting quite close to each other. From where Derek and Etienne were standing one could see that under the table the two men were holding hands. They were silent for the most part, and looked into each other's eyes, smiling softly and whispering when they did speak.

Etienne saw it and smiled a little and then glanced to Derek to see if he had noticed. Their eyes locked for a second and then they both looked away.

Soon the men stood and instantly changed from the tender, lovers' attitude that they had had to rough, swaggering masculinity as they made their way through the crowded room and into the street.

Both Etienne and Derek knew that they would go find some quiet, sheltered place, and in the security of that place, their naked bodies would find love and affection.

Derek smiled a little regretfully and wished that it were he and Josh, or better yet, he and Thomas who were now walking from the room to find a quiet place to share their love.

His gaze met Etienne's again, and he smiled.

Josh lay fully clothed on the huge double bed that dominated Lucien's room. Lucien sat beside him, one hand smoothing down Josh's hair, and then moving to his ear to trace softly the outline of it.

"Are you sorry that we didn't go to town with the others?" he asked.

"No, I'm not. Are you?" Josh asked. His hands were busy touching and caressing Lucien's chest and shoulder. They moved to the buttons on the tunic that Lucien wore, and one by one he unfastened them.

"Don't be silly," Lucien said, bending down to touch Josh's cool forehead with a soft kiss. "There's nowhere I'd rather be than here with you. You know that . . ."

"Yes. I just wanted to hear you say it." Josh parted the tunic and slid it slowly from the man's shoulders. Lucien wore nothing underneath the shirt, and his smooth, tanned body, firmly muscled and hard from many hours of work, shone warm and inviting and golden in the dim light.

"I said it. I meant it. You're an irresistible young man." His own hands were busy unbuttoning Josh's uniform jacket.

"Young?" Josh questioned, with a smile. His fingers were busy touching and caressing Lucien's chest. His thumb moved to the man's nipple and squeezed gently, smiling even more, and the man took a quick, deeply indrawn breath and closed his eyes.

"I'm thirty-one years old. You're no more than twenty. I was ten years old when you were born," Josh said. His hand moved down to Lucien's flat, softly downed stomach and moved across the hard ripple of muscle.

"Yes, but I'm so much more experienced than you, so that makes me older," he said. He put his hand on Josh's arm and pulled him up a little so that he could pull the jacket from his shoulders.

Josh lay back down, and let Lucien's hands move freely over his slowly rousing body.

"Does it make a difference who's older?" he asked.

Josh moved his hand from Lucien's stomach to his lap and felt the tight, restraining material of his trousers over the urgent manhood.

"Not a difference in the world. The only thing that matters is that we two are here, right now, at this moment, in this room, and that I am waiting for you like this, and that you are waiting for me like this . . ." He moved his hand to Josh's loins and felt the heavy manhood that pulsed and rose hard against his palm as he pushed down on it.

"I like that," Josh said, and he thrust his hips slightly upward, feeling the heavy-sweet touch of the man's hand.

They were working slowly, very slowly. There was no need for haste or hurry at all. They were alone together and they wanted to explore and taste every facet of lovemaking.

Lucien touched the heavy buckle of the belt Josh wore, and slowly undid the catch on it. Then he moved his finger to the first button, then the next, and the next, until they were all unfastened. He reached down and tasted the rich goldenness of Josh's body and his tongue moved to the masculine sweetness of the man's navel.

"And I like that!" Josh said. His hands moved to Lucien's trouser buttons and slipped each one from its fastenings as Lucien had done to his.

"It is nice being together here like this, isn't it?" Lucien asked.

"Oh, yes! Oh, God, yes!" Lucien stood and slowly and tenderly removed each of Josh's boots and then pulled the stockings from his feet.

He straightened then and smiled down at the man who was lying on the bed.

"Do you want to remove my trousers, or shall I?" he asked.

"You do it. It'll be quicker that way," he said.

Lucien removed his boots and socks and then slid his trousers down over his hips, letting them fall to the floor. He stepped out of them and sat again. As under the tunic, Lucien wore nothing under the trousers, and he sat now, fully nude, his rising, evident manhood springing swiftly and fully from his loins.

"Now you . . . but let me do it. I want to be your slave," he said, his hands moving to Josh's trousers.

"You want to be my slave? But you don't know what I might ask of you."

"Does it matter? I'd do anything, anything at all," he said.

Lucien's hands slid the tight cloth from Josh's hips and down over his ankles. He tossed the trousers to the chair and removed the white linen underwear the man wore.

Now they were both nude, and Lucien lay down next to Josh. Their warm bodies were touching.

"Anything? You'd do anything for me?" Josh asked, and then their lips met again, and Josh tasted the rich sweetness of Lucien's mouth. His tongue moved in slow, soft circles, exploring the depths of the man's mouth and lips, becoming familiar with the angle of every surface.

"Yes! Anything you ask. I want to share with you what I feel for you. Everything that I feel for you, with no reservations," he said.

"I want that. I want to know everything there is to know about you, about your body."

"And I want yours. I want you here . . ." He touched Josh's nipple with a long kiss, his teeth taking the tender flesh in little nibbling bites that made Josh gasp and writhe under him.

"And here . . ." His mouth and tongue moved lower, exploring the depths of Josh's navel and reveling in its sweetness.

"And here . . ." Still lower he moved, bypassing the heavy throbbing of Josh's lean saber, to taste the warmth of the man's inner thighs.

"And here . . ." His mouth moved up further to touch, with his lips, that heavy ridge at the juncture of Josh's legs.

"And here . . ." He moved even further up, touching the hard length of Josh's erection in one long continuous kiss. He moved up to the very tip of it.

"And here . . ." His mouth closed down on Josh. A hot dark sweetness that made Josh gasp and cry out as Lucien moved down, taking the whole of Josh in his demanding mouth.

"Why don't we be frank with one another?" Etienne asked. They had had more than one drink now, and they were both loosening up. Their mutual sexual need had become more and more apparent.

"Of course. Why not?" Derek returned. The thought of what the two men who had left the saloon a short while before were now doing inflamed and disturbed him. With each passing hour, his need for sex was becoming more and more telling. He now, for the first time, looked more closely at Etienne. He took in the grace and power of the man. He was not overly masculine in his actions, but he carried himself so well that he became attractive in that very femininity.

Etienne leveled his gaze point-blank at the man.

"You're in love with Josh, aren't you?" he asked.

"Yes and no," Derek answered, calmly and steadily. "You see, I have a lover. He's somewhere in Virginia now. I won't see him until this war's over. We have a little farm near San Diego. Someday soon we'll be back there, together."

"But in the meantime, now that you're separated, you can't help but feel an emotional attachment to such a handsome, virile young man as Josh?" Etienne said.

"Yes, I guess it's just that I'm lonely . . ."

"That's part of it. But don't forget that you're also a virile young man. You need a lot of sex. You needn't be ashamed to search it out," he said.

"That's what I've been trying to explain to Josh. The only thing I did wrong was to be the first man in his life," Derek said.

Etienne raised his eyebrow slightly at this trifle bit of news.

"Yes. I was the first man to touch him. The first. I almost wish now that it had never happened. He says he's in love with me."

Etienne took another sip from his drink. "That's only natural. I fell in love with the first man I'd ever been to bed with. I got over it though. So will Josh. In fact, I think that very thing's happening now. Believe me, Lucien is one man who is able to make another forget everything. He's such a demanding man that another man who's with him has no time for anyone else."

"Yes, I would imagine that he is. Nevertheless, I need Josh," Derek said.

"Need him? Need him, or do you just need sex? You seem like a man who needs a great deal of attention that way."

"Yes. I guess I am. It's just that Josh and I seem to work so well together . . . I mean that. We seem to know just what the other one needs and wants, and we're right there to supply the solution," Derek said.

"I know how that goes. I felt the same way once," Etienne said, "but I soon found out that it wasn't just one man that I needed. That any—well, almost any—man would do."

"I don't know . . ."

"In case you haven't noticed, Derek, I'm propositioning you. It's been a long time since I've had a man, and I need you desperately," Etienne said sincerely.

Derek started to interrupt, to interject a comment.

"No, please. I realize that you're the kind of man who prefers younger men, and I know that you probably don't find me particularly attractive, but at the same time I'm probably different from any other man you've ever known. You see, I don't like to be touched."

Derek raised his eyebrows incredulously.

"It's true. You see, when I was very young, my father forced me to marry a young girl that I didn't love. She loved me very much and I had no idea that the reason I didn't love her was because I was one of those men who preferred other men. To make a long story short, she bore me a son, Lucien. Our life went along smoothly. If we were not the most ideally romantic couple, we were at least the most outwardly stable twosome. I was young then, and very handsome, and there were many women chasing me.

"They had no idea that the reason I rejected them was because I preferred men, not because I was loyal to my wife. Eventually, when Lucien was scarcely four years old, my wife and my father found me in the stable with a young gentleman friend of mine from New Orleans.

"My wife committed suicide that very evening and my father never forgave me for it. That terrible night left its mark on me. I can't bear now to have a man touch me. I can touch them. I can do everything and anything to them, but I can't let them touch me. I get violently ill if they do. So you see, you're not the only one with a sad tale to tell. Everyone has one if you search deep enough for it," Etienne said.

"I'm sorry. I didn't know," Derek said.

"What I'm trying to tell you is that I want you. If you allow me to have you, I'll do everything I can to make you happy. Everything that is, short of letting you touch me. It can be nice."

"I don't know . . ."

"Please . . . you won't regret it! I swear it!" Etienne pleaded.

Derek closed his fingers tightly around the glass he was holding. He did need it! He did want it! He wanted so desperately to have a man's mouth around his lengthening flesh, to touch and kiss him and take him thoroughly and completely.

"Yes! Now! I want you to touch me all over . . ." His voice was rough and harsh with need and desire. He wanted this man to use him in every sexual way, to drain him completely.

"Come with me. I know a place. Come with me now!" Etienne said.

They hurriedly left the saloon and walked out into the cool evening.

They walked down the planquette to the livery stable where the carriage was parked.

Etienne headed the horses out onto the wide river road and along it, going downriver.

As they rode along, Etienne reached over and ran his hand over the smooth maleness of Derek's inner thigh. Derek lay his head back against the seat and spread out his long lean legs in front of him. Etienne grew bolder and ran his hand up to the bulge where Derek's strength pushed tautly against the tight material of his trousers.

"Oh, hurry!" he moaned. "This place, is it far?"

"Not far. We'll be there in a few minutes. Be patient."

"I can't! Not with you doing that!"

"There's more. Oh, so very much more. Just wait," Etienne promised.

"Hurry! Please hurry!"

"And I want to touch you here . . ." Lucien's hand moved around the small of Josh's waist to his buttocks, touching them with fire and need as he moved. His fingers slipped lower, touching the dark-hot entrance to the man's body.

"Here is where I want to touch you the most. Right here!" His finger plunged in, and then two fingers, feeling and exploring the deep inner recesses of Josh's body.

"Oh, God, yes! Like that! Do it like that!"

"Now I must hurry! You've driven me too far to wait! I have to have you now!" He placed his hands under Josh's legs and shoved them up, up and over his shoulders. He positioned himself and then quickly spat on his hand and lubricated his wide, blood-filled dagger.

He moved the massive instrument to the hotness of Josh's body and poised there.

"Is this it? Is this what you want?" he asked.

"Oh, yes!" Josh's fingernails clawed into Lucien's back, urging him forward, urging the deadly length of him to bury itself totally into the opened wanting of his body.

Lucien moved then with one terrible and swift motion of his body, sinking fabulously inch by inch into Josh.

"This is what you wanted, isn't it?" he asked.

"Oh, God, yes, Lucien! Yes!" Josh clinched his muscles tightly and hotly around the massive wedge.

———

Etienne turned the carriage onto a narrow, dark lane, and past a grove of trees. Ahead, the dark frame of a cabin stood starkly outlined against the starlight sky.

"This belongs to my foreman. He's in New Orleans now. It's empty."

"Good! Let's hurry!" Derek said.

They hurriedly parked the carriage, tying the horse to a low-lying branch from a nearby tree. They hurried into the cabin and Etienne felt his way to a table, dimly seen in the dark light from one of the open windows, intending to light a lamp.

Derek had made his way to a small cot set against the opposite wall of the cabin.

"Never mind the light! Come here," he urged.

"Yes! I'm coming!"

Etienne went to the cot and found Derek lying there, half nude. He had already removed his uniform jacket and his boots.

Etienne rapidly stripped the rest of the uniform from the man's body, letting the clothing drop carelessly to the floor.

"Yes! That's right!" Derek almost sobbed, as Etienne's mouth moved down his chest, pausing at his navel to tongue and nip, and then moved yet further on to the hard pulsing maleness of the man.

"Yes! Now take it in your mouth!"

Etienne moved quickly now, plunging himself down on the ready willingness of Derek, his mouth making slow, hot, lazy circles around the man's flesh.

"Yes! Oh, God, yes!"

"Make it last, Lucien! Please, I want it to last!" Josh sobbed and moved his body under the younger man who had embedded himself firmly into Josh.

"Yes, my darling. I will make it last. I'll make it last as long as you want." He reached down and touched Josh's closed eyelids with a kiss, and then another kiss, and another.

"Do you like this?" Josh asked, pushing his hips up so that Lucien was buried in him up to the hilt.

"Yes! Oh, you don't know how much I like it!"

"Touch me, Lucien. Make me come with you! Help me come with you."

"Yes, I want you to be there with me. You're so good for me, so good!"

Lucien moved up slightly and reached down for Josh's throbbing lance that pulsed between them and poked rigidly into his stomach.

"You're ready!"

"Yes! Are you?"

"Almost. Wait for me."

"Yes, I'll wait. But hurry!"

"Yes! Almost!"

"Hurry!"

"Is it now?" Etienne paused for a moment to look up through the darkness at Derek.

"Yes!"

"Do you want me to take you now?"

"Yes!"

"Now?"

"Yes! Now! Now!"

"Is it now?" Lucien paused for a moment to touch Josh's lips with a kiss.

"Yes!"

"Do you want me to take you now?"

"Yes!"

"Now?"

"Yes! Now! Now!"

PART FIVE

The World Split Open: Life and Literature After Stonewall

The Stonewall riots of June 28, 1969, were not a quirk of history. They were the explosive culmination of a myriad of factors, some clearly identifiable as intrinsic to gay culture, others not. The Gay Liberation Movement would never have taken the form it did had it not been witness to the radical movements of the sixties (the second wave of feminism, Black Power, the hippies, Yippies, the anti-war movement, the Free Speech movement, sectarian groups, and unions). All of this took place in the context of the invention of the birth control pill, the sexual revolution, the relaxing of censorship laws, and the emerging drug and youth counterculture.

The increasingly sexually explicit gay novels that had been available since 1967 were also a manifestation of a new politics of homosexuality. Their message wasn't simply that discrimination against homosexuals should stop, but that there was an inherent "politics" about sexuality itself. The freedom to express sexual desire was seen as the logical extension of protection from societal prejudices and legal restraints. And the struggle for the political and sexual freedom of homosexuals was inseparable from larger battles for social justice. This political understanding is reflected in many of the post-Stonewall gay male pulps. *Gay Revolution* places sexual liberation in the context of cold war politics, and *Gay Rights* explicitly addresses a host of discriminatory behaviors against women, homosexuals, and the disabled. Even the *The Gay Haunt* places its ghostly, comic shenanigans in the broader context of the politics and ethics of the closet and of personal responsibility.

But this emphasis on politics was not new for the gay movement, or, for that matter, gay fiction. Looking over the history of gay fiction from the forties, we can find many critiques of racism and anti-Semitism. Often this took the form of an overt criticism of prejudiced characters. In John Horne Burns's *Lucifer with a Book* (1949), the priggish Mr. Pilkey, headmaster of an elite New England prep school, has a run-in with one of the school's few Jewish students:

> Mr. Pilkey simply stood and stared at the tall muscular boy. His pet peeve was the Jewish liberal. Here was one ready made. The Principal's granite Puritanism found nothing but decadence and subversiveness in Jews who pretended to be intellectual and progressive. They set on edge his Republican teeth. For such liberalism (it was really chaos, a lack of sense of values) always led to free love and Communism.

This critique of prejudice occurs in gay novels as diverse as Stuart Engstrand's *The Sling and the Arrow* (1947), Hubert Creekmore's *The Welcome* (1948), and John Selby's *Madam* (1961). In Carson McCullers's *The Member of the Wedding* (1946), Meyer Levin's *Compulsion* (1956), and John Rea's *The Custard Boys* (1961), the authors also wove a critique of racism into the plots of their novels. African-American writers such as Chester Himes in his prison novel, *Cast the First Stone* (1952), and Charles Wright in *The Messenger* (1963) routinely call attention to the connections between racism and anti-gay prejudice, as does, of course, James Baldwin.

The critiques of racism and anti-Semitism in these novels almost always are linked to a larger critique of traditional masculinity and, by extension, normative heterosexuality. As we have seen, this was part of the postwar public discourse about what it meant to be a man. Richard Brooks's *The Brick Foxhole* (1945) argues that this masculinity (and its manifestation in war) causes and reinforces accepted structures of destructive social privilege, such as racism, anti-Semitism, misogyny, queer hatred. Cast as a psychological thriller, *The Brick Foxhole* revolves around the murder of a gay man by Monty Crawford, a pathologically violent soldier and former policeman who hates Jews, Blacks, Irish, Italians. Brooks (who was to later become a major Hollywood film director) catches the hysteria and the incipient violence in the all-male world of the barracks, the "brick foxhole" of the title. Written at a breathless pace, *The Brick Foxhole* captures the tumultuous and threatening social changes engendered by the war:

> "What do you mean, Hank? Trouble?"
>
> "Yes sir. Sure's you're born. Made the biggest mistake of our lives letting them [African-Americans] into the war. Lots of Southern niggers going to camp up North. Getting ideas. And a lot more going over to France and all those whorehouse countries. Well, you know how they treat niggers over there? Well, all those niggers will be coming home with big ideas. They're going to think that they own the good old U.S.A. They'll want more money for working, and you know as well as I do how they don't produce worth a doggone now. And just look what the niggers are doing right in New York. Raping girls and stealing and beating up people. Why it ain't safe to walk the streets anymore."

The climax of the book comes when a fellow soldier, Pete Keeley— who has a vision of how all hatred in the world is the cause of hurt and pain—confronts the killer:

> "Keeley?" called Monty softly. "Where are you, mick? Where are you, you Irish sonofabitch? Where are you, Jew-lover? Where are you, Papist bastid? You ain't fit to wear the uniform. Come out! Come out and fight!"
>
> "You've got to die, Monty."
>
> "Me? Why? What did I do to you? Tell me, what did I ever do to you?"
>
> "You're alive . . . that's what you've done to me. You're alive. And this is war and you've got to die. This is the war that kills the enemy and you're the enemy."
>
> "You're crazy drunk, Pete Keeley. We're on the same side. We beat the Japs together. You 'n me."

"No, Monty. You're the enemy, too. And you've got to die."

Brooks's sweep is panoramic. On the dust jacket of the cloth edition, Richard Wright notes that "His [Brooks's] is the harder battle, for it is to reveal—while living with it!—the greed, the blindness, the racial hatred, the stupidity, the emotional confusion, the easy thinking and shallow feeling that govern so wide an area of our existence." The book is not only a cry against specific intolerances and prejudices, but also a devastating condemnation of a world being ruined by masculine violence and hatred. By placing the murder of a gay man at the center of the novel, Brooks makes it the fulcrum upon which his entire philosophical and social message rests.

It is important to remember that books such as *The Brick Foxhole*—while surprising to contemporary readers who imagine that a progressive politic about homosexuality could not exist in the 1940s—did not exist in a vacuum. Beginning in the forties and into the 1950s it is possible to locate a sympathetic trend in popular social criticism that paved the way for a new understanding of homosexuality. By today's standards the language and sometimes the suppositions of these works seem prejudicial, but for their times they were groundbreaking and laid the foundations for a more liberated way of viewing homosexuality.

Philip Wylie's 1942 *Generation of Vipers* (published six years before the Kinsey Report) was a scandalous bestseller in its unrelenting attacks on American culture; its most famous target being the American mother. Along with pointing to the debasement of sexuality in advertising, the hypocrisy of American religion, and the increasing number of bisexual individuals, Wylie notes that:

America is still populated with male ignoramuses who stand ready to slug a nance on sight and often do so—and who know about female homosexuality only as a shady and inscrutable washroom joke; but there is, nonetheless, an ever increasing practice of homosexuality through all the country. It is common in the navy, the army, and in colleges both for men and for women.

Psychologists have shown that the urge toward the experiment [of same-sex activity] is thoroughly normal in the young, although its continuance in maturity may be regarded as infantile. They have also shown that men who are inborn sluggers of nances are motivated by a sense of shame and fear caused by the fact that they have engaged in life-long psychological battles to repress and to conceal miscellaneous homosexual urges in their own personalities. They have further shown that the true function of the homosexual aspect of every personality is to afford a base for psychological projections which will make the opposite sex understandable. Such demonstrations make it clear that homosexuality should be dealt with as a type of behavior important in relation to private neuroses. To treat it as a fiendish manifestation, like ax-murdering, is silly.

Americans generally treat it like ax murdering. To them it is horrifying, repulsive, loathsome, and altogether beyond the pale of the thinkable. The fact that it goes on all the time means only that millions of people have dangerously guilty consciences. A guilty conscience is a terrible peril to an individual; collective guilt is a profound and imminent menace to groups. Our guilt is august.

There were many contemporary critiques of the alleged homogeneity of the fifties. Novels such as Sloan Wilson's *The Man in the Grey Flannel Suit* (1955), and social critiques such as William H. Whyte's *The Organization Man* (1956), C. Wright Mills's *The Power Elite* (1956), and Vance Packard's *The Hidden Persuaders* (1957), were all acclaimed books that focused on the alienation, materialism, and conformity of American culture. Psychologist Robert Lindner's popular books included his *Must You Conform?* (1956), in which he argued that in American culture, "nonconformity and mental illness or disease have become synonymous." While he views same-sex desire and behavior as originating in sexual repression, Lindner also understands homosexuality as a social, even political, refusal to conform to the heterosexual norm.

None of these men probably imagined a world in which gay porn novels would be sold on newsstands, or that the nascent homophile movement would become so prominent and influential in securing rights for a mostly despised minority. They certainly could not have imagined that their psychological and sociological theories would be reflected in a new popular literature, often overtly sexual, aimed at an increasingly open gay market. And yet, in many ways, the political concerns and understandings that are the underpinnings of *Gay Revolution* and even of Bruce Benderson's *Kyle* have their origins in these earlier works. The overtly progressive political sentiments that we find in many of the gay porn novels of the late sixties were not simply a response to a newly emergent Gay Liberation Movement, but also a reaction to a long literary and social tradition of political writing and thinking.

MARCUS MILLER

Gay Revolution

Pleasure Reader, 1969

Dr. Ashbury knew one thing about his new drug, methialine:
It changed ordinary men into raging homosexuals. He knew it
because he had experienced the transformation himself. Dr.
Ashbury had always suspected that this was true, but he wondered how methialine brought this ingredient to the surface
and made it dominant. And this was only one of the questions
that tormented him. Once men had tasted methialine and become homos, was this effect permanent? Was there an antidote
to reverse the process? And most important, what would happen if he slipped his drug into the water supplies all over the
world, filling the globe with homosexual love? Since Ashbury
was a practical man, he decided to try it and find out.

This plot summary—well, teaser, really—for the 1969 *Gay Revolution* shows how sophisticated the gay pulp imagination had become. Published during the birth of the Gay Liberation Movement,
Gay Revolution draws upon two paranoid themes that surface in
the popular culture of the period. The first is embodied in the film
Invasion of the Body Snatchers (1956), where one by one the

protagonists realize that the entire world is turning into "pod" people, and they can do nothing to stop it. Easily interpreted as a parable of encroaching fascism or communism (although the political sentiments of the filmmakers were liberal), it pushed enough cultural buttons to be remade two more times in the next forty years. The second paranoid narrative was one that ran rampant in the second half of the sixties: The fear that hippies would put LSD into a city's drinking water, and soon the whole country would be tripping.

In *Gay Revolution*, Marcus Miller turns these fears on their heads and creates a world in which personal, social, and political salvation comes with what is called "the Transformation." We meet Bill and Adam, two CIA agents, whose job it is to track down the nefarious Dr. Ashbury and find a solution to the nightmare of queer contamination. If this plot had been used a decade earlier, it might have resulted in the standard *Body Snatchers* story of predatory homos taking control. In Miller's novel, however, the Transformation actually brings about positive change: Crime has nearly disappeared, sex has replaced violence, and the world is returning to something that looks safe and reasonable. Adam, however, still has some concerns:

> When he thought about their jobs, he began to get a little worried. Perhaps the country might still have need for the CIA, but from where things stood, things did not look too encouraging. Russia seemed to be in a different mood since a new brand of leadership had seized power and the lifeblood had been drained out of the cold war. It was very difficult for any country to maintain an interest in the cold war when hot sex was abounding at every street corner. He began to wonder if Dr. Ashbury hadn't the right idea after all. People who indulged in pleasures of the flesh had little desire to kill, unless, of course, inspired by jealousy or hurt feelings. There was always that possibility. The thought of countries reacting similarly fanned a small spark of hope that their jobs would be saved.

Miller takes the slogan "Make Love, Not War" to its logical conclusion. But Miller goes much further and critiques heterosexuality itself—obviously, heterosexual sex is not doing anything to make the world a better place. By reversing the traditional narrative's perspective—this is *Body Snatchers* from the pod person's point of view—Miller raises the vital question that is always faced by opponents of sexual freedom: Who wouldn't want to have a good time? The answer from moralists and status quo defenders has always been that if everyone did what they wanted, the world would fall apart. But by imagining a world in which the reverse is true—in which things actually become much better—Miller advances a strong argument for the politics of pleasure. Like the science fiction novels of H. G. Wells, Philip Wylie, and Samuel Delany, *Gay Revolution* uses the phantasmagoric as political critique. But even more than that, Miller's moral is about a unified world. At the end of the novel, after Bill and Adam have made the Transformation and become lovers, we are told: "But all Adam could see were the years of pleasure ahead of them. Years which would be filled with meaning once more instead of haunted days trying to live like an alien in this world. Now they belonged, truly belonged. They belonged to the world and not just to each other."

Marcus Miller published sixteen gay-themed novels and a number of heterosexually themed books between 1966 and 1970, including *Boy Meets Boy, Gay Stud, Gay Swap, Locker-Room Lovers,* and *Mother Truckers.* Most of them were published by the Adult Books and Phenix Companion Books series of Greenleaf Classics. All of his novels are out of print.

In this chapter Bill and Adam are hot on the trail of the enterprising Dr. Ashbury and are beginning to realize how widespread the Transformation has become.

Chapter 7

In the restaurant, Bill Crane was paged shortly after he'd placed his order. He went to the telephone booth which the waitress had pointed out to him and picked up the receiver. The last person he would have expected to be on the other end of the line was Governor Piper.

Adam ate heartily, his spirits having risen when he felt he was at last back among his own kind of people. The waitresses and all of the airport personnel seemed ordinary heterosexuals and he was pleased. Everything seemed all right . . . until he saw his companion returning from the telephone booth. Bill's white-faced expression was grim and immediately affected Adam's appetite.

"What's wrong?" he asked hesitantly, anxious to ward off bad news.

"Real bad," Bill sighed and took his seat again. He fumbled for a cigarette and, catching sight of his food, pushed the plate to one side in disgust.

"That was Governor Piper," Bill continued after exhaling a cloud of smoke carelessly into his companion's face. "He just got word that Washington . . . well, it's all queer . . . including our boys. He wanted to warn us not to take the plane out. He even intimated that they may be out looking for us because he's had word from Washington to dismiss the state police from Fairview and to reopen the highways to traffic."

Adam Hood's face drained of color. He put his fork down, his appetite completely ruined. His hand trembled so violently that the fork fell to the floor with a clatter, and he too lit a cigarette. The shock had been too much for him to be able to say a word. It was too enormous a tragedy to be assimilated entirely in a few seconds. Finally, his voice returned.

"Where do we go from here?" he asked.

"I really don't know," Bill sighed. "We'll think of something. Right now, I think I'm going to drink some of this coffee and we can both think about it."

They both consumed two cups of coffee each and several cigarettes later had still not come up with any ideas.

"Adam, what will happen to the human race? At this rate, it will die out in a few generations! Hasn't anyone thought of that? And what about the animals? I didn't notice any in Fairview, but suppose the animals who have drunk this water are affected. Will it upset the delicate balance of nature?"

Adam Hood took a deep drag on his cigarette and looked at his companion. "Well, in any case," Adam said, "we wouldn't be around to see it die out. I grant you that those are valid questions, but artificial insemination would also work equally as well. I don't believe whoever is behind this wants everything to die out. There has to be a mastermind or a master plan behind all this rigamarole. I don't know what his motive is, but you can bet that it's a good one, at least, to the person who thought of it."

For several minutes they did not try to keep up the conversation because of the landing of a large transcontinental jet whose whistling engines drowned out every other sound. The giant plane taxied nearer the building and jockeyed into position, helped along by several small tractors as it sidled up to the exit ramp. Adam took more notice than usual, for it was very odd for a plane of this size to land so near to him. He'd always been on them or at airports where the view was obscured by various other buildings, and the only thing he'd ever actually observed was the plane touching the ground. The actions of the ground crew amused him. But he also had another reason. He was fearful that other agents may have been sent to pick up him and Bill. But then, he thought, they probably think that it'll catch up with us eventually. Why should they go to that much trouble?

Some of the passengers from the plane began to stream in through the restaurant door and Adam watched them carefully, but they were only the usual passengers, businessmen, women with children, elderly ladies, and one or two gray-haired men. But they bore the distinctive air of the people of Fairview.

Adam and Bill exchanged glances. They did not have to voice their opinions. All of the passengers were obviously queer to them. It wasn't that their actions were of the opposite gender, but their general relaxed attitude gave them away. All the heterosexuals employed at the airport wore the same worried expressions which Adam and Bill had seen on each other's faces, on the faces of the state troopers and the governor. These people were smiling and chatting gaily, just as though the tragedy which had overtaken civilization hadn't happened, or was a great boon to mankind.

"Don't drink any water," Adam warned. Bill nodded in understanding.

"Do you think this is how it's spreading?" he asked.

Adam nodded.

"Place to place. In this day and age, it would be possible to spread it completely around the world in a matter of two or three days."

Adam noticed that five or six men had gone into the men's room. Five minutes later, none had returned. He imagined the group orgy that must be going on.

"Let's get out of here," said Bill. "This place is beginning to make me nervous."

Adam nodded. They got up, paid the check at the cashier's desk, and then returned to the government car. It had gotten hotter as the sun rose higher and Adam flicked on the car air conditioner as they drove from the airport.

"Adam, what are we going to do?" The tone of Bill's voice sounded odd to his partner, almost bordering upon panic. He had never quite heard that sound before in Bill's voice, no matter how tough the going had gotten, and they had been in some tight spots together in the past.

"I think we ought to get a motel room, take a good hot shower, get a paper, and turn the television set on full blast. That way, we can get some idea of how this thing is progressing. We don't really know what the latest news is."

Bill agreed. Neither of the two men had had any sleep the previous night and they were beginning to feel tired. The import of what had happened hadn't helped to lighten the fatigue, either.

They chose a motel on the outskirts of the next largest town. Adam noticed that the owner eyed them suspiciously as they registered, looking them up and down as though fearful that they were two traveling queers from Fairview, but he said nothing.

Once inside the motel room, Adam stripped hurriedly and stepped into the shower while Bill laid across the bed poring over an early edition of a newspaper he'd picked up from a box at the airport.

Refreshed from the shower, but still almost falling asleep, Adam brushed his teeth as Bill came in and unceremoniously sat on the toilet reading the paper.

"Adam, you won't believe this," Bill said. "There's an article which says that the Pope has called a council meeting of Vatican dignitaries to decide whether or not the Church will continue to condone heterosexuality! Can you believe it?"

Adam did not answer, for at the moment he was rinsing his mouth. Then Bill, disgusted with the many articles in the paper which were complete turnabouts from what he was used to reading, threw the paper down on the floor and prepared to take his shower.

At the moment, Adam wasn't really interested in reading the paper or in hearing any more about the tribulations of mankind. He just wanted some sleep. His mind was reeling with memories of things the way they used to be. All of his friends and acquaintances in Washington, even old man Perkins, the hypochondriac, were now queer. It was hard to imagine, hard to believe. Little by little, with the adaptability of the human mind, he was beginning to accept the reality of the situations, but these things took time. He threw himself across the bed, and in moments his heavy-lidded eyes closed and he was asleep.

He slept soundly, but his dreams were troubled. In these dreams, he was continually running from groups of people who screamed as they ran after him, holding glasses of water which they were trying to make him drink. He was followed by Perkins, the hypochondriac in the CIA office, and several of his coworkers. They were all smiling and cheerful as they begged him to drink heavily of the water. He struggled as he ran, fell, got up and ran again, only to be eventually caught. He fought to get free, but four men held him down while Perkins poured the water down his mouth. Adam awoke with a start, his body drenched in sweat. When he looked about him, he realized that he'd been having nightmares. Bill was sound asleep on the adjoining bed, his blond hair falling on the pillow and his face as innocent as a babe's.

Adam got up from the bed and picked up the towel which he'd used earlier. It was still damp, but with it he managed to absorb the cold sweat covering him. He turned the television set on, keeping the sound down to a minimum so as not to disturb his partner.

His attention was immediately arrested by a cleanser commercial which depicted a female plumber displaying the glories of the product to a pretty young housewife. Near the end of the commercial, when the camera had shown how the cleanser had demonstrated highly superior performance over its leading competitor, the female plumber put her arm about the housewife's shoulder and kissed her. A masculine voice was then heard to say that if one used Nova Cleanser, *anything* could happen!

For the first time, Adam realized how swiftly New York was catching up with Fairview, only with their television networks, they were able to reach the masses. Apparently, Madison Avenue had adapted to the current trend. They surely didn't waste any time.

The program was just beginning. In spite of his own feelings about what was happening, Adam could hardly suppress a smile as the title of the show unfolded: *As the World Turns Gay.* He hated soap operas, but he was anxious to see what the TV boys had done to them. He wasn't surprised to find that the characters in the stories who had been so normal just a few days previously were now affected by the water and the story had been hastily rewritten to conform to this fact. A handsome young doctor was explaining to his alcoholic wife (who hadn't drunk any water) why he was leaving her in favor of his longtime buddy.

Adam switched channels. He found a camera ad which was devoted to displaying the versatility of the equipment at a group orgy on the beach. Boys and girls were displayed together, but each sex more or less stuck to itself, although there appeared to be friendly conversation between members of both sexes. Two young boys avidly watched as two girls performed an oral ritual as old as Sappho and photographed them in action. One of the photographer's friends was eagerly stroking his eager flesh and reaching around greedily to touch his buddies, who were equally as exciting.

On another channel, Adam's attention was once more arrested. He immediately recognized the United Nations Security Council and it was apparent that a debate was in progress. A Russian was in the process of delivering a long oratory, his voice droning on and on in a language which Adam always found completely unintelligible.

"The Soviet Union's representative," a voice broke in in English, "claims that his country has long been devoted to the type of love erroneously titled 'Greek' and that it was in his country that homosexuality flourished before it had spread to its neighboring nations. The representative of Greece has hotly contended this argument and claims to have positive evidence that Greece has for ages been correctly termed the cradle of homosexuality. But, as this meeting has continued, it has become increasingly apparent that other countries such as Turkey, Iran, France, and Egypt wish to make similar claims.

"Fortunately," continued the narrator, "the differences of opinion are of a totally different nature than the issues which formerly came before the Council. Russia has relaxed her effort to dominate the world due to internal struggles which every nation on earth is experiencing at this very moment, as power, formerly held by heterosexuals, is being wrested by normal, peace-loving peoples of the world. The new Russian premier, Alexei Cogsugeroff, has assured his people that the barriers will soon be lifted and that they will once again be allowed to travel the world freely and unencumbered. Washington has reiterated that if Russia truly wants peace, it is amenable to discussion. Already, talk is that many atomic installations are being dismantled throughout the globe.

"Cuba has openly declared that its ports are once again open to American tourists, although there has been no significant change to date. The American people, rejoicing in their newfound freedom, do not seem at all anxious to travel at the moment."

Adam listened with unbelieving ears, yet he knew that the spoken words were not a dream. This was actually happening! As the full import of the United Nations meeting soaked into his consciousness, he thought of his relatives in the affected cities. He hated to think of his brother-in-law, an ex–football hero, engaged in some nefarious activity in a men's room somewhere, or his young nephews wallowing on the beach with their buddies as he'd seen the youngsters on the camera ad doing. Yet, he knew in his heart that this was precisely what they were doing, for the men in his family had always been highly sexed. He refused to let himself think about his sister or any other female relative, for that matter. He found it too repulsive to contemplate. The men, well . . . at least, men had always been sensually inclined.

He tried to let his mind drift toward childhood memories, for he had had a pleasant childhood, and then, the world had been sane. He was preoccupied with these thoughts when Bill awoke.

Adam looked at his partner as the man rubbed his eyes and

stretched his limbs. Then, he saw the old, familiar expression return to his face when the man's mind once again returned to the dilemma in which they found themselves.

"Jesus, what's that? The UN?" he asked.

"Yeah," said Adam. "You should hear the latest. Russia is claiming to be the cradle of fruitdom and some other countries are fighting back. Cuba has announced an about-face and is willing to join the world again. Everything's screwed up."

Bill Crane moaned and laid his head in his hands.

"Oh, God, what will we do? What will we do?" he asked of no one.

"It looks like the beginning of the end," Adam said flatly, lighting a cigarette. "We can't go on like this indefinitely. Sooner or later . . . well, we're bound to come into contact with the chemical, one way or another. I suppose it's inevitable." When he saw Bill's chagrined look, he added, "Might as well face up to reality, Bill. Something as big as this can't be sidestepped. It's not like avoiding narcotics and refusing to take anyone else's cigarettes. We have to have water to survive and . . ." He didn't finish the sentence. No sense in torturing both of them.

"There *has* to be an antidote to this," Bill said. "Adam, if a drug can do something like this, then another drug could undo it. Doesn't that seem logical? I mean, everything seems to have an opposite."

"Sure." Adam smirked. "But you and I aren't chemists. We don't even know what the original drug is, for that matter, and we couldn't do anything about it even if we did know. Bill, it seems to me that if Washington isn't doing anything to find this antidote, then apparently they're either satisfied with the new status quo, or else, there isn't any alternative drug. We have some of the finest scientists . . ."

Adam paused in midsentence. From the trend in the conversation, he immediately recalled his acquaintance with Dr. Orenson in Los Angeles. He was a professor at an obscure college just outside L.A., yet he was one of the country's foremost authorities on drugs and pharmaceuticals. Adam had first made his acquaintance while on a narcotics case, and a friendship had grown up between them, although they only corresponded at Christmastime.

"Wait a minute, Bill," Adam said. "I've just thought of someone. If Dr. Orenson hasn't any idea of what this drug is, then no one has."

Adam immediately began to rummage through his wallet for a small card on which he had written the doctor's telephone number. After three minutes, he finally found it and placed a long-distance call. He let the telephone ring six times and was just about to hang up when the receiver was lifted off the cradle on the other end of the line. Adam was relieved to hear Dr. Orenson's resonant voice.

"Dr. Orenson, this is Adam Hood. Yes, the agent with the CIA. I and my partner are in a motel in the Midwest where we were sent to investigate the start of . . . well, of everything that seems to be happening all over the country and the world. Things seem to be out of hand at the moment and we're cut off from Washington. I called because I knew that if anyone knows anything about what this drug or chemical is, it has to be you."

"Yes, Adam. Nice to hear your voice." Dr. Orenson seemed pleasant enough, but as Adam talked on and it became apparent that he was not affected by the drug, the chemist's voice chilled somewhat noticeably.

"Why are you so insistent, Adam? I mean, after all, if our own government and those of other countries seem completely satisfied with the arrangement, why try to continue the fight alone? For what purpose?"

"Dr. Orenson . . ." Adam hesitated. "I hate to ask, but have you . . . I mean . . ."

"Yes, Adam, I'm affected, if that's what you mean. It slipped up on us rather suddenly, and then I began getting those headaches which were troublesome, but soon over. Of course, I know what the drug is and I even spoke to the man who is responsible for putting it into the water supply, but you needn't worry about it being harmful."

"Who is it, Doctor?" Adam was insistent. "Who is behind all of this?"

"What good would it do to tell you?" Dr. Orenson asked. "Adam, I'm afraid that you've gotten yourself all in an uproar over nothing. This is the best thing that could have happened to mankind all around. Can't you see it? Or are you too blinded by your own heterosexual prejudices to believe that anything could be superior to your own way of thinking?"

"Dr. Orenson, who is the man?" Adam ignored the words which bit into his ego. To hear them from this man whom he had so admired made them doubly biting.

There was a slight pause on the other end of the line. "All right," Dr. Orenson sighed. "I suppose if you meet him, he might be able to satisfy your curiosity and convince you of the humanitarian aspect behind his ambitious scheme. His name is Ashbury. Dr. Alton Ashbury. He is originally from the East, but at present he's here in Los Angeles. I believe he's awaiting the arrival of the president, who had flown to Hawaii to avoid . . . the inevitable. I understand that the entire island has been affected, including our august Chief of State and that he is now amenable to speaking with Dr. Ashbury to gain a new perspective in order to run the country along totally different lines."

Adam felt his stomach sink down to his knees. So, even the president was queer! Well, with all of Washington gone the way of the world, it probably was inevitable, as Dr. Orenson had suggested.

Try as he might, Adam found it impossible to be uncivil to the chemist. He had admired and respected him for too long a time to suddenly turn against him, especially when he was affected by something which had nothing to do with choice. It wasn't as though he had been queer all along and then had come out with the revelation.

"Dr. Ashbury is staying at the Ambassador in downtown Los Angeles," Dr. Orenson volunteered. "You'll not find it difficult to meet him. Of course, he's usually surrounded by a group of admiring people, but he's not guarded or any of the silly nonsense of the past. I believe that even the president will eventually do away with his personal bodyguards. Times will be different, Adam. You'll see."

Adam found it impossible to share the chemist's confidence in the security of the new world.

"Doctor . . . just between old friends . . . ," Adam stammered. "My companion and myself would like to avoid contact with this drug. As it is, we've avoided drinking water like the plague. I suppose we could live on fruit juice or some other substitute liquid . . .

but, well, do you know of any sure way that we could keep from inadvertently coming into contact with it?"

"Well . . ." Orenson paused. "I suppose you could manage to live on the fruit juice, but it would become monotonous. Then, too, it will be almost impossible to avoid contact through your food. Many dishes are cooked with water added and I don't mean only soups. Eventually, you'll become affected, no matter how hard you try. Soft drinks will become just as sufficient as a glass of water from the tap and so will beer. You can't consume alcohol only, and your body will require liquid. So, you see, Adam, I'm trying to tell you that the best thing would be to stop fighting it. It's not really so bad as you believe." Then his voice assumed a confidential, intimate tone as he advised, "Why don't you just drink some water and have it over with. You and your friend. You're torturing yourself needlessly over this matter."

"No, thanks, Doctor," Adam sighed. "As long as we're breathing, we'll fight it."

Orenson's voice sounded resigned. "Well, if that's your wish, it's your life and not mine. I was only trying to spare you the unnecessary torment of living left-handed in a right-handed world. It won't be pleasant, Adam, but I wish you good luck."

"Thanks, Doc," Adam said and hung up.

BRUCE BENDERSON

Kyle

Crusier Classics, 1975

Not all post-Stonewall pulps were interested in progressive, community-building politics. Once the idea of a vibrant gay movement came to fruition, many writers turned to deeper questions of psychology and emotion. How would the new culture of homosexual liberation shape a gay man's inner life?

Bruce Benderson's *Kyle* (1975) takes up these concerns: It is the spooky, unsettling story of a man's unsettling relationship with a boy whom he knew as a child, then tricks with as an adult, and who is also the famous western star Colin Pomeroy. But that is only part of the problem—"Kyle" seems to be everyone and no one at once; at times he denies who he is and shifts identities with disconcerting ease. Like Thomas Pynchon's V or Woody Allen's Zelig, Kyle seems, at times, hardly to exist.

Benderson is concerned with memory, desire, and illusion. Like many gay writers of the seventies, he is interested in disturbing the apparent stability of post-Stonewall gay life. Take, for instance, this Christmas party scene, in which four-year-old Kyle and Bruce are taken into their grandmother's bedroom:

With a surreptitious gesture she produced a small, pearl-handled revolver from a sequined evening purse. She tested the barrel to be absolutely sure that it was not loaded.

"Your grandfather don't like to let you play with this, honey. Don't tell him," said the old girl.

Kyle took the revolver without a word of thanks and began trying to pull the trigger while he caressed the pearl handle. His grandmother undressed him until he was naked against the rumpled silk sheets. Then she brought him a glass of milk, gave me my flannel pajamas to put on, and left us alone.

The rest of the evening floats in my memory intact, like an illuminated miniature. I remember Kyle lying naked against the white satin pillowcase, sucking on the glass of milk, while he played with the pearl-handled gun. He had regarded me through his heavy lashes. I had wondered about what there was about his sulky nakedness that seemed so complete.

"Bang, bang," he had said. He had not even bothered to point the gun directly at me. He had never been much for cops and robbers.

Then he had taken a drop of milk on his finger and touched it to his breast. It hung there on his tiny nipple. "Mommy lovths babyth milk," he had said.

I thought of his disconsolate mother sitting in the corner of the living room.

He let the gun rest on his chest and spread his arms apart. "Come, baby," he cooed probably to me, in a high tiny voice.

As evidenced by this selection, Benderson's writing is at once creepy and original. *Kyle* seems to have been clumsily edited by the publisher; there are many gaps in the narrative that make little sense. Even as it stands, however, it is an evocative piece of writing that is emblematic of a time and place.

Bruce Benderson is the author of the novels, stories, and essays *Meet Me at the Baths, The United Nations of Times Square, Pretending to Say No,* and *User.* He writes about the junkies, whores, and hustlers of New York's Times Square. His work has been praised by Manuel Puig, Dennis Cooper, and Hubert Selby Jr. He lives on New York's Lower East Side. *Kyle* is out of print.

In this selection, which occurs halfway through the novel, Bruce and Kyle are just finishing having sex, and Kyle, once again, makes a mysterious exit. Bruce, thinking that Kyle is headed for an assignation, decides to trap him in his lie only to find himself in a strange situation and no closer to the elusive Kyle than before.

Kyle thrust up into me, moving his ass off the floor, holding me by the hips. I watched his head tilt back, his mouth fall open. Then he lowered himself; and before I had a chance to catch my breath, thrust into me again with such force that we were both carried off the ground.

His hand moved to my pubic hair and seized it roughly. Holding me only by this, he jiggled my body vigorously up and down so that my throbbing hole worked against his cock. Then he took my cock and fucked it in his hand until I thought it would burst. He began to thrust into me with such force that I was thrown into the air, landing ever more firmly on his shaft. In and out he thrust, until I felt his charging cum fill me entirely, and I rode it like a hungry shark rides a wave, until my own cum met his boiling sand and I dissolved into a million tiny grains on his body.

Never before had I felt so completely possessed by Kyle. Without taking his cock out of my hole, I fell forward and wrapped my arms around his chest and shoulders, which were wet with perspiration. I thrust my grateful tongue into his open mouth.

"Let me sink into you forever," I managed to whisper; but I felt the muscles of his body tightening into the discrete identity of this world again, and his cock retreated from my hole. He pulled me gently off him.

"Lay with me," I begged.

Kyle was slipping into a pair of red bikini briefs. Then he took them off and put on black ones. He put on a pair of pale yellow slacks and a silky pale yellow shirt. "What are you doing?" I asked weakly.

Kyle was relaxed, fluid, unaware of my scathing need. "I feel like a butterfly tonight," he said. "I shall wear yellow. It looks so lovely and light outside." As he swept to the bathroom, the shirt billowed out behind him, and the light shone through it.

"Where are you going?" I called out.

He answered from the bathroom. "To the audition. How many times do I have to tell you!"

And then I heard the sound of tap water, which I augmented with my tears.

Why was I weeping? Kyle had done nothing to me. There was no real relationship between my fears and what was actually happening. A smothering, phantom jealousy had enfolded me. I wanted Kyle to be with me and he was going to one of his silly auditions that never came to anything anyway. Was he really going to an audition?

Searching for something tangible on which to leash my fears, my mind rested again on the matchbook collection. In the hysteria of my need, I manufactured Kyle's new lover from the last matchbook, the one marked Grasshopper. He was going to see him, I told myself. Yes, it was obvious. Wasn't that the latest matchbook in the collection? The whole thing began to twist into the mangled logic of my longing for complete possession of Kyle, the lost cousin of my past. Raising myself on one elbow, I made one last attempt.

"Don't go," I called weakly, but my voice was far from penetrating the noise of the water from the tap. In a few moments Kyle was out the front door with a fast good-bye flung over his shoulder.

At this point, listening to the steady drops from the hastily shut faucet, I fell completely, and the image of little cousin Kyle was obscured by something blacker. At this point my reason began to drown.

With curled, burning fingers I dug the pasteboard from the back of the closet. I seized the last matchbook, ripping it from the board.

"All these lovers," I muttered. I flung the thing back into the closet.

Under the word *Grasshopper* was an address. I took a taxi to it. I was going to beat Kyle and surprise him with his lover.

The Grasshopper was on Stevenson Street, and by the time the driver had found it, I had run up a large fare. This is because Stevenson Street is one-way the opposite way every other block. And it is for this reason that the Grasshopper chose this street to situate itself. It's not the kind of club which would want to make itself accessible to nice grandmothers from the Midwest. It's a tiny hole-in-the-wall next to a welfare hotel in the industrial section of the city. Inside, it is painted black and illuminated only by violet and green lights.

I was in such an emotional confusion when I walked in that I asked the man at the bar, "Are you the Grasshopper?" meaning to ask, *"Is this* the Grasshopper?"

To my surprise, he answered, "Yeah, I'm the Grasshopper. Why?" He was a mammoth, muscular brute, almost like the drawing on the matchbook.

I found my self unable to answer him. "Give me gin," I said breathlessly, "and tonic."

He tossed the ingredients together. Then he set the glass across from me with exaggerated care, letting his hand rest on it for too long a time. He stood watching me with a smile that looked slightly cruel at the corners of his mouth while I paid up.

A black curtain opened in the far wall. A black man in a black suit came out on a little wooden stage and said, "Tonight we have a special show for you. Sepia, 'the largest sequin in the world,' is appearing for your pleasure."

A green spotlight came from somewhere, and the black man was replaced by the largest dress in the world covered with gleaming green sequins. Soon my eyes were adjusted enough to the glare to let me know that I was watching an enormous drag queen in a red lacquered wig and gigantic, trembling rhinestone earrings. A pink carnation was pinned to the green-sequined dress. She began to speak toward me, or rather, her mouth began to move, and the words "Thank you. Thank you very much" came from a speaker on the opposite wall. Then there was the sound of applause. A fat lady's comedy routine came from the speaker and she began to mouth it, making jokes about her weight, pausing at the right places on the record, adding the appropriate gestures, and nodding at the recorded applause in between.

It was with consternation that I realized I was the only person besides the bartender in the audience. This condition continued until three Oriental men in identical suits entered, holding cameras. One of them approached the bartender.

"What'll ya have?" said the muscle man.

The Oriental man's face clouded over with confusion. "Gin," he said finally. "One, two, three. Three gin!"

The bartender made three gin and tonics. The man smilingly paid and took the drinks away. Now the fat drag queen began to alternate, sometimes playing her act to the three foreign tourists and sometimes to me.

I wondered why she felt it necessary to mouth a comedy routine. I knew that performing drag queens sometimes felt insecure about their singing voices but I had not known any of them were afraid to speak. With anxiety the fantasy came to me that she had no voice except those borrowed from records. The fantasy was augmented by the reaction of the three Oriental tourists. It was obvious that they spoke little English and did not understand the comedy album; but they knew when to laugh because it was clearly marked by the audience reaction on the record.

The Orientals laughed and applauded politely at each interval. I began to wonder if *their* reactions were recorded also, and if they were merely mouthing their laughter. I became irrationally afraid, and focusing my mind on the image of Kyle, I saw it melting into his image as a four-year-old, which finally retreated from me altogether.

"Are you all set?" It was the voice of the bartender standing near me, but I could have sworn it was not exactly synchronized to the movement of his lips. In consternation I turned to look at the loudspeaker behind me. His hand was on my arm.

"I said are you all set?" The bartender was speaking to me. He let his hand rest on my wrist. Immediately I thought of the drawing on the matchbook cover, and with this thought I was reminded of my mission to find Kyle.

"Have you see Kyle?" I said.

Suddenly a needle scrape came from the loudspeaker as the record ended in the middle of the routine. The female impersonator was left on stage, bowing in confusion. The Oriental tourists applauded as she made her exit with difficulty.

The bartender was very close to me now. He peered down the length of my seated body. "Don't remember any Kyle," he said. "Supposed to meet him here?"

"Maybe."

"Hmmm. Full of mystery. How'd you know I was the Grasshopper?"

Paranoia begets craftiness. My imagined loss of Kyle and the fantasy that he was meeting someone here had turned me into a crackerjack detective. "I've heard of you," I said, leaning toward him.

He seemed pleased. "Oh, yeah, and what have you heard."

"Sure you don't know any Kyle?"

"Can't remember. Don't know everybody's name who comes in here."

"You'd remember this one."

He raised his eyebrows. "What he tell you about me?"

"Said you knew how," I said ambiguously, grasping for strategy.

"Oh yeah? Likes that kind of thing, huh?"

I wasn't quite sure what he was referring to. "Yeah," I said.

"What about you?"

"Sure," I said. "Where do you think I could find this Kyle?"

"Maybe at my house. Who knows?" said the Grasshopper, laughing. "That is, if you wanna come."

I nodded.

He poured me a thick green liquid. "Chartreuse," he said. "On the house."

Along with one emaciated go-go boy and two other drag queens, I saw the comedy act of the largest sequin in the world four more times before closing time rolled around. Then the muscular bartender led me to a green sports car and we sped to an unfamiliar suburb of the city. He lived in a little white storybook house with a green picket fence, but inside, the storybook flavor was turned topsy-turvy.

"What are these?" I said, studying the series of black-and-white photos on the wall.

"Photography's kind of my hobby," said the Grasshopper.

The pictures were pornographic and poetic at the same time—and bizarre. Beautiful naked men in costumes of animals, birds, and insects doing sexually submissive things. One of them, in a feathered and sequined outfit like a bird, was tied by his arms to a perch. Another, wearing a dog's tail, dog's ears, and a furry blouse, was being whipped by a naked young man while his helper fucked the boy-dog in the ass. Most bizarre of all was a portrait of a naked boy in great pain, covered with bleeding bites. Behind his shoulder stood the bartender with the black mask of a fly, sporting antennae, conical eyes, and black fangs.

I moved toward the door, but the Grasshopper had thrust another glass of Chartreuse into my hands. "Where's Kyle?" I asked.

"Huh? Kyle? I told you I never heard of him."

"But you said he was at your house."

"I was only joking." He ran his fingers through my hair and held me by the scruff of the neck. He began to lead me toward another room.

"This really isn't my scene," I said.

"Oh yeah," he said, becoming annoyed, "that why you waited until we were all the way out here to tell me?"

He pulled me roughly toward him. His shirt had come unbuttoned, exposing his enormous pectorals. He held me by the hair. He was several inches taller than me. "Get in there!" he said. "I've got just the costume for you."

He opened the door and shoved me into a tiny green room. There were all sorts of costumes hanging up on the walls. Before I could examine them he opened the door of a little green iron cage and threw me inside. I rattled the bars. "Let me out of here! Are you crazy?"

"In a minute I will," he said. "Don't play so innocent."

He was right. Had I really expected to find Kyle here?

The Grasshopper returned with a bundle under his arms. He let himself quickly into the cage and shut it behind him. I cowered in the corner.

"This won't hurt yet," he said.

Forcefully he stripped me of my clothes and tossed them into the corner. Then he put a pair of brown rabbit-skin leggings on me, with the ass and crotch cut out. With elastic he fastened a little white cotton tail above my ass and some long brown ears to my head. He pulled my cock and balls so that they hung over the furry edge of the leggings.

"There, I knew you'd make a good rabbit." He let himself quickly out of the cage.

Presently he returned in a costume that took the breath out of me. His body was naked except for a thick belt of brown feathers about his waist. He was enormous, with granite arms as powerful as a blacksmith's. His body tapered at the waist and then flared out into bulging, boulderlike thighs. His ass looked as if it had been sculpted out of enormous blocks of marble. His head atop powerful shoulders was concealed by the mask of a hawk, which had been executed with much attention to detail. It had a large curved beak of yellow ivory and tiny slits for his eyes with yellow glass hawk's eyes pasted above. He was wearing yellow hawk's feet with enormous black claws attached.

I gasped and cowered against the rear wall of the cage, covering my face. "Please—no."

But the Grasshopper had shed language with his clothes. Only a rustling sound, laughter like dried leaves, came from within the mask. His cock had swollen to an enormous size.

He stepped into the cage and slammed it shut. Then he came up to me and grabbed the rabbit ears. The strong elastic strained against my chin.

When I reached up to try to pull it away from my face he grabbed my wrists in one strong hand and held them over my head. My kicking feet slipped out from under me and into the air. He lay me on the ground and put one clawed foot on my cock and balls.

"No—no—please," I begged.

He poked a claw between my thighs. Then he grabbed me by the ears again and raised my head. He pulled my head to his erect member. Desire augmented my fear. I opened up to him as he rammed his cock down my throat. It filled me completely, choking me.

Finally he stood me up and held me by the waist. Lifting me into the air so that I was bent over his arm, he began to rub the crack of my ass with his thumb. When he found the opening of my asshole his thumb slid rudely in, parting me abruptly.

His thumb was like a cock inside me, and he began to work it around my asshole in a circular motion, readying its path for the charge of his enormous cock.

Meanwhile, he held me in the air. My kicking legs only served to allow him further entrance into the hole. I began to feel actually like a helpless animal under the power of some superior animal. I imagined the ludicrous figure I cut, held almost upside down in the air by this enormous man, with my rabbit ears pointed down and the cotton tail above my hole twitching in apprehension.

Finally, he lowered me to the floor and turned me over on my back. He held my ankles through the leggings in each of his hands and spread my legs way over my head.

Without bothering to lubricate either his tool or my hole, he positioned the enormous strawberry head. Then he thrust and I was parted completely. I felt as if I had been cleaved in two. Yellow stars filled my head like grains of spilled powder. I felt myself losing consciousness.

His second thrust sent me surging back to myself in a spin. "Stop!" I screamed. "Please! You're too big!"

The waves of sharp pain moved into my thighs as his efforts redoubled. He pinned my legs over my head until I was nearly flattened out double-jointed, and he plunged into me over and over.

When he had fucked me for a while, and my hole had adjusted to his enormous member, no longer offering any resistance, he grew tired of his efforts and pulled out of me. He held my shoulders pinned to the floor and let my legs down.

Before I had time to catch much breath he had parted the cheeks of his ass with his hands and sat on me. He bore down on my face until I thought he would crush it. I could hear him gasping sharply above, hear his hand slapping his own enormous member as he forced my lips and teeth into his hole. He spread his ass cheeks and pressed against me until I thought my whole head would be swallowed by his asshole. In the frenzy of his efforts he grabbed my erect cock and squeezed it with his strong fingers.

Finally he stood me up. I backed against the wall of the cage. He came toward me. He held his erect tool in his hand.

"I've had enough," I gasped. "Please."

My tool, however, was still thrusting upwards, rigid between my legs. He was watching it with his hawk's eyes.

I prayed, begged heaven, that he would at least speak. I could not stand the sight of the silent, staring animal face, the rigid claws. I wanted him to perforate the illusion with the sound of a human voice. Apparently, he was aware of the effect of not speaking. I heard only his rasping breath through the large curved beak of the mask.

The creature moved toward me. I shut my eyes tight. I felt a warm liquid dousing my face and trickling down my chest. Then I felt the tip of his cock against my closed lips. I opened my eyes and pushed his pissing cock away from my face, but he thrust a thumb between my lips and with the fingers of the other hand yanked my jaws apart. Then he thrust his cock deep into my throat.

In order to keep from choking to death, I had to swallow the warm liquid that filled my throat. I was swallowing his piss!

He leaned into me until he had emptied a good part of his bladder. Then he held me by the hair and withdrew his cock.

He turned me around and pressed me against the bars of the cage. The flat metal poles cut into the flesh of my chest. Holding me by the armpit with one hand, he moved my hips up with the other hand to gain access to my ass. He put the tip of his cock into my hole and thrust it up me. This time I opened to him without resistance and fell limply against the bars of the cage. A strange sensation traveled up my spine. I felt as if my flesh were turning into warm water.

I realized that he was pissing inside of me. The warmth was almost a soothing sensation after the brutality of his previous thrusts.

I let him fill my hole with piss. He was moaning in a swoon. But now, just as I had let myself relax, he began to thrust in and out of me again, as if he wished to mangle me against the bars of the cage. The entire cage began to rock in the rhythm of his movements and I let out pitiful moanings.

In an effort to relax completely, which I knew would be the only way to absorb the violence of his thrusts, I let myself go completely limp. The muscles of my bladder let my own piss move to the head of my penis, and now I felt it trickle in a thin stream down my legs.

As soon as the Grasshopper became aware of this, he pulled out of me and turned me toward him. He held his hand under my cock and caught a palmful of piss. Quickly he moved his hand under the mask. I heard him sucking the liquid greedily into his mouth. Dazedly I pissed all over his body. It covered his stomach and moved down his thighs in long trickles. This only increased his excitement.

He turned his back to me, reached behind him, and grabbed me by the hips. Bending slightly over, he took my cock and positioned it over his own hole. Holding my cock in his fist, he rubbed the head around his asshole, lubing it with the drops of piss which remained. Then he stuck the head of my cock in his asshole.

He put his hand around my buttocks and pulled me into him. I slid in to the hilt. He held me there for a second. The warmth and moisture of his slippery hole seemed to penetrate my cock and travel into the root of my spine until I thought I would turn to liquid and flow into his body. My thighs were pressed against his buttocks. My balls were crushed against the backs of his thighs.

He took four fingers and inserted them into my asshole. Boosting me onto my toes by the pressure of his fingers in my hole alone, he moved me even further against him. I was afraid that his four fingers would cleave my ass apart. To escape from those fingers, I pressed up against him until the bones in my groin made an indentation in the cheeks of his ass.

My balls had fallen between his open thighs. He pressed the thighs together suddenly and caught my balls between them. He increased the pressure, squeezing my balls until I began to groan and I thought they would burst between his legs.

Meanwhile, he had tensed the muscles of his asshole and gripped my cock in a vise of fire. He began flexing his sphincter, milking my cock so that the cum was drawn painfully toward the tip. I could not shoot a load, however. There was no room to shoot inside his ass, because the muscles gripped me with so much tension.

Finally, he let up a little and I began to thrust in and out of him. To increase the strength of my inward thrusts, he kept the four fingers in my ass so that he could pull me against him. Then he would let up with the fingers until my cock had withdrawn to the tip, and suddenly, the four fingers would bear down in my asshole again and thrust me against him.

I held his stomach in my hand and my nails dug into it. Soon I grabbed his balls and began pulling them away from his thighs, squeezing them in my hands. I thrust into him as hard as I could, as eager to move up the tract of his asshole as to escape his digging fingers in my ass. I grabbed his cock and yanked it as if I would rip it from his body. He bellowed in pain, but only sent his ass harder against my groin.

I pumped harder and harder into him, throwing my lesser body against his larger bulk. I felt my cum gathering in my balls like licking flames. Then it swelled up into the root of my penis and traveled in a thin burning line to the tip. I began hitting his chest, his armpits, his stomach, with my clenched fist, screaming and cursing as my cock charged into his asshole.

Finally with open hand, I gave his erect cock and hanging balls sharp, quick slaps from the side. Each time his member bounced back from a blow, I hit it again.

He was gasping, almost screaming high in his throat when I felt my cum spurting into him. As it hit his asshole he moved against me in spasms, his ass muscles clenching and unclenching to be sure to milk the cock of every drop. Finally, his hand curled around my thigh and caught my balls through the backs of my thighs. He squeezed them and yanked on them as my cock finished spurting into his body.

I was finished. I crumbled to the floor behind him.

But he was not finished. He stood over me holding his hard pulsing member in his hand. He lifted me by the rabbit ears and brought my mouth to his cock. I was filled with a wave of nausea and exhaustion.

"N-no . . . ," I said.

In the fury of his passion he held the back of my neck and pulled me roughly against his tool. I held my mouth tightly shut. He started to pull my jaw open. I spun away from him and crawled to the other side of the cage.

He came up to me and turned me on my back with one of the mammoth clawed feet. He placed the foot on my stomach. One of the claws pointed toward my groin. Its claw touched the head of my penis.

Pinning my shoulders down, he spread his legs and kneeled over me. The hanging balls hit my chin. The head of the enormous cock butted my lips. Still I kept my lips tightly shut.

He sat on my chest. I felt the backs of his thighs loosen as did the muscles of his buttocks. With some effort he produced a feeble trickle of piss. It hit my lips and rolled down to my chin.

Finally the Grasshopper removed the mask. The face was florid and sweating underneath. The dark hair was tousled, the black eyes hard and glittering and watery.

"Listen," he said in a voice that was almost a growl, "I don't like it when my tricks quit after they come. I always come too."

A wave of resentment against him rose within me. I compressed my lips tighter and moved my head to the side. He laid a stinging blow against my face with his open palm. Then he hoisted me to my feet and threw me to the ground again, this time facedown. He pulled my thighs apart and lay down on top of me.

He was going to fuck me for the third time. I didn't know if I could take it.

"Motherfucker," he said.

Before I knew it I felt the hot member parting me. It lunged deep into my asshole and forced my thighs apart. An unusual burning sensation originated at my asshole and traveled in waves up my back.

He encircled my chest with his arms and took each of my nipples in thumb and forefinger. Then he pinched them until I thought the blood would burst through. His mouth, now free of the restraints of the mask, took my ear whole. Then the teeth began to pierce the lobe. I moaned, struggling, but he fastened his mouth to my neck and sunk his teeth in.

Now I could feel his loosely hanging balls slapping my thighs. His thrusts pressed my body against the floor with such force that my ribs were bruised. His mouth moved to my mouth. He bit my lip until I tasted blood.

To increase the friction around his cock, he moved my legs together and thrust back and forth in the sheath of my flesh. I could feel every inch of his enormous member as it slid out almost to the tip and then came traveling back to the hilt with renewed fury. I felt the waves of blackness rising in my head and belly again. I let my head fall to the floor and stretched my arms straight out above it. I prayed that it would end soon.

But it went on and on; the thrusts becoming wilder and wilder. Soon he held my hips in his hands and rocked them forwards and back, so that my hipbones grazed the floor with each thrust and my knees knocked against it. Then his rhythm became spasmodic. He began to lunge in and out of me with no conscious control. The penis vibrated wildly against the interior of my asshole. I felt the hot liquid filling me. He spurted and spurted, lunging violently into me; and when I thought he had finished coming he began to spurt again and fell into a frenzy, moving against my body as he growled and whined low in his throat.

Finally it was over. His enormous weight lay on me, pinning me to the floor, the tool still hard in my burning asshole. Then he yanked it out and stood up. He hoisted me to my knees. He thrust his cock in my face.

"Clean it off," he said.

I licked the swollen member clean of come, mucus, and shit.

He ripped my costume off me. "Fold it up nicely," he said. Apparently that was a part of my role in the ritual. He tossed me my clothes and walked out of the cage.

I lay on the ground, trying to raise myself on one elbow. The slightest movement sent sharp pains through my burning asshole. I felt as if he were still in me. I managed to fold up the costume and pull my clothes on. I was reaching for my shirt when my gaze swept past one of the photographs on the wall of the room. It was a color photograph of Kyle. Naked, except for two gigantic butterfly wings attached to his shoulders, he was caught struggling in a giant net. His hair was very short and very blond. Two tiny, iridescent wings were attached to either side of his hanging cock.

The Grasshopper came back into the room, zipping his pants. "Kyle," I said. I rushed to the picture, separated from it by the green bars of the cage.

"Kyle."

"Who?" said the Grasshopper. "I told you I don't know him."

VICTOR JAY

The Gay Haunt

Traveller's Companion, 1970

The impact of the Stonewall riots could be felt on the world of gay pulps. Because the turnaround time on writing and production was so swift, it was possible to include changes in the world of politics soon after they happened. By 1970, some pulps were mentioning the Gay Liberation Movement, and in 1971 Richard Amory's *Frost* was dedicated to "my brothers and sisters in the San Jose Gay Liberation Front."

New venues and publishing opportunities also opened up. Olympia Press had always welcomed gay material (their Paris imprint published *The Gaudy Image* in 1958), but their New York imprint, which began in 1967, had hardly published any books with primary gay content. But between 1970 and 1973 Olympia's Traveller's Companion series issued fifteen gay male erotic novels that were up to the usually high standards of the press. Olympia Press was a step up for gay erotic publishing. Authors had more control over their work; the books were sold in bookstores, not just newsstands; and most important, the books were treated with respect by both critics and readers. What would have been sold as porn from the pulp factories in California now became literature (or, at least, classy erotica).

Another difference was length. The average gay pulp novel ran between forty thousand to forty-five thousand words. A novel in the Traveller's Companion series could run up to sixty-five thousand words, giving the author space to actually develop plot, characters, and ideas. Olympia Press also prided itself on its literary excellence. The back cover copy of Amory's *Frost*, for instance, ends with a nod to Chaucer's Nun's Priest by adding, "Amor Vincit Omnia— eventually!"

Victor Jay's *The Gay Haunt* flaunts its literary antecedents. It's a witty social comedy about a gay man who tries to advance his career by marrying the boss's daughter, only to discover that the ghost of his late boyfriend has other plans. Gay readers of the time would quickly have recognized that Jay was drawing on both Thorne Smith's enormously popular 1926 novel, *Topper* (later made into a film and then a television series), and Noël Coward's 1941 play, *Blithe Spirit*. Both are noted artifacts of gay male culture that feature ghosts who come back to get involved in the sexual activities of the living. (They are, in fact, the specters of queerness in a heterosexual world.) Jay draws his basic plot from the Coward play, in which the spirit of the late wife wants to ruin her former husband's marriage, but takes his tone from *Topper*, where the ghosts are a fun-loving, madcap couple who decide that the stodgy, conventional protagonist needs some loosening up. Jay's hero gets loosened up so much that he even enjoys a little sex with women, something he was not looking forward to in his impending marriage.

Victor Jay is the pseudonym of Victor J. Banis, who also wrote under the names of Don Holliday, J. X. Williams, Lynn Benedict, and Jan Alexander. Banis was one of the marvels of pulp publishing and penned an enormous volume of work. He published three other gay pulp novels as Victor Jay, sixteen as Don Holliday, and seven as J. X. Williams. He also wrote scores of heterosexual pulps.

Paul, the protagonist of *The Gay Haunt*, is about to marry the boss's daughter, only to be sidetracked by his late lover, Lorin (as well as several other very alive men). In these chapters Paul has just finished having sex with Don (his future wife's cousin) when Lorin drops in. Within a short time, things get even more complicated.

Chapter 14

M̲y, you are the hot one," Don said when I released him from a long, torrid kiss.

"You ain't seen nothing yet," I warned him. "Let's get out of these clothes, okay?"

He cast a glance in the direction of the door. "Maybe we ought to leave the clothes on, in case anyone comes in. That can be embarrassing. I wouldn't want anyone to think I came here just to trick."

I flipped the lock on the door. "No intruders, okay?"

"Well . . ." He still looked a little hesitant. I came back to where he was standing and kissed him again, running my hands over the full little mounds of his ass. That, apparently, was where the switch was hidden. "All right," he said brightly, wriggling against me.

I gave his butt a smack. "Out of the clothes," I said. Naked I felt I had a better chance of keeping him here. Lorin was one of the few people I had known who went around crowded rooms naked. I was hoping Don was a little more modest.

I was already undressed by the time he had shed his briefs. He looked quite delectable, in fact, so the effort I was making was not merely a matter of caution. As for my fears about taking Margo's cousin to bed, they no longer seemed valid, since he thought we had done it already.

We kissed again, and I fell backward, taking him with me to the bed. I rolled him over and inserted a tongue in his ear, making him squeal. His naked flesh felt like velvet to my roaming hands. This was altogether a pleasant task I had set myself.

We rolled onto our sides, facing one another. He pulled slightly away from me and slid downward, working his way down to my crotch. My cock was certainly more than ready for him by the time he got there. I gasped with excitement as he clasped it and brought his mouth to the head; the lips slipped warmly over it. He sucked it deep into his throat.

I scrambled around on the bed, careful not to interfere with what he was doing, and managed to get into a sixty-nine position. His own cock tasted sweet and young and altogether delicious. I sucked on it hungrily, my nose buried in his balls. I had a splendid view of his ass, with its dimpled cheeks and the soft inviting valley between. I cupped my hands over the soft mounds, massaging them lightly. He pushed back gently against my hands.

I pressed him forward slightly, rolling over again until he was above me and I was on my back. I licked at his dangling balls and then began to work my way beyond, pulling his cheeks apart as I licked my way upward. My tongue reached the core and he sighed happily, pushing back against my face.

I slid back, between his legs, and got to my knees behind him. It was just too good not to crawl into. I didn't need any lubricant either. The spit he had gotten on my prick and the spit I had left on his ass were all that was necessary. I brought the head to his hole and worked it carefully in. He bent further, lifting his ass up, to make the entry easier for me.

He was hot and tight, clinging to my rod as I thrust in. I paused, waiting until I felt the muscles relax slightly, then going a little deeper.

"Oh, give it to me," he murmured, wriggling his little ass slightly.

I did. I drove it home, filling his ass with eager cock. He welcomed it greedily, groaning with pleasure as he sat back on it. It went in to the hilt, the entire shaft disappearing as his ass brushed my balls. It was sheer heaven! No wonder Lorin had had such a pleasant time!

Fucking Don, however, got progressively wilder. It was somewhat akin to riding a bucking bronco. He was certainly not the sort to just sit or kneel there while you poked. He began to swing his hips, gyrating them much as he had done when we were dancing. My thrusts were almost unnecessary. He bounced and bobbed and twisted and writhed, and my cock kept feeling harder and bigger and hotter until it was close to exploding. We were both sweating, our bodies making little slapping sounds as they came together.

It was not long before I felt that familiar, delightful ache in my balls. Deep down inside me a knot of tension was beginning to grow. It swelled, seeming to fill me entirely, and then it was rushing down and out, erupting into the hot receptacle of his ass, and I was clinging fiercely to him, groaning and gasping for breath.

It took several long seconds to regain my senses. Finally, reluctantly, I slid my prick from the still-tight opening. I pushed him down on the bed and reached for his cock. It felt wet and sticky to my grasp.

"I'll bring you off," I said, lowering my head toward him.

"Not necessary," he whispered.

"Of course it is. Fair is fair."

"Not necessary," he repeated. "I already came. While you were fucking me."

I felt more carefully. He wasn't kidding. I had heard of guys who got so excited getting fucked that they shot without anything more being needed, but this was the first time it had ever happened with me. With Lorin a little hand action had been employed if we wanted to come together.

"Well, I'll be damned," I said. I fell back on the bed and gave his ass a pat. "You're pretty good."

"So are you," he said. After a pause, he added, "you know, I wish Lorin had been with us. I've never had a three-way, but with you and him I'll bet it would be fun."

I sat up on the bed. "Look, about this Lorin business," I said, measuring my words carefully. "I think you had better forget all about what you told me."

"What's that?" he asked.

"About seeing Lorin. People will think you were drunk, if they're being kind, or maybe even crazy."

"Why?" he wanted to know.

"Because," I said again. "Lorin is dead. He is six feet under the ground."

"Tosh," Lorin said, popping into view. "I may be three sheets to the wind, but that's all."

"You see," Don said, giving me a triumphant look. "I told you." He seemed quite unperturbed by Lorin's unusual manner of entrance.

"I thought we had an agreement—" I said angrily to Lorin.

"He's already seen me tonight," Lorin interrupted. "So it seems pointless to keep hiding from him. Anyway, we met before."

"Five years ago," Don said.

"More recently than that," Lorin said. "At Paul's. That was me in bed with you."

"You?" Don's eyes widened in surprise. He looked at me, then Lorin, and back to me. "Well, isn't that funny? I was wondering why your cock wasn't as big."

"I didn't hear you complaining," I said, vaguely offended. I couldn't see any necessity for telling him all this.

"He's been telling everyone you were dead," Don said to Lorin.

"Well, I am, sort of," Lorin explained. "But it's really all very complicated, and I don't know that anything is going to be accomplished by going into it. Why don't we just agree that this will be a secret between the three of us, and that will be that?"

"Sure thing," Don said brightly. "As long as a guy is groovy and good in bed, what do I care about his background or where he comes from?"

"That's the spirit," Lorin said. He turned to me, obviously intending to charm me into a better humor. "See, everything is fine."

"I'm not sure." I leaned a little closer and peered at him. "You're drunk. I didn't think ghosts got that way."

"No law against it. And you're a fine one to talk."

He was right, I was squiffed too, and feeling it more than ever, having burned off a little energy with Don. "I suppose we should have some coffee," I said.

"Like hell," Lorin replied. "I've worked too hard to get this way. Honestly, every time I'd get a drink mixed, somebody would come along and take it right out of my hand."

"Besides," Don chimed in, "why go to all the trouble of getting that way just to not be?" He frowned as a new thought crossed what for want of better description could be termed his mind. "Only, what will we drink? There's nothing in here."

Lorin gave a wave of his hand. "There is now," he said. A magnum of champagne and three glasses appeared on the dresser.

"I thought you waved wands to do that sort of thing," I said. "Or is that for fairy dragmothers?"

"If I waved my wand, it would come," Lorin said. "I haven't had anything tonight, and I got awfully horny watching you two guys."

"That's no problem," Don said quickly.

"A child after my own heart," Lorin said.

"It's not your heart he's after," I offered.

"But first," Lorin said, ignoring my comment, "a glass of the bubbly." He poured the sparkling liquid into the three glasses and handed them around. I figured, what the hell, and emptied my glass. Lorin filled it again almost at once.

"Gee," Don said, sighing happily and looking from one to the other of us. "All we need now is a roaring fire in the fireplace."

"That's very simple," Lorin said, weaving a little unsteadily. He was obviously having a grand time showing off. Of course, I had not been very appreciative of these stunts since he came back, so it was logical he would delight in having a better audience. "Fire is something of a specialty where I come from."

He waved his hands again without even looking from the champagne he was pouring. A warm blaze appeared at the wall behind him. I emptied my glass again and lay back on the bed. Sometimes it's wisest not to argue with the fates. I couldn't at the moment rid myself of either of them, so I might as well relax and enjoy them.

"To love," Lorin said in the way of a toast, lifting his glass in what I considered a rather flashy gesture.

Don lifted his in return. "I never met a man I didn't love," he said, finishing off the golden liquid in one fell swoop.

Lorin came closer and filled my glass again. I tried, and confirmed that one cannot drink lying down. I sat up and lifted the glass to my lips.

I didn't drink, however. The flicker of flames beyond Lorin caught my attention. My first thought was that Elliot had one huge fireplace in his bedroom. Then I remembered what should have occurred to me before—Elliot didn't have a fireplace in his bedroom. And Lorin hadn't thought to conjure up one to go with the fire. As a result, half the room was now ablaze.

Chapter 15

Lorin!" I cried, pointing.

He turned and saw the fire. "Well, for heaven's sake, what happened there?"

"It's that damn fire you started," I said. "There was no fireplace there."

"Never occurred to me," Lorin said, looking thoughtfully at the flames licking up to the ceiling.

"Well, don't just stand there staring," I cried. "Put the damn thing out!"

"I don't know how," he said.

"What?"

"Where I come from, we learn to start them. There's never any reason to extinguish them."

The noises of the party, which I had thought were getting unusually loud, were a roar now, and I realized that the fire was the general topic of discussion. Somewhere in the distance, but growing louder, I recognized the sound of a fire siren.

"Where are our clothes?" I asked gruffly, getting off the bed.

"I put them all on the chair," Don said.

"I don't see any chair," I said, looking around.

"It was over there," Don explained, pointing to where the fire burned brightest.

"I don't know why you're worrying about clothes," Lorin said. "It seems plenty warm in here. I was glad to get rid of mine again."

He was naked once again by this time. That, however, was not much of a consolation. "You realize," I said, "that we could be burned alive."

"In my case, that would be difficult."

"Don and I could end up joining you," I said.

"That wouldn't be so bad," he said, screwing up his face thoughtfully. "I mean, we do make an attractive threesome, and we could have such fun."

"Lorin!" I snapped.

"Oh, all right, if you're going to be fussy about it." He looked annoyed. "There's a window over there, and a fire escape outside."

"I don't suppose you could produce some clothes for us, could you?" I asked. The closet was unreachable by this time, and the bedroom was like an inferno. But I was nonetheless a little reluctant to go running out dressed as we were.

"I think you both look lovely," Lorin said.

"God damn it, I don't feel lovely," I said, not caring if I hurt his feelings. The fire was hurting my feet. "Get me some clothes, right now, or I'll report you as a failure as a spirit."

"All right, all right, don't get all uptight. Honestly!" He made a movement of his hand and stamped his foot twice. There was suddenly a beaded evening gown on the bed before me.

"What in the name of heaven is this?" I demanded, holding it up for inspection. It looked like a Salvation Army reject.

"You seemed in such a hurry I didn't take time to shop around," Lorin explained.

"I think it's gorgeous," Don said, taking it and fingering the material.

"You wear it then," I said, yanking a blanket off the bed and wrapping it around me. The window was stuck. I had to take one of the pillows to it and knock the glass out.

"Careful," I warned the others, climbing through with my blanket tucked about my legs.

Don actually had taken time to put on the gown. It looked more than a little weird; even if it had been a lovely gown, and he a qualified drag queen, it would have looked strange without wig, makeup, shoes, or any such garnishes.

"You really aren't going down on the street with that on?" I asked.

"It's chilly out here," he said, lifting his skirts.

The fire escape was over an alley. Below we could see a part of the street, looking like a beehive of activity. Red lights flashed on and off, sirens still wailed, and over it all was the hubbub of countless voices. I felt more than a little silly in a blanket, accompanied by one naked man and another in a beaded gown, but the only alternative was remaining where we were, which could mean being burned alive.

"Let's go," I muttered, starting down. Don followed close at my heels, taking pains not to trip over his skirt, and Lorin trailed, seemingly in no particular hurry, although of course he was in no particular danger. Being dead has its advantages, that was plain.

I had hoped we might escape detection, but there was just too much going on below, and too many people. And we were a conspicuous trio. Fortunately Lorin remained behind me so that, surprisingly enough, Don and I got most of the attention.

Perhaps the greatest irony of all was that by the time we got to the street, sticking as close to the walls as possible for shelter, most of the excitement was over.

"It's all under control," one woman assured me. "Fire's practically out. They're looking for the damage now."

I was wondering if we couldn't possibly go back up the fire escape and avoid the embarrassment of a frontal entrance, when Lorin gave my blanket a tug.

"Look," he said, pointing.

I looked, but saw nothing unusual—nothing unusual, that is, at the site of the fire. There were crowds, mostly in the other direction, and a hook and ladder truck parked at the curb, apparently not needed.

"I don't see anything but a fire truck," I said.

"That's it," he said. "I've always wanted to drive one. I didn't dare before, I was afraid I'd get killed. But now I don't have to worry. Come on, let's go for a ride."

"Are you crazy?" I asked, staring wide-eyed. "Maybe you can't get killed, but I can."

"Oh, that's what's wrong with you, Paul, always nitpicking." He was already headed toward the truck. "I'm going for a ride. Anyone who wants to join me climb aboard. Don, how about you?"

"It sounds scary," he said. A smile flitted across his features. "But it sounds like fun too. Wait for me."

Everybody of course was paying attention to the apartment building. No one noticed Lorin, naked as a jaybird, helping Don, in his beaded gown, onto the truck.

"You can't drive this thing alone," I yelled. "It takes two people to drive one of these jobs. One up front and one back here."

"Well, what are you standing there for?" Lorin yelled back, already at the wheel. He waved his hand and I was suddenly sans blanket. I threw a hand over my cock and looked around for some place to hide. The truck was the nearest place. I made a jump for it just as it started to roll.

Someone shouted and I blinked. I suppose I had thought someone might manage to stop Lorin, or perhaps he was only kidding, or perhaps he might not even know how to get it started. But before I could even reconsider and jump off, the siren suddenly split the air and we were roaring away with more speed than I would have thought the mammoth machine capable of.

"Lorin!" I shouted at the top of my lungs, clinging frantically to a handle of some sort or other and aware that, bare-assed, I was not only conspicuous but a damn good target if anyone decided to shoot.

He shouted something back. It sounded like "Steer the back end!" We were roaring down the street, siren screaming. For the moment he was all right, although the rear end was weaving back and forth dangerously. But he'd never get this beast around a corner without some help back here, and if he piled up now, I had more to lose than he did. I swallowed, and scrambled up to the seat and the extra wheel positioned back there to take care of the wide-swinging rear.

In his own way, Lorin could be quite thoughtful. A big tumbler filled with champagne suddenly appeared on a tray before me. I took the glass and the tray disappeared. The champagne helped with the fluttering in my stomach. I didn't mind at all when it refilled itself. Ahead of me I could see Lorin's naked back. Don was standing, silvery gown fluttering behind him, and hanging out one side.

Behind us there was a considerable uproar. People had shouted as we went away, but by now there were other sirens and red lights roaring away from the curb in hot pursuit.

"Lorin," I screamed, not at all sure he could hear me. "They're after us."

He decided, apparently, that they would have to catch us first. I tried to sit down, but the combination of cool night air and leather did not make the seat comfortable. I jumped when my balls touched the cold seat, and sent the back end of the truck sweeping wide to the left.

"Easy," I told myself, bringing it back in line. I wondered helplessly if there were some way of stopping my half without bothering the front end, but I wasn't sure enough to risk anything.

We were suddenly taking a corner. I put all the muscle I could into the huge wheel before me. Somehow the rear end managed to get around the corner as well. I was so engrossed in that concern that it was a moment or so before I realized that we were on the Sunset Strip. Of course, with the sirens and lights going, the traffic was no problem.

But the Strip was always crowded, with everything from hippies to Midwest tourists. And even in that exotic scene we were a striking sight, two of us naked and one more or less in drag. Lorin was brandishing a champagne glass as though blessing the crowds. Someone cheered and I toasted him with my glass as we swept past. I tried keeping a hand over my crotch, but found that impossible without spilling my champagne, which I felt increasingly important.

I looked over my shoulder. The police and fire vehicles were a veritable parade in hot pursuit, and gaining rapidly on us. I tried shouting at Lorin, and signaling, but he had chosen to ignore me for a time, basking as he was in the glow of considerable attention, which had always delighted him.

He suddenly gave me a signal for another turn, and almost before I knew what was happening we were screeching around another corner, the rear end swinging wide as I fought to keep it under some kind of control. I hadn't even begun to establish any such control when Lorin was taking us around yet another corner, this one looking altogether too small for the truck to fit into. It was an alley, in fact; I realized he was trying to dodge our pursuers, although the idea of hiding a multi-ton fire truck seemed rather far-fetched to my way of thinking. But of course, I reckoned without Lorin's talents, those that he had acquired in the last five years. I looked back to see that the entrance to the alley was a solid wall of rosebushes and trellises, hiding us from view. Sirens shrieked and lights flashed through the growth as the chasing vehicles went racing by.

I let out the breath I had been holding, as nearly as I could calculate, since we left the apartment building. Lorin was already scrambling down the front end.

"Better move," he yelled. "They'll be back in a minute."

"Where would you suggest we go?" I called back. "I'm going to look a little conspicuous on the Strip."

"Move up in the world," he called. He worked the appropriate switches to send the huge ladder suddenly climbing upward.

"I will not," I said. I had no intention of perching atop a ladder until discovered by the police, and unless I wanted to break into one of the apartments in the building beside me, I couldn't see that the ladder was going to take me anywhere.

The sirens were suddenly growing louder again. The police were coming back. Lorin was right, of course; in a minute or so they would discover the hidden alley.

I looked back to where Lorin had been, but he and Don had disappeared. I looked around frantically. One side of the alley was a high wall which I had little chance of getting over and which apparently only bordered a parking lot anyway. The other side of the alley was a line of apartment buildings. I ran to the one nearest me, trying a door that apparently led to laundry facilities. It was locked.

Up seemed the logical direction after all. Maybe I could find an empty apartment and borrow some clothes. Without clothes it mattered little which way I went, I was bound to stand out like a sore thumb.

I looked up. One window on the fourth floor was open and dark. It offered the best possibilities. I guided the ladder as close to it as I was able in my inexperience and began to climb hastily upward.

I made it none too soon. I had just reached the ledge outside the open window when a police car stopped at the end of the alley. I balanced on the ledge and gave the ladder a shove—no use leaving too obvious a trail. Then I hoisted myself up to the high sill and wriggled through the window.

The room inside was pitch-dark. I could only guess how far the floor was, and what might be on it. But I damn well couldn't stay where I was. I took a deep breath and dropped through—and landed, not on the floor, but on a bed. The bed was occupied. I found myself suddenly amidst a profusion of flesh.

Chapter 16

My God!" a male voice said from beneath me. "We're caught! It's my wife!"

"Your wife?" a female voice said. "I didn't know you had a wife!"

"I beg your pardon," I said, trying to extricate myself from the tangle of arms and legs. "But I'm not your wife, sir."

A hand felt along my leg, reached my cock, and grasped it. "You're right," the woman said. "He's not your wife, Henry." The hand stayed where it was, stroking with what seemed more than casual interest. My own hand was imprisoned under an ample derriere. I squeezed, and the ass squirmed a little.

"Who are you, then?" the man demanded.

"No one you know," I said. "I was just passing by and thought I'd drop in." I felt along the curve of the ass to the thighs, and between the legs. I reached a rather puny set of balls.

"Not now, Doris," the man said. "I want to get to the bottom of things."

I had already accomplished that myself. My foot was resting against another thigh. Presumably that belonged to the woman. I felt with my foot and thrust my big toe right into a warm cunt. She giggled.

"That tickles," she said. She had continued to feel my cock, long past the point where my sex could be in question, with the result that it now was bone hard and standing erect.

"I want to know what's the big idea, interrupting people like this," Henry said. "I've got a good mind to call the cops."

"I wouldn't," the woman said, changing positions so that she was lying alongside me. "Think of the publicity. Think of your wife. What if she read the papers?"

"I don't think she can even read," he said. "Say, whose side are you on, anyway?"

By this time she wasn't on her side at all, she was on her back, tugging ambitiously to get me on top of her. I offered nothing more than token resistance. In the first place I didn't have much of an alternative. By this time the neighborhood was crawling with cops, and I could hardly leave in my current state of undress. I needed a place to hole up, in a manner of speaking, and she was offering me one. In the second place I was somehow miraculously aroused. I suppose it was the result of the earlier excitement, the drinking and that wild chase on a fire truck; whatever the cause, I was primed and ready. We managed to get into position and there was hardly any resistance when my prick slipped into her warm sheath.

"Henry, you're a rat," she said over my shoulder, wriggling her butt happily in response to my deep thrust. "You didn't say anything about a wife to me."

"Must have neglected to mention it," Henry mumbled. "But damn it, Doris, that's got nothing to do with this. We've been set upon by a madman. Heaven only knows what he intends to do with us."

"If he does to you what he's doing to me," she said, "you've got a streak in you I didn't suspect."

"What are you talking about?" There was some shuffling about and a hand moved along my leg, over my ass, and down to the point where Doris and I more or less became one. They felt my balls suspiciously.

"Thank you," I said.

"Doris!" The lights came on, blinding me. I blinked a few times before I got a good look at Doris. She wasn't all that bad—a little hard-looking, but basically pretty. Henry was fat and bald and looked highly piqued at the situation.

"Hey, you look as good as you feel," Doris said, gazing appreciatively up at me. She raised her butt up to meet me. I had paused when the lights came on, not certain of Henry's reaction. But I figured if Doris didn't care what he saw, why should I? I took up the fucking again.

"What are you doing?" Henry demanded.

"You mean you can't tell from looking?" I asked. "Maybe I'm doing something wrong."

"You're doing everything right," Doris said, beginning to pant a little.

"This is the limit," Henry said.

"Not far from it," I admitted, moving a little faster. I was rapidly approaching a climax, and from Doris's breathing and her increasingly frantic movements I felt pretty sure she was right along with me.

The doorbell rang. Doris seemed oblivious to the sound. "Aren't you going to answer that?" Henry asked.

"You get it," she said, clinging tightly to me.

Grunting angrily, Henry got up and walked to the door, his limp dick flopping ineffectually against his leg. As the door opened, I got a glimpse of men in blue.

"Ah hah!" one of the policemen said, seizing Henry's arm. "You're just the guy we were looking for."

"What is this?" Henry asked, struggling to free himself from the grip. "What's this all about?"

"Don't give us that innocent routine," the officer said, holding firm. "We've been chasing your fire engine around town, and when we found it in the alley, we knew you had to be in this building somewhere. Come along now."

"There's some mistake," Henry said. "I've been here with my lady friend all evening."

"*Your* lady friend?" The cop looked past him to where Doris and I were still joined together. Caught in the act, so to speak, it had seemed a bit pointless to try to hide what we were doing.

"Don't mind us," Doris said. "We won't be long."

I was fucking hard now, pulling it nearly out, then slamming it all the way back in.

"Is that all you?" Doris asked me.

"I think so," I said. "Although with all these people around we can't be sure."

"Do you know this guy, lady?" the officer asked, indicating Henry.

"Never saw him before in my life," Doris said without breaking rhythm. "My boyfriend here and I were just spending a quiet evening together when that guy climbed in the window and dropped on top of us."

"Doris!" Henry was quite shocked. "This is preposterous," he told the policemen. "I've known this young lady nearly a year. We spend many evenings together."

"What a terrible thing to say," Doris said. "You ought to be ashamed of yourself, mister. Why, think how that would look if it came out in the papers. Think of what your wife would say."

"Certain grounds for divorce," I said, really pouring on the steam now. I could feel my climax welling up with me, ready to explode.

"And a fantastically expensive alimony," Doris agreed, writhing and thrashing wildly about.

Henry looked completely nonplussed. "I've never had anything like this," he said.

"Neither have I," said Doris. She sank her teeth into my shoulder and her body jerked spasmodically as she reached her climax.

"Okay, buddy," the policeman said, "it's off to the station with you. You've got a lot of explaining to do." Two other policemen grabbed Henry and led him forcibly from the room.

"Hey," another policeman said, for the first time getting a good look at Doris and me. "What are you doing?"

"It's done," I said, letting out my breath in a long sigh. Doris's frantic climax had brought me off as well, and I had just finished shooting a healthy load of come into her.

I turned to look at the policeman still lingering in the door. "Would you fellows mind?" I said. "It's a little drafty in here."

JOHN IRONSTONE

Gay Rights

El Dorado Editions, 1978

It would be easy to say that John Ironstone's *Gay Rights* (1978) was unique in the annals of gay pulp and porn because one of its main characters is a radical nun who had spent time helping rebel forces in Zimbabwe. This is only one surprising detail in a story that focuses on the struggle of a Gay Student Union (at the University of Indiana at Bloomington) to bring a sex discrimination suit against the university, and the battle of Brian Dushan, a gay, blind social worker, to be reinstated to his job after being fired because of his sexual orientation. Written in the aftermath of Anita Byrant's campaign to repeal the Dade County gay rights ordinance—a fine example of how quickly gay pulp novels could respond to real world politics—the story also charts the Bloomington Human Rights Commission's struggle to get a gay rights law enacted.

Gay Rights is a fine example of how gay male magazines and pulps responded to the post-Stonewall world of gay politics. References to Vietnam creep into many of the novels, as do allusions to Nixon, Watergate, African-American civil rights struggles, and gay rights organizing. Some books threaded this material throughout the narrative; others made it more explicit. *Shootout in Cheyenne* (1977), a gay western by Burt McClain published by the Blueboy Library, seems at first to be only about the historical conditions of Western living that would encourage men to turn to one another for love and sex. But then it ends on this upbeat note, a year before Bryant's campaign and California's Proposition 18, which would have forbidden the hiring of homosexuals in the state's public schools:

> Homosexual civil rights are still at issue in this, the country representing itself as the beacon of liberty to the rest of the modern world, although through education of the population the homosexual's preferred lifestyle is finding increasing acceptability and tolerance in the majority's domain. Largely due to our Puritan inheritance and the periodic influences of McCarthy and his ilk, homosexuality was heretofore touted as a "disease" and "perversion," yet once again through education and exposure understanding and acceptance are definitely on the increase.

Gay Rights is overtly political, and Ironstone is both a realist and a pragmatist. Although the book is headed for a happy ending—with which this excerpt ends—the final political outcome is more somber, as the Bloomington Human Rights Commission is essentially dismantled by the state supreme court, and Brian's case against his boss is voided.

Pulps never underestimated the harshness of the closet and the reality of persecution, which were the driving forces behind most of their plots. What is remarkable here is that Ironstone has made this situation overtly political. The fantasy world of the pulp novel could no longer exist in a make-believe space independent of the real world. Ironstone ends his novel with a polemic that is as touching as it is vigorous:

> But no man or woman's rights will be safe as long as the rights of any are threatened. Whether it be by judicial fiat as in Indiana, or by referendum as it was in Miami, your rights can be taken away from you. Perhaps you have never felt free to enjoy your rights. Perhaps you have never known the sweet taste of freedom to be yourself. Freedom is something that can

hardly be understood until it is felt and until it is lost. We will never give up! The closet is a horrible place to die! Never will we be forced back into it! Never!

John Ironstone published pulp novels from 1976 to 1978. These included a sequel to *Gay Rights,* entitled *Gay Rights 2;* a thriller, *Disco Danger;* and an adventure story, *In Search of Gold.* Except for both volumes of *Gay Rights,* which were published under the El Dorado Editions of Maverick Publishing Inc., his books were published by Blueboy Library.

In this first excerpt we see Brian Dushan and his lover, Davey Carter, at home in the morning after the former has been fired from his job. The second excerpt, at the very end of the novel, gives Ironstone's political views and brings us the "false" happy ending of the book.

Chapter 8

Brian's alarm lock went off at seven o'clock even though he no longer had a job to go to. He wanted to preserve as much of his daily routine as he could to keep from drifting into a fog of hopelessness and uselessness. He pushed back the covers sleepily and swung his feet over the side of the bed. Davey moaned and pulled the covers over his head. He had been up late the night before studying, so Brian let him get a little more sleep. He didn't have a class until eleven.

Dushan rubbed his hands across his belly and felt the disgusting layer of flab that was building up. He shook his head. Had to get more exercise. He got up in the silent, black apartment and headed for the bathroom. He didn't bother to turn the lights—they bothered Davey and did Brian no good. The tile floor of the bathroom was cold. It was getting into the cool of the year. He stripped off his Skivvies and dropped them into the hamper. He stepped up to the toilet, touched his toes against the cold porcelain of the base, lifted the lid, and took a hearty morning piss.

He needed a shower to get himself going. He opened the door of the shower stall and turned the water on. The sound of the rushing water for Brian was like turning out the lights for a sighted person—it dulled his ability to hear and separated him further from the world around him. But the hot water drumming on his skin was delicious. It stung and prickled and soothed all at the same time, relaxing him and awakening him. His mind seemed to clear and begin functioning properly.

After he had scrubbed himself until his skin was tender to the touch, he dried off, feeling the warm, damp air on his body like his lover's breath. He ran his fingers over the stubble on his jaws and opened the medicine cabinet. He picked up the can of shaving cream and his razor. One of the hardest things that Davey had had to learn when he began living with Brian was to put everything, every single thing, back exactly where Brian had kept it so that Dushan could find it without fumbling. Brian ran the hot water in the sink and shook the can of shaving cream.

Stop and wait a minute here and make sure that you are understanding what I'm telling you, please. He is blind. He is standing in front of a mirror in a pitch-black bathroom and is preparing to shave himself with a safety razor, not an electric one. He didn't cut himself very often, less often than I do, and I have a beard. If you think that this was no small accomplishment, try it with your eyes closed tomorrow morning—only have a friend handy to get you to the hospital for a transfusion!

Put your hands over your eyes so that just two small slits are left at the bottom. When I do it, I can see only the sides of my nose, my mustache, and part of the keyboard of my typewriter. This is all that my friend Brian ever sees. He shaves with his fingers, running them along behind the razor blade to feel his skin and to make sure that he has shaved off all the whiskers. Davey says that it is an awesome performance. Davey stumbled in and turned on the light as Brian was rinsing off the last of the shaving cream.

"There's only one towel left," Brian said. "I'll have to do the laundry today." There was a laundry room in the basement of the apartment building where they lived, so he could manage it easily enough. Carter grunted and took a long piss himself. He was very slow to waken in the morning, stumbling around muzzy-headed for a half hour or more after he got out of bed. Not very communicative, either. But amorous! Oh, yes, always amorous in his horny-sleepy-foggy state!

He shook the last drops off the tip of his prick and focused one bleary eye on his lover. Brian was wiping his face off on a hand towel, naked, glowing. The heat of the shower had him hanging heavy. The bright bathroom light picked up the two dimples where the columns of his thighs tucked into the flare of his hip bones. A drop of water hung like a diamond in the golden hair that ran up to his belly button. He looked extraordinarily sexy!

Carter took him into his arms, plastering his naked body against Brian's. Dushan laughed. He knew what was on Davey's mind! He felt the thick short cock pressed against his leg, felt the strong arms holding him tightly, felt his lover rubbing his scratchy cheek over his freshly shaven one. Carter was nuzzling his lips around Brian's ear. "You want to take a shower with me?" Davey growled.

Brian was soaping up the washcloth. He was going to scrub Davey's back for him, but when he took him in his arms and ran the cloth over Carter's neck and shoulders, Davey turned it into a hot, soapy embrace. Their hot cocks were trapped between their bellies, and Davey was hunching himself around on Brian's slippery flesh. Brian forgot about the washcloth and began washing Davey's face instead with his tongue and lips.

Carter leaned his head back and surrendered himself to Brian. His own tongue was out, touching Brian's as Dushan licked across his mouth and chin and cheeks and nose and eyes and forehead, curling around the intricacies of his ear, loving and claiming each turn and whirl for himself. Carter shuddered from the chilly thrill of it in spite of the heat of the shower.

Brian's hand with the washcloth began to move again, scrubbing over the firm muscles of his back. Then Brian let the cloth slip out of his hand so that nothing would be between his sensitive fingertips and Davey. He traced each of the muscles, felt each bone of his spine, caressed the broad, clipped angel's wings of his shoulder blades, the hot, hairy little nests of his armpits. In the front, his tongue ran over Davey's neck, licking the strong cords of his sinews, the bumpy cartilage of his voice box, touched the throbbing of his pulse in the arteries of his throat. Down, down to the twin hollows between the base of his neck and the delicate arches of his collarbones, tasting the water and the flesh. Over the broad plains of his chest, the slender hollow of his breastbone, the firm swelling of his chest muscles, the exciting, hard points of his nipples. He knew every hair that grew around the little tits, every goose-bump that circled the nipples. His lips were burning with the touch of Davey's skin, hotter than white coals, searing the knowledge of him into his heart.

Davey leaned back against the wall, his hands on Brian's head, the water drumming against the backs of his hands and wrists and seeping through the wet hair. He moaned and felt weak as Brian's mouth traced the edge of his rib cage and his hands gripped the hemispheres of his ass. He leaned over, wanting to raise Dushan up, to kiss him some more, to make it last longer, but Brian was insistent, resisted.

He swung his head around it, left it for later, ran his tongue in one long lick from the tip of Davey's pelvis, down the shallow joint between his belly and leg, down to the hair of his crotch. He felt the hot, rigid rod against his cheek as his tongue delved into the narrow space between leg and cock root, knew the heaviness of the root and the thin, delicate veil of flesh that began below it, the soft, thin wall of the bag that held Davey's balls.

The hair was tough, wiry, and wet; the skin so incredibly soft and supple. The muscles of Carter's scrotum contracted under the tickling touch and lifted up the rubbery eggs of his balls to Brian's lips. He forced Davey's legs apart with his hands, bent down even further to push his face up under the tight nuts to lick at their tender undersides. Davey's cock was against his forehead, arching up over his hair. Brian's tongue darted along the deepest roots of the phallus, behind the balls to the center of his lover's crotch. His fingers came to meet him from the other side, slipping between the firm globes of Davey's ass into his crack, seeking the tight button of his asshole.

Carter's knees were wobbly, too weak to hold him up if he hadn't been resting his weight against the shower wall. He wanted to be taken. His only will was to have no further will. His hands were limp on Brian's head, letting him do what he wished. His balls were sucked into Brian's eager mouth, first one and then both, circled by the strong lips, sucked into the hungry mouth where the agile tongue teased and probed them. A finger was worming its way into his butt, gently but insistently. He willed his surrender, felt the finger slide in, hot and hard and itchy with soap, up, up into him, burrowing into his body, feeling, wriggling, touching the back of his prostate, causing his cock to surge with hot blood.

Brian sucked on the nuts, rolling his head around in tight circles to tug on them, heat them to boiling, licking and loving them, tasting the flesh, feeling the wiry hairs, feeling the hot cock jerk with excitement. He sent another finger after the first, tugging and twisting against the unwilled tightness of the ring of muscles that guarded the opening, feeling them, making them loosen for him, preparing. Twin goads—hot jointed bones, tendons, filled with blood pounding, millions of tingling nerve endings knowing, touching, experiencing each tiny fold, each furrow of the most delicate flesh, the lining of Davey's body.

Carter's hands were on each side of Brian's head, from jawbone to spine, pulling him, urging him up. This time Dushan agreed. He released his lover's balls and gave one hot twirl of his tongue around the hard twitching shaft of his cock, sucked the clear, cool fluid that was oozing from the tip. He stood up straight, his hands still in Davey's crack, pulling him up, up off his feet, holding him between his body and the wall, spreading the legs, hooking Davey's thighs over his hips, running his tongue and mouth over Davey's face again. Davey whimpered with anticipation. His tongue welcomed Brian's with a frenzy of licking kisses over his face, into his mouth, thrusting hungrily over the other tongue, twining with it like mating snakes.

He put his arms around Brian's neck, his legs around his lover's waist. Brian's back and belly were a single column of twisting, strong muscle, strong enough to hold them both up. Davey's spine was pressed hard against the tiles, the grooves between the smooth plates ridging the flesh of his back. His legs were spread wide, his pelvis tilted up, his ass open, his cock thrust back against his own hard belly. Brian's hands cupped his butt, the fingers digging into the soft, relaxed muscles, holding him open.

Dushan leaned closer, let the head of his aching cock run along the ridge of Davey's cock root, back to his asshole. Carter twitched in his arms and put his hands down to guide Brian's shaft. His fingers pressed the head of the cock to the opening of his body, guided it and held it as it pressed in, spreading him open before its broad nose. He tilted his butt up a little further as the knob slipped in. He pushed out, relaxing himself, thrilling to the invasion.

Brian paused until he sensed that Davey was ready. Then he

shifted his lover's weight up on his hands and pressed in. It was so heavenly glorious. It altered his being. His body became a rigid arch with his cock as the apex. Every part of him was connected to the broad cockhead. Every part shared and knew the pleasure of the fiery heat of the flesh that spread open and gripped it so fiercely. The heat, the tightness, the chemical tingling of the soap, the slipping movement of his lover's body over his, encircling, sucking, pulling him into it. His face was twisted with the intensity of it, his lips pulled back from his teeth as he sucked ragged breaths of steamy air into his lungs. Nothing, nothing could ever, ever . . .

He was in all the way. Davey felt the rough hair over Brian's cock pressed hard to the base of his cock under his balls, felt the bag of Brian's balls against his butt. He was filled utterly, crammed and bursting. It was good, so good. He was ravaged with lust, tearing his mind free from its moorings, melting it down in delight. He wanted to get fucked! Hard! Now! He bucked his hips up against Brian as best he could. His fingers sank hard into the flesh of Brian's neck and back, gripping the muscles and demanding the attack of his lover. He was trembling all over.

Brian pulled back and thrust in hard, slamming Davey's whole body up the slippery surface of the shower wall, shaking him to the very foundation of his heart. His cock was hard and horny, a rigid spear, plunging in and out, slapping his fat balls into his lover's butt. He gripped Davey's waist and held him tightly against the wall as he fucked him. He twisted his hips, rolling them to give a corkscrew twirl to the thrusts of his cock up Davey's asshole. He snapped his shaft in and out like a piston until he began to lose the rhythm of his strokes.

His head dropped forward, seeking Davey's, seeking the thrill and communion of mouth on mouth. The climax was near. Their heads bobbed against each other with the force of Brian's thrusts, lips sliding over licking tongue, half-words moaned and swallowed. Then, joining in orgasm, first Davey, jetting his cream over the hard ridges of his belly, sending spasms of passion through the ring of his asshole, bringing Brian off with him. Brian slamming Davey up against the wall, lifting his body on his cock, rivers of hot cum jerking and gushing up through his cock, into Davey's gut to bathe the tender flesh and the throbbing spurting head of Brian's cock.

Moans, murmurs, shudders of pleasure, too good for words, too well known and felt to be spoken. Then inevitably postclimax, the water of the shower turning cold, cramps in stretched muscles' detumescence, legs lowered back to the ground. Smiles, kisses, but also shampoo and soap to wash up. Yelping in happy dismay as the last of the hot water gave out. Toweling each other off vigorously to fight off the final chill of the water.

Chapter 10

If you've read any of my books before, you know that I like happy endings. Not your modern, modified, limited, mostly ironic, tiny-little-ray-of-hope-after-the-Dark-Night-of-the-Soul happy endings. I go in for the pull-out-all-the-stops histrionic happy ending. I like 'em sappy-happy with the forces of evil crushed or driven far away, the good guys triumphant in each other's arms thinking about a nice roll in the hay. It's probably the effect of reading too many Dickens novels during my formative years.

Well, this book doesn't have a very happy ending, and I thought in all fairness that I had better warn you in advance, Gentle Reader. No, I'm not going to give you a three-hanky ending like the one the greatest sob sister of them all, Ernest Hemingway, provided in *For Whom the Bell Tolls*. I'm not going to kill off one of our heroes and leave you to weep over his grave à la Patricia Nell Warren. I hate morbid endings like that, and anyway, this is political porn I'm writing, spiritually uplifting and socially redeeming, but also based closely on fact.

That's the Mother that messed it all up—fact, the real world. The events in the newspaper dictate the shape of my fiction, and we have once again been fucked by the Fickle Finger of Fate. Not a true catastrophe, no catharsis, just a pain in the ass. But when has the Famous Finger ever come equipped with K-Y? So, we're going on a roller-coaster ride, my friend, beginning with mere unpleasantness, taking a swoop up toward the stars, ending with a nasty pratfall that isn't very funny. Please fasten your seat belts.

Starting with the merely unpleasant, we turn to Alfie. Alfie did not get all better when the doctor kissed him on the top of his pointed head. God, I don't like Alfie, but there's not much of Alfie left to dislike. He decompensated, as the psychiatrists say. He came unglued. He took a header into the deep end of the pool when there was no water in it. He had constructed (with the aid of his loving parents) all of his personality around hating his natural self, loathing his feelings for other males. He wound up the mummy-bands of his outer personality very tightly around the core of this inner putrefaction. When the boil was lanced, there was very little left of Alfie. He lapsed into a frankly psychotic state and eventually had to be committed for long-term care. They are trying to put him back together a little bit at a time. John is praying for him. I only wonder.

Denny is doing a lot better. No miracles though. He is still silly, clumsy, and a klutz. He has virtually no self-confidence, and he breaks into tears at a butterfly's fart. But he has a lot of new friends to help him. He's making it (barely) in school with the help of Tommy and others who help him do his work and explain it over and over to him. He really isn't that dumb—Alfie was right about that. He just spends most of his time thinking and worrying about himself. He's very much a passive-dependent type and probably always will be. He gets on your nerves after a while, but, by God, at least he's not nasty. He's really a very nice kid once he gets his attention focused on something outside himself. He can be very caring then. How caring are you?

Well, anyway, Brian got a package in the mail. He wasn't expecting anything, and he never went to the mailbox downstairs even when he was. It had a combination lock on it, and he couldn't get the damned thing open. So, Davey brought it up when he came home from classes. It was just a little package, small enough to fit in the mailbox. It was from the DDU.

"Maybe something you left in your desk," Davey said, dropping it into Brian's lap.

"It's a tape cassette," Dushan said, feeling it through the wrapping.

"Open it, open it," Davey urged him.

Brian opened it. There was a sheet of paper and the cassette inside. He handed the paper to Davey. "It's from Joyce, your secretary," Carter said and began to read it to his lover:

Dear Brian,
I found this the day that you got fired, and I've been keeping

it in my desk ever since. I'm sorry I didn't give it to you right away, but I was afraid that I would get in trouble about it and maybe lose my job. It's not easy finding a job, and I guess you know that. I guess that's why I'm sending it to you. It's not fair what they did to you, and I hope you ruin the bastards!

Joyce

P.S. I got the typewriter hot like you asked me to.

"What in the hell is she talking about?" Davey asked when he had finished reading the letter.

"I don't know." Brian shrugged. "Play the cassette."

Davey got out the machine and stuck the cassette into it. Brian's voice spoke from the little tape recorder. He sounded irritable and upset. There were frequent loud clicks from when he had turned the microphone on and off. The tape said:

"Rationale on Phillip Kinkaid, Social Security Number 265-82-0082. Type it on a separate 834 form, Joyce. Medical Evidence: [Click!] Dr. William Gilliken, TP [Click!], 4/1/77; Dr. M. B. Sell, Psychiatric CE, 8/1/77; Central State Hospital records of admission, oh shit! [Click!] 2/22/77 to 3/29/77. This twenty-one-year-old wage earner alleges disability due to, quote, Too crazy to work, unquote. Medical evidence shows a sociopathic personality, adjustment reaction of adolescence, and a borderline IQ of, damn it [Click!], 89."

"Is she supposed to type in all the *shits* and *damn its*?" Davey asked with a laugh.

"Hush!" Brian waved his hand excitedly. "I think I remember this case. I think it's . . ."

The tape continued for a minute with Brian's voice dictating the details of the rationale. Dushan was smiling with great eagerness showing on his face. Davey was puzzled at why his lover should be so interested in hearing the decision on a case Brian had once adjudicated for the Disability Determination Unit. Then Brian's voice on the tape broke off with the loud sound of the microphone being put down on his desktop. But the recording didn't stop. There were funny little sounds coming from it as from a radio which had not quite been turned all the way off.

"Turn it up! Turn it up!" Brian shouted with delight. Davey fumbled with the controls on the recorder and turned up the volume to its highest. The sounds were still very distant, but the words could be clearly heard:

". . . even bothered to deny it!"

"Deny what, Mr. Thompson?" (Crash of a door slamming.)

"You were kissing him! On the lips! In public! Right where anyone could see you! Don't try to lie to me about it either, because I saw you do it!"

As the tape continued, Brian was hopping up and down in his chair, hugging himself. "I forgot to turn it off! I forgot to turn the damned machine off! It was sitting right there on my desk, right in front of all of us, recording the whole damned thing, and I didn't even know it!" He slapped his hands on his thighs. "Shit! Of course, I even heard it running, but I couldn't figure out what the sound was. Listen! Listen to it! Every goddamned thing we need right there on tape for us! Whoopee! I'm going to take Joyce out for a champagne dinner!"

His voice on the tape echoed him: "I'm telling you that I have rights, and I know what they are. I intend to have my rights observed. I am not giving up my job!"

Carter was standing by the coffee table staring down at the little tape recorder, the little deus ex machina. He closed his gaping mouth with a snap as the tape ran out and stopped. "I don't believe it. It's just incredible! We'll slaughter them!"

"Call Weinstock! Right now! I can't wait to play this tape for him!"

Carter called the director attorney of the Commission and told him their tale of blessed luck. He was so excited that he could hardly make himself understood. The words came pouring out in a torrent of glee. Barry wanted them to bring the tape over immediately. They brought it to him, guarding it as carefully as if it were the original Ark of the Covenant.

They played it over a couple of times in Weinstock's office and rejoiced over it. Then Barry got on the telephone to Franklin's office. His round little face was splitting with grins that he could hardly contain, but he kept his voice as calm and measured as he could.

"Hello, Franklin? This is Weinstock over at the Human Rights Commission. How are you today? Fine, fine, glad to hear it. Unh-hunh. I'm calling you because we've turned up some new evidence in the Dushan case. Yes, that's right. Well, I think it's going to be some help for us. Yes. Yes, I'd like very much to share it with you. As a matter of fact, I think it would be very helpful if Mr. Thompson and Mr. Simpkins could examine it as well. Do you think you could arrange that? Unhhunh. No, I assure you that it won't be a waste of their time. Right. You contact them and set up a time that is convenient for them. Anytime will be all right for me. I'll make special arrangements for it. I sure do. You call me as soon as you get it set up. Right. Fine. Good-bye."

He burst out in laughter as he hung up the telephone. "God, I can't wait! This will be one of the high points in my legal career. Let me get out that consent decree and dust it off. I want to check it over again and see if we can't screw even more out of them than I first proposed. They haven't got a fucking leg to stand on now!" He chortled in devilish delight!

"When will it be, Barry?" Brian asked.

"I don't know. It will depend on them. I want to have them all here when I spring it on them. I'll call you as soon as I find out. You keep the tape in your possession and be careful with it, okay? Don't even play it again until it's time!"

The meeting was arranged for the next Monday afternoon. Certain things regularly happen on Mondays. One of them was the monkey wrench that got dropped into the happy ending of this book. Brian and Davey were in Weinstock's office an hour early. Both of them were dressed as formally as possible, ready to be in at the kill. Dushan kept the tape recorder and tape clutched in his lap. Davey kept hopping out of his chair to stand behind Brian's and put his hands on his lover's shoulders. He was so fiercely proud of Brian that he could hardly contain himself.

Franklin came in right on time, leading Thompson and Simpkins behind him. They were all holding themselves stiffly, suspicious as could be, and with good reason. Simpkins avoided looking into Brian's blind eyes, but Thompson stared at Dushan and Carter and allowed himself the luxury of a small sneer of distaste. He thought he could afford to be cruel since he had the upper hand. A true prince!

"Now, what is all this, Weinstock?" Franklin said, sitting down on the couch. Thompson and Simpkins sat down with him. The other two men were inelegantly popped up into the air when Simpkins dropped his weight onto the sofa. They recovered their dignity as best they could while Brian and Davey turned their chairs to face the couch, and Weinstock seated himself behind his desk. His fingers played idly with the consent decree that he had redrafted in preparation for the meeting.

"It's a tape recording," Weinstock announced. "Play it for them, will you, Brian?"

"What tape is this?" Franklin began.

"Just listen to it first, then we'll talk about it, okay?" Weinstock said, smiling.

Brian's fingers were cold and trembling with excitement as he pushed the button to begin the tape. He began it from the start. Franklin was completely mystified by the strange jargon of the rationale, but Thompson and Simpkins knew immediately what Brian's recorded voice was talking about. They knew where the tape came from at any rate, and Thompson began to turn pale. Simpkins was slower on the uptake.

When the sound of the microphone clunking down onto the desk came, Brian twirled the volume control up to the highest. Thompson's voice came squeaking out of the machine.

"That's you, Mr. Thompson!" Simpkins blurted out.

"Thank you for identifying him, Mr. Simpkins," Weinstock said smoothly, and Franklin winced visibly. Thompson had his hand over his mouth, staring at the machine and looking very, very sick.

"You had no right to make a secret recording," Franklin began to bluster. "Why wasn't this evidence brought forward from the start?"

"Shut up," Weinstock said simply. "Just listen."

"Sick! You are a queer! If you were normal, you would say so! I am truly disgusted! Do you hear that? Disgusted with you, Dushan. I always thought you were a nice boy, doing a good job, even if you were blind. But now! This! You leave me no choice. Your services at the Disability Determination Unit will no longer be required as of . . ."

"Turn it off! Turn it off!" Thompson said.

"Don't you want to listen to the rest of your speech?" Brian said. He was gloating a little bit, I must say.

"You can't admit it into evidence!" Franklin shouted. "I'll move to have it suppressed!"

"The hell I can't!" Weinstock countered. "The tape recorder was sitting right out on Mr. Dushan's desk in plain sight. He consented to the making of the recording, even if he didn't realize at that time that he was making it. You're caught, Franklin, flat screwed!"

"We'll see what the court has to say about this! We'll—" Franklin continued.

"Shut up, you goddamned fool!" Thompson bellowed at him.

Franklin snapped his mouth shut as ordered.

Thompson got up from the sofa, ignoring Brian and Davey. He walked over to Barry's desk and leaned over it confidentially. "All right, Weinstock. What do you want for that recording?"

"I'm glad you realize your position, Mr. Thompson," Weinstock said, leaning back in his chair. "We won't give you the recording, of course, but what we want you to do is sign this consent decree." He turned the papers around to face Thompson. "You're getting off very easy, I would say. If the recording had turned up after you testified to your story before the Commission, you might have set yourself up for perjury charges."

"Your solicitude for my welfare touches me, Weinstock. What is this? What does it say?" He snapped his finger against the papers.

"It's a consent decree, Mr. Thompson," Franklin began to explain.

Thompson turned his head slowly over his shoulder to look at his lawyer. "Will you shut up, you asshole? Ironclad case, you said!"

Franklin was finally enraged to the point of risking his job. "You told me you fired him because he was a drunk! You were lying to me all the time! It would have been an ironclad case if you had been telling the truth, God damn you!"

Thompson ignored him. He was a realistic man when it came to the terms of power. He knew that he had his ass in a sling, and he wanted to know how to get out of that position with a minimum of pain to himself. Weinstock had the gun. Therefore, he talked to Weinstock. "What does it say?" he repeated.

"You don't admit that you have done anything wrong. The consent order cannot be used against you in any other suit."

"Good, what else?"

"You will rehire Mr. Dushan with a full reinstatement to his former rank and all benefits, including back pay."

"All right, anything else?"

"I was going to ask for damages, but Mr. Dushan would not agree to the demand."

Thompson turned around and looked at Brian for the first time since the tape had been played. "Why?"

"I don't want the extra money. I want to have my job back and to do it as well as I can. I want to sit in front of you every day and know that you had to admit that you were wrong. I want my presence in front of your eyes day in and day out to remind you of what you did and that you COULD NOT GET AWAY WITH IT!" Brian was shouting and pounding his fist on the arm of the chair.

"You're right!" Thompson snarled. "I would gladly pay a thousand dollars out of my own pocket just so I never had to see your face again!" The bile of his hatred was choking him, turning his face purple-gray.

"Where do I sign this goddamned thing!?" he demanded of Weinstock.

Weinstock smiled again and flipped to the last page of the document. "Here. We'll need your signatures, too, Mr. Simpkins, and yours, Mr. Franklin. There are three copies. Be sure to sign each one of them."

Gay Novels, 1940–1969

These are novels and short story collections with significant gay male content published by mainstream American houses between 1940 and 1969. It is by no means a complete list but rather an indication of what was available to gay and lesbian readers before Stonewall and Gay Liberation.

1940

Long recognized as an American classic, Carson McCullers's *The Heart Is a Lonely Hunter* presents us, in the character of the Jewish deaf mute John Singer, with a coded portrayal of a gay male outsider who is the moral center of the novel.

1941

Carson McCullers, writing about a variety of sexual experiences including homosexuality, sadism, voyeurism, and fetishism, once again contemplates the boundaries of eroticism, outsider status, and the fragility of "normal" in *Reflections in a Golden Eye*. Similar themes are dealt with in Harlan McIntosh's astonishing novel, *This Finer Shadow*, which is one of the first books to overtly use psychoanalytic theory to discuss and try to understand sexual and gender variance. Its odd, dreamlike narrative places it outside the realm of realism.

The novel's drag ball, during which many of the characters take on alternative identities, is a fascinating cross between camp and deadly serious psychological fiction.

1944

While Charles Jackson's *The Lost Weekend* became such a bestseller (as well as a Hollywood box-office hit a year later) that its title became common English usage for alcoholism, few critics mentioned the fact that Don Birnam, the book's hero, was driven to drink because of tormented feelings over his homosexuality. Mark Connelly's *Deadly Closets: The Fiction of Charles Jackson* (University Presses of America, 2001) is a fine analysis of the underlying gay themes in all of Jackson's work. Kenneth Millar's *The Dark Tunnel* is a fairly routine World War II spy thriller, but here the Nazi spy is a transvestite homosexual who keeps fooling everyone, including the butch college professor hero who is quite smitten with him. While playing with anti-queer stereotypes, the book is a fascinating look at representations of homosexuality during the war. Millar went on to write detective novels under the name of Ross Macdonald. *The Dark Tunnel* was published as a mass market paperback in 1950 by Lion Books, which reissued it in 1955 under the title *I Die Slowly,* and in 1972 by Bantam Books.

1945

The Brick Foxhole by Richard Brooks (who would later become a distinguished Hollywood director) is an amazing novel whose pivotal action turns on a queer bashing and murder by a U.S. solider on leave in New York, but locates this deed in the context of how notions of masculinity were distorted by the war and society. When it was made into the 1947 film *Crossfire* (directed by Edward Dmytryk, with a screenplay by John Paxton), the murder victim was changed from a homosexual to a Jew, and the story became one about anti-Semitism, not fear of sexual variance. (Collectors of camp arcana should note that Brooks was collaborating on the screenplay for the 1944 camp classic *Cobra Woman* the year before *The Brick Foxhole* was published.) While the narrator of Christopher Isherwood's *Prater Violet* can be read as homosexual (as is the case in most of Isherwood's novels), this book's exploration of anti-Semitism is representative of the many novels published during these decades that juxtaposed their gay content with other themes exploring issues of social justice. William Maxwell's *The Folded Leaf* details the love between two young men in middle-class midwestern America in the 1920s. Not quite closeted, the original jacket copy for the novel noted that "this is a Damon and Pythias story written with candor and generosity for the modern age" and that it details "the passion and the touch of Greek splendor below the surface of casual college athletics."

1946

Christopher Isherwood's *The Berlin Stories* (originally published as *Mr. Norris Changes Trains* and *Goodbye to Berlin* in 1935 and 1939 respectively) was given a major reissue that was followed by John Van Druten's 1951 Broadway adaptation, *I Am a Camera*, and the ensuing Hollywood film version of the play in 1955. Van Druten's play served as the basis for the 1966 musical *Cabaret*. In the film version of the musical, and in later stage revivals, the main character's homosexuality was made explicit. If critics ignored the implicit homosexuality of *The Lost Weekend*, they had to deal with the explicit homoeroticism of Charles Jackson's *The Fall of Valor*. As much a meditation on the effects of World War II on American masculinity as the story of a married college professor's grappling with his homosexuality ("The Powerful Story of a Man's Conflicting Loves" reads the jacket of the 1948 Signet paperback edition), the novel was labeled "daring" and "honest" by some critics, but generally received mixed-to-negative notices. Carson McCullers's *The Member of the Wedding*—another examination of outsiders in a Southern setting—deftly explored connections between race and sexual and gender orientation. Gladys Schmitt, already known for her popular mainstream historical novels, introduced an explicitly sexual relationship between Hebrew Bible lovers David and Jonathan in *David the King*; critics, for the most part, made no comment.

1947

John Horne Burns's *The Gallery*—which featured the explicitly homosexual section "Momma," about homosexual GIs spending an evening together at a gay bar in Naples in 1944—was a prime example of how integral discussions of homoeroticism and male-male relationships were to the postwar novel. Critics lauded Burns as one of the new leading lights of American fiction. John Mitzel's *John Horne Burns: An Appreciative Biography* is a great analysis of Burns's work and one of the few studies of this writer. Stuart Engstrand had already published three highly praised novels before *The Sling and the Arrow*, his exploration of what we would now call a transgender identity. He was inspired, according to the book's jacket copy, to write the novel after "rereading [Wilhelm] Stekel's writing on abnormal psychology." Like *This Finer Shadow*, it is a perfect example of how popularized psychoanalytic theory affected both contemporary fiction and public discussions of homosexuality. Willard Motley's *Knock on Any Door*, which looks at the life of "Pretty Boy" Nick Romano, an Italian-American street kid from Chicago's slums, was a tremendous bestseller. Motley, who was a black homosexual progressive, was hailed as a great American novelist and compared to James T. Farrell and John Dos Passos. The successful 1949 film with John Derek and Humphrey Bogart deleted the substantial subplot of Nick's hustling and his redemptive relationship with a gay man who loves him. *The Great Snow* was Henry Morton Robinson's second novel, but he already had a noted reputation as a poet and critic (he published, with Joseph Campbell, *A Skeleton Key to Finnegans Wake* in 1944). This novel is a frank and disturbing portrayal of a macho father coming to grips with the reality that his young son is homosexual. Finally published in the United States, *Abel Sanchez*, Miguel de Unamuno's great 1917 Spanish novel, based on the story of Cain and Abel, is a philosophical inquiry into the meaning, and fairness, of life. While never thought of as a "gay novel," its sprawling plot features homosexual themes that are vital to the concept and shape of the novel. Calder Willingham's *End as a Man*, detailing the sadomasochistic and homoerotic underpinnings of a Southern military academy, was a scandalous success. Critical of mainstream anti-Semitism and racism, the novel is emblematic of popular fictional critiques of masculinity that appeared after the war. Willingham's novel became a popular stage play in 1953 and a film in 1957.

1948

Truman Capote's *Other Voices, Other Rooms* caused a stir not simply because of its implicit gay content, but because the dust jacket photo of its twenty-four-year-old author—looking fourteen, brimming with sullen eroticism, his hands resting on his crotch—created an equal media stir. Capote's work, along with the novels of Carson McCullers and the work of Tennessee Williams, created in the popular imagination a subgenre of Southern gothic that highlighted sexual deviance. Not as extravagantly baroque in emotions or style as Capote's work, *The Welcome* by Hubert Creekmore, set in the 1930s, tells the story of a man returning to his small, Southern hometown from an urban life in New York, to encounter the complications of being a single man in a tightly coupled community and discovering that his boyhood best friend is now married and still in love with him. John Howard has an excellent analysis of Creekmore's works in *Men like That: A Southern Queer History*. Klaus Mann's *Pathetic Symphony: A Novel About Tchaikovsky*, written in 1935 when he was a refugee from Nazi Germany, was finally published in English in the United States. Long viewed as simply emblematic of the author's own emotional struggles—like Tchaikovsky, Klaus Mann was to take his own life—it is now viewed as a far more sophisticated work of imagination that critiques anti-homosexual prejudice. Betty Smith's *A Tree Grows in Brooklyn* became an American classic when it was published in 1943. In her bestselling *Tomorrow Will Be Better,* her working-class heroine is married to a quiet young man who begins to discover his homosexuality. Gore Vidal's *The City and the Pillar* was perhaps the postwar homosexual novel that garnered the most notoriety, and criticism, for its explicit homosexual theme. Critic Roger Austen claims that "in the nineteenth century males could kiss each other but not disrobe; in the twentieth century they could undress together but not kiss; in *The City and the Pillar* they do both." Vidal revised his novel in 1965, the most salient difference being that the hero does not kill, but rapes, his unreciprocating beloved. Tennessee Williams's collection of stories *One Arm*, which featured several overtly homosexual stories, was released in a limited edition the year after his highly touted, award-winning *A Streetcar Named Desire* was produced on Broadway.

1949

Isabel Bolton's *The Christmas Tree* is the elegantly written, *New Yorker*ish novel of a gay man and his partner dealing with his former wife and child over the holidays. *Lucifer with a Book* by John Horne Burns details the homoerotic goings-on at a New England boarding school. Like Willingham's use of an all-male microcosm in *End as a Man,* Burns uses this setting to produce a harsh critique of postwar masculinity, sexuality, racism, and anti-Semitism. Michael De Forrest's *The Gay Year* was published by the Woodford Press, a small publishing house started by novelist Jack Woodford, whose sexually explicit work earned him the reputation of an "American Rabelais." The Woodford Press was noted for its adult, sexual content. Not very well written, and certainly not particularly sympathetic to homosexuality, the book's scenes set in theaters, gay bars, and Greenwich Village apartments have an authentic ring of truth about them. *The Gay Life* was to be reissued in cloth by Castle Books (and in paper by Lancer) during the 1950s and 1960s, usually with the author listed as "M. de F." *The Divided Path* by Nial Kent (pseudonym of William Leroy Thomas) is a sensitive story of a young man growing up in a small town and discovering his homosexuality through his feelings for his heterosexual best friend. After a separation during which the protagonist comes out and his friend joins the armed forces, the book ends on a hopeful note of possible romance. The novel's publisher, Greenberg, a small firm in New York City, frequently published novels and nonfiction with gay male or lesbian content. *The World Next Door* by Fritz Peters is a narrative tour de force. Told from the point of view of a schizophrenic central character—a closeted veteran coming to grips with his sexuality—the narrative moves from relentless internal confusion to clearer, healthier consciousness. Reflecting the postwar preoccupation with psychoanalysis, mental illness, and homosexuality, the novel is both unusually sophisticated and psychologically astute for its time, although the ambiguous jacket copy on the Signet paperback reads: "The Gripping Story of a Man's Triumph Over Dark Powers Which Threaten to Destroy Him." Thomas Hal Phillips's *The Bitterweed Path* is a compelling story, set in the post-bellum South, of a father and son, wealthy landowners, who are both emotionally attached to a poor young man who works their land. Drawn more from the biblical story of David, Jonathan, and Saul than from themes or tropes in twentieth-century Southern literature, the novel is a mature exploration of homoerotic relationships. Phillips wrote several other novels and is noted for his work in Robert Altman films, including supplying the voice of never-seen presidential candidate Hal Phillip Walker in Robert Altman's 1975 *Nashville*. John Howard's introduction to the 1995 University of North Carolina Press reprint of the novel is an excellent introduction to the novel and its author. *Stranger in the Land* by Ward Thomas is a startling, perceptive thriller about a gay man who decides to murder his heterosexual, some-times lover when the man threatens blackmail. The novel shares its quaint New England town setting and the backdrop of World War II with *Lucifer with a Book*, and Thomas, like Burns, deftly links queer hatred and male supremacy to other social ills and points out tactics to combat them, such as his protagonist's realization that "the invert must copy from the Negro and the Jew all their tricks of survival in the stronghold of white Nordic supremacy."

1950

James Barr's *Quatrefoil*, published by Greenberg, is an overtly gay novel of two naval officers who, against all odds, fall in love and dream of a life together. Eschewing the sexual and emotional turmoil of Vidal's *The City and the Pillar* and the dark exploration into American masculinity that defined Willingham's *End as a Man*, Barr's novel is a celebration of masculine homosexual love and devotion. In the novel's second half, one of the protagonists returns to his hometown in Oklahoma to sort out his new, complicated sexual feelings; this lengthy section not only draws upon a tradition of regional writing but anticipates some of Barr's later writings. *A Long Day's Dying* by the twenty-three-year-old Frederick Buechner was hailed as an important new American novel by a young genius. This highly literary, ironic comedy of errors features gender- and sexually ambiguous characters and was a critical and popular success. While there is little overt homosexual content, the publishers certainly pitched the novel to a gay audience with jacket blurbs by Isabel Bolton, John Horne Burns, Leonard Bernstein, Christopher Isherwood, and Carl Van Vechten. (Interestingly there is a character named George Motley, whose name must surely have echoed, for literate readers, Willard Motley.) Buechner was later ordained as an Episcopal priest and has written numerous novels and works of popular theology. A. J. Cronin, author of such "classics" as *The Citadel* and *The Keys to the Kingdom,* was a very mainstream, widely read, highly respected novelist. This makes the overt homoeroticism and the implicit, positively portrayed pedophilia of *The Spanish Gardener* even more surprising. As with many books with homosexual content in the 1950s, Cronin is also interested in seriously critiquing accepted ideas of American masculinity. Harrison Dowd was an intimate of Edna St. Vincent Millay's and a major figure in the Greenwich Village arts scene in the 1930s. *The Night Air* is his only novel. He worked frequently on the Broadway stage, where much of this novel takes place, and in Hollywood. *The House of Breath* by William Goyen is a poetically impressionistic story of ambiguous gender and homoerotic relationships set in a small Texas town. While the content was resonant of *Other Voices, Other Rooms,* Goyen's elliptical style—which at times feels like a forerunner of magical realism—was completely original. The themes here appear in many other Goyen works, most strikingly in his 1983 novel, *Arcadio.* *Strangers on a Train* was Patricia Highsmith's first novel. While its homosexual characters—murderous, psychopathic, weak—are hardly "positive," the genius of Highsmith's work is that she makes them the book's moral center because the rest of the world is even worse. The 1951 Hitchcock film removed most of Highsmith's cutting, ironic, and nasty edge. Charles Jackson's collection *The Sunnier Side* (the title was a rebuke to those who had found the content of his earlier work distressingly sordid) contained the story "Palm Sunday," about a man remembering a boyhood involvement with an older man. Alberto Moravia's *Two Adolescents* is an unsentimental account of Italian street life, boys, and homosexual behavior. While the material is, in some respects, similar to Motley's let's-understand-the-poor attitude in the cityscape of *Knock on Any Door,* Moravia's Italian neorealistic roots are unsparingly harsh. Roger Peyrefitte's *Special Friendships* (published in France in 1944) has become a classic midcentury homosexual novel. The story of two boys whose romance in a Catholic boarding school flourishes in spite of the rule against "special friendships," but still ends in tragedy, was made into a popular 1964 film directed by Jean Delannoy. Peyrefitte's *Diplomatic Diversions* (published in the United

States in 1954) and *Diplomatic Conclusions* (published here in 1955) are considered semisequels, although they contain very little explicit homosexual content. Gore Vidal's *A Search for the King* charts the story of the faithful troubadour Blondel for his master, Richard the Lion-Hearted, who has been kidnapped by the Austrian duke Leopold after the Third Crusade. Although there is no explicit sexual relationship between Richard and Blondel, contemporary homosexual readers would have known of the relationship that has historically been suggested between them. George Sylvester Viereck's *Men into Beasts* was technically a prison memoir, though it looked like a pulp novel when it was published as a "Gold Medal Original" paperback. Its cover featured a naked inmate being beaten by guards. Although Viereck was heterosexual and had a notable career as a poet and novelist—as well as a philo-Semite *and* a supporter of Hitler (he was imprisoned for sedition during World War II)—the cover copy played up the book's substantial, and highly sympathetic, homosexual content. Selling nearly two million copies, Viereck's book was probably the first "cross-over" pulp with explicitly homosexual content. *The Invisible Glass* by Loren Wahl, the pseudonym of Lorenzo Madalena, was published by Greenberg. Set in Italy during the Allied invasion, it details the complicated sexual relationships between soldiers. It also, even more daringly, dealt directly with racial prejudice in the army and how this affected sexual relationships. It was republished in an abridged paper edition in 1952 with the title *If This Be Sin*. This edition was later revised and issued in another paperback edition as *Take Me As I Am*. In 1965, Guild Press republished *The Invisible Glass* under its own imprint. The book's title comes from a quotation by W. E. B. DuBois. Tennessee Williams's *The Roman Spring of Mrs. Stone* contains only undercurrents of homoeroticism, but this tale of a widowed, aging actress purchasing love and affection in Rome can easily be read as a gay male story. *The Dog Star* by Donald Windham charts the wanderings of a young teenage boy in the South during the Depression after his best friend commits suicide. While the boys were never lovers, Windham makes the erotic attachment between them clear. This theme—present in *The Bitterweed Path* and *The Folded Leaf* as well as many other less erotically charged novels—runs through much U.S. postwar literature and is a prime example of the culture's coming to grips with the new ideas about masculinity and sexuality that came about because of the war.

1951

Derricks, a collection of seven short stories by James Barr, featured not only mostly homosexual-themed work, but showed that Barr was comfortable writing in a wide range of genres, from Booth Tarkington regional romance (with a pedophilic twist) to the James M. Cain tough-guy double-double-cross thriller. Truman Capote's *The Grass Harp,* like *Other Voices, Other Rooms,* presents us with a pre-sexual boy who lives with outsiders. This Edenic world, related in elegant language, of intense boyhood crushes and lovable eccentrics was one (although obviously not the only) way of bringing implicitly homosexual content into the mainstream. Paul Goodman's *Parents' Day,* about a teacher in a progressive school who falls in love with one of his male students, is a remarkable work that explicitly promotes a sexual liberationist ideology and not only poses the question "Is it permissible to have sex with a student?" (the answer is a very slightly qualified "yes") but, more interestingly, broaches the more complicated question "Exactly what constitutes sexual relations?" Goodman's groundbreaking analysis of youth, sexuality, and social freedom, *Growing Up Absurd,* was published in 1960, but many of the themes in that book are present in this novel as well. The historical novel, particularly aimed at a postwar female audience, gained enormous popularity in the 1950s, and Norah Lofts's *The Lute Player*—detailing the life and loves of Richard the Lion-Hearted—is a fine, literate example of the genre. What distinguishes this book is the author's refusal to shy away from her protagonist's homosexuality (which is far more explicit here than in Vidal's *A Search for the King*) and his love for the page Blondel. Unlike Mary Renault and Marguerite Yourcenar, who idealized their characters' homosexual relationships, Lofts takes a more critical view, reflecting both the prejudices of her time and what she understands as the assumptions of medieval Europe. The relationships between Richard, his wife, Berengaria, and Blondel are also discussed, in non-primary ways, in Margaret Campbell Barnes's

1944 *Like Us They Lived* (revised in 1954 as *The Passionate Brood*) and in Jean Plaidy's 1977 *The Heart of the Lion*. *The Ballad of the Sad Café* by Carson McCullers charts the tormented lives and loves of misfits and social outcasts in a small town. McCullers populates her world with characters who are physically singular—the plot revolves around an erotic triangle involving a possibly lesbian Amazonian woman and a homosexual hunchback dwarf who are loved by and in love with a con man—but the underlying appeal of her message, especially to homosexual readers of the time, is that "the most outlandish people can be a stimulus for love." Alberto Moravia's *The Conformist* examines the intersections of sexuality, identity, and politics and how fear of sexual otherness can cause a fascist mentality. The novel was the basis for the 1969 award-winning film of the same title by Bernardo Bertolucci. Fritz Peters's *Finistère* (the title comes from the Latin meaning "the end of the earth") is an astonishing novel of a young American teen's love for, and relationship with, a physical education instructor at his French school. Peters is nonjudgmental about the affair, but the tragedy happens when the boy's mother and (closeted) stepfather interfere. This novel is a prime example of how fictional intergenerational relationships were viewed with far more acceptance in the years after World War II. Grace Zaring Stone was a popular novelist (her 1930 novel *The Bitter Tea of General Yen* was a bestseller and a popular 1933 film with Barbara Stanwyck), and her taking on a homosexual theme in *The Grotto* was unusual. The jacket copy of the cloth edition states that Stone "has dared to write frankly about a tragic problem—the struggles of a mother to save her son from becoming a homosexual," but the novel, and its characters, are far more complex. Much of Russell Thacher's *The Captain* reads like a routine World War II naval tale (it was compared by critics to *Mr. Roberts* and *The Caine Mutiny*), but the moral center for the novel is a polymorphously perverse sailor who sleeps with and loves other men and who stands in stark relief to the uptight, by-the-rules eponymous character. Philip Wylie's *The Disappearance* was a science fiction thriller predicated on the idea that, for some unexplained scientific reason, women and men begin living in different physical spheres, and some of the men begin to have homosexual relationships. This is a fascinating fictionalization of some of the controversial, very progressive ideas about homosexuality that Wylie had discussed in his 1942 social critique, *A Generation of Vipers*.

1952

John Horne Burns's *A Cry of Children* is set in Boston, where its protagonist has an affair with a young woman, even though he was possibly lovers with her brother when they were in the service together during the war. Burns is more elliptical with the sexual material than in *Lucifer with a Book*, but the story has undeniable power and clearly the marketing of the novel—the Bantam paperback touts it as being about "young love in the bohemian fringeworld"—created an ambiguity that could draw homosexual readers. While Patricia Highsmith's *The Price of Salt* (which she published under the name of Claire Morgan and which was reprinted in some later editions as *Carol*) contains no gay male content, its tender handling of lesbian relationships is radically different from the acute irony and edge that she brings to her homosexual male portraits. Although well written and serious, this novel has none of the brilliance, or psychological acumen, of her other work. *Cast the First Stone* by Chester Himes was a seriously cut version of his original manuscript. Set in a prison, it freely describes and discusses homosexual behavior in nonjudgmental ways. Himes, an African-American who spent a great deal of time living in Paris as an expatriate, wrote a series of popular detective novels as well. *Cast the First Stone* was reissued in 1998 with its original text and title, *Yesterday Will Make You Cry*. Douglas Sanderson's *Dark Passions Subdue* is a fascinating look at the lives of young gay men living in and near Montreal. At times overly dramatic, Sanderson has a fine ear for dialogue, and while his politics and insights could not be called "gay liberationist," his understanding of his characters is sympathetic and nuanced. Sanderson would later go on to write popular mystery and "tough guy" novels under his own name and as Malcolm Douglas and Martin Brett. Russell Thacher's *The Tender Age* is a coming-of-age story of a young man trying to figure out how to live in a changing world after World War II. Reminiscent of *The Catcher in the Rye*, Thacher's novel deals with indifferent parents and hypocritical social standards. Its sixteen-year-old male protagonist—who is nicknamed Bunny—develops a strong crush on an older male neighbor and sustains his troubled, incipiently erotic, relationship with his "strange" best friend. Angus Wilson's *Hemlock and After* is a comedy of intellectual manners in which a noted British novelist and progressive activist discovers his homosexuality late in life and begins to divide his life—resonant of Wilde's "Bunburying"—between city and country, family and homosexual friends, only to discover that life is far more complex than he had imagined.

1953

William Burroughs's novel-memoir *Junkie* was published as a drug-exploitation paperback original by Ace. Written under the pseudonym William Lee, it told, with horrifying explicitness, the details of a life committed to shooting drugs. Although it is clear that the author/narrator is homosexual, the book is far more concerned with drugs than sex. (*Junkie* was bound with Maurice Helbrant's *Narcotic Agent* in this Ace edition.) *Scotland's Burning* by Nathaniel Burt deals with the power plays and erotics of a private boy's school, which caused it to be compared to John Horne Burns's 1949 *Lucifer with a Book*. Burt, a noted composer as well as a writer, attended the prestigious St. James Preparatory School in Maryland, the model for the school in *Scotland's Burning*. He was best known for *The Perennial Philadelphians* and *First Families*, about the American "aristocracy." Donald Webster Cory, who wrote the enormously influential *The Homosexual in America* (1951), edited a collection of homophile stories entitled *21 Variations on a Theme*, which was published by Greenberg. It included pieces by contemporary authors such as Sherwood Anderson ("Hands"), Paul Bowles ("Pages from Cold Point"), James T. Farrell ("A Casual Incident"), and William Carlos Williams ("The Knife of the Times"), as well as by such canonical authors as Henry James ("The Pupil"), Guy de Maupassant ("Paul's Mistress"), and D. H. Lawrence ("The Prussian Officer"). *21 Variations on a Theme* was the first anthology of homosexual-themed fiction from a mainstream publisher, and it set the standard for future collections, such as Stephen Wright's *Different: An Anthology of Homosexual Short Stories* (1974), Seymour Kleinberg's *The Other Persuasion: An Anthology of Short Fiction About Gay Men and Women* (1977), and David Galloway and Christian Sabisch's *Calamus: Male Homosexu-*

ality in Twentieth-Century Literature—An International Anthology (1982), all of which duplicated stories that originally appeared in Cory's book. Charles Jackson's short story collection *Earthly Creatures* contained several stories with homosexual themes—"Outlander" and "Romeo" being the most prominent. The book received positive notices, but some critics were still disturbed by what they saw as Jackson's continual insistence on examining the more sordid aspects of life.

1954

Rodney Garland's *The Heart in Exile* is a moving exploration of a man discovering his sexuality in midcentury London. Written as a psychological thriller, it has, at its core, a plea for social tolerance of the homosexual. Rodney Garland is the pseudonym for conservative British journalist and political commentator Adam de Hegedus. *The World in the Evening* by Christopher Isherwood is a plainspoken, emotionally detailed account of several complicated male-male relationships and the effects on the people in them and those connected with them. Isherwood's sheer matter-of-factness about homosexuality (it is neither a social nor a political issue) is unique for the time, as is his portrait of a Quaker character who views his homosexuality in a clearly, and distinctly, political light. Gordon Merrick's second novel, *The Demon of Noon,* is a romantic intrigue featuring a mix of heterosexual and homosexual activities in France after the war. It was released in paper as *Lovers in Torment.* His first book, *The Strumpet Wind* (1947), a World War II spy thriller, had garnered him a strong reputation and included implicit but inconsequential homosexual content. Merrick would go on to write the 1970 bestseller *The Lord Won't Mind* and a series of popular male-male romances. John Selby's *The Man Who Never Changed* details the life a career-driven conductor who seals himself off from all nurturing relationships—including his best male friend who loves him—to further his career. The homosexual content here is matter-of-fact and very sympathetic; it is better to be homosexual and capable of love than heterosexual and emotionally isolated. Selby was a writer and critic of some note, and as chief editor at Rinehart he published, in 1952, Charles M. Schulz's first Peanuts book. Tennessee Williams's story collection *Hard Candy* contains several pieces with explicitly gay male content. These stories—exploring the loneliness of the human condition as well as sex with hustlers in movie theater balconies—delivered the lyric melancholy and poeticized sexual fervor that was expected from him at this point in his career. Marguerite Yourcenar's *Memoirs of Hadrian* was a highly literary re-creation of the Roman emperor's life and his love of the beautiful Antinoüs. Most critics treated its unabashed praise of homosexual love—she offered no psychological excuses and made no liberal pleas for understanding—with cautious respect and emphasized that Hadrian's sexuality had nothing to do with the modern world. Homosexual readers had an alternative reading, and Yourcenar's novel became ubiquitous on the bookshelves of gay men and lesbians. Yourcenar (whose real name was Marguerite de Crayencour) was the first woman elected to the august Académie française. She came to the United States at the beginning of World War II and lived for many years on Maine's Mount Desert Island.

1955

When Lonnie Coleman published *Ship's Company,* he had already garnered, with his first five novels, a considerable reputation as a Southern writer dealing with serious social issues. A collection of interconnected short stories about life on the USS *Nellie Crocker* (even its name sounds queer), it featured two explicitly homosexual stories, "The Theban Warriors" and "Bird of Paradise." Like Thacher's *The Captain,* Coleman's presentation of homosexuality in a World War II setting was rendered naturalistically and presented as ordinary. It was the cold war that fueled Rodney Garland's *The Troubled Midnight.* A fictional version of the British spy scandal involving Guy Burgess and Donald Maclean, the story is not particularly sympathetic to its protagonists. This material was later dealt with, far more empathetically, in Julian Mitchell's play *Another Country* (and the 1984 film) as well as in Alan Bennett's short plays *An Englishman Abroad* and *A Question of Attribution.* The dark, dangerous edge that Patricia Highsmith brought to homosexuality in *Strangers on a Train* was made more potent in *The Talented Mr. Ripley,* which featured an engaging, murderous sociopath as hero. "Tom Ripley's not such a bad person," Highsmith once said in an interview, "he only kills when he has to." Unfortunately Highsmith's homosexual antihero—who repeatedly gets away with murder—could not translate unpunished to the screen. In the 1960 *Purple Noon,* Ripley is apprehended by the police, and in the 1999 film *The Talented Mr. Ripley,* he is punished by having to murder the man he loves. Audrey Erskine Lindop's *The Outer Ring* is a sympathetic, overly circumspect, look at a man who is struggling with his sexuality, his relationship with his father, his marriage, and his psychoanalysis. In the end Lindop's main character decides to accept his homosexual feelings but remain married, but her attitude toward homosexuality is quite enlightened for the time. A paper edition, whose jacket copy inaccurately proclaimed it "A Surging Novel of Forbidden Love," was released in 1956 by Popular Library under the title *The Tormented.*

1956

Like Vidal's *The City and the Pillar,* the topic of James Baldwin's *Giovanni's Room* is less homosexuality than the struggle to sustain a loving gay identity in a queer-hating culture. The "tragic" endings in each book are more critiques of oppression than a commentary on homosexuality itself. Also, like Willard Motley in *Knock on Any Door,* Baldwin chose to write here about white Americans and Europeans, a choice that garnered rebukes from many black literary critics. Lance Horner's *The Street of the Sun* is a historical potboiler about the slave trade and class relationships in nineteenth-century Cuba. Overheated in all of its descriptions of (heterosexual or homosexual) lust, power, and money, it is an entertaining, if ultimately silly, romance about sexual rivalry between two half-brothers. *Compulsion* by Meyer Levin was a bestseller that became a Broadway show in 1957 and then an extraordinarily popular 1959 Hollywood film. Based on the Leopold and Loeb murder case of 1924—which Levin had covered as a young reporter—the book is an almost journalistic account (Levin relies on the court transcripts) of the murder, the trial, and the complicated sexual relationship between its protagonists. Tom Kalin's 1992 film, *Swoon,* was a queer retelling of the story critiquing the anti-Semitism and the anti-homosexual context of the trial. Interestingly, Levin was married to Tereska Torres, the author of the bestselling 1950 semi-lesbian pulp *Women's Barracks,* and he also translated many of her later novels, some of which have overt lesbian content. Like Marguerite Yourcenar's *Memoirs of Hadrian,* the novels of Mary Renault set in ancient Greece were not only popular and critical successes but garnered a wide gay following who experienced them as affirmations of contemporary homosexual lives and experience. (Renault, the nom de plume of Mary Challans, was a character in Thomas Otway's *Venice Preserv'd,* her favorite Restoration play.) *The Last of the Wine* detailed the life of an Athenian who prospers as a merchant and has a series of homosexual and heterosexual attachments. Undoubtedly the fact that both Yourcenar and Renault were women (both of whom were quietly lesbian as well) made their narratives of male homosexuals more palatable to the mainstream heterosexual literary establishment. Gerald Tesch's remarkable *Never the Same Again,* an account of a love affair between a thirteen-year-old boy and a thirty-year-old man in a small midwestern town, would probably not be able to find a publisher today. Tesch takes a generous view of the relationship and never condemns it. Even the cover copy on the 1958 Pyramid paper edition asked the open questions "Was Their Relationship Too Intimate? What Would You Decide?" As in *Finistère,* the villain here is a closeted homosexual who also desires the boy, and the relationship explodes in scandal when he exposes it. Gore Vidal's *A Thirsty Evil* includes three unapologetic, homosexually themed short stories: one of a Princeton football player turned hustler in Key West; another of two gay students being expelled from a prep school; and "Pages from an Abandoned Journal," in which a social-climbing, pretentious heterosexual discovers his true sexuality and becomes a social-climbing, pretentious homosexual while completely misunderstanding the natural purity of the deep love he felt for a dear friend when he was a teen.

1957

Margaret Campbell Barnes's *Isabel the Fair* is a historical romance detailing the life of Isabel, wife of the homosexually inclined English king, Edward II. Barnes, appropriately for fiction written for a female audience, takes Isabel's side, reflecting a 1950s women's magazine view of a marriage in trouble. While Jack Kerouac's *On the Road* contains only a fleeting reference to one of its main characters having been a hustler when younger, the whole novel, when viewed through the lens of what we know about Kerouac's relationship with Ginsberg and Neal Cassady, can easily be read as a (closeted) homosexual novel and as such had a huge influence on the popular American conception of the beat movement. While presented as a prison memoir, *Behind These Walls*, Christopher Teale's touching look at male-male relationships (both erotic and emotional), reads in every way like a novel. Clearly inspired by George Sylvester Viereck's *Men into Beasts*, Teale avoids the hard-boiled, tell-all tone of many 1950s prison memoirs and is far more interested in describing the intimate relationships between prisoners than exposing the horrors of the institution. James Yaffe's *Nothing but the Night* is another retelling of the Leopold and Loeb case. Set in a contemporary U.S. high school, the novel does not dwell on the sexual relationship between its main characters, but makes it clear that an erotic connection exists between them and is the basis for their actions.

1958

The narrator of Truman Capote's *Breakfast at Tiffany's* is obviously a gay man, although this is never explicitly stated. Capote's creation of Holly Golightly—that naïf who is part drag queen and part fairy—was an embodiment of a certain type of 1950s gay sensibility. The 1961 film, with Audrey Hepburn, manufactured a not quite convincing romance between the narrator and Golightly. Lonnie Coleman's *The Southern Lady* is a coded tale of homosexuality and race. The novel's narrator (a Southern novelist who resembles Coleman himself) challenges a proper Southern lady about her racism while hiding his own secrets. Like many of Coleman's earlier works, as well as his Beulah Land trilogy, this novel is concerned with the complicated intersections between race, gender, and sexual orientation. *Koptic Court* by Herbert Kastle is a panoramic view of mid-1950s urban life set in an aging, once grand apartment building in Brooklyn. The homosexual content is dealt with sympathetically and intelligently and juxtaposed neatly with themes about racism, anti-Semitism, the Holocaust, labor organizing, and political extremism. Kastle is a great naturalistic writer, observant and empathetic, with the eye of a journalist. *Koptic Court* was released in several paper editions as *7 Keys to Koptic Court*. Kenneth Martin was only sixteen when he published *Aubade*, a remarkably unsentimental coming-of-age story about a young teen falling in love with an older medical student. Its simple, elegant prose masks a deeper understanding of human relationships, and it stands along with similar but better known works such as Alan Sillitoe's 1959 *The Loneliness of the Long Distance Runner* and David Storey's 1963 *Radcliffe* as fine examples of British lower-middle-class, slice-of-life fiction. *Confessions of a Mask* by Yukio Mishima (the pen name of Kimitaka Hiroaka) is an autobiographical novel of the author's coming to terms with his homosexuality. The book is not only an exploration of how the author has to wear a "mask of normality," but also hints at the sadomasochistic sexual fantasies that were to be salient in so much of the author's later work and life. *Let No Man Write My Epitaph* by Willard Motley is a sequel to his bestselling *Knock on Any Door* and follows the life of Nick Romano's illegitimate son and namesake as he tries to overcome his addiction to drugs. According to the book's flap copy, Nick Jr., like his father, relies on mentors: "the protective friendship of loyal men of the slums and . . . a freelance writer who found Nick while he was dredging beneath the surface of Chicago's muck." *The Bell*, Iris Murdoch's fourth novel—near the beginning of her long oeuvre that explicated how various forms of traditional Greek philosophy might be used to understand the complicated intersections of sexual and emotional relationships—is a startling story of intergenerational love, religious belief, and redemption. Dennis Murphy's *The Sergeant* is a Freudian tale of repressed sexual desire erupting in violence when an officer, barely cognizant of his homosexual desires, becomes obsessed with a beautiful soldier. Unexceptionally written, the story, essentially a non-metaphoric retelling of Melville's *Billy Budd*, nevertheless carries some illustrative power when it is read in the context of popular 1950s conceptions of masculinity, homosexuality, and psychoanalysis. Mary Renault's *The King Must Die* continued her look at ancient Greek lives and here explored the exploits of Theseus from his slaying of the Minotaur to his rise to King of Athens. James Dean had only been dead for three years when Walter Ross published his bestseller, *The Immortal*, which was clearly based upon the late star's life. Here young, hip screen idol Johnny Preston—who dies in a tragic accident at the height of his film career—is polymorphously perverse in his sexuality, although clearly more drawn to men than women. "Johnny didn't care" notes the cover copy of the paper edition. "He'd try anything. Fast cars . . . books . . . bongo drums . . . marihuana . . . people. For him an experience was neither good nor bad, but something to be bitten into like bread, tasted like wine and spat out like garbage." While this is a work of fiction, Dean's homosexuality was apparently well-known enough for such public speculation. Mario Soldati's *The Confession* is a brilliant and sometimes shocking look at religion, sexual repression, and homosexuality. The novel, published in Italy in 1955, examines how the misogynistic theology of a Jesuit school leads the fourteen-year-old protagonist to believe that acting upon his homosexual desires is a perfect way to avoid sin. William Talsman's *The Gaudy Image* had been published in Paris, by the Olympia Press, and distributed underground (after problems with the U.S. Customs) in the United States widely enough for the novel to garner a reputation. Crossing Genet's underworld characters with the flaming queens of Tennessee Williams's New Orleans, this fanciful mixture of erotic gangster camp is unique in gay writing of the time.

1959

William Burroughs's *Naked Lunch* is, along with Ginsberg's *Howl* and Kerouac's *On the Road,* central to the canon of beat literature. Its disturbing, hallucinogenic mixture of boy love, violence, drugs, and apocalyptic fantasy caused it to be banned for years, but its effect on gay male writing—from John Rechy to Dennis Cooper—has been unmistakable. Breaking wildly free from conventional narrative, Burroughs provided an alternative to the traditional modes of expression that other gay writers were safely exploring to tell their stories. While he did not emulate Burroughs's radical break from narrative, Lonnie Coleman's *Sam* is as remarkable a break in content. An unapologetic look at the life of a middle-class homosexual—including his trips to the baths, his ugly fights with his lover, and his struggle against betraying his own sense of self—this novel was a landmark for gay male fiction. Coleman was already a respected novelist, and *Sam* did nothing to hurt his career. Allen Drury's *Advise and Consent* was a bestseller and became a 1960 Pulitzer Prize winner; a play and a hit 1962 Hollywood movie soon followed. A political thriller that turns on the suicide of a principled Mormon senator from Utah who was being blackmailed because of a homosexual past, the novel's theme was completely in sync with the rampant paranoia that had existed, for at least a decade, about the influence of homosexuals in American politics as well as a reflection of national hysteria about sexual deviation. Drury, who was deeply closeted, was essentially sympathetic to his gay characters, and the book does not exploit the theme, but uses it to expose the deep fear of homosexuality as well as the mercilessness of the political process. Gore Vidal's 1960 Broadway play *The Best Man,* which dealt with a similar theme, was made into a film in 1964. Martin Mayer's *A Voice That Fills the House* is an insider view of the feuds and skullduggery in the opera world. There are many gay male characters—including a white police detective with a younger African-American lover—and Mayer treats everyone with an impudent sense of humor and irony. The sheer overabundance of homosexual characters and the nonchalance with which they are viewed make this a unique book for its time. William Miller's *The Cool World* is a naturalistic look at young men in Harlem street life, told in the first person by a "cool" hustler and gang member who is extraordinarily likable. His sexuality is open to a wide variety of acts and partners, and Miller is a nonjudgmental observer. James Baldwin wrote that it was "one of the finest novels about Harlem that has ever come my way," and it is certainly one of the few books of the period that deals primarily with African-American lives. *A Room in Chelsea Square* by Michael Nelson (the original British edition listed no author) is a sprightly, slightly nasty cultural comedy loosely based on the friendship of millionaire arts patron Peter Watson and *Horizon* editor Cyril Connolly. Nelson's knowing prose is a cross between Nancy Mitford and Evelyn Waugh (with a hint of Ronald Firbank), and the novel pushes its archness to the near breaking point, but, in the end, succeeds perfectly. *Malcolm* was James Purdy's first novel and set the stage for what were to become his major themes throughout his career. Here youth and trust are destroyed by love and sex—homosexual and heterosexual—and Purdy's laconic, ironic prose, which borders on surrealism in his early work, leads us to understand that there is much more happening than we are being told. Rather than the classic coding of sexually variant material, Purdy's often deadpan and elusive style was more indicative of his exceedingly odd emotional ambiance. Before Mary Renault wrote her novels set in the ancient world, she published *The Charioteer* (1953 in Great Britain), an outright plea for tolerance of homosexuals that examined the lives and loves of three upright English soldiers in a military hospital during World War II, although the emotional and erotic involvement of two of them began at a public school years earlier. Sincere and well written, *The Charioteer* lacks the passion of its author's less preachy historical works.

1960

Giorgio Bassani's *The Gold-Rimmed Spectacles* is set in 1938 Ferrara, Italy, as the fascists are passing anti-Jewish laws. Similar in theme to Bassani's masterpiece, *The Garden of the Finzi-Continis* (which has minor homosexual content), this novel features a homosexual Jewish doctor as the protagonist. It was made into an Italian film in 1987. There is no avoidance of homosexuality in Alfred Duggan's *Family Favorites*, a lively, and often very funny, portrait of Elagabalus, one of the more perverse of the Roman emperors. The flap copy notes "the truly fantastic debaucheries of the brief reign are described with keen insight and a dry wit amusingly appropriate for the extravagance of the occasion," and Duggan, a respected historical novelist, is enthusiastic and unflustered by his material. As the narrator notes: "I don't like male prostitutes. Nobody does. At the same time nobody objects if a man falls in love with another man, because that has been made respectable by the example of antiquity." Alexander Federoff's sprawling *The Side of the Angels* contains many fascinating descriptions of gay life in New Orleans, Washington, and New York in the late 1940s. Two of the many, many characters here are gay men who attempt to negotiate a complicated affair, and while the author is clearly not writing from inside the gay world, he is a fairly accurate observer of public gay life and acutely aware of the myriad forms that social intolerance plays in gay men's lives. *A Separate Peace* by John Knowles has been a staple of U.S. high school reading lists for four decades. This may be the reason why it is hardly ever classified as a "gay novel," even though the relationship between the narrator and his best friend falls decidedly into the elegiac model of teenage homoerotic romance begun with William Maxwell's *The Folded Leaf*.

1961

Charles Gorham had already drawn several gay characters in his early fiction, most notably *The Future Mr. Dolan* and *The Gilded Hearse* (both 1948), but *McCaffery* is a full-fledged portrait of a working-class Irish boy who becomes a hustler and call boy. Gorham's novels, literary works with pot-boiler topics (prostitution, alcoholism, street crime), were known for their bluntness and realism. *McCaffery*'s power lies not so much in its exposé of male prostitution, but in its protagonist's troubled, sexualized relationship with his brutal father. For all of its flaws, Gorham has produced a powerful novel about sexuality, masculinity, and families. *The Nearness of Evil* by Carley Mills is a fictionalization of the notorious 1943 Lonergan murder case in New York, in which a socialite heiress was murdered by her husband, who was also involved with her homosexual father. Mills is a jaunty writer who delivers on his jaded, soul-weary, café society material, but never reaches the level of intelligence or social analysis that Levin produces in *Compulsion* or Vin Packer does in *Whisper His Sin,* both based on famous murder cases. In 1997 Gordon Merrick's *The Good Life,* also based on the Lonergan case, was published posthumously, finished by his lover, Charles Hulse. Factual information on the Lonergan murder can be found in *The Gay Metropolis: 1940–1996* by Charles Kaiser. John Rae's *The Custard Boys* is a short novel about schoolboys in the English countryside during World War II. Thematically somewhere between *Good-bye, Mr. Chips* and *Lord of the Flies*, it is a commentary on British intolerance and anti-Semitism as well as an astute look at British class differences and the damaging ways that war defines masculinity. The main character, a thirteen-year-old boy, is torn between his intense sexual relationship with a new friend and his alliance with his gang. In order to avoid being called a coward, he makes a choice that ends with tragic results. Rae's novel is simply written, quite sexy, and very powerful. John Selby's *Madam* is a clever, sardonic look at the life of a flamboyant, bigoted, controlling, mean-spirited noted woman journalist—a sort of anti–Auntie Mame—who has to deal with her openly gay son. Selby's tone scuttles between satire and scorn—not quite campy, but clearly in the know—and almost always hits its mark.

1962

James Baldwin's *Another Country* is an amazing breakthrough for the American novel in dealing with sexual identity, race, and eroticism as his characters—white, black, heterosexual, lesbian, gay, bisexual—all collide in the jazz and beat worlds of late 1950s Harlem and Greenwich Village. This is one of the few novels to actively investigate the intersections between race and sex, between class and art, during this period. The "Ambrose" section of Christopher Isherwood's *Down There on a Visit* charts the existential isolation, and rejection by mainstream society, of a man who has been driven to living on an island to escape the homophobia he has faced in his life. As with *The World in the Evening,* Isherwood produced an articulate and sophisticated political and literary analysis at a time when homophile groups—just over a decade old—were in the process of producing their own. Vladimir Nabokov's *Pale Fire* is a brilliant work in which the line-by-line exegesis of a long poem reveals a complicated plot—part thriller, part haunting love story—that is built around a homosexual obsession. Mary Renault's *The Bull from the Sea* continued the story of Theseus where *The King Must Die* left off. Her historical novels were now becoming so popular that they were beginning to be discussed as "classics."

1963

Jean Genet's *Our Lady of the Flowers* is one of the most important works about homosexuality in modern literature—perhaps the most important. Not only is it shockingly and amazingly written, but it defined, at this early moment, a homosexual political and criminal identity that would eventually be, in a more Americanized form, known as "queer." While Genet is more perverse than what we would now usually call "queer," this vision was not only deeply disruptive at the time of its 1963 American publication, but even more amazing when you realize that Genet's original was written in 1943. *Making Do* by Paul Goodman is in some regards a sequel to *Parents' Day* in which the now older Goodman-like central character—who is married and a parent, has a reputation as a noted political commentator, and works for progressive political causes—begins a complicated affair with a young man. A reflection of Goodman's own concerns, this is also a brilliant snapshot of a post-beat world in which the personal is becoming inextricably (and often publicly) linked with the political. Eric Jourdan's *Two*—published in France in 1955 under the title *Les Mauvais Anges*—is the beautifully written, tortured story of two boys who love each other with such a frenzy that one passionately murders the other and then kills himself. Clearly not about sadomasochism or self-hatred, the story, influenced in part by the erotic philosophies of Genet and Georges Bataille as well as by the doomed romantic fictions of Françoise Sagan, is disturbing and unique. Although French critics praised *Two* as a work of literature, it had no U.S. cloth edition and was published as a paperback original. Portions of John Rechy's *City of Night* had already been published in various small literary magazines such as *Evergreen Review*. But no one was ready for the shock that this novel of a male hustler would have on critics and the reading public. In a stream-of-consciousness, almost documentary style that was reminiscent of Kerouac but riddled with explicitly sexual details, Rechy exposed not only the loneliness of the male hustler, but the increasingly fragile existence of urban life in the United States as well. One brilliant stroke of designing genius on the part of Grove Press, Rechy's publisher, was to put a stark black-and-white photograph of Times Square on the book's jacket. Before this, books with gay content were usually packaged and promoted with coded images of single men or soft color schemes. This photo literally brought gay nightlife out of the closet and made it indisputably visible. Charles Wright's *The Messenger* was critically acclaimed—James Baldwin gave it a rave blurb. It is a sophisticated, knowing novel of a young African-American man who drifts from sexual situation to sexual situation and never quite finds himself or his identity. Wright hits perfect jazz notes of urban isolation in his spare, taut prose, and his main character becomes emblematic of a new "lost generation" that is searching for some meaning in contemporary life, race, sexual identity, and relationships.

1964

Christopher Isherwood's *A Single Man* was a breakthrough even for a writer who had dealt openly with homosexual themes in his earlier work. Short, unsentimental, and powerful, it tells the story of a middle-aged gay man who is grieving over the recent accidental death of his longtime lover. Isherwood's plainspoken style—a prose version of Frank O'Hara's "then-I-did-this-and-then-I-did-that" type of poetry—amasses detail upon detail, giving readers complete access to the private life of an ordinary man dealing with the undeniably brutal fact that life goes on. *Cabot Wright Begins*, James Purdy's absurdist fable of the alienation of modern life—which features, among other items, a sympathetic rapist and a platonic gay interracial couple—was yet another example of his perverse, humorous take on a world that is ridden with racism, dislike of sex, and hatred of homosexuality. Like Rechy's work, portions of Hubert Selby Jr.'s *Last Exit to Brooklyn* had appeared for years in literary magazines, yet the publication of the book was a major cultural shock. Violent, unsparing, and shocking, Selby's world of hustlers, closet cases, drag queens, hoods, whores, and longshoremen was a bleak and daunting portrait of urban life. If Willard Motley's urban novels were a plea for understanding and tolerance, Selby's hellish vision—related in a post-beat, jazz jargon that was totally unique—signified that understanding, even if possible, was just not enough.

1965

Sanford Friedman's *Totempole* charts the life of a young Jewish man who grows up and falls in love with a prisoner of war during the Korean War. Written with enormous attention to psychological and emotional detail, Friedman's novel is also notable for its treatment of homosexual love during wartime. While many homosexually themed novels emerged from World War II, this work—entrenched in the Korean War and the larger cast of the cold war, but drawing upon those earlier works—presents readers with a new level of discussion and understanding. *Rogue Roman* by Lance Horner is a Roman sword-and-sandal epic with lots of homosexual sex and violence. Horner—and co-author, Kyle Onstott—would revisit ancient Rome in their 1966 homosexual epic, *A Child of the Sun*. Both of these popular novels drew upon the vast reputation and sales of earlier Onstott novels—such as *Mandingo* (1957), *The Tattooed Rood* (1960), *Drum* (1962), and the Falconhurst series—set in the pre–Civil War American South. While these novels dealt mostly with heterosexual sex (although featuring an uncommon amount of homosexual activity as well), their vivid and abundant descriptions of male bodies and genitalia made them the mainstream equivalent of softcore homosexual porn. Roger Peyrefitte's *The Exile of Capri* is a caustic turn-of-the-century literary romp, with semitragic overtones, in which an exiled nobleman (who entertained schoolboys "in a peculiar manner") is visited by such figures as Oscar Wilde, Gide, Proust, Norman Douglas, and Baron von Krupp. Hugh Ross Williamson's *A Wicked Pack of Cards*, published in England in 1961, was released in the United States by Guild Press four years later. This small gay publishing house with a reputation for publishing pornography was an odd choice since Williamson, a noted British writer of historical novels, plays, and poetry (often with religious themes), had most of his other work published here with more mainstream publishing houses. A mystery with a great surprise ending that revolves around the images of the Tarot—T. S. Eliot's "wicked pack of cards"—it is smart, involving, and ultimately quite moving. Gillian Freeman's *The Leather Boys* was also published by Guild. Originally released in England in 1961 under the pseudonym Eliot George (although she had already published three novels, Freeman did not use her real name), the book examines the lives of several working-class boys who spend their time riding motorcycles, not working, and figuring out how to live in a society that makes little sense to them. The novel's focus is far more on the social welfare state and the end of empire than on homosexuality—although its main characters do, to their endless surprise, fall in love. Freeman's nuanced ear for the language of South London slums, and her wickedly observant eye for the details of home and street life, made the book vibrant. It was made into a critically successful film in 1963, with a screenplay by Freeman. Donald Windham's *Two People* is an unassuming, and somewhat unconvincing, story of a thirty-five-year-old man on vacation in Italy whose wife leaves him. He then has a passionate affair with a seventeen-year-old Italian boy and decides that he is now gay. Windham's easy, comfortable style and the sheer lack of emotional conflict here is refreshing for the time.

1966

The Occasional Man, James Barr's first novel since 1950, is a startling story of an older gay man who seeks a younger, working-class man who is just coming out. Set on New York's Lower East Side, it is funny and often frightening in its intensity. As much concerned with social status, money, and class as with sexual orientation, this is a mature, sophisticated work that has been neglected. Released only in paper in the United States, it received a cloth edition in England two years later. George Baxt's *A Queer Kind of Death* was a surprisingly gay mystery that borrowed themes and ideas from Patricia Highsmith but maintained its own unique, perverse twists. Baxt went on to write a series of campy, celebrity-driven mysteries, most of which maintained a gay sensibility if not content. *Sorcerer's Broth* by Rodney Garland is a crime thriller in which the unsuspecting lover of a bank robber gets more than he bargained for in a holdup that goes awry. Deftly mixing the genre material with the emotional content, Garland produces a curious blend of popular fiction that avoids making arguments for social tolerance, but manages to transcend its basic mystery formula. Jean Genet's *Miracle of the Rose* is a continuation of themes that were present in *Our Lady of the Flowers,* but here Genet becomes far more interested in various types of masculine genders as he moves from being a "passive" homosexual to taking a more butch, active role. Genet's prison world—in which all relationships and love are doomed—becomes a metaphor for the outside world in which the same is true. Leaving the urban Chicago of his earlier novels, Willard Motley set *Let Noon Be Fair* in a small Mexican village that is being developed as a resort. A wide assortment of characters include gay men and boy lovers. Motley lived in Mexico during the writing of this novel and for the last years of his life, and it is fascinating to see his social concerns transmogrify and adapt themselves to a new setting. Mary Renault's *The Mask of Apollo* examined the lives of men in the beginnings of the Greek theater.

1967

Christopher Isherwood's *A Meeting by the River* examines the lives of two brothers—one a married man who has returned to his wife after a passionate homosexual affair and other attractions to men, and the other on the verge of taking his vows as a Buddhist monk. Isherwood is less concerned with homosexuality here than with looking at what it means to have a spiritual inner life. Here the rejection of being gay, and the return to married heterosexuality, is a moral and ethical failing because it is predicated upon a rejection of the true self and an acceptance of conformity as a way of life. In *Eustace Chisholm and the Works,* James Purdy deals with homosexuality in a more forthright fashion than in his earlier works. Yet the novel—which ends with a character being nailed to a barn door and eviscerated—is as morally complex, odd, and gothic as his other work. There is nothing easy about Purdy's vision—like Genet's, it is based on physical and moral destruction being one of the gateways to salvation—and its triumph is in its ability to discomfort and disturb. If the sexual activity in *City of Night* was described obliquely, John Rechy took the opposite approach in his next novel, *Numbers,* which featured a great deal of promiscuous homosexual male activity described in surprising detail. Rechy's critique of gay male life and sex as being compulsive, while reflecting psychoanalytic thinking, was clearly written from an insider's perspective. Irving Rosenthal's *Sheeper* is a great autobiographical novel of the author's relationship with writers such as Allen Ginsberg, Herbert Hunke, and Alexander Trocchi as well as his drug use and his ever-evolving plan to write the story of his life. This is a novel in the beat tradition, but Rosenthal's trip "on the road" is through his own mind. Odd, elliptical, and overtly sexual, *Sheeper* is an important, highly original, and mostly forgotten example of beat writing. Rosenthal first became famous when, as editor of *The Chicago Review,* he printed an excerpt from William Burroughs's *Naked Lunch.* After a legal furor over the alleged obscenity of Burroughs's work, he resigned and moved to San Francisco, where he founded and edited the avant-garde magazine *Big Table.*

1968

Michael Campbell's *Lord Dismiss Us* is an English boarding school novel that radiates intelligence and, thanks to a degree of satiric distance, never resorts to the sentimental. Examining a range of homosexual attachments—from schoolboy crushes to relationships between boys and older men—the book treats all this positively, even as it views the closed world of the school as a slightly campy, overly theatrical milieu in which the heart can find many manifestations of love. Pier Paolo Pasolini's novels *A Violent Life* and *The Ragazzi* both deal with the lives of Italian street boys in postwar Italy. Deftly mixing poetic language with working-class vernacular and slang, Pasolini added a new dimension to Italian neorealist literature. Interweaving his homoerotic imagination with his communist sympathies and deeply antiestablishment views, Pasolini invented a new aesthetic in which the sexual was inexplicably bound with the political. *Myra Breckinridge* by Gore Vidal confounded critics and many readers with its out-of-control, topsy-turvy, transsexual view of U.S. culture and sex. Shocking in some of its sexual details, amazing in its dissection of gender and sexual norms, and illuminating in discussing how Hollywood has either elevated or destroyed American culture, Vidal's angry, vivid, and viciously satirical novel marked a turning point in U.S. culture.

1969

Genet's *Funeral Rites,* published in France in 1947, details its narrator's sublime, agonizing confusion as he grieves for his late lover, who was killed in the Resistance, while he grapples with his intense sexual attraction to a collaborator. Like Genet's other work, it is a study in the desire to transcend the mundane world through both the transfiguration and degradation of love and sexual desire. Since the late 1950s, Juan Goytisolo has been considered one of Spain's greatest living writers as well as one of its fiercest cultural and political critics. (He began living in exile in Paris, where Genet was a mentor, during Franco's regime.) *Marks of Identity* was his ninth novel, but his first with overtly gay content. Drawing, in some part, from autobiographical details, *Marks of Identity* broke new ground for Goytisolo. Not only did it break from the realism of his earlier work, but in it he expanded his critique of traditional Spanish culture to include not only racism and backwards religion but repressive gender and sexual roles as well. *Marks of Identity* was the first in a trilogy that was later to include *Count Julian* (1974) and *Juan the Landless* (1977). *Fire from Heaven* was the first in Mary Renault's eagerly awaited trilogy about Alexander the Great. In this novel, and the subsequent volumes, *The Persian Boy* (1972) and *Funeral Games* (1981), Renault dramatizes Alexander's military career and his love for Hephaistion and the eunuch Bagoas. In many ways, these three authors are emblematic of a new time. Genet's hatred and rejection of the normal, Goytisolo's ability to imagine and act on myriad—political, emotional, and psychological—transformations, and Renault's love and desire all helped set the stage for the Stonewall riots and Gay Liberation.

BIBLIOGRAPHY

Adams, Stephen. *The Homosexual as Hero in Contemporary Fiction*. New York: Barnes & Noble, 1980.

Austen, Roger. *Playing the Game: The Homosexual Novel in America*. Indianapolis: Bobbs-Merrill, 1977.

Bergman, David. "The Cultural Work of Gay Pulp Fiction." In *The Queer Sixties*, edited by Patricia Juliana Smith. New York: Routledge, 1999.

de Grazia, Edward. *Girls Lean Back Everywhere: The Law of Obscenity and the Assault of Genius*. New York: Random House, 1992.

de St. Jorre, John. *Venus Bound: The Erotic Voyage of the Olympia Press and Its Writers*. New York: Random House, 1994.

Gertzman, Jay A. *Bookleggers and Smuthounds: The Trade in Erotica 1920–1940*. Philadelphia: University of Pennsylvania Press, 1999.

Hatton, Jackie. "The Pornographic Empire of H. Lynn Womack: Gay Political Discourse and Popular Culture, 1955–1970." *Thresholds: Viewing Culture* 7 (Spring 1993), 9–32.

Kennedy, Hubert. "*Quatrefoil* Broke New Ground," *The Harvard Gay & Lesbian Review*, III, 1 (Winter 1996), 22–24.

Levin, James. *The Gay Novel: The Male Homosexual Image in America*. New York: Irvington Publishers, 1983.

Norman, Tom. *American Gay Erotic Paperbacks: A Bibliography*. Burbank, Calif., 1994.

Perkins, Michael. *The Secret Record: Modern Erotic Literature*. New York: William Morrow, 1977.

Sarotte, Georges-Michel. *Like a Brother, Like a Lover: Male Homosexuality in the American Novel and Theater from Herman Melville to James Baldwin*. New York: Anchor Press/Doubleday, 1978.

Stryker, Susan. *Queer Pulp: Perverted Passions from the Golden Age of the Paperback*. San Francisco: Chronicle Books, 2001.

Summers, Claude J. *Gay Fictions: Wilde to Stonewall*. New York: Continuum, 1990.

Young, Ian. *The Male Homosexual in Literature*, second edition. Metuchen, N.J.: Scarecrow Press, Inc., 1982.

Zimet, Jaye. *Strange Sisters: The Art of Lesbian Pulp Fiction, 1949–1969*. New York: Viking Penguin, 1999.